FIC   King, Benjamin,
       1944-

       A bullet for
       Stonewall.

$17.95

DATE			

A BULLET FOR STONEWALL

A BULLET FOR
STONEWALL

By BENJAMIN KING

A Novel

PELICAN PUBLISHING COMPANY
Gretna 1990

Library of Congress Cataloging-in-Publication Data

King, Benjamin, 1944–
    A bullet for Stonewall / by Benjamin King.
        p.   cm.
    ISBN 0-88289-768-3
    1. Jackson, Stonewall, 1824–1863—Fiction.
    2. Chancellorsville, Battle of, 1863—Fiction.
    3. United States—History—Civil War, 1861–1865—
    Fiction.   I. Title.
    PS3561.I473B85   1990
    813'.54—dc20   89-25552
                                                                CIP

Manufactured in the United States of America
Published by Pelican Publishing Company, Inc.
1101 Monroe Street, Gretna, Louisiana 70053

FIC

*To my wife Loretta
and
Special Thanks
to
Pierre Kirk
and
Nancy Reinfeld
for their assistance*

A BULLET FOR STONEWALL

CHAPTER 1

Washington, D.C.
December 22, 1862

THE NIGHT WAS bitterly cold, but the man stood under the street lamp and calmly puffed on his cigar. He stood erect so that in the shadows he appeared even taller than he actually was. Beneath the top hat he was balding but that hardly mattered. He was broad-shouldered and had a handsome face with a high forehead, straight nose, and strong jaw. He was well dressed in a warm overcoat which covered a blue broadcloth dress coat with gold buttons.

The man could have been a dandy out for a stroll after an exclusive Washington party but he wasn't. He was Salmon Portland Chase, Secretary of the Treasury. On nights like this persons of his rank were normally found by their fires at home. A strong gust of icy wind whipped down the street and the secretary hunched a little in the cold. One might be considered a little crazy for being out in such inclement weather. There were plenty of political enemies ready to hang that label on Chase, anyway, and he knew it. But he was out in the cold for a reason and that reason was moving past him.

The wagons creaked and groaned slowly through the bumpy streets of the Nation's Capital carrying their cargo of human misery. These were the wounded from the Battle of Fredericksburg coming to Washington for treatment. Even in the cold the secretary could smell the filth and decay coming from the wagons. Occasionally, moans and cries could be heard above the sounds of iron-bound wheels moving over the cobblestones. From one of them a pitiful voice pleaded, "Oh, God, please let me die." The Union Army was transporting the wounded in wagons because there were not enough ambulances.

General Ambrose Burnside had bungled badly. He had made a frontal attack against an entrenched enemy and over 12,000 Union soldiers were now dead or wounded. Chase knew he should have been able to prevent a tragedy like this. At one time he could have. That was early in the struggle when Simon Cameron was the Secretary of War. In those days, Chase had been the main bulwark against Cameron's corruption and incompetence. Now, Edwin Stanton was the Secretary of War and he ran his department with an iron hand. Because of that and Secretary of State William H. Seward's indifference toward him, Chase found himself being moved further and further from the center of control.

It was true that running the Treasury Department was a heavy burden in itself. As Secretary of the Treasury, Chase had to fight constantly against senators who sought patronage for their supporters. Otherwise he would not be able to retain honest and efficient administrators in the department. He had begun in 1861 with an empty treasury and his policies were beginning to bear fruit in the form of substantial loans. Nevertheless, he knew he could contribute more if only the president would listen to him. He had protested to Lincoln on the seventeenth and offered to resign, but the chief executive had refused to accept his resignation. Even though Chase hated slavery he advised the president to let the Southern states go peacefully in 1861. He was positive that a solution to the crisis could be found without resorting to war. The attack on Fort Sumter had shown just how illusory his hopes were.

The attack had plunged the nation into a terrible civil war with no end in sight. Chase was determined to do anything that would bring it to a successful close. He smiled bitterly at the irony. There had to be way to destroy the Southern Confederacy and with it the vile practice of slavery. There had to be a way without all this senseless bloodshed.

The wagons stretched as far as Chase could see in the lamplight—and beyond. There had to be a way to end the conflict without these horrendous casualties and Chase was determined to find it. He walked to his carriage. As he drove home, he continued to see the wagons, hear the creaking of their wheels and the cries of agony, and smell the stench of wounded bodies. The tragic scene filled him with a terrible anger.

Department of the Treasury
Washington, D.C.
January 13, 1863

Chase had stopped keeping his diary in October of the previous year. He had neither the energy nor the desire to continue it, as one misfortune for the nation followed another. He knew that the unfortunate Burnside would soon be replaced by another commander. The most likely candidate was Major Gen. Joseph T. "Fighting Joe" Hooker. Hooker would then be the Union's man of the hour, but so many others had also appeared in that role. There had been McDowell who lost at Bull Run, and "Little Mac" McClellan who had taken the army up the Peninsula, won nearly every engagement and wound up in full retreat. While that was going on, the braggart Pope lost his coat and hat to Stuart, and nearly an entire army to Lee. McClellan tried again and with odds of nearly three to one, had failed to destroy Lee's army at Antietam. Then there was Burnside. The litany was endless. But for the Rebels there was no litany. There were only Jackson, Stuart, and Lee—imperturbable and unbeatable.

Chase picked up his pen and put it down. He rose from his blue upholstered chair and strode across the gray carpet to the window. The day outside was rapidly drawing to a close and he was tired. Tired minds often play tricks on the unwary and for a fleeting second he was back under the lamp post watching the wagons transport their pitiable cargoes. When he blinked he was no longer Secretary of the Treasury. He was once again the small boy who had gone to visit his uncle's farm. Salmon and his uncle had gone to chop wood for his aunt to cook supper and he and his uncle were walking through the barn on the way to the wood pile. Suddenly he was frightened by a rattlesnake which was coming out of one of the stalls. Chase screamed and jumped back as his uncle swung his ax. The heavy blade severed the snake's head from its body and young Salmon clung to his uncle's arm. He watched in horrid fascination as the the headless serpent continued to twist and writhe for several seconds until it lay still.

When Salmon P. Chase blinked again he was back at the window of his office, but everything had changed. He now understood the problem and the solution. No animal could survive once its head was cut off unless it had multiple heads and the animal he had in mind had only one. Chase went back to his chair and sat down. This was a decision so momentous that he had to record it. Once again he picked up the pen but his hand trembled. He put the pen down and he began to feel uncomfortably warm as beads of perspiration broke out on his forehead. What he was thinking was not honorable. Gentlemen did not order the deaths of other gentlemen, even if they were on opposite sides. This was the United States in 1863, not Florence during the Renaissance.

The secretary had always prided himself on his calm and reason. He had always been in complete control of himself. Now his brain was rushing unchecked to the ultimate solution of the problem. He was, by nature, not a violent man, but his logic was cold, precise, and murderous. Was this not war? What if thousands could be saved at the cost of one enemy soldier? Was that not what war was all about? Was gentlemanly behavior just another excuse for doing nothing? There had to be someone with whom he could discuss the problem. He discussed everything with his daughter Kate, but this was something he didn't want even her to know. It had to be someone with whom he could discuss the problem on a realistic and practical level since his idea had already progressed far beyond the abstract. The person he needed to discuss his solution with had to be knowledgeable and deeply concerned with the fate of the Union. He also had to be politically astute enough to realize that once he was associated with the plan, he dare not reveal it.

Chase strode to the coat rack, retrieved his coat and hat, and left the Treasury. He let his feet carry him without consciously thinking about where he was going. Instead of hiring a carriage he walked the several blocks to the neat house near the Capitol. He ascended the steps and pulled the handle that rang the bell. The time between the ringing of the bell and the housekeeper's arrival seemed like an eternity. During that eternity Chase decided at least a hundred times to give the plan up and a hundred times he resolved to see the thing through. Mrs. Lydia Smith, the senator's octoroon housekeeper answered the door. She was a handsome woman who moved with a natural grace, and Chase could understand why the capital was rife with rumors about the senator and his housekeeper.

"Mr. Secretary," she said with a surprised look. "We didn't know you were coming."

"I apologize for arriving unannounced," he said. "But I must see the senator. It's of vital importance."

Mrs. Smith ushered the secretary in and gave him a worried look. She was used to the senator receiving visitors at all hours, but this was the first time that Chase had ever come alone to the house and he looked agitated and upset. She could only assume that something terrible had occurred.

"I'll inform the senator that you're here, sir," she said and scurried down the hall. She returned a moment later.

"The senator is in the parlor, Mr. Secretary. May I take your coat and hat?"

Chase was so deep in thought that, at first, he didn't realize that she was speaking to him. "Oh, yes, thank you." He was beginning to perspire again.

Senator Thaddeus Stevens was sitting on a chair in front of the fire with a shawl around his shoulders. Even in this homey setting he looked grimly forbidding with his firm jaw and piercing eyes. He wondered what had caused Salmon Chase to come knocking at his door unannounced and in an agitated state.

"Mr. Secretary," he said rising. "It's nice to see you."

Stevens offered his hand to Chase and the two men shook hands. He noticed that Chase's palm was sweating.

"Thank you for seeing me at such short notice, senator," the secretary said. He took a handkerchief from his pocket and wiped his brow.

"Please have a seat," Stevens said. The senator motioned to a chair opposite his own and watched Chase carefully. Perhaps the secretary had had another falling out with the president.

"Thank you," Chase said. He sat in the chair his host had indicated and let out a great sigh.

"May I get you anything, Mr. Secretary?" Stevens asked politely.

"That is very kind of you senator, but if I may I would like to come directly to the point."

Stevens was beginning to get concerned. "Problems at the Treasury?" the senator ventured, trying to get some indication of what the matter was.

"No sir. This has nothing to do with the Treasury and nothing to do with the government," Chase replied. "I am in need of assistance in another matter which is confidential and private. I have a plan which, if successful, will shorten this war and bring victory to the Union."

The senator's expression changed from one of curiosity to interest. Although many others regarded Salmon P. Chase as a fool, Thaddeus Stevens did not, but he wondered how a man could have a private plan for winning a war which thousands of troops could not. "What is your plan, Mr. Secretary?"

The secretary rose from the chair and began pacing back and forth. He presented his plan as if he were presenting a client's case to a jury.

"We have been at war for nearly two years. During that entire time, the rebel armies have shown themselves quite superior to ours in attaining victory. Although this has mitigated somewhat in our favor in the west, it continues to be the case in the east which is the most critical theater of the war.

"You may ask why. We are superior in population, farming, and manufacturing. Our armies are larger and better equipped. Our navy has swept all but a few raiders from the seas and continues to tighten our hold on the South and its ports. Nonetheless, the war continues without abatement and without any improvement in our position vis-a-vis the rebels. Only the Emancipation Proclamation appears to have stayed the hand of the Europeans from recognizing the Confederacy as a nation.

"The answer to the question is simple. The Southern armies have better leaders than ours. Lee, Jackson, and Stuart have accomplished amazing feats against our generals. This, then, brings up another question. What would the South do without these men?"

Stevens looked at him with great interest but said nothing.

"The South would be in a difficult situation at best, I think,"

Chase continued. "However, it would be expecting too much of fate to assist us in removing all of these men in one fell swoop. Therefore, I propose that we take charge of the situation and eliminate the most important of these men as quickly as possible. I assure you, the blow would be most crippling to our foes."

"You propose to kill Robert E. Lee?" Stevens asked.

Chase looked directly at the senator. "Not Lee," he said after a slight, dramatic pause. "Jackson."

The senator looked puzzled.

"Who has singlehandedly won more victories for the South than any of its generals?" Chase asked. "Whose troops are known as 'foot cavalry' because they move with such celerity? Who is capable of transmitting Lee's strategic plans into actual movement of troops?"

A light shone in Stevens' eyes and his thin lips moved in a slight smile.

"It would be like separating the body—or at least part of it— from the head. But why come to me?" Stevens asked.

"What I need," Chase concluded, "is the right sort of man to carry out the plan. I was hoping you might know someone who could direct me to such a person."

The senator looked at him briefly without saying a word. Stevens did, indeed, know of such a man, but his first impulse was to say no. Plans of this sort had too great a tendency to become public knowledge and backfire politically on the originator. On the other hand, Chase's idea had incredible potential. If it worked it would deprive the South of effective leadership and bring the rebellious states to their knees without further bloodshed. The Confederacy would be crushed in a single, telling blow. Chase waited impatiently as Stevens made his decision. The air hung heavy with the silence.

"If you are able to find such a man, his services will cost a great deal of money," Stevens finally said. "It may even cost a great deal of money just for intermediaries." His voice was calm as if he were discussing his housekeeper's budget.

Chase had not even thought of money, but he said, "Money is no object." As the custodian of the nation's funds, he would worry about that issue later.

A brief smile—if it could be called that—flickered across Stevens' thin lips. He rose from the chair and retrieved a pencil and a piece of paper from a small table. He wrote a name and an address on the paper and handed it to the secretary.

"Go to this place the day after tomorrow at seven in the evening and ask for the name on the paper. He will put you in contact with the man you require. If he requires payment, it must be made in gold as a man in your position must appreciate."

It was Chase's turn to smile briefly. It was Chase who had opposed the issue of greenbacks in lieu of gold when the war began.

"I trust this is all you will need," Stevens continued. "I wish there were more I could do."

Chase understood that Stevens was henceforth washing his hands of the whole matter. They both knew that in this age of professed chivalry a plan such as this could damage one's political future, even if it were successful. Actually, Chase was relieved. The plan was his and he did not want to share it with anyone. Now he could control it from beginning to end.

"Thank you, senator. I will treat this information with the utmost confidentiality," the secretary replied, taking the folded piece of paper.

Once again they shook hands. This time the secretary seemed much calmer. The senator managed another brief smile. At the senator's signal the housekeeper retrieved the secretary's hat and coat and helped him on with it. He thanked her, wished her a good evening, then walked out the door and down the steps to the street. Before Chase looked at the paper the senator had given him he took a deep breath and let the cold air sting his lungs. The name on the paper was "Mr. Joseph Fitch" and the address was a place in a run-down area near the Navy Yard.

Southeast Washington D.C.
January 15, 1863

The Chain and Anchor was a sailors' tavern in an alley near the waterfront. Under ordinary circumstances Chase would have hesitated to enter the alley in daylight, much less at night, but these were not ordinary circumstances. The secretary was a man with a purpose and nothing was going to sway him from it. A figure emerged from the darkness of the alley and Chase, convinced he was about to be attacked, tensed and raised his cane to defend himself.

"Well, well," a heavily-painted prostitute said, looking Chase over with an approving glance. She was surrounded by the odor of cheap perfume and cheap whiskey. "What have we here?"

Chase did not answer. He sighed in relief and brushed by her.

"Damned snob!" she called after him.

The alley was covered with slush and it reeked of stale beer and urine. A few feet from the dimly lit door, a man Chase took to be a sailor was vomiting. Chase went straight into the tavern. The patrons stopped talking and cursing and stared at him as he walked to the bar with an air or authority totally foreign to his present surroundings.

"What'll it be?" The bartender asked. He smelled like the alley.

"I'm looking for Mr. Joseph Fitch," Chase said in a nervous voice that was slightly louder than normal.

The bartender nodded toward the back table. A man in a shabby overcoat and tophat was sitting in the dimmest corner of the room. Chase strode over.

"Mr. Fitch?" he asked.

"Jesus Christ," the man swore. "Did your mother have any kids with brains?"

"I beg your pardon . . . "

"Shut your mouth and sit down!" Fitch commanded.

Chase opened his mouth and looked around. Everyone was staring. He sat down quickly.

"You crazy to come down here dressed like that, mister. Don't you know there are people around here that would kill you for them shiny buttons on your coat?"

Chase didn't need a lecture. He wanted to get down to business. "Look, I'm . . . "

Fitch held his hand up. "Rule one, no names. The day may come when you don't want to know me and I don't want to know you. Rule two, pay first. Ten dollars—gold."

Chase's thrifty instinct told him not to pay it and leave, but he reached in his pocket and tossed a coin on the table. Fitch smiled revealing rotten, stained teeth. The shabby man picked up the coin, and bit into it. Satisfied, he put it into a small purse.

"Now, what can I do for you?"

"I am told you can put me in touch with a man who is an expert at eliminating competition."

"Wife's boyfriend?" Fitch asked with a leer.

Chase didn't answer and Fitch shrugged.

"No matter," the intermediary said. "But, it will cost you another ten."

"It's worth twenty, but you won't see another cent until I meet the man I'm looking for," Chase said.

Fitch looked him over. He had taken an instant dislike to the haughty man sitting across from him and would have enjoyed having a few friends teach him where he stood, but he was a potential customer for Anderson and that made him untouchable.

"All right, I'll deliver the time and address to you in two days where do you live?"

Chase was learning quickly. He didn't want Fitch anywhere near his lodgings. "I'll meet you in front of Brown's Hotel at 7:00 P.M. Do you know where it is?"

"It's on the corner of 'The Avenue' and 6th, across from the National."

"That's the one. I'll wait half an hour."

"I'll be there."

Without another word Chase stood up and left. As soon as he was out the door two large, muscular seamen rose as if to follow. They looked at Fitch, but he shook his head and they sat back down.

On January 17, the evening specified, Chase waited patiently in his carriage. At precisely 7:15, Fitch delivered a sealed envelope.

"Thank you," Chase said.

"Aren't you forgetting something?" Fitch asked.

"What?"

"My money."

"It's not your money until I see the man I need to see."

"Bastard!"

"Would you prefer I call the police?" Chase asked.

Fitch disappeared.

When Chase opened the envelope his jaw dropped. He read the instructions twice to make sure he was reading the address correctly. He was expecting another meeting at a place like the Chain and Anchor, but the note read:

Dear Sir:

Please get a reservation for two for supper at the Willard Hotel for the evening of January 19th at 8:00 P.M. Tell them you are expecting a friend named Anderson. If you are alone, I will meet you. I am looking forward to making your acquaintance.

Sincerely,

ANDERSON

Chase studied the note. The script was neat and precise, but its character was neutral as if it had come from a child's primer. The secretary pocketed the note, a little disappointed. He had hoped that the handwriting would reveal something of the character of the man he was to meet. The next morning he sent a clerk to make the reservation. The two-day wait was vexatious, but at precisely 8:00 P.M. he entered the Willard Hotel. The opulence of the hotel's interior never failed to impress Chase. Everything was lavishly decorated with stained hardwood paneling, upholstered furniture and crystal chandeliers. The maitre d' hotel nodded at the secretary and showed Chase to his table. The secretary sat down and waited, nervously drumming his fingers on the table. Would the man Stevens had recommended show up? When the waiter arrived he ordered oysters, roast beef, boiled potatoes, and a bottle of wine. The meal was excellent and for a moment he forgot the war, his plans, and the man he was supposed to meet. He was in this reverie when reality intruded.

"Good evening, Mr. Secretary," a pleasant voice said.

Chase, his fork halfway to his mouth, looked at the source of the voice. Instantly, he knew it was the man he was supposed to meet and he stared. The secretary stared not because the man was remarkable, but because he was so unremarkable. Chase had expected a more robust and adventurous looking man. Instead, the man was of medium height and build. His short hair was brown and his hands were white as if the man wore gloves all the time. He looked neither young nor old and Chase guessed he was in his mid-thirties.

"Mr. Anderson?" the secretary inquired. He did not extend his hand.

"The same, sir," the man replied and did not seem to care whether the secretary offered his hand or not.

"Have a seat."

The man who called himself Anderson bowed very correctly and sat across from Chase. His speech was undistinguished but refined. His manners were polished as if he were born to genteel society.

"How did you know I was your client?" Chase asked.

"My assistant pointed you out to me. Now, how may I assist you, Mr. Secretary?" he asked calmly.

Before Chase could answer, the waiter arrived. Anderson ordered soup, fish and potatoes, and a white wine. It was then that Chase decided that there was indeed something extraordinary about the man. His eyes. They were gray, but there was nothing unusual in that. His eyes held neither warmth, nor mirth, nor anger. In fact, they showed no emotion at all. If one considered the adage that the eyes were the windows to the soul, then Anderson had the drapes to the windows of his soul drawn tight. This, in itself, was enough to offend the secretary, but there was something else and he couldn't put his finger on it. Anderson's eyes did express interest, but it was more than that. It seemed to Chase that Anderson could, perhaps, see everything, but that wasn't quite it, either. Finally Chase realized that it seemed if Anderson could see through everything. It was as if neither he, Chase, nor anything around him had any substance.

Chase found this quite unnerving, but he was used to unnerving situations when practicing law and he didn't allow his reaction to show. With the ability to see through things the man would make an excellent spy, Chase thought. Spy. The word had a loathsome, reptilian connotation. Spying was a dishonorable trade and a spy was to be trusted less than a serpent. From that point on, the secretary thought of Anderson only as "The Spy." Regardless, these were desperate times and spies were as necessary as artillery and muskets.

As soon as the waiter left, Chase outlined his plan as he had with Stevens. He carefully explained the background to his case and the facts bearing on it. Then the secretary presented his plan clearly and concisely, followed by what he expected the results to be. There were two interruptions by waiters, and Chase had to stop talking until they left. Throughout, Chase's presentation, the Spy exhibited an intense interest as he continued to eat his supper with slow, careful bites. He neither seemed to relish the meal nor dislike it. The Spy acted as if an undertaking of this magnitude were an everyday occurrence. This nonchalance irritated the secretary but Chase, the shrewd lawyer, did not let his irritation show. Perhaps, in the Spy's world undertakings of this sort were an everyday occurrence. The Spy listened without comment until Chase finished. When the secretary was silent the Spy sipped some wine and looked directly at Chase.

"The cost for this operation is $100,000 in gold." Chase's eyes went wide, but the Spy ignored the reaction and continued. "I do not expect you to pay the full amount in advance, of course. For operating expenses I will need $10,000, half in gold and half in paper from a reliable bank or in greenbacks. This sum is not part of the payment. The operating expenses will be delivered to Fitch on Friday, the twenty-third of this month. That should be sufficient time for you to raise the money. The payment for the full amount will be forwarded to me after I accomplish the task. Fitch will give you the address when you give him my operating expenses. Since your target is such a public figure, you will know almost immediately when I succeed. If the task is not performed by the first of June, this year, you may assume that I am dead and need not forward the money.

"In addition to the money, I will need passes for the War Department. One should be for a civilian and the other should be for a military man, an officer. The names are to be left blank. I will also need passes allowing me to go freely through the picket lines. Here, again, the names are to be left blank.

"This is the last time you and I will meet. Should we happen to see each other accidentally on the street you will pretend you don't know me. If we are introduced you will accept whatever name is given. If I need anything I will contact you through Fitch who will give his real name. As soon as I leave this dining room our contract begins. I am not boasting when I say I have never failed in a commission. My services are expensive, but are guaranteed. Since there is nothing in writing, I pride myself on the character of my clients, and from what I have seen you are a most honorable man. Unfortunately, sometimes even honorable men are tempted to do things which are, shall we say, foolish in the extreme. Perhaps it is the times. The point is, Mr. Secretary, that betraying me in any way would be most hazardous to your person."

The Spy was so casual, he might have been remarking on the weather. He communicated the threat without any malice. "If you have no questions, Mr. Secretary, I will take my leave."

Chase could think of no questions. He merely nodded and the Spy got up from the table.

"Good night, Mr. Secretary. It has, indeed, been a pleasure."

Chase watched him leave. When the Spy was gone, Chase sipped some wine and was surprised at the way he felt. The irritation and the nervousness were gone. He knew without a shadow of a doubt that he had hired the right man to execute his grand plan to save the Union. Chase wondered why a man like Anderson did what he did. It was undoubtedly the money, but there had to be more. Perhaps it was the sense of danger and high adventure. Chase understood that some men became addicted to danger the way that others became addicted to opium.

Anderson stepped into a carriage and gave the driver the address he wanted. He had no doubt that he could do exactly as the secretary asked. A plan was already forming in his mind. The Spy would have laughed had he known what Chase was thinking about him. Danger and high adventure were the last things that interested him. He had succeeded in his past commissions because he planned them thoroughly and executed them without a flaw. He did this because he understood the foibles of other people's judgment and observation. The Spy had no such weaknesses. Regardless of the situation he remained objective. As for the money, it mattered only as a measurement of the intricacy of the planning and the difficulty of the execution. Even before the secretary's offer, the Spy had enough to live comfortably for a long time. Commissions were his life's work. He loved the planning, the watching, and finally the result. From each commission he learned a little that helped him with the next. His previous commissions were his past. Whatever came before was dead. It was dead because he had purposely killed any link with it. It had been boring.

Anderson came from a decent, prosperous family which had provided him with an excellent education and a good career. Anderson found it all very boring, and when war came it appeared to offer interesting and exciting times. He enlisted in the local regiment, and after the usual delays in camp, the regiment marched off to its first battle. The battle was an insignificant affair as battles go, but Anderson distinguished himself by leading a company of men in an assault on an enemy position when all the officers had been killed or wounded. The position was taken, but Anderson was wounded in the arm severely enough to be hospitalized.

In the hospital, Anderson learned that he was breveted a lieutenant for his bravery. By then he had decided that the army, with all its silly rules, was also boring. There were too many ridiculous popinjays strutting about in uniform, giving people ridiculous orders. The Spy decided to leave his country's service then and there. His only concern was for his family's self-esteem. He felt he owed them that much. As an ambulatory patient, Anderson had a chance to walk around. As an officer he was required to do nothing. In his long, boring walks around the hospital he happened to see a man being wheeled about in a chair. This man bore a striking resemblance to Anderson, and he had a wound in about the same place in his shoulder. That was when Anderson conceived his first plan. He didn't realize it was a plan at the time but at least it was interesting. He liked to remember his first plan because it taught him several valuable lessons that would make his commissions successful. Instinctively, he knew he would need money. He wrote his parents for money and they graciously sent what they could to their heroic son. He then attempted to find out where this *doppelgaenger* of his was, but when he walked into another ward, the orderly asked him what he was doing there. Anderson explained that he was looking for a friend and the orderly brusquely told him that he didn't belong in the ward and would have to leave. Orderlies were large and muscular. They had to be to hold down patients undergoing amputations. Anderson left.

Lesson One: In order to go where you want without any trouble you must look as if you belong.

Later that day the doctor came to check on Anderson. The doctor was wearing a white smock over his uniform and was carrying a folder which contained patient records. The doctor told him that his wound was healing properly and that he could soon return to his regiment. As soon as the doctor left, Anderson donned his uniform and went looking for a white smock. He found one in a large closet. He went to a filing cabinet full of patients' records, removed a folder and walked purposefully through the wards looking for his twin. No one questioned him and a few even greeted him with "Hello Doctor." There was one bad moment, however. In one ward an orderly came up and took his arm. A patient's wound had begun to bleed again. Anderson told himself not to panic. He walked over and looked at the man.

"Quickly," he shouted at the orderly. "Clean the wound again and bind it."

The orderly did as he was told and the bleeding stopped. He told the soldier that he would be all right and told the orderly he had done a good job. They both thanked him and he moved on.

Lesson Two: If you want to look like you belong, you must act like you belong.

When the Spy found his double, the man was delirious. His wound had become septic and he was dying. Late that night, Anderson, dressed like an orderly, wheeled a gurney through the darkened, quiet wards. He returned to his unconscious double's beside and placed the gurney next to the bed. It was difficult rolling the unmoving body onto the gurney, but he finally managed it. Anderson returned to his own bed and placed his double into it. He was going to let the man die in peace but, as he was about to leave, the man woke up.

"Water. Please may I have some water?" the dying man asked in a croaking voice.

Anderson froze. What if the man had come awake after he had left? Without a word, Anderson smothered him with a pillow.

Lesson Three: Never leave anything to chance.

Anderson, still acting like an orderly took charge of the body and had it shipped to his parents as himself. He repaid their kindnesses by giving them the dead hero son they deserved.

He returned to the hospital and forged a certificate of medical discharge. He chose the name Anderson because unlike his own it was common, but not an obvious alias like Smith or Jones. Next he needed a base of operations. His first thought was to go to California, but he decided against it. It was too far away from the majority of the population. He considered many other places. He rejected the Confederacy because it was a new country and its currency was unstable. There were several large and important cities that seemed like good possibilities, and after a week of careful consideration he decided upon Washington, D.C. It seemed to suit his purposes best because there were more people with power in the District of Columbia than in any other city. Washington also seemed to be the most amoral city of all.

Upon his arrival in the District, Anderson took a room in a very modest hotel until he could find something less expensive and even less noticeable. During his sojourns through the city he assumed the guise of a rather fussy, innocuous little man who had found employment as a clerk and required rooms. After several days of searching, he arrived, carpet bag in hand at Mrs. Wellman's Boarding House. It seemed like the perfect place. The rent was reasonable and the table was ample. When Anderson applied for the room, Mrs. Wellman inquired if he were Irish, a salesman or an actor.

"An actor?" Anderson shrieked in undisguised horror. He picked up his bag. "Madam, I refuse to stay in any place that houses actors."

"Please, Mr. Anderson, you misunderstand," the lady said apologetically. "I don't allow Irishmen, salesmen, or actors. I run a respectable place."

"Oh," he said, relieved. "That's different. In that case, I would like to see the room." Anderson walked around the room, prodding the bed, looking in drawers and checking for dust. Finally, he announced that he would take it.

Mrs. Wellman's was filled with nobodies. Fortunately, they were mostly employed nobodies. There were two convalescing officers down the hall, but all they did was drink and play cards, which was fine with Anderson. There were two clerks who worked in government offices, a bank teller, and a retired music teacher who played the piano in the parlor every evening. Anderson represented himself as a finicky little busybody who paid his rent promptly and ate most of his meals at the boarding house. He made himself enough of a pest that the others avoided him.

With a place to stay that was still a drain on his modest resources, Anderson began to look for work that interested him. He discovered that if he frequented certain establishments looking clean but slightly shabby, there were errands to be run and a few dollars to be made if you weren't curious. Anderson's employers soon found that he was intelligent, reliable, sober (a rarity), and closed-mouthed. His horizons expanded. He spied for the North and for the South. He also spied for the English and the French. Anderson even worked for the Pinkerton Detective Agency, an association that would eventually benefit him a great deal. The Spy found working for Pinkerton interesting but it still wasn't exactly what he was looking for. Mr. Trowbridge provided the next step in his quest.

Mr. Trowbridge was a troubled man. It seems his wife found the company of another man preferable to his. The trouble was, he couldn't find out where either his wife or her companion might be. One evening in a tavern, Anderson overheard Mr. Trowbridge's complaint and introduced himself. He offered to solve the gentleman's problem for a sum of $100 in gold or the scrip of a good bank. Anderson found the couple in three days. He led Trowbridge to their room where Trowbridge burst through the door. The lover escaped in his underwear and the Spy had to stop Trowbridge from beating his wife long enough to get paid. To his surprise, Trowbridge gave him a $20 bonus. A smiling Anderson walked down the stairs to the sound of Trowbridge beating his wife senseless. Anderson's reputation spread rapidly. In a few months he had gone from waiting in bars to being much sought after for solving "domestic cases." His clients were mostly men, but Anderson owed his ultimate success to a woman. Mrs. Lorena Stolley, a very handsome woman, sought his assistance in finding whom her husband was seeing and where. She offered to pay in advance.

"Because I'm going to kill both of them when I find them." The woman was obviously distraught.

"Aren't you afraid you'll get caught?" Anderson asked. He was curious not sympathetic.

"I don't care," she said crying into her handkerchief. "He's betrayed me."

Solving Mrs. Stolley's problem suddenly interested Anderson. "Wouldn't it be better if your problem were solved and you were not suspected?"

"Can you do that?" Mrs. Stolley asked.

"I think it can be arranged for—say $1,000?"

Mrs. Stolley smiled shyly at him. "That sounds very reasonable, Mr. Anderson."

"The only other thing I need is a sample of your husband's handwriting."

Mr. Stolley was a very careful man and it took the Spy nearly a week to find the small house in Georgetown that was the errant husband's trysting place. Unfortunately, Mr. Stolley wasn't careful enough. He always entertained the pleasant looking young woman on Wednesdays. He spent other evenings out with friends who covered for him on the trysting night. Whenever his paramour was due, Stolley would give the housekeeper the evening off. On a Tuesday afternoon, the Spy put his plan into effect. Dressed as a carpenter, he visited the house claiming that Mr. Stolley had engaged him to do some work. He told the housekeeper that he needed to make some measurements in order to give Mr. Stolley an estimate. The housekeeper let him in. During the course of making measurements, the Spy unlatched three windows on the ground floor. He completed his work, thanked the housekeeper and left.

The following night the Spy returned with a club made of sand in a heavy sock, a rope made into a noose and an envelope. None of the windows he had unlocked had been relatched. When he climbed in the window nearest the kitchen he could hear Mr. Stolley and the lady upstairs. The Spy made his way quietly up the stairs and tied one end of the rope to the banister over looking the foyer of the house. He then tiptoed to the bedroom and waited until Mr. Stolley and his mistress were finished. They were pleasantly exhausted and the last thing they expected was an intruder. The Spy crawled along the floor and picked up one of the woman's silk stockings carelessly dropped there. The first blow of the club knocked Stolley senseless. The woman didn't have time to utter a sound before the stocking was wrapped tightly around her neck. It took her longer to die than the Spy expected and he was afraid that Stolley might come to, but he had hit him very hard and the man was still groggy when the woman lay still. Anderson lifted the semi-conscious man to his feet and moved him down the hall where he slipped the rope around Stolley's neck and pushed him over the banister. While Stolley jerked around attempting to save himself, Anderson returned to the bedroom and placed the artistically forged note near the woman's body. In the note, Mr. Stolley apologized to his wife for his betrayal and explained that he was taking the only honorable way out.

The housekeeper found the bodies the next day and went for the police. Upon examining the evidence, they came to the obvious conclusion Anderson had orchestrated. Stolley had murdered his mistress and killed himself out of remorse. The authorities then gave the tragic news to Mrs. Stolley who feigned the bereaved widow. Anderson earned his $1,000 and Mrs. Stolley showed how grateful she was for an entire week. After the Stolley commission, the Spy prospered. He never kept track of the money he made. What mattered was the difficulty of the commission.

Washington, D.C.
January 23, 1863

Joseph Fitch delivered the passes to the Spy. The man he knew as Anderson seemed well pleased.

"Very good, Joseph. Very good," the Spy said. He handed Fitch a twenty dollar gold piece. "Now tell me what you are supposed to do."

"I am to go to the house of Mrs. Lydia Ratliffe and watch the house for any army officers that visit. I am to find out who the officers are and where they work. I am to report to you daily."

"Very good. What else?"

"I am to clean up, get myself some good clothes, and I ain't supposed to get drunk."

"Excellent. Now be on your way. There's work to do."

Fitch left the room and walked downstairs. He left Mrs. Wellman's Boarding House wondering why Mr. Anderson didn't stay in a fancy hotel like the National or Willard's. If Fitch had bothered to think, he would have realized that to a man like Anderson, anonymity was an asset. Of course he didn't think. If he had the Spy never would have hired him. Fitch let the thought pass. It was no business of his. Anderson, or whatever his name was paid well. Fitch's share of the work would be $500. That was a lot of money for just a few errands and keeping your mouth shut. One thing you didn't do was cross Anderson. The ones who tried were at the bottom of the Potomac feeding the turtles. The Spy watched Fitch amble down the street toward his destination then closed the curtain. He sat at the small table and began to finalize his plans. Now all he had to do was catch the right fish and he would be headed south in perfect company.

It took Fitch nearly three weeks to do as he had been asked. It was surprisingly good work. The spy already knew about Lydia Ratliffe and her intelligence gathering operation. Lydia Ratliffe was an attractive and, from all accounts, a wealthy widow who enjoyed male company and gathered information for the Confederacy. Nearly everyone knew about her except the War Department and the District Police. The Pinkerton Detective Agency had its suspicions, but Ratliffe's high-placed friends kept protecting her. For the Spy's purposes the situation was ideal.

Mrs. Ratliffe was also one of the most charming women in Washington and her legendary parties were attended by the elite of the city. Congressmen, army officers, and government officials regularly attended the parties which were held at the Ratliffe mansion. After observing the mansion over a period of time, Fitch discovered that among the partygoers there were two army officers who were regular visitors to the Ratliffe residence. On Sunday, February 8, he stood with the Spy on a dark corner opposite the mansion. As usual, the lady was entertaining and the house was brightly lit. Carriage after carriage drove up to the door to let off visitors. The spy recognized many of them immediately. Two of them, Montgomery Blair and Caleb Smith were members of Lincoln's cabinet. In addition to the politicians there were scores in uniform. Fitch watched each carefully.

"There's the colonel," Fitch said quietly pointing out the man. "The one with gray hair."

The Spy lifted his field glasses to his eyes. The officer was Lieutenant Colonel James Swanson, a volunteer officer from Massachusetts. Swanson's regiment had been disbanded when his men's enlistments were up in April 1862. His reason for remaining in Washington was to get another regiment. There had been four new Massachusetts regiments through the city since, and he had joined none of them. Instead, he had attended every official party—invited or not—and had become enamored of Mrs. Ratliffe's charms. The colonel was costing the state of Massachusetts a lot of money. He was not only useless to his home state and the Union, he was also useless for the Spy's purposes.

"That's the other one," Fitch said in strained whisper. "That's Major Ellison."

No one saw the Spy smile. He focused his field glasses on a tall, distinguished looking officer. If he knew human nature, the major was his ticket to the Confederacy. He checked his watch. He would wait fifteen minutes. He watched quietly as more distinguished guests arrived for the widow Ratliffe's soiree. Another uniform would hardly be noticed. When the fifteen minutes were up the Spy told Fitch to go home and get some sleep. He then stepped out of the shadows wearing the uniform of a captain of cavalry and a very natural looking mustache. The Spy walked across the street to the large house. A colored servant at the door stopped him.

"May I see the captain's invitation?" he asked haughtily.

Since so many arrived without invitations, the Spy assumed the man was looking for a bribe. When in Rome . . . The Spy handed the man a greenback and the servant bowed gratefully. The Spy walked in and another servant took his hat. Mrs. Ratliffe certainly didn't skimp on the entertainment. There was a full orchestra and plenty of French champagne, not to mention enough food to feed a regiment. The Spy took a glass of champagne and made his way through the crowd. He introduced himself to several superior officers, saying that it was nice to see them again. They smiled coldly and acted as if he were something akin to dirt and that was just what he wanted. He had been seen and if they saw him again later there would be recognition and the knowledge that he belonged in uniform. Some of the women at the party looked at him hungrily and he put that away for further reference. He dumped several glasses of champagne into potted plants, giving the impression that he was drinking heavily. It took him a while to find Major Ellison.

The major was in his late thirties or perhaps early forties. He had dark hair and a full beard with a touch of gray. In uniform, he looked quite handsome and several of the ladies in the assembly thought him attractive enough to give out some nearly blatant invitations. It was soon obvious that the major was a painfully shy man especially where women were concerned. It was also obvious that the major was in love with Mrs. Ratliffe to the point of distraction. The Spy watched Ellison as he acted like a smitten teenager and followed their hostess around like a puppy. It was obvious to anyone who had eyes that the lady could have cared less. The Spy followed them and learned that the major was not without skill as he managed to maneuver Mrs. Ratliffe into a more or less private alcove. The Spy placed himself around a corner of the alcove behind a large plant. When they began to talk he peeked around the corner. Mrs. Ratliffe and the major were so involved in their conversation that they didn't realize they were being observed.

"My darling why don't we marry and move away from here? Then we don't have to worry about this war coming between us." The voice was whining and pleading.

"Charles," she said in a long dramatic drawl. "You know I cannot desert the cause. I must carry on my work here until we are triumphant. Only then can I think of my own personal happiness. I thought you understood that."

"I do, my dove. It's just that we never seem to have any time alone together anymore and I can't stand to be away from you." He took her hand in his and kissed it. The expression on her face was somewhere between irritation and revulsion.

"If you really loved me, you would help me," she said petulantly.

The major looked pained. "I bring you everything I can, my dove."

"None of it is ever important," she snapped. "I think you just use it to take advantage of my affection for you. You are most callous, Charles."

"Oh, please, don't think ill of me. It's not true."

"Now, I must return to my guests." In a graceful, but contemptuous gesture she slipped away from him and moved back into the throng. The major stood in the alcove as if he were mesmerized and his gaze followed her. The Spy, pretending to be drunk, staggered around the corner and accidentally bumped into the major.

"Who was that?" the Spy asked.

"The most wonderful woman in the world," the major said dreamily.

The Spy smiled. He had his man.

CHAPTER 2

Washington, D.C.
February 9, 1863

THE SPY KNEW that most plans fail for two reasons. The first was that the planner did not pay sufficient attention to detail. The second was that the executor, no matter how enthusiastic he might be, was not sufficiently familiar with the purposes of the plan to be flexible when something unexpected occurred. The Spy was determined to avoid both reasons for failure. He was meticulous in laying his plans. He wrote them down to the smallest detail in a notebook. His notes were made in his own cipher. After a day or two, he reviewed them and subjected each aspect of the plan to the most intense scrutiny. Once he was satisfied that the plan was as good as theoretically possible, he memorized it thoroughly. He then burned the notebook. It was this almost pathological determination not to leave any trace of himself that contributed to his success.

In the execution of his plans the Spy had no equal. He avoided danger wherever possible. He did this because he always understood his adversary better than the adversary understood himself. This was where most plans were weakest and where he excelled. He had always caught the object of his attention totally unaware, so that by the time the object knew what was happening—if he ever knew what was happening—it was too late. The part of the plan involving Major Ellison was a typical situation.

In order to discover the major's habits, traits, and weaknesses (other than Mrs. Ratliffe), Anderson had to observe him in the most minute detail over a course of days if not weeks. It is one thing to watch someone from across a street. It is quite another to become part of a person's routine, observe him every day, and not be considered someone unusual. The work was tedious and boring and very dangerous, for if the quarry suspected anything the entire plan could be ruined. The Spy knew all of this and took great pains with this part of his plan. He never trusted the important parts, regardless of how uninteresting they might seem, to others. He did them himself. Only peripheral matters were entrusted to underlings like Fitch.

In the matter of underlings, the Spy was equally careful. He preferred getting people to accomplish his ends without them really knowing what was going on. An appeal to their vanity or patriotism and a little hard cash usually accomplished the task. However, underlings were sometimes unavoidable. At first he had had a difficult time with them. One man tried to blackmail him and a woman had wanted to stay with him. He had disposed of them quickly and efficiently. The word spread: Anderson pays well, but don't cross him. He usually looked for certain attributes in his subordinates, and Fitch had most of them. He was not overly curious, he stayed sober when he had to be, he kept his mouth shut, he was dependable, and he was an excellent observer of other human beings. These were the reasons that Joseph Fitch had been with him longer than any other assistant. He did have three weaknesses: whiskey, cockfighting, and women. The order of preference depended on his particular appetite at the moment. During commissions, Fitch avoided all three. Between commissions, the Spy insured that Fitch had enough money to stay dissolute until he needed him again.

In order to learn the intimate details of Major Ellison's life, the Spy first had to discover precisely where he spent most of his time. Fitch had already done this for him by watching the Ratliffe house. When the major left the Ratliffe mansion, Fitch followed him home. He stayed by Ellison's door the entire night and, in the morning, followed the unsuspecting major to the building where he worked. By asking around, Fitch learned that Ellison had a desk in the War Plans office. The preliminary work was completed. Now the Spy had to learn exactly where in the building Ellison worked and what he did.

To do this, the Spy would have to penetrate the War Department security system. This, he knew would not be difficult. In fact, he was greatly amused by the Army's idea of security. The War Department system revolved around a series of passes for those buildings it considered vital to protect. There were three sets of passes. One set was for people who worked in War Department buildings. A pass was assigned to each individual who worked in a particular building and the individual kept his or her pass. The second set was for people who did not work in a particular building, but needed access to it. This category included contractors, visiting officials and officers from other agencies, and the navy. The third type of pass allowed access to any building in the War Department. This pass was for people whose duties required them to frequent more than one building, such as the Under-Secretaries of War, generals and couriers. To army officers who questioned little, this system seemed more than adequate. It might have done some good had there been some controls on the system but there were none.

The first thing the War Department did was hire a contractor to print the passes. The contractor printed as many numbered passes as the contract called for. No one checked to see if additional copies had been run or to whom they had been sold. It was rumored that one printer made more money selling a few additional passes than he had from fulfilling the contract for the War Department. At the end of the war, the army congratulated itself on the success of its system because no counterfeit passes were discovered. It never occurred to them that real ones were too easy to come by. The army continued to believe that its system worked perfectly.

Once the passes were printed, they had to be signed and issued. Naturally no one of any importance was going to spend days signing hundreds, if not thousands of passes. So the onerous duty of "Building Guard Officer" was passed to some underling. Usually this was a lieutenant, but sometimes a captain found himself the lowest member on the totem pole. It is not difficult to imagine the attitudes of these functionaries toward their duties. The officers of good quality were chafing at the bit to get into action where they could win fame and promotion. The others were content with their lot and were not about to do anything that might get them noticed so they would be sent into action where they end up in a pine coffin. Therefore, no one dared criticize the system, assuming they noticed. Once the passes were signed, they were given to a sergeant or a corporal who would issue them and record the number of each one, the person to whom it was issued, and the date it was issued. On the outside of each building the War Department considered important stood two or more guards. These were privates armed with single shot muzzle-loading rifles. The presence of these two guards announced to the world that the War Department had something inside the building that it considered worth guarding.

At the entrance of the building there was also a sergeant or a corporal at a desk. The sergeant's duty was to check the passes of those who worked in the building as they entered. If he had been on duty for a few days and was reasonably sober, he could recognize these people without their passes. His most important duty was to issue a pass to those who wanted to enter the building, but did not work there. In addition to issuing the passes, he entered in a ledger the number of the pass issued, the time the person entered the building, and the time he left. This was also the procedure for those carrying passes for the entire War Department. For identification, the sergeant relied on the military papers of the person requesting entry. If the person was not military, the sergeant would rely on letters, visiting cards, or even the person's word. It depended on the sergeant's attitude or his mood. The Spy speculated that the system might successfully keep out someone trying to impersonate the president if the sergeant were a close relative of Mr. Lincoln.

There was another side to this system of guarded buildings. There were places that the War Department did not consider important enough to restrict access to. The Commissary Department and the harness shops were two of them. There were, of course, guards, but these were posted to prevent theft and pilferage, not to protect information. A reporter or someone masquerading as one could walk into the main office of the Commissary Department and learn that the department was issuing 160,000 rations per day to the Army of the Potomac. Likewise the harness shops could tell him the number of harnesses available, the number lost, the harness being made, and the number in need of repair.

In order to gain access for a quick look where he would have to go inside the building, the Spy decided to dress as a courier. Uniformed men are least suspicious to soldiers. In order to look and act as if he belonged, he carried a dispatch case. In the case were the kinds of routine dispatches that are the lifeblood of every army. To anyone giving them a close scrutiny they would appear genuine. They were made by a man who lived near the Chain and Anchor and specialized in the creation of any and all documents required by his clients, whether they were false bills of lading or genuine War Department passes. His services were expensive but valuable. The Spy used him because he found that he was a more talented forger and the Spy was not one to let ego get in the way of a well executed plan. The dispatches were his backup in case his presence in the building were questioned. He would show the dispatches to the person questioning his presence and innocently ask assistance. It was a ploy that never failed. If no one questioned him, he would deliver them to a convenient recipient.

On a cold Tuesday morning, the Spy presented himself to the sergeant in the large War Department building on the corner of 17th and G streets across the street from the White House, which was looking pathetically run-down. To anyone who cared to notice, he was a captain of volunteer cavalry, so typical of those who entered and left the building every day. The sergeant at the desk looked at his identification and his pass and wrote "Captain Donald Henderson, 6th Pensy Cvlry" in the ledger and the number of his pass. The Spy entered the building and was pleased to find that the other part of the army's security system was in effect. On every floor was a large sign indicating which offices were on that floor. On each door was a sign indicating who occupied the room. The generals had the largest signs, the colonels the next largest, and so forth. The Spy made a mental note of the fact that a Major Thomas of the Surgeon's Department worked on the first floor in room nine. A short walk up the stairs revealed that the Plans Office was on the third floor. Major Ellison worked in the the fourth office on the right. The Spy opened the door and walked into the room. It was full of officers and clerks working diligently at their desks. Only one or two seemed to notice him but no one acknowledged his presence. He had a dispatch case and that undoubtedly meant extra work. The spy walked around the room twice, memorizing the layout of the room and closely observing the major busily working at his desk. Finally, he stopped at a clerk's desk.

"Excuse me," he said smiling an embarrassed smile.

The clerk looked at him with an annoyed expression. "Yes?"

"Excuse me," the Spy said again. "I think I got turned around. Could you direct me to Major Thomas' office?"

The clerk looked around the room. "Does anyone know a Major Thomas?"

"First floor, I think," someone said.

"Thank you," the Spy said with genuine gratitude. "Thank you very much."

The Spy left the room and went downstairs to room nine where he handed a befuddled surgeon, whose specialty was diseases of the lungs, a case full of dispatches concerning artillery mules. The major snorted that the damned army was totally fouled up. The captain agreed, saluted, and left.

The Spy put the first part of the plan into effect. A cleaned up and well dressed Joseph Fitch temporarily took rooms in the same boarding house on 22nd Street that housed Major Ellison. He thought the second part would be more difficult, and take a long time. However, it took him only one day to find a way to stay in the War Department Building on a permanent basis. The building was run by a custodian named Alfred Hull who kept it clean and tidy. His position was a reward for a favor he had done for a senator. He was paid a salary and given a sum of money with which to maintain the building. A shrewd custodian could pocket a tidy sum each year if he managed his accounts correctly, and Hull was shrewder than most. He hired mostly women, who worked cheaper, then required them to give him back some of their pay in order to keep their jobs. If they struck Hull's fancy they were required to give a little more. The Spy made no judgments. It was the system and he saw no reason to change it. He only needed to understand it in order to use it. It required only one evening to follow Hull to his favorite tavern and then home to find out where the janitor lived.

The Spy prepared very carefully for his meeting with the custodian, and decided to present himself as a Pinkerton Detective. The credentials he would present to the custodian were quite genuine. Since the Spy still did work for the Pinkerton Agency between commissions, they let him maintain his credentials. It was worth it for the minimal effort required. The Spy was already wearing the disguise he intended to use. He only wanted the janitor to see one person. The Spy had gained his expertise with disguises as the result of a commission he performed for a famous actor. Part of the actor's fee for Anderson's help in divesting himself of a troublesome wife was a series of lessons about acting and makeup. The actor, who was considered a genius in the way he changed his appearance on stage used much less makeup than his contemporaries.

"Create an illusion and let it live and breathe," the actor told Anderson. "Don't suffocate it under a slab of pancake."

The Spy always followed the actor's advice.

The Spy knocked loudly on Alfred Hull's door late one night. "Mr. Hull!" he called impatiently.

Hull opened the door and eyed Anderson suspiciously.

"Mr. Hull," the Spy said, showing Hull his badge, "my name's Anderson. I'm a Pinkerton Detective."

"So what do you want with me?" Hull asked warily.

Good, the Spy thought. If he feels guilty about something it will make things much easier.

"May I come in?" the Spy asked. "This is not something you'll want your neighbors to hear."

"Yeah, I guess so." Hull stood aside and let Anderson into the dingy little room.

The Spy stepped into the room and looked around. He said nothing at first, trying to discover just how guilty the custodian felt. Anderson didn't care what Hull had done just as long as the fear helped Hull make the right decision. Hull was beginning to look at him fearfully. Very good.

"There is a Rebel spy in your building," the Spy told him. "I want you to put me on as a janitor so I can watch him."

"What if I don't want to?" It was a halfhearted attempt at bluster.

"If you hire me, I will work for no pay. In addition to that you will be paid $25 per week for your services and cooperation. If you refuse, we have to assume that you are in league with this spy and I will have you arrested and charged with treason."

The janitor's jaw dropped. "You wouldn't."

"This spy has done untold damage to the nation, sir," the Spy said pompously. "He must be apprehended. I consider anyone who stands in my way no worse a traitor."

The janitor looked and him and rubbed his unshaved chin. "You did say $25 a week, didn't you?"

"Naturally, we don't expect to saddle honest citizens with financial burdens."

"All right, sure," Hull said with a sigh of relief. "I'm patriotic. Tell the sergeant at the desk you want to see me. What'll I say the name is?"

"Do you hire Irishmen?"

The janitor laughed. "Hell no."

"Germans?"

"They're all right."

"The name is Herman Stein."

"See you in the morning, Mr. Stein."

On the following morning, the Spy, sporting workman's clothes and a thick German accent appeared at the door of the War Department building on 17th and G. He stated with some difficulty that he was looking for Mr. Hull who had promised him a job. In due course, the janitor arrived and took him to an office where he was given a pass. He then went to work. The Spy did whatever job Hull assigned without shirking. He swept halls, carried out ashes, and cleaned rest rooms. He ran errands for government workers too lazy to walk to lunch by getting their lunches for them. In the first week he made over two dollars in tips. If a government worker wanted him to do something he didn't want to do he would tell them "Nicht undershtandt zu goot" and they would leave him alone. By the end of the second week, Anderson, the sweeper of floors, and Fitch, the roomer, had learned a great deal about Major Ellison.

The major was a man of spartan and rigid habits. His rooms were devoid of any decoration, save for the inexpensive Currier & Ives lithographs that came with the furnishings. The only personal item in the room other than his clothing and toilet articles was on his dresser. This was a daguerreotype of Mrs. Ratliffe. Next to it was a desiccated red rose. His only jewelry was a cheap gold washed ring in the form of a lion head with cut glass eyes which Lydia Ratliffe had given him as a token. Every morning, the major rose promptly at 5:00 A.M. He was then shaved and dressed by his valet. After a large breakfast of ham and eggs with coffee, biscuits and jam, the major read *The National Intelligencer* and walked the five blocks to the Plans Office of the War Department.

On Sundays he attended the small Presbyterian church near his rooms before going to work for half a day. The major arrived at work at precisely 6:30 A.M. He worked steadily, writing plans or reviewing dispatches until approximately 9:00 A.M. when he went to the bathroom for a period of no more than six minutes. When he returned he drank a cup of coffee while he continued his work. At noon, he gave a soldier money to buy a sandwich and a bottle of beer. He didn't tip the soldier, but once a week bought him a lunch. Ellison ate his sandwich while he worked and continued until 2:30 P.M. when he once again had to use the bathroom. After his trip to the bathroom, the major had another cup of coffee and worked through until 6:30 P.M., at which hour he walked home to take supper. If he ate in his rooms the supper would be light. If he ate out which he did twice a week, his supper would be quite heavy, accompanied by his favorite red wine and followed by cheese, brandy, and a cigar.

During the day various dispatches would arrive and the major, as the senior officer in the room, would sign for and read every one. If he considered them important enough for Mrs. Ratliffe to send south, he would take them home and copy them. On Wednesday and Friday evenings he took a carriage to Mrs. Ratliffe's. His visits lasted anywhere from a few minutes to well into the evening. Once he did not leave until the wee hours of the morning. The Spy speculated that he was being rewarded for a particularly important piece of information. At the end of two weeks, the Spy terminated his employment at the War Department. Hull, who was $50 richer, was sorry to see him go.

Shortly after the Spy ended his career as a janitor he made another visit to the neighborhood of The Chain and Anchor to see the artistic forger. This time he commissioned a set of two dispatches. One was another set of routine dispatches concerning the supply of salt pork to a particular division. It seemed the pork had not been properly preserved and a number of men had become ill. The other dispatches contained the details of Hooker's advance on Richmond to start in March. The Union Army would catch the Confederate Army in winter quarters, and, for once, steal a march on them. The movement orders for the entire Army of the Potomac were included. There were two copies of the same orders, each done by a different clerk. There were also other documents that even made the forger raise an eyebrow, but he said nothing. The Spy was pleased. The forger's work was most impressive and the Spy happily gave him the the $350 in gold that they had agreed upon as the fee.

The War Department
Washington, D.C.
February 23, 1863

On Monday, the Spy once again appeared as "Captain Donald Henderson, 6th Pensy Cvlry." He passed through the entrance to the building with no trouble and went straight to Major Ellison's office. The garrulous captain irritated the major and Ellison signed for the dispatches almost without comment. On Wednesday February 25, the Spy delivered his second set of dispatches.

"I'd like to see the expression on Bobby Lee's face when he finds out that Fightin' Joe Hooker is in Richmond before he wakes up," the Spy said.

The major looked at him. He had a distant look. The Spy knew what Ellison was thinking. Here was a way to further ingratiate himself with Lydia Ratliffe.

"Uh, yes, that's right captain. Very good."

"Please sign for them here, sir," the Spy said producing a receipt.

The major looked down at the receipt. It said only one copy and the captain had delivered two. Ellison's jaw dropped. This was a fabulous piece of luck. The major could hardly contain himself.

When the Spy left the War Department, Fitch was across the street, ready to follow Ellison. The Spy climbed into a closed carriage, gave the driver an address, and changed into civilian clothes en route. His destination was a tavern in a neighborhood not quite as bad as that of the Chain and Anchor. There he met an attractive young woman named Irma Lindman. Miss Lindman was an actress who was having difficulty finding work. Despite her ill fortune she was well dressed and obviously trying to maintain her dignity. The Spy bought her lunch which she began to eat hungrily.

"Miss Lindman," he said. "I must confess that my assistant was not totally candid with you. I am not the owner of a theater, although I do require your talents as an actress."

She gave him a filthy look that told him that she was not a prostitute. That was even better. Before she could tell him so he continued.

"My name is Anderson and I'm with the Pinkerton Detective Agency," he said showing her his credentials.

She looked at him with the suspicion that any thespian might regard a member of the police. The Spy pretended not to notice.

"We are on the trail of a spy who works in the Provost Marshal's office. Whenever we try to trap someone we suspect is a spy, this man warns him and our quarry is able to escape. Tonight we have set a trap for him but we need the talents of a trained actress such as yourself. In addition, there is a substantial reward for the capture of this man. Your share would be $100."

Lindman's eyes lit up at the mention of the money.

"All you have to do is pretend you are a certain officer's fiance. This man has betrayed you and his country for a beautiful Confederate spy to whom he plans to give some valuable information before they run off together this evening. I will give you the correct address. You must notify the desk sergeant at the Provost Marshal's office of these facts at 5:30 P.M. this evening. After you have notified the sergeant, you will be paid and say nothing of this again.

Miss Lindman sipped her beer and smiled. "One hundred dollars?"

"Yes."

"How do I know if this is on the level."

"All you have to do is walk right back into the Provost Marshal's office if you are not paid."

"I guess I don't have anything to lose," she said. "All right."

At the proper time, Anderson met Miss Lindman near the Provost Marshal's office. The Spy followed the actress at a discreet distance and listened to her tell the desk sergeant what had happened. She was very convincing. On the way out he handed her five $20 gold pieces.

"Your country will ever be in your debt, Miss Lindman," he told her, tipping his hat.

"I'll bet," she said sarcastically and disappeared into the night.

At 7:15 P.M., three men and an officer from the Provost Marshal's office intercepted Major Ellison outside Lydia Ratliffe's house. He was carrying the extra copy of the dispatches that the Spy had given him earlier in the afternoon. The Spy watched from a dark corner across the street as the Provost's men arrested him and dragged him to a prison wagon. The major kept looking over his shoulder at the house. His expression was one of disappointment and disbelief.

The Spy found no time to congratulate himself. The next phase of his plan would be the most difficult. He had to convince Lydia Ratliffe that he was a Confederate sympathizer who had important information that had to be taken south. Despite her outward appearance of a frivolous woman who gave lavish parties, Lydia Ratliffe was an experienced operative in the network of Colonel Raymond Longfellow, General J.E.B. Stuart's legendary chief of scouts. She was intelligent, shrewd, and naturally suspicious. The Spy knew it would be useless to try the same tactics with her as he had with Ellison. Mrs. Ratliffe would be leery of a new person in her midst immediately after Ellison's arrest. Therefore, instead of the methodical approach, he was going to have to panic her.

From observation, the Spy knew that the lovely Mrs. Ratliffe had three weaknesses. She was genuinely loyal to the Confederate cause. This meant that there was something she considered more important than herself. This was a concept that the Spy understood in others even though it was foreign to his nature. Her second weakness was her fear of discovery, which would be great indeed once she found out that Ellison had been apprehended practically on her doorstep. The lady's third weakness was men. By all accounts, her appetite for male company was legion. This last weakness the Spy had already rejected. It would take too long to exploit. His only hope was to panic the lady which was why he had had Major Ellison arrested. The Spy then took a calculated risk. He waited three days. This would insure that the news of

Ellison's arrest got to the attractive widow. It would also insure that Ellison would be sufficiently desperate.

Forrest Hall Military Prison
Georgetown
February 28, 1863

The Spy was surprised at the appearance of Forrest Hall Military Prison in Georgetown. Instead of high walls, iron bars, and a heavy gate, he found a three-story brick building with a stone facade that was right on the street. Next to it was May's Bakery and Confectioners complete with candy canes in the window. The Spy presented his credentials as Major Harold Waters of the Judge Advocate General's Corps. He was there to see to the defense of one Major Charles Ellison. He requested a private room in which to have a conference with his client. This was a standard request and the Spy was led to a small conference room where he waited for his client. Had he been a compassionate man, the Spy would have undoubtedly felt pity for the major. Ellison had aged at least a decade in the past three days. The military lawyer introduced himself and bid his client sit down. The Spy explained the major's situation as succinctly as possible.

"What you're trying to say is that they're going to hang me."

"Not necessarily, major. You could get your sentence reduced to twenty years at hard labor if you told the Provost Marshal who your contacts are."

"No!" He said. "I'll never betray her."

The Spy breathed a sigh of relief. "Mrs. Ratliffe will be glad to hear that."

"You mean Lydia . . . "

The Spy put his finger to his lips. "Please be quiet and listen. I am here to rescue you, but you must help me."

"How? I don't understand."

"I will be here tonight with a guard to obtain your transfer to the penitentiary. Be ready to leave at a moment's notice and say nothing."

Hope gleamed in Ellison's face. "I knew she wouldn't let me down."

"I'll be back later to discuss the rest of your case, Major Ellison. Is there anything I can get for you in the meantime?"

"No thank you, Major Waters. I have everything I need now."

At 7:00 P.M. the Spy appeared at the prison. This time he was Major Joshua Gordon of the Provost Marshal's office. He was assigned to transfer the prisoner Major Charles Ellison to the penitentiary. He had only one guard. The Spy asked if the prisoner was dangerous.

"No sir," the sergeant of the guard replied. "This one's a pussycat. Arrested for treason. They ought to stretch his neck, if you ask me."

Major Ellison was led out to the waiting area. Under the Articles of War, an officer kept his rank until convicted and sentenced, so he was dressed in full uniform. The guards at Forrest Hall Military Prison were taking no chances. Since Ellison was charged with a serious crime they had put him in irons. The Spy signed for the prisoner and the keys. He hoped the irons wouldn't prove too much of a problem. Outside, Fitch, dressed in the uniform of a sergeant, sat in the driver's seat of a wagon that had four rows of seats. Beneath the last seat was the body of the driver from whom Fitch had stolen the wagon. The Spy helped Ellison into the seat behind Fitch.

"All right, sergeant, the prisoner is secure," the Spy told him.

Fitch snapped the reins and the team started the wagon forward. When they came to an intersection, the Spy instructed the driver to turn right.

"But the penitentiary is to the left," the driver protested and pulled the wagon to a halt.

The Spy pulled a pistol from under his cloak. "Drive to the right, like I told you," he said.

"No," the driver said reaching for his rifle.

The Spy's pistol exploded in the dark. The flash blinded Ellison but he heard the sergeant cry out and fall off the wagon with a thud. The Spy climbed into the driver's seat and urged the horses forward. Fitch waited until the wagon was out of sight then got up and stripped off the uniform that he was wearing over his street clothes. He tossed them in an alley and started the long walk home. He had bruised his elbow in the fall and he rubbed it. It hurt but he smiled. If everything went well tonight, he had only one thing left to do and his part in this commission was over. He would have $500 to spend and he knew the woman who would see the first part of it.

A few blocks from the shooting, the Spy stopped the wagon underneath a gaslight. "Quick, let me unlock those irons," he said. The irons took a while to get off but they finally got them open.

"I don't know how to thank you . . . " Ellison began.

"Save it. I was hoping I wouldn't have to kill that guard," the Spy said. His voice was tinged in panic. "We have to leave the wagon and find someplace to hide."

"Lydia will hide us," Ellison said. "Let's hire a carriage quickly."

They hastily left the wagon where it was and walked toward Pennsylvania Avenue where the were sure to find a carriage for hire. No one gave a thought to two army officers walking up a street on that cold night. By the time they reached "The Avenue" they were just two of many. Ellison hired a carriage and gave the driver Lydia Ratliffe's address. If this doesn't panic her, the Spy thought, nothing will.

The Spy paid the driver and checked quickly to insure they weren't being watched. The house was well lighted so they moved quickly to the front door. Ellison banged on the door loudly with the huge brass knocker. Daniel, the colored servant who the Spy had bribed previously, answered the door. Obviously, he had been expecting someone else.

"Major Ellison," he said staring in amazement. "We heard you was . . . "

Ellison pushed into the house. "Where's Lydia?"

"Uh, Mrs. Ratliffe . . . " Daniel called.

"Lydia!" he called.

The Spy wanted to smile but didn't. There was one thing you could say for Major Charles Ellison. He was true to type.

Lydia came down the stairs.

"Daniel," she said to her servant. "What is the . . . Charles," she screamed. "What are you doing here?"

"I need help, my dove."

"Help? Are you insane? They arrested you right across the street. They're probably watching the place right now. Are you trying to get us all hanged?"

"But, Lydia . . . "

"No buts. Get out right now!"

She was on the verge of panic and the Spy had to play this one carefully.

"I thought you said she'd help," the Spy said sharply to Ellison.

Lydia noticed him for the first time.

"Who is this?" she screamed at Ellison.

"I'm a friend," the Spy told her.

"He's the one who helped me escape," Ellison told her. "He had to shoot a guard."

"I can't believe you'd be so stupid to escape from prison, shoot a Yankee soldier, and walk in here. I have half a mind to turn you in myself."

"I don't think you want to do that," the Spy said firmly. "You'd only be putting a noose around your own neck."

"What do think I have around my neck with you here in the house? Just who are you anyway?"

"I told you. I'm a friend."

"With friends like you we could all go to the gallows."

"I helped Major Ellison escape because I need a way out. I have been under deep cover. I only see a contact once a month. I wasn't supposed to break it except under orders, but two days ago I saw something that was too important to delay. I thought this was the best way. I could help Ellison and he could help me."

"Colonel Longfellow never told me about you," the widow said.

"He couldn't have," the Spy replied calmly. "I work for General Beauregard."

Lydia looked at him. He didn't want her to have time to think.

"Why don't you hide us tonight and get us out tomorrow night. We head south and you never see us again. No harm done."

"How do I know you're not one of Pinkerton's men?" she asked.

"Look, I don't want to do this, but I'll show you what I have. However, it has to be to you alone. If you don't believe me then, we'll leave. Fair enough?"

She was curious. "Fair enough. Let me see it."

"Alone."

"Give me your gun."

"No. I don't trust you anymore than you trust me."

She hesitated a moment. "All right. Come with me."

The Spy followed her to the small alcove where he had first seen her with Ellison. He handed her the letter. As she read it she gasped.

"It can't be."

"Do you doubt the signature?"

"No, I've seen Stanton's signature plenty of times before. That Yankee bastard!"

"Mrs. Ratliffe, please." The Spy sounded amazed that a lady would use such language.

"All right," she said. "I'll help you, but I can't get you through the Yankee pickets yet. I don't have any of the new passes."

"I helped myself to some before I left."

"Just how did you happen to get your hands on that letter?" she asked. She was still suspicious.

"I was carrying messages for the Secretary of War. I always read his mail."

She looked at him but said nothing. The crisis had been passed.

"Daniel, get the attic room ready."

"Yes, Mrs. Ratliffe." The servant disappeared.

"The attic room is a bit cramped but no one will find you. If I had my way I'd have you out of here right now."

"I realize the position I have put you in, Mrs. Ratliffe, believe me. Had there been any other way, I would have taken it. Your contribution to the cause will never be rewarded enough." Lydia seemed genuinely flattered by the last remark.

"The room is ready," Daniel said.

"Follow Daniel," she told them, hurriedly. "I'll see you in the morning."

The Spy said nothing else. He followed behind Daniel and Ellison. It didn't seem like a trap, but he had his pistol just in case. Daniel, carrying an oil lamp, led them up the stairs to the attic. When he was nearly at he top of the stairs he slid back a portion of the wall revealing another set of steep, narrow steps. There were only about six steps and they led to a low room above the attic. Daniel lit a lamp. The space was less than four feet high. There was no place to build a fire but the place was not uncomfortable because the chimney ran up through it. The Spy also noticed that the space was not musty. It was apparently used quite often. There were two mattresses and plenty of blankets on the floor. Daniel, undoubtedly used to such visitors, had left a small basket of food and two bottles of beer. In the corner was a chamber pot. "All the comforts of home," the Spy said. "Thank you, Daniel."

"My pleasure, sir."

Daniel walked backward down the steps. The Spy waited until the servant slid the panel back in place then relaxed. They were safe until morning. He was hungry. In the basket he found cold chicken, bread, butter, a jar of pickled oysters, and some potatoes made into a salad. He opened the jar of oysters and a bottle of beer. Ellison was not even paying attention to the food. The Spy, acting the interested friend turned to him.

"Aren't you hungry?" he asked.

"No, thank you, Waters. Or is it Gordon?"

"Actually it's Anderson. Something wrong?"

"I guess I just realized that after tomorrow it will be a long time before I see Lydia again."

The Spy thought Ellison was a damned fool.

"She's a wonderful woman," Ellison continued. "I'm sure you can see that. I love her and I put her in danger. I'd die before I'd let that happen again."

That could be arranged very easily, my friend, the Spy thought.

"Now I must do something to make myself worthy of her affection again. What do you think I should do? Should I apply for service with the Confederacy?"

"That sounds like the right thing to do. Now, eat something. You need to keep up your strength."

"I think I'll apply for a commission in the infantry," Ellison said more to himself than to his companion.

I don't think you need to plan that far ahead, the Spy said to himself. The Spy sat on one of the mattresses and stretched out. He pulled the blankets over himself. He had to get some sleep tonight. It would probably be his last full night of sleep for some time, but there was one thing left to do. He waited until Ellison fell asleep, then he quickly removed his clothes. He folded what he wanted to hide in a bundle, then hid it in the eaves near the chimney. He hoped that Daniel wouldn't see it.

In the morning, Daniel gently woke the Spy. Major Ellison was already up. He looked as if he hadn't slept at all. The Spy didn't mind if the major stayed tired. It would make keep him tractable until the time came to deal with him. Daniel led them down the

stairs to a washroom. There they cleaned up and put on civilian
clothes he had left for them. Then they went down to have breakfast with their hostess. She seemed to be in a slightly better mood.

"It appears I owe you an apology, Mr . . . "

"Anderson, Mrs. Ratliffe. At your service."

"The papers are full of your exploit. The guard you shot was
found dead last night." Her tone was sarcastic as she passed him
the newspaper. "It will make it ten times more difficult to get you
out of Washington than normal. You'll have to wait a few days."

"I don't know about Major Ellison, Mrs. Ratliffe, but I am leaving tonight and if you care for him, you'll have him leave with me.
He's not used to avoiding anybody's patrols."

Lydia looked at Ellison and her expression seemed to soften.
The spy scanned the story. Fitch had done his work well. Daniel
served them a good breakfast, but Ellison only picked at it.

"You'd better eat heartily, major," the Spy told him. "Good
meals in the Confederate army are few and far between."

"The Confederate army?" Lydia asked.

"Why yes," the Spy told her. "When we get through the lines,
Major Ellison is applying for a commission in the infantry."

The widow beamed. "Why, Charles, how noble." She got up,
went to him and kissed him on the cheek. As far as the Spy could
tell, the sentiment was sincere. Ellison blushed fiercely and began
to act like a new man. He devoured his breakfast as if he had been
starving.

The rest of the day was uneventful, but Anderson kept an eye
on the street. Shortly after three in the afternoon the Spy noticed
two Pinkerton men in his favorite observation place on the opposite corner. They were waiting for someone.

"I think we'd better get back in the attic," the Spy said. "There
are Pinkerton men across the street and unless I miss my guess,
they're waiting for troops. They probably want to search the
place."

"It won't be the first time," Lydia said.

Ellison and the Spy followed Daniel up the steps again and the
servant was just sliding the panel back into place as a heavy
pounding shook the door.

"Open up in the name of the Provost Marshal?"

Even from his secluded hiding place the Spy could tell how little subtlety the soldiers had. Not once did they knock on walls or ceilings, but they thought they were extremely clever looking in drawers and closets and peeking under beds. Searching a house took training and experience. These recruits had neither and they found nothing. When they left it was dark and time for Anderson and Ellison to go. As unobtrusively as possible the Spy retrieved the bundle from behind the eaves. Lydia gave them instructions to go through Georgetown and over the aqueduct to cross the Potomac. They were then to head south to Falls Church. This way, she assured them, they would avoid most of the Yankee patrols. She then gave them valid passes to get them through the Confederate lines.

"We are going to need our Yankee uniforms. It will help," the Spy told her.

"You're crazy. If you're caught in a Yankee uniform, you'll be shot as a spy."

"The Yankees will not be looking for two officers in uniform. They'll be looking for a pair of fugitives being very furtive about their movements."

She gave him an angry look. She obviously did not like being told what to do in her milieu. "You're very bold," she told him.

"It's the only way to get out of a city swarming with Yankee patrols. Give us the uniforms. We'll hide the Confederate passes where they'll never find them."

"It's your funeral," Lydia said. The tone of her voice was genuinely unkind, but she was admitting he was right.

Ellison and the Spy dressed in Union uniforms and waited until 7:00 P.M. Daniel brought two horses around to the front of the house. The Spy and Ellison mounted and they rode away. When the Spy turned south to the Long Bridge, Ellison stopped.

"What's the matter?" the Spy asked.

"You're going to the Long Bridge."

"That's right."

"That's the most heavily guarded bridge."

"That's true. It's also the last bridge they expect us cross because it is the most heavily guarded. You can go to Georgetown if you like. I'm going to the Long Bridge," the Spy said spurring his horse forward. "If you go with me, say as little as possible. We have to hurry. They'll be taking the planks up soon."

Ellison hesitated a moment then meekly followed him. They rode due south until they came to the Long Bridge. The guard stopped him. The Spy smiled inwardly. The War Department's wonderful security system was working again. They had increased the number of guards on the bridge, but there was still only one bored sergeant checking passes.

"May I see your pass, sir?"

The Spy handed him the orders of Captain Donald Henderson of the 6th Pennsylvania Cavalry. As he did he spat off the opposite side.

"Where are you going, sir?"

"Out of this place and back to my regiment. You can have this here city, sergeant." The Spy had made his voice gruff and his speech coarse.

"I know what you mean, sir," the sergeant said enviously.

"Did you boys catch that son-of-a-bitch yet?" the Spy asked.

"Not yet, sir," the sergeant answered. "But when we do they'll hang him."

"Hangin's too good for the bastard," the Spy said. "They ought to geld the son-of-a-bitch."

The sergeant laughed and saluted. "You're right about that, sir. Have a good trip."

"Thanks sergeant," the Spy said, returning the salute.

The Spy could only hope that Ellison would follow instructions. Nervously, Ellison pulled out his papers and held them out. He cleared his throat. Without meaning to, Ellison had done just the right thing. Instead of looking like he was hiding something he looked like a typical field grade officer who wanted the sergeant to check his papers and let him be on his way. The sergeant, not used to field grade officers in a hurry at this time of night, only gave Ellison's papers a cursory check. The sergeant saluted and the two officers started on their way south. The Spy felt exhilarated. His commission was going well. Ellison headed south to an uncertain future. He looked back over his shoulder and thought of Lydia Ratliffe.

As they moved away from the city of Washington, security became less and less stringent. By the time they passed Occoquan, the sentries were only concerned with the color of the uniform they were wearing. Except for a few cavalry skirmishes, it had been a very quiet winter since Fredericksburg and the guards weren't jumpy. They found the going south of Occoquan very difficult. The roads were so muddy that the Spy had to agree to an overnight stop in Aquia, although he didn't like it. They stayed in a small inn and the Spy paid the innkeeper in advance, explaining that they would be leaving early in the morning and would not require breakfast.

"Do you think we're safe?" Ellison asked once they were inside the room.

"Lower your voice!" the Spy said in a sharp whisper. "We won't be safe until we're across the Rapidan. These people will turn you in for the reward at the drop of a hat." None of what he said was true, but it kept Ellison on edge and off balance. The Spy waited until Ellison fell asleep and then retrieved the bundle he had hidden behind the chimney in Mrs. Ratliffe's. He unwrapped it and removed his clothes. He redressed rapidly, then he lay down and rested comfortably until 5:00 A.M. Ellison spent a restless night and hardly slept. They traveled south in the dark. These roads weren't bad because they had been improved by Yankee engineers. At Stafford Court House they turned west. The going turned rough again and it took them much longer than expected to reach Hartwood. The Spy made Ellison push on even though he wanted to stop.

"We have to cross at night, Ellison, and tonight will be overcast. Once we get across the Rapidan we'll be safe and your troubles will be over."

"If I can get off this horse, you mean."

"The penalty for riding a desk most of the war," the Spy said with a friendly grin.

Ellison had no reply as they pushed on. Instead of turning south and going directly to Richard's Ford, the Spy headed west. It was dark by the time they crossed the Rappahannock at Ellis Ford. Now it was rough going across country to the Rapidan, since the Spy wanted to avoid Richardsville. He wasn't too sure who was in possession of it and he didn't want to find out since they were still in Yankee uniforms.

"How much farther?" Ellison asked.

"Not much more than an hour or so and we should be safe."

Finding a ford in the dark is no mean feat, but the Spy had no problem. He had been across the fords many times. Unionists weren't his only clients. Before entering the ford he stopped.

"What's the matter?" Ellison asked in a normal tone.

"Lower your voice! The pickets can hear you," the Spy snapped in a harsh whisper.

"Oh." Ellison lowered his voice. "Why are we stopping?"

"Nature," the Spy said sliding off his horse and disappearing into the trees. Ellison remained mounted.

Once out of sight, the Spy quickly removed his overcoat and tossed it aside. He stripped off the Union uniform he had worn when he freed Ellison. Beneath it was the Confederate uniform he had so carefully hidden. He covered the Yankee uniform with leaves and put his overcoat back on. He returned to the point where Ellison was waiting.

"Follow me," the Spy told him.

Trustingly, Ellison followed him into Ely's Ford. They crossed without incident and began heading south toward Chancellorsville when the Spy stopped. He could just make out the small guard hut in the trees. They had a fire going and when the wind blew his way, the Spy could smell their bacon. The Rebel army wasn't any better at guarding themselves than the Yankees were. The Spy motioned Ellison forward.

"Over there," he whispered to the major. "A guard hut."

Ellison peered through the trees. He wasn't able to see the hut or the Spy's arm moving up. If he did catch the movement, he wasn't able to react. The report of the pistol exploded in the dark and the flash lit up the night for a fraction of a second. The .36 caliber pistol ball shattered the major's cheek and blew off part of his nose and he fell of his horse with a moan. The pickets were aroused. The Spy jumped from his horse and hugged the ground as bullets buzzed overhead. Somehow the bullet had failed to kill Ellison and the major lay on the ground semi-conscious and moaning loudly. The Spy crawled over and put another bullet in his head. The firing stopped. The pickets were unsure of themselves. The Spy removed Ellison's wallet from his coat and took his papers.

"Help," the Spy shouted. "I'm over here."

"Stand up and show yourself," a southern voice demanded.

"Don't shoot. I'm walking toward you right now."

The Spy cautiously removed his overcoat and stood up. He raised his hands and walked toward the pickets.

"Thank, God," he said when he saw the ragged Confederate soldiers. "Thank God."

The pickets blinked in disbelief as a major in a muddy gray uniform emerged from the trees.

"Now don't that beat all," the sergeant in charge of the little group said. "What in hell's name was you doin' out there, major, and what in hell was you shootin' at?"

"I'm carrying dispatches for General Lee, Fitzhugh Lee. He's supposed to be in Orange or Culpeper. I'm new here and got lost in the dark. I crossed the river and figured I was mixed up and started back. When I did someone was following me. I waited in the trees until whoever it was came close. I fired my pistol and missed, but you men got him. It was a Yank."

"It was?"

"He's lying over there. Can I put my hands down?"

"Oh, sure, major, sure," the sergeant said excitedly. "Show us this Yank."

The Spy took them to Ellison's body and they put it on the horse to take it back to the hut. In the lantern light, Ellison's wounds were hideous. It would have been impossible for any but an intimate friend to recognize him. The Spy went through his saddlebags. He carefully removed any clue to Ellison's identification, but left the blank passes.

"Just as I thought. You'd better call your officer."

"Why?"

"Look in his saddlebags. Civilian clothes and passes. This man was a spy."

The sergeant grinned. This was the most exciting thing that had ever happened in this part of the line. They had traded shots and other things with the Yankee pickets, but they had never caught a spy. The sergeant looked at the items in the saddlebag. The major was right. The Spy looked over at the sergeant's men. They were viewing Ellison's saddlebags greedily.

"Eat his food and take his money," he whispered to the sergeant. "But turn the body, horse, and papers over to your officers. There might be something that's important."

The sergeant looked at him and smiled. "Thanks major, you need anything?"

"Just to be on my way."

"Take the road south until it ends. Turn right where the sign points to Wilderness Tavern. That's the road to Orange Court House."

"I am much obliged to you and your men, sergeant. Not just for the directions, but for saving my life."

"Sure thing, major," one of the men called after him. " 'Cept these Yankee officers jus' gettin' too easy to kill." The rest of them thought that was very funny and laughed, as the major spurred his horse up the hill.

Anderson was relieved to be rid of Ellison. He had been a wearisome companion. What mattered was that the plan was still on schedule. The Spy wondered in passing if Mrs. Ratliffe would be glad to be rid of him or whether she would weep at the news of his death. The Spy dismissed it from his mind. Major Charles Ellison was no longer his concern.

CHAPTER 3

Headquarters
Third Virginia Cavalry
March 1, 1863

CAPTAIN RICHARD JORDAN returned to his tent after a breakfast of cornbread and chickory coffee. He had to remove his hat and stoop a little to enter. Whoever made tents for the army made no provisions for men of average height, much less those like Jordan who were taller. With his broad shoulders, light brown hair and mustache, he looked like a typical cavalier, so often pictured in one of the popular illustrated weeklies. Jordan had what women described as pleasant features with a strong chin and blue eyes, but this morning he looked anything but pleasant. He was scowling at the stack of reports that took up all the space on the tiny camp table in the middle of the tent. With a heavy sigh, he began reviewing and signing them one by one. Reports, reports, reports. He hated reports. It was the army's way of punishing those who were insane enough to accept the increased responsibility of command. In November he had been promoted to captain and appointed to command C Company, Third Virginia Cavalry. Since then, he had spent more time filling out reports than he had in the saddle.

How many men fit for duty?

How many men sick?

How many horses fit?

How many horses with glanders?

How many men on furlough looking for horses?

How many carbines?

The questions went on and on. The question that counted was never asked. How many troopers could he put into the field? Out of 60 troopers authorized he could put 21 into the field against the enemy, and not one of them, himself included, was a real prize. This winter was the hardest of the war and he and his men were thin and their clothes were tattered. Jordan's prize possession was a warm overcoat he had taken from a dead Yankee.

The horses were also in bad shape. They were gaunt and ill because there wasn't enough fodder. Despite it all, morale remained high. The big problem was Company "Q." Company "Q" was the result of the Confederate government's inability to furnish horses to the cavalry. Each cavalryman in the Confederate army had to furnish his own mount. The government paid him an allowance for its upkeep. If the horse was lost and it was not the cavalryman's fault he was paid a "fair price" for it and given a furlough to return home and buy a new mount. Thus, he was assigned to Company "Q." If a man lost his horse and it was his fault, then he had to replace it at his own expense. If he could not replace it, he was transferred to the infantry. The system was the worst of all possible worlds. It meant that even in the best of times, men who were desperately needed in the ranks were away from the unit. It also meant that the services of a trained cavalryman could be lost to the army just for the loss of a mount. Fortunately, the Yankee cavalry was kind enough to furnish additional mounts from time to time. Jordan signed the last report and called for his orderly.

"Simpkins!"

The boyish face of Corporal Simpkins appeared through the flap of the tent. "Yes sir?"

"Take these to headquarters, please." Jordan handed the corporal the stack of papers.

"Yes sir." Simpkins carefully put the reports in a leather case to protect them from the weather. Simpkins was a nice young man, but he was one of those misguided souls who had a strange reverence for army paperwork. The corporal saluted and left the tent to trudge across the muddy field to regimental headquarters. Jordan stared at the tent flap blankly. It took a few seconds for him to realize that his inspections and reports were completed and he had a little time to himself. He leaned back on his chair savoring the idea. Perhaps he would have some time to read one of the books he had purchased in Richmond the previous October.

Richmond! The book left his thoughts as an image of home filled his senses. When he closed his eyes, he was in his parents' house on Grace Street. Before the war his father had been a draper and an importer of fine fabrics. The Jordans were not slaveholders. Theodore Jordan, Richard's father, employed several freed colored tradesmen, who joked and laughed with the young Richard when he ventured into his father's shop. It gave Jordan a very different perception of Negroes than many of his countrymen. One pleasant memory faded into another and Jordan found himself with his father in warehouses on Cary Street where his father went to inspect the fabrics that had just been unloaded from ships that had sailed up the James River. Theodore Jordan was a careful man and he personally inspected every bolt of cloth in a shipment. For a young boy it was an exciting place, and everywhere there was the sweet aroma of cured tobacco waiting to depart on the very ships that had brought the cloth. Now the only ships that came up the James were Yankee warships. The elder Jordan had been forced to move his business to Wilmington, North Carolina where he now imported war supplies instead of cloth. Alice Jordan, Richard's mother had stayed in the house in Richmond because it was the family home. Jordan could almost taste her bread and butter pickles. The thought of them made him grin.

Somehow, Jordan's best friend, Bobby Maysfield, always knew when Alice Jordan had put up a batch of her pickles. He loved them and would sneak them the way other boys would sneak cookies. If he had been naughty, Mrs. Maysfield would threaten to "Go see Dick's mother and tell her not to make any more pickles for such a bad little boy." Invariably there would be a jar of pickles for Bobby at Christmas and one for his birthday. Jordan's nostalgic smile faded when he remembered that Bobby had been wounded at Fredericksburg in December. The wound had not seemed too bad and he hoped that his friend would mend quickly. Not everything pleasant on Richard Jordan's mind had to do with home. One thought made him blush. Jennifer Leigh Franks was a widow he had met twice since last November. No woman had ever made him feel so warm and so alive.

"Are you alone, Dick ?"

Jordan was so surprised by the voice that he nearly fell over in his chair. At first he thought the person he was looking at was just another pleasant memory, but when he blinked, the young man with the unruly shock of red hair and mischievous smile was still there.

"Bobby," Jordan cried, jumping up. He embraced his friend. "It's really you. You're back. The wound? Has it healed?"

"Good as new," the lieutenant said, raising his right arm. He grinned and blushed at his friend's display of genuine affection. "On top of that, I think I gained ten pounds which is more than I can say for you." He poked Jordan in his flat stomach.

"You do look great, Bobby. It's good to have you back."

"Not only that," Maysfield said with a mock conspiratorial whisper. "I have also brought you some contraband." From behind his back, he produced a package wrapped in brown paper and tied with string.

"What's this?"

"It's from your family. I stopped to see your mom. Your dad was in Wilmington. She says everyone's fine and sends their love."

Jordan took the package from his friend. "I wonder what it could be," he said.

"For heaven's sake, open it up and find out," Maysfield told him. "I've carried the damned thing all the way from Richmond and I'm curious as hell!"

Jordan placed it carefully on his bunk and untied the string. In it was a new gray uniform with the three bars of a captain on the yellow collar, and gilt buttons down the front. On the sleeves were trefoils of gold thread. It made him very self-conscious of his shabby appearance. He looked down at himself.

"Well isn't that a pretty sight," Maysfield said in admiration. "Put it on."

"Not until I get a bath," Jordan said emphatically. "The critters in these clothes are not going to inhabit the new ones."

"I know what you mean," Maysfield said grinning.

Jordan started to rewrap the package and felt something hard. "What's this?"

"I don't know," his friend said. "Your mother gave it to me wrapped and told me to be careful with it."

Jordan unfolded the uniform carefully and began to laugh.

"What's so funny?" Maysfield asked, perplexed.

"Mom certainly put one over on you, Bobby."

Maysfield looked over Jordan's shoulder. Wrapped in the uniform were two jars of pickles, a wax-covered cheese, and a small salt-cured ham.

"It's not fair," Maysfield said. His feelings were hurt.

"No wonder mother didn't tell you, Bobby. She was afraid you'd eat the pickles."

"That's what she gets for making the best bread and butter pickles in the state. I should have looked in and eaten every one." The expression on his face was one of genuine pain.

"I don't doubt that you would have. Well, you deserve a reward for carrying them up on the train," Jordan said tossing a jar to his friend. "But not the whole jar."

Maysfield grinned and began opening the jar then said "Damn me for a fool, I almost forgot." He pulled two envelopes from his tunic.

Jordan took the envelopes and looked at them. One was from his mother. The other was addressed to "Lieutenant Richard C. Jordan, 3rd Virginia Cavalry, C.S.A." in a firm even script. He recognized his brother's handwriting immediately.

"How . . . I mean . . . "

Maysfield looked at him sympathetically. "His ship is operating off North Carolina. There was a raid and then a truce to recover the wounded and bury the dead. One of our officers has relatives in the north and asked him to deliver a letter. It happens all the time from what they tell me. He wrote one to your mother and to your sister. Your father doesn't know."

Tears welled up in Jordan's eyes. He had not seen his brother since the war began. "I don't know how to thank you, Bobby."

"I'll leave you two alone," Maysfield said sympathetically. He took a knifeful of pickles, set the jar on the table and left the tent.

Jordan sat on his cot and carefully opened the letter.

January 25th 1863

Dear Dick,

I don't have much time to write as the truce is only to last for two more hours. One of your officers has kindly offered to see this letter forwarded. He is a nice fellow who has relations in New Jersey. It makes me wonder why we are fighting this war. I am fine and hope you are well. It has been a long time since I have seen you and find myself wondering what you look like. I bet you look dashing on your horse. I've grown a beard and have been promoted. If things go well, I will have my own ship soon. I hope its one of the new ironclads. As exciting as it sounds I wish I were back home. That's assuming Dad will let me back in the house. I miss you and Mom and Hannah and, yes, I miss Dad, too. Probably him most of all. Write if you can and when you get back home kiss Mother for me and give Dad a hug only don't tell him it's from me. I'd like to hear how Hannah is doing. I haven't heard anything about our sister since she married and moved to Atlanta. I'm glad for her. The war will never touch her there. Take care of yourself and don't do anything foolish.

Your loving brother,

DANA

Jordan sniffed and carefully folded the letter before putting it back in the envelope. When he was younger he idolized Dana. The whole family had been proud of their eldest son when he graduated from the Naval Academy in 1856. When the war came, Dana announced that his loyalty lay with the Union. Theodore Jordan became furious. He denounced his son and called him a coward and a traitor to Virginia. Unfortunately, Dana had his father's temper and lashed back. Richard Jordan would never forget his brother's words before he stormed out of the house.

"You, sir, are the traitor. You have betrayed this country and you will bring ruin upon the South and this state. May God forgive you for I certainly shall not!"

Their father fumed and their mother wept openly. Richard and Hannah ran after Dana as he strode out the door. Dana, with tears in his eyes, stopped and embraced them both. Richard Jordan begged his older brother to reconsider.

"Dick, there are times in life when you must do what you think is right no matter what others around you may feel or say. That's what I have done. I just hope you won't hate me for it," Dana said wiping his eyes.

"I'll never hate you Dana," Dick Jordan told his brother.

Shortly after Dana left, their father went to the family lawyer and had Dana disinherited. Thereafter, he forbade the mentioning of Dana's name ever again. Several days later, Richard Jordan made his own choice. The federal government was attempting to impose union by force. In the younger Jordan's eyes it was tyranny and, with Bobby Maysfield, he volunteered for the Third Virginia Cavalry.

Richard Jordan sighed and wiped his eyes. He offered a silent prayer for his brother's safety. The war had begun as a great adventure with expectations of quick victory and lots of glory. It was now nearly two years old and no end was in sight. Jordan decided that dwelling on the morose wasn't about to do him any good so he took his fork from his field chest, opened the jar of pickles, and took two mouthfuls. I'm going to read a novel, he decided. He would have to start over because he could no longer remember which of the books he had begun. He closed the jar, wiped his hands, and looked in his trunk for the books. One was *The Last Days of Pompeii* by Bulwer. The other was *Barry Lyndon* by Thackeray. He decided on the former because he liked the illustrations and it was so far from his own time that it would help him forget it. Jordan stretched out on his cot, opened the book and began to read slowly, savoring every word. He read the "Blind Girl's Song" twice and silently hoped that he would never be blinded. A few pages later Jennifer filled his thoughts. He had to see her again. I think she likes me, he thought.

Jennifer Leigh Franks was the widow of Colonel Tom Franks. Jordan had met Franks once or twice before he was was killed at the head of his regiment at Sharpsburg. He was a likable man with an infectious laugh. Jordan had met Tom Franks' widow barely two months after her husband had been killed. Despite the fact that she was in mourning, she allowed General Stuart to hold a gathering of his officers in Oakview Manor, her home. Jordan had been one of the officers and he remembered how sad her lovely eyes were. His heart melted and he knew he had to see her again. He had his wish in January. In memory of her husband,

Mrs. Franks kept open house for the officers of the Army. Jordan passed by to pay his respects and was invited to dinner. This time she was less sad, but the same magic occurred. Jordan could remember every detail of her dark curly hair and pretty face. Her eyes were green and she had the warmest smile. To him she had the face of an angel. Jennifer had a slim waist but the rest of her figure was full and feminine. Jordan blushed at the last thought. It was improper to think of the woman he loved that way—before marriage. Love? Marriage? Did he dare? He decided it best if he concentrated on the book.

Corporal Simpkins entered the tent without announcing himself. He stood stiffly in front of Jordan's desk and saluted. "Sir, I have a dispatch for the captain."

"Put it on the table, please," Jordan told him.

"If the captain will forgive the impertinence, I think he should read it immediately. It is not a routine dispatch. It's from General Stuart's headquarters."

Jordan's brow furrowed in curiosity. Simpkins was right. Captains did not routinely get dispatches from the commanding general's headquarters. The captain rose and held out his hand. Simpkins gave him the dispatch. It read:

February 26th 1863

To: Captain Richard Charles Jordan
Cmdng, Co. C, 3rd Virg. Cav.

Sir:

You are requested to report to this Headquarters at your earliest possible convenience.

R. CHANNING PRICE
Maj., Adjutant.

"Earliest possible convenience" was polite army parlance for "right now." It made Jordan feel uncomfortable.

"Saddle my horse will you please, Simpkins. I have to go to headquarters."

Simpkins smiled. "Another promotion, sir?"

Jordan shrugged. "The way this is written it could be a court martial." He wondered if he had done something wrong.

Jordan put on his jacket and saber, then donned his hat and the warm Yankee overcoat. He picked up the dispatch and walked across the field to headquarters. A clerk was sitting in the headquarters tent.

"I need to see the regimental commander," Jordan told him.

"I'm sorry sir," the clerk replied. "Colonel Owen is ill. You'll have to see Major McClellan.

"Thank you." Jordan walked over to the adjutant's quarters. He liked Henry McClellan. He was a pleasant man who knew a lot about what was going on. Some mistrusted him because he had three brothers in the Union Army and one of his first cousins was George B. McClellan, twice commanding General of the Army of the Potomac, but Jordan thought him as loyal to the Confederacy as any man he knew.

"Dick, how are you?" he said looking up from his stack of paperwork.

"I don't know, sir," he said, handing McClellan the dispatch. "What do you know about this?"

McClellan took the dispatch and read it. He shrugged. "I don't know a thing about it. Usually these things come through channels. It's the first I've seen or heard of this. I don't know what to make of it."

"Do you think I should go?"

"By all means, but it's highly irregular. Let me know what it's about when you get back."

"I definitely will, sir." Jordan saluted and left.

The fact that Major McClellan didn't know anything about this didn't make him feel any better. Jordan appointed Lieutenant Smith to command the company while he was gone. He packed his new uniform and the cheese and ham from his mother's package and filled his canteen. If he hurried he could make it from Culpeper to Stuart's headquarters south of Fredericksburg in about five hours, providing the roads weren't too bad. He left shortly before nine in the morning. Fortunately the weather had been cold so the roads were firm. For part of the afternoon there were snow flurries and a sharp wind and Jordan was thankful for his captured overcoat. He reached Stuart's headquarters a little after 3:00 P.M. It was in a pine woods near the Telegraph Road. A sentry directed him to a large tent where groups of officers sat at tables reading dispatches and making out reports. Jordan reported to a major and presented the dispatch that had summoned him.

"Oh," the major said, with a smile. "You're very prompt, Captain Jordan. We didn't expect you until tomorrow, but since you're here, I can tell you that your orders require you to report to Colonel Longfellow at his headquarters."

Jordan, of course, had heard of Colonel Raymond Longfellow, Stuart's Chief of Scouts. Who in the cavalry hadn't? He was rumored to be the Confederacy's master spy with all of that word's ugly connotations. But, Jordan had never met him and wondered what the Chief of Scouts wanted with him. "Are you sure you have the right Captain Jordan, major?"

"Oh yes, As it says in the dispatch. Captain Richard Charles Jordan of the Third Virginia Cavalry? Are you not he?"

"I am he."

"Then you are to report to Colonel Longfellow's headquarters forthwith."

"Where is the colonel's headquarters?"

"Ah," the major said. "They are on the Johnson farm east of Chancellorsville. I'll show you on the map."

Jordan followed him to a table where the major unrolled a map. He nearly groaned when he saw where the farm was. It was only a two hour ride from where the Third Virginia was camped.

"Thank you, sir," he said, and left the tent wondering if this part of the army knew where the other parts of the army were.

The ride to the Johnson farm on a tired horse was cold and miserable. It was past 10:00 P.M. when he arrived. There were quite a few units camped around it and it took him a while to find the colonel's adjutant. The adjutant was surprised to see him.

"We weren't expecting you for a day or two, captain. I'm sure the colonel will be happy to learn you're here early. You can meet him in the morning. I'll get Sergeant Masters to take you to your room."

The major called for an orderly and a private appeared. "Find Sergeant Masters and tell him Captain Jordan is here," he said.

The orderly disappeared and returned with an average size man in a sergeant's uniform. Sergeant Masters had dark brown hair and he was clean shaven. He was a little younger than Jordan and he had a relaxed way of moving that was decidedly unmilitary. He saluted with a smile.

"Welcome to Colonel Longfellow's headquarters, captain."

"Take Captain Jordan over to the house and see that he gets a warm bed," the adjutant told the sergeant. Masters nodded.

"Thank you, sir." Jordan saluted.

The sergeant led Jordan up a narrow path which brought them to the back of a large white farm house.

"The Johnsons own the house and live here but they let the colonel use the overseer's house as a headquarters. They have two sons in the army so they're pretty nice. The old man is a real fire eater and hates Yankees, so it's best not to say anything that could be construed as favorable to the gentlemen in blue, if you know what I mean. Otherwise, you'll get one of his tirades."

"Thanks for the warning," Jordan replied. "What does Colonel Longfellow want with me, sergeant?" Jordan ventured.

"Even if I were privy to that information, I wouldn't be at liberty to discuss it with you, sir. I'm sure the colonel will explain everything in detail tomorrow morning."

The sergeant's evasive answer didn't help Jordan's frame of mind, and his concern must have shown on his face.

"You really don't need to concern yourself with it until morning, captain," Sergeant Masters said with a disarming smile. "Until then, I'm sure you can use a good night's rest."

Masters showed him to a small room on the second floor. There was a washstand and a small bed with clean white sheets.

"I'll have the girl bring you hot water for a bath. If there's anything else you need she'll take care of you. I'll come get you at six in the morning for breakfast."

"Thank you, sergeant."

"My pleasure, sir."

Masters left and a few minutes later a colored woman brought a tub of warm water, soap, and clean towels. She was a young woman and would have been attractive if it had not been for the look of terror in her eyes. She watched Jordan carefully as she set down the tub and brought in some towels.

"Ah's Rebecca," she said. "Ah brung you hot water an' towels."

"Thank you," he said.

"If you needs sumthin' else, Ah's down de hall," she explained.

She groveled and acted like a trapped animal as she backed toward the door.

"Thank you, Rebecca. I don't need anything else. All I want to do is take a bath and get some sleep."

Rebecca gave him a brief, forced smile, but watched him suspiciously as she closed the door. It wasn't difficult to figure out why the woman acted the way she did. She had, no doubt, been beaten and probably raped. Jordan had seen it before and it always upset him. No one should be treated like that, even a slave, but he was too tired to dwell on it.

He bathed quickly, enjoying the hot, soapy water and the clean towels. He lay down between the smooth, clean sheets and was thankful for the luxury of the bed. Despite his fatigue and his desire to sleep, he couldn't help wondering what Colonel Longfellow wanted with him. Jordan wasn't a spy, so that couldn't be it. He also wondered if the stories about the colonel were true? One story said that he knew what decisions the Yankees were making before Lincoln. Another said that he actually attended Lincoln's cabinet meetings. Then another thought occurred to him. Perhaps Longfellow was planning a raid and needed good cavalry officers. Yes, that had to be it. Jordan felt comforted and smiled. It would be fun raiding the Yankee rear areas again. He fell asleep.

Jordan woke up, shaved, and dressed in his new uniform before the sergeant arrived to fetch him. Masters looked at him and smiled.

"Sir, if I may be so bold, you sure look a hell of a lot better than you did last night," Sergeant Masters said.

Jordan felt a little self-conscious. "It's a new uniform. A gift from my father."

"Don't see many fine uniforms these days," the sergeant said sincerely. "It's very handsome, sir."

"Thank you, sergeant. It's very kind of you to say so."

"Not at all, sir. Now, if the captain will follow me, I think he is in for a treat."

They went downstairs to the dining room where Mr. Johnson and his wife were having breakfast with a group of officers. The house was comfortably and expensively furnished. Mr. Johnson looked as if he were in his fifties and he had a rather dour expression on his deeply-lined face. He was dressed in a black frock coat with a white shirt and no cravat. He looked like a preacher or a deacon of the church. His wife was a plump woman who wore a pale yellow dress with a lace shawl over her shoulders. Although she sat at the table, she wasn't eating. She merely sat, crocheted, and watched. At first glance she seemed a pleasant enough woman, but when she looked at Jordan she reminded him of a bird of prey with cold, beady eyes. Most of the time, she watched the old slave serving breakfast. He had the same fearful look as the girl.

There were four officers at the table. Smith, Aldritch, and Houston were majors. Tate was a lieutenant colonel. They were all in good spirits since they had received assignments to their units. The breakfast could only be described as sumptuous. There were eggs, ham, biscuits, and hotcakes with plenty of real coffee. Jordan, unaccustomed to such luxury ate with polite but undisguised relish.

"Are you here for assignment, Captain Jordan?" Tate asked.

"No, sir," Jordan said proudly. "I command Company "C', Third Virginia Cavalry. I was told to report to Colonel Longfellow this morning."

"That's funny," Major Smith said haughtily. "You don't look like a spy."

"Colonel Longfellow is a scout, I believe," Tate said.

"Scout, spy. It's all the same, if you ask me," Smith continued humorlessly. "It's a wretchedly dishonorable business and no real gentleman would have any truck with it." He was looking directly at Jordan when he made the last remark.

Everyone at the table looked at Smith then at Jordan. I suppose they think I should feel insulted, Jordan thought. It's ridiculous. Well, they'll get no duel out of me. If I'm going to kill anyone it's going to be Yankees.

"I've never met Colonel Longfellow," Jordan said, pretending not to notice Smith's remark. "I understand he's very highly regarded."

Smith glared at him but before he could say anything else, Mr. Johnson changed the subject.

"Where are you from, Captain Jordan?" Mr. Johnson asked. Jordan was grateful for the question.

"Richmond, sir."

"Lovely city. Whereabouts?"

"Grace Street, sir."

"Ah," Johnson nodded, obviously approving. "What does your daddy do?" he asked, taking a bite of a biscuit.

"He used to import fine fabrics," Jordan said. "But since the Yankees seized Norfolk, he imports war supplies through Wilmington."

"Damned Yankees always ruining people's livelihood!" Johnson snorted. "Damn near ruined mine! I'll tell you, son, we are well rid of the Yankee race. Those tradesmen and factory workers are lower than niggers. That's why they can't hold a candle to our southern boys."

"Yes sir," Jordan said, glad he had been warned by Sergeant Masters.

"That damned Lincoln will burn in hell, you mark my words! It's sinful the way he talks about freedom for the niggers. They was meant to be slaves. It's in the Bible. This Emancipation Proclamation is against the will of God. When this war is over no one is going to stop me or anybody else from selling slaves. The African race must be kept in its place if we are to keep this world in accordance with the word of God."

Jordan wanted to leave the table, but he couldn't be impolite. This was the Johnsons' home and Johnson had a right to his opinion. Nevertheless, Jordan didn't believe in slavery. No one had the right to place another in bondage. Jordan felt the South had made a big mistake by making slavery an issue, and when The Emancipation Proclamation had gone into effect on January 1, it was a grave blow to the Confederacy's hope for recognition as an independent nation by the European powers. It would have been best to repudiate slavery immediately but hard liners like Johnson refused to relent. All of the others seemed a bit embarrassed by Johnson's polemic except for Major Smith whose family also held slaves. It was a relief when breakfast was over and Jordan managed a smile in the direction of his host and hostess.

"Well, nice talkin' to you boys. Just kill a few Yankees for me and Mrs. Johnson and we'll be happy."

Sergeant Masters came to get him and grinned when he saw the expression on Jordan's face. "I see you've met our charming host and hostess," he said with a wry smile.

Jordan wondered what this sergeant's job was. He had a rare sense of humor. Jordan was beginning to like him. "Thanks for the warning. It helped."

The sergeant led him down a path past two barns to the overseer's house.

"The colonel's inside, sir," the sergeant said. "I'd better lead the way."

Jordan followed Masters inside. He expected the neatness of a military headquarters with people in the proper uniform. Instead he found a room with filing cabinets crammed against the walls and tables covered with maps taking up the available floor space. The people inside were all busy huddling around maps, looking in file drawers, or weaving in and around the tables trying to go someplace. Not one of them looked at Jordan or Masters.

"Back here," Masters said, indicating the way.

Masters led Jordan to the back of the house and knocked on a closed door.

"Come in."

Masters popped his head in the door. "Captain Jordan to see you, colonel."

"Ah, send him in."

Jordan stepped in the door and saluted. "Captain Richard Jordan reporting, sir."

The man returning the salute didn't look like any colonel he had ever seen. Longfellow was dressed in a buckskin jacket with colonel's stars on the collar. Beneath the jacket was a gray vest with gilt buttons that said CSA. His black woolen trousers had leather inserts. The colonel was tall and he was balding. The hair remaining on his head and his beard was brown with streaks of gray. His eyes seemed to shine as if he'd just heard a funny story. On a peg on the wall was a black slouch hat with gold cords. He was smoking a long cigar. From the looks and aroma it was a very expensive one. He extended a large hand.

"Welcome, Captain Jordan. Your father is Theodore Jordan of Richmond, is he not?"

"Yes sir."

"I thought so. I knew him in Mexico. You favor him."

"Thank you, sir."

Colonel Raymond Longfellow was an amiable man unaffected

by his rank. He seemed more like an uncle than a colonel, but behind the pleasant exterior he seemed to be carrying a great burden. Jordan decided he liked him.

"Have a seat, take off your hat, and relax. That's a nice uniform. Don't see too many regulation uniforms these days."

"It was a gift from my father, sir."

"Ah, leave it to a draper to insure his son has a proper uniform. I envy you, captain. I really do," the colonel said sincerely. "Can I get you something? A drink, perhaps? "

"No thank you, sir. It's a bit early."

The colonel looked at him and smiled. "Just as well, I suppose. You have no idea why you're here, do you?"

"Quite frankly, sir, I don't."

The colonel's face maintained its cheerful exterior, but his voice became very serious. "The reason you're here is that I need a smart young man to go to Washington for me."

Jordan's jaw dropped. The room was quiet. "I — I'm not a spy, Colonel Longfellow," he stammered.

The colonel didn't comment on the remark. "Do you mind if I call you Dick? That's what your friends call you isn't it?"

"Yes sir, and I don't mind."

"Dick, I'm going to ask you a question. I want you to answer it truthfully no matter how much you think I might dislike the answer. Agreed?"

"Yes sir."

"How's the war going?"

Jordan thought for a moment. "I suppose in the field it's not going too badly. Sharpsburg was a setback, but we've recovered. The thing that's hurt us most is the Emancipation Proclamation, because the Europeans are very sensitive about slavery. But, if we win another victory like Fredericksburg, I don't see how the Yankees can continue. They'll have to grant us our independence."

"That's a well-thought-out appraisal," the colonel said. "Now, let me fill you in on what else is happening and I have to admit that some of it doesn't look good." The colonel unrolled a map and laid it on his desk. He held the corners down with three glass paperweights and a dragoon pistol.

"This is a map of the United States and the Confederate States that shows the current battle lines. Only fools like our esteemed congressmen in Richmond can fail to notice that we have lost nearly a third of our country since the war began," he said bitterly. "In the east we have won every battle except Sharpsburg, as you said. My boy, all those victories have accomplished nothing so far."

Jordan felt as if he had been slapped in the face. "Nothing? We have beaten the Yankees against overwhelming odds time and time again. You call that nothing? Sir, that is something. Something very important."

"It is? Has it brought us closer to peace?"

Jordan didn't answer. It hadn't.

"How many times have we whipped the Yankees, and how many times have they come back to try again?"

Jordan said nothing. He knew the colonel was right.

"To make matters worse, almost all of the fighting has been done on our soil. Now look at the west," the colonel told him.

Jordan looked at the map. Red lines showed the deep penetrations that the Yankees had made into the western borders of the Confederacy.

"If you look at this the picture doesn't seem as rosy. New Orleans has been captured and the Confederacy has been nearly cut in two. The only place holding it together is Vicksburg. If Vicksburg falls we will be in serious trouble."

"I thought Vicksburg couldn't be taken unless the Yankees could get across the river."

"They haven't been able to yet, Dick, but just remember, Grant is no McClellan and Sherman is no Burnside. Unfortunately for us, the Union generals in the west know their business a lot better than their counterparts in the east. Equally unfortunate is the fact that we have no one of the caliber of Lee or Jackson in the west since Albert Sidney Johnston was killed at Pittsburg Landing. I have recommended that either Joe Johnston or Beauregard go back to the west but Davis insists on retaining Bragg." The colonel paused for a moment and took a deep breath. "Sorry, I got carried away."

Jordan looked at him. "Granted, what you say is true. What are you leading up to?"

The colonel looked directly at him. His eyes were no longer mirthful. "It comes down to this, Dick. This is our year. We are still intact as a nation and our armies are victorious. The enemy, although not totally beaten, is demoralized and many of its two-year volunteers are going home. It is now time to take the war to the enemy. What I tell you now must not go beyond this room."

Jordan nodded in agreement.

"We are going to invade Pennsylvania this summer. It's not going to be a half-hearted march to get supplies like the one that ended at Sharpsburg. We are going to fight the war on northern soil and make the Yankees pay the price of having an invading army in their country."

Jordan grinned. He felt like cheering, but he knew there was more.

"We intend to make this invasion fully supplied with the Army of Northern Virginia intact. Unfortunately, we are short of everything, especially medicine, uniforms, and shoes. It appears that we have captured enough muskets and artillery to supply more troops than we have. There is clothing, medicine, and shoes waiting for us in Indiana, but we can't get to them."

"Indiana?" Jordan asked incredulously.

Colonel Longfellow grimaced. "We had a front in Washington that we set up before the war. It was, for all intents and purposes, a legitimate business. The business had a legitimate account at a bank in Washington. Since the beginning of the war, all we had to do was place an order with payment in gold to one of several firms in the north. Once the payment was made the material, cloth, medicine, gunpowder—whatever we needed was shipped down the Mississippi to Vicksburg."

"You mean to say that Yankee businesses are selling us supplies to fight their own country?"

"Don't be surprised. It's not only the Yankees. We have businessmen who sell cotton to them and pocket the money. The world isn't exactly full of idealists, Dick."

"Obviously something happened to this arrangement," Jordan said.

"Obviously," The colonel said bitterly. "Things were going along well; too well. Our man in Washington began to get cocky. He had nothing but contempt for the Pinkertons because they never seemed to suspect him. I tried to tell him that they weren't geniuses, but they weren't idiots, either. He should have realized that after they arrested Mrs. Greenhow and moved her to Old Capitol Prison. He played the Pinkerton detectives for fools once too often and they arrested him. The worst part is that when they caught him, they caught him red-handed and confiscated the money in our account. They also severed our contact with the Yankee firms we dealt with. What we need is someone with a business background who can pass for Yankee to carry $100,000 to our agent in Washington. We checked your record. You spent two years at Harvard, did you not?"

"Yes sir," Jordan answered. "I trust you're talking about a $100,000 letter of credit, sir."

"No, Dick, I am not talking about a letter of credit. I am talking about $100,000 in gold," the colonel solemnly replied.

"In gold?"

"Gold, Dick. The Confederacy has no more credit. We are nearly bankrupt. What we would like you to do is become an agent for our front company for a while. Believe me, I wouldn't ask this of you if I could find an experienced agent with the necessary qualifications this quickly. You know business practices and you've lived in the north. You'll fit in a lot easier than most others I can think of. We have to close the deal with the northern firm in the next week or so. Deliver the gold to our contact, get the invoices, and return. That's all. Naturally, any information you pick up in Washington will be extremely useful. When you return, bring back as many newspapers as you can. They're always very helpful."

"Newspapers?"

"Yes, newspapers. Ours are as bad as theirs. They do nothing but give away information in the name of 'Freedom of the Press.' Take this New York paper," the colonel said, holding up a copy of the *New York Tribune*. "It lists the number of sick per 1,000 in the Army of the Potomac, then it lists the total number sick. That way we know the strength of the enemy."

"How do you know they haven't tried to deceive you?"

"Good question. If we relied on only one source we wouldn't know, but the scientific gathering of information requires confirmation from several sources. Some may even be contradictory. Put together it gives us a clear picture of what the Yankees are trying to do.

"What I would like you to do is take a day to think about it and then tomorrow morning tell me what your decision is. Whatever you decide will be accepted without question and there will be no reflection on you. I would just like to add that you shouldn't let a misplaced sense of chivalry interfere with a service your country desperately needs."

Jordan looked at the colonel. It was one thing to risk one's life in battle for something you believed in. There, the worst thing was not death, but mutilation and—worse—the surgeon's knife. At least one could bear his scars proudly after the war. It was quite another to be something that both sides despised. No matter how much it might help the nation, your ultimate fate is at the end of a rope and an unmarked grave.

"Please, Dick. Think it over. I'll answer any question I can if it will help."

"What happens if we don't win this year?"

"There's the presidential election of '64. If we can continue winning, the North may be war weary enough to vote Lincoln out and elect someone who will be willing to let us go. That's the chance we have next year, but it's not as good as the one we have now. Nothing is better than a clean military victory. That's something within our reach. I dare say not even Grant and Sherman would be a match for Lee, Jackson, and Stuart. Do you know the Europeans have already begun studying Jackson's Valley Campaign. There's a Prussian observer with Lee who claims Jackson's the new Napoleon." The colonel shook his head in respect. "Imagine that; Jackson, the new Napoleon."

Jordan smiled.

"Did I say something funny, Dick?"

"No. I know 'Old Jack' is a genius and God knows if I weren't in Stuart's cavalry I'd want to be in the Stonewall Brigade. But when you see him sitting on his horse, sucking on a lemon with his hand in the air, it's kind of hard to imagine him as a Napoleon."

The colonel grinned broadly. "I see what you mean. You're right."

Jordan stood and saluted. "Permission to leave, sir?"

"Come back in the morning or anytime you'd like, Dick, and thank you."

Jordan walked out into the cold morning. He looked around at the comings and goings of the headquarters. Around him thousands of men were camped. How many would die this year and how many would die next year if the war didn't end? If they didn't get him to volunteer who would they get? There were thousands of questions he needed to ask, but he doubted the colonel could answer them. He certainly didn't feel like eating lunch.

The colonel watched him leave. Dick Jordan was a fine young man and although he told Jordan much of the truth, he had not been completely candid with him. If he had told Jordan the un-varnished truth, the captain would not have felt as if he had a free choice. A man had to have some hope. Longfellow was clinging to his by a slender thread. He knew what few men on either side knew. If we don't win this year we can never win. If we lose, God help us!

CHAPTER 4

Colonel Longfellow's Headquarters
March 2, 1863

EARLY MARCH IS the bleakest time of year in Virginia. In 1863 it was overcast and cold and it snowed frequently. In the western part of the state, the snow fell so hard that travel in the mountains was impossible. In the eastern part of the state, the snow seldom amounted to much, but it did add to the moisture in the ground. When the sun came out, the ground thawed and where wheels or hooves tried to move there was heavy, clinging mud. Military operations slowed to a standstill and both armies waited for April or May when the ground would dry out and the skies would clear. Then they could return to the science of killing each other.

The morning that dawned the day after Richard Jordan's first meeting with Colonel Longfellow was little different from the ones that preceded it. It was cold and overcast and a bitter wind blew in from the north. The bright side of the weather was that the roads were partially frozen and wagons full of bacon and hardtack could now reach the hungry Confederate Army.

When Jordan awoke, he knew that he was going to Washington for Colonel Longfellow. He tried to find some logical reason for wanting to go. It wasn't from a sense of not having done enough as a patriot. He had been in every major battle since First Manassas and in quite a few skirmishes that did not have names and never would. It was certainly not for want of adventure. He had

had enough to last a lifetime in the past two years. There would be no disgrace in declining, but he was going. No matter how hard he tried he couldn't put his finger on the reason why.

Richard Jordan was a young man. He lived in a young era in which one scientific discovery after another was being made. He was a member of a young army that had succeeded in spite of the numbers arrayed against it; an army that had absolute faith in itself and its leaders. Neither Jordan nor the army he proudly served could imagine a situation so difficult that it could not be overcome by sheer force of will. Both felt they were invincible. Had he been a more mature man, acquainted with the vagaries of fate, Jordan might have been aware of the tinge of desperation and urgency in the colonel's voice. Whether he understood or not, Jordan was responding to that urgency. While other, more aristocratic members of his society might eschew working as a "scout," Jordan would not. He came from a solid and successful business family and understood the need for someone going to Washington regardless of what his friends might say or think. Colonel Longfellow had chosen well.

Jordan had the dining room to himself for breakfast. Neither of the Johnsons was present and their servant offered no explanation. The other officers had left the previous morning to join their units, so Jordan, thankful for the peace and quiet, ate heartily. He imagined it would be a long time before he would enjoy food as ample as this. When he was finished he walked down the path to the overseer's house where Colonel Longfellow had his headquarters. Jordan didn't bother to knock. He entered the chaos and walked around the tables until he was out of the room. No one paid any attention to him. The door to the colonel's office was open and Longfellow was sitting at his desk smoking one of his long cigars and signing reports. He looked up as Jordan approached his desk. His face was neutral but his eyes held the question.

"I've decided to do it, sir," he said.

The colonel's face broke into a wide grin. "Good," he said. "Good."

The colonel rose from his chair and offered his hand. "Thank you, Dick. I want you to know how much I appreciate your decision. We were about to have a meeting on the plan. Since you're part of it now you might as well sit in and meet all the players. Come with me. We have a lot of work to do."

Jordan followed him to another room. This one was shocking in its neatness. It had obviously been a sitting room. There were lace curtains, flowered wallpaper, and comfortable furniture. A huge map of the United States and the Confederacy had been tacked up on one wall. In the center of the room was a large table surrounded by chairs. On the table were neatly-rolled maps and some books. There were three other men in the room. Two were in uniform, one was not. One of the men in uniform was the same Sergeant Masters who had been Jordan's guide. The colonel gave the sergeant's first name as Tarleton. The other man in uniform was a lieutenant of cavalry named Edward Patterson. Lieutenant Patterson was in command of a platoon of cavalry controlled by Colonel Longfellow. The man in civilian clothes was introduced as Mr. Frederick Harmon. Harmon looked like a prosperous backwoods businessman. He had a pleasant face and a full beard.

"Gentlemen," the colonel said. "May I introduce Captain Richard Jordan of the Third Virginia Cavalry."

The three nodded in welcome then they all sat down at the table. The sergeant selected a map and unrolled it. It was a detailed map of the roads in the area bordered by Orange Court House, Fredericksburg, and Washington, D.C. The sergeant held the corners of the map down with the books.

"Gentlemen," the colonel began. "You all know the plan, but I will review it for Captain Jordan's benefit. We are going to transport $100,000 in gold to Washington to buy needed supplies for our army. The supplies will be shipped from Indiana to St. Louis and then to Vicksburg via riverboat. The supplies will then travel to the east and there they will be used for our invasion of Pennsylvania this summer. Unfortunately, our agent in Washington was arrested by Pinkerton's men, so Captain Jordan has agreed to take his place. Sergeant Masters will accompany him. Now, I am going to discuss the details of the plan and each of your parts in it.

"In two days, Mr. Harmon will bring the gold from Richmond on the Richmond, Fredericksburg & Potomac Railroad. The gold will be transported in two boxes marked 'Musket Parts' and will arrive at Guiney's Station at approximately 2:00 P.M. The gold will be removed from the train along with other military cargo and will be transferred to one of five army supply wagons as if it were an everyday occurrence. Lieutenant Patterson and his men will provide the escort. This part of the operation must appear as if it were routine. In the meantime, Sergeant Masters will travel to Orange Court House and pick up the sutler's wagon we have been preparing for the trip. Captain Jordan will stay out of sight until it's time to move north. I will brief him on his part in detail, later. Three days from now you will all assemble at Ely's Ford. Before dawn, you will cross the ford with both wagons. Once across, Lieutenant Patterson's force will provide security while the gold is transferred to the sutler's wagon and concealed in the false floor. Captain Jordan and Sergeant Masters will be sutlers to the Union Army traveling north for more supplies. The wagon will be empty except for a few bottles of whiskey which they can use for bribes."

Acknowledging Jordan and Masters, Longfellow continued. "You will drive north to the Richardsville Road, then turn east. Once you cross the Rappahannock at Richard's Ford you will be in Yankee country. Your papers should help there. Drive north to Harwood, then west to Stafford Court House. Then you will travel north to Occoquan. At Occoquan, you will head northwest to Falls Church. There you will find Wilson's Livery. Mr. Wilson is our agent. I will give you the password with your orders. He delivers produce and hay from his farm to the Washington area. The gold will be transferred to one of his wagons at that point.

"Sergeant Masters will remain with the gold and Mr. Wilson will drive you, Captain Jordan, to Harper's Ferry where you will catch a train to Baltimore. Once in Baltimore you will catch another train south to Washington as if you were any other businessman going to Washington to conduct business with the U.S. Government. In Washington, you will be staying at Willard's Hotel. For this onerous duty, President Davis has directed that you be given extra pay."

Everyone laughed at the joke.

"Once in Washington, captain, you must contact the agent and place our order. Once the contractor has the gold, you and Sergeant Masters will leave Washington by the fastest and safest route. Are there any questions?"

Jordan nodded. "Yes, sir. I do have one."

"Yes, what is it?"

"With the roads as difficult as they are, wouldn't it be easier to transport the gold with mules?"

"If this were a purely military operation, the answer would be yes. The reason we are using a sutler's wagon is that they are seldom questioned in the rear areas of the Union Army, so it gives you and Sergeant Masters an excellent cover. Even if you are stopped, the wagon provides a place to hide the gold well enough so that, when you are searched, the odds are it won't be found."

"Thank you, sir," Jordan said.

"Now if there are no further questions, you gentlemen can get started and I can give Captain Jordan his confidential instructions."

All three men nodded. The military men didn't bother to salute. They rose and left the room. The colonel waited until he and Jordan were alone and closed the door.

"The reason I don't want you involved in any other part of this operation is that I'm sure some of my people are being watched. You are new, and if you are not seen with them, you will remain undetected."

"Yes sir. I understand."

"We don't have time to devise a fictitious identity for you, so you will have to use your own name. This way you won't accidentally respond to a name other than the one you are using. You are an agent of Dedham & Sons of Baltimore, an actual firm that is a contractor to the Army of the Potomac. It is a Union company but one of its employees is among our agents, so you will be covered. Dedham & Sons is in the process of completing a contract for the Army of the Potomac and you are looking for a new one on which to bid. I have a prospectus of the company and the name of our agent at Dedham & Sons. Should you be questioned, he will verify your employment with the company. This is where we need your expertise. You must go to several government agencies and get contract information. This will do two things. It will cover you and it will give us information on the planned size of the Union Army in the coming year. The person who will put you in touch with the Yankee contractor is Mrs. Lydia Ratliffe. She is an attractive and wealthy widow whose society is much sought after. You will have her address before you leave. She entertains extensively and has contacts everywhere. The Pinkertons and the army have searched her house, had her under surveilance, and questioned her associates, but no one has ever been able to penetrate her network. I understand she even has an admirer in the War Plans Office itself. She is quite remarkable. Once you make contact with Mrs. Ratliffe, she will invite you to a party. That is where you will meet the representative of the contractor from whom we are ordering the supplies. Before you leave I will give you the list of supplies required. You must impress on him that we must have the shoes. That is the one thing we are critically short on that we cannot get enough of from the enemy. Next we need the medicine and the cloth."

The colonel paused to see if Jordan had any questions. Jordan had none, so he continued.

"The next question is what to do with you from now until the rendezvous at Ely's Ford. Despite General Lee's prohibition against them, I suggest a short furlough. You can't stay here, so you can either go to Orange Court House, which admittedly is nothing to write home about, or you can be on your way and perhaps stay over for a day or two at Oakview Manor. The owner is Mrs. Franks, the widow of Colonel Tom Franks, who was killed at Sharpsburg last year. She has written General Lee and has extended an open invitation to officers of the army despite the fact that she is still in mourning."

"I am acquainted with Mrs. Franks, sir," Jordan told him without revealing any of his feelings. "She allowed General Stuart and his officers to use her home, even though she had recently received news of her husband's death. I am in need of a bit of quiet, so I'd be most happy to accept her kind offer."

"Very well, then. Just make sure you travel in uniform and say nothing about your mission. You are not to change clothes until after you are across the river. If the subject of your presence comes up, just tell Mrs. Franks or anyone else that you have been scouting north of the river for Yankee activity and are tired."

"Yes sir."

"Last, but not least, unbend a little. Too many 'yes sirs' and 'no sirs' may make some people in Washington suspicious."

"Yes s . . . " Jordan laughed and so did the colonel.

The following morning Jordan saddled his horse and packed his few belongings. Longfellow provided him with instructions from Dedham & Sons in Baltimore. Mrs. Ratliffe's address was in cipher.

As he led his horse out of the barn, Jordan heard a strange noise in the adjacent outbuilding. He walked over and peered in the open door. The slave girl Rebecca was hanging by her wrists from a beam so that her feet couldn't touch the ground. She was stripped to the waist and Mr. Johnson was wielding a whip. Every time the lash struck her bare back, Rebecca sobbed. Mrs. Johnson was off to the side watching. There was an expression of great satisfaction on her face as she whispered hoarsely, "Hit her again!"

Jordan felt the bile rise in his throat and he mounted his horse. He spurred it on in the bitterly cold morning until the Johnson farm was out of sight. Jordan was not able to get the image of the hapless slave woman and her tormentors out of his mind until the roof of Oakview Manor appeared over the trees.

Oakview Manor derived its name from the famous grove of tall oaks that hid the house from the view of anyone on the road. The entrance to the manor was a large wrought iron gate that had been made in England in the 18th century, but the Franks family was so proud of its hospitality that it boasted that the gates had never been closed. The gate marked the beginning of the mile-long drive to the manor. The road wound its way through the grove and ended at the house. In the summer it was green and shaded. Squirrels played in the trees and birds sang in the branches. On this bleak March afternoon, the trees were bare and the only sound was the dead leaves rustling in the wind. When Jordan cleared the grove and sighted the house, he was so excited that it may as well have been spring.

Oakview Manor was typical of so many homes in that area of Virginia. It was built of the local grayish brick. The central portion of the house was built before the Revolution by the first Franks who had been a well-to-do merchant. After the War of 1812, the two wings were built and the Georgian portico added. In the back were the outbuildings for the laundry room and the kitchen. The first time Jordan saw the house, he thought it large, cold, and foreboding, but once he met Jennifer, it seemed to emanate warmth.

Jennifer Franks sat at the large mahogany desk and made the entries for the sale of several loads of hay to the cavalry in her ledgers. Tom had shown her how to check the books before he was appointed to command his regiment. He didn't think he was going to be gone long, but he felt it was something that she should know even though Lucas, the house master, did all the actual bookkeeping. That now seemed a different world. It was a good thing that she had an aptitude for figures, because she had to see to every penny herself. Oakview, like the rest of the Confederacy was barely keeping body and soul together.

Oakview's money crop was tobacco, but there were two crops of it in the warehouse and no way to sell it. The last time she tried to ship a tobacco crop, the transportation cost nearly as much as her profit. The railroads were too busy hauling war supplies to transport tobacco to a port. Even if Jennifer managed to find a way to get it to a port, there was no guarantee she could sell it. Every dock in the Confederacy was jammed with unsold tobacco and cotton. The Yankee Navy was slowly strangling the South and the only way to make a profit was to find someone who was taking a shipment to Bermuda on a blockade runner. That way a large profit could be made in gold instead of paper money which was losing its value daily.

The previous year she had to make ends meet by selling fifty of Oakview's one hundred and twenty-three slaves. She didn't want to do it, but she had to in order to save Oakview Manor. Slaves were the only commodities that were maintaining their real value, and Jennifer was able to run the plantation at a profit by the sale. That would have left seventy-three slaves, except that fourteen had run away since they learned about the Emancipation Proclamation. Most had been field hands but one escape bothered her a great deal. Lucas or Luke had been her house master. He ran the house and kept the accounts. He also had a permanent pass that allowed him to go to Fredericksburg, Orange Court House, or Culpeper without supervision. Often he did just that, staying overnight to buy supplies for the manor. Luke had been in the family for all of his thirty-eight years and was one of the most trusted members of the staff. The Franks never mistreated their slaves. Neither Tom Franks nor his father ever owned a whip. Throughout all the trouble with the Underground Railroad, Oakview had never lost a slave. She couldn't understand why Luke would want to run away, and his flight bothered her very much. It would have bothered her even more if she knew that her former house master was now First Sergeant Lucas Franks, "K" Company, 56th United States Colored Infantry, and that he had already seen action against Confederate troops.

Jennifer made her last entry and closed the books. At least the farm was making money and that would see them through the next year. She was able to sell produce to the local communities and hay to the army. So far she had not been bothered by the new law allowing the army to "impress" whatever they needed. This meant the soldiers could seize whatever they wished as long as they paid a "fair" price in devalued paper money. It was tantamount to theft and Jennifer could not understand how a government, created to escape Yankee tyranny, could pass such a law. Money was a serious problem. Jennifer was always careful to spend any as soon as it came into her hands before it lost more of its value. Prices had more than doubled in just the last six months. Butter was up to $3.50 a pound, coffee was $50 a pound, and flour was $300 a barrel. It was rumored that some of her neighbors were converting all their scrip to gold or even Yankee dollars. Jennifer absolutely refused to do that. She would not join the ranks of the faint-hearted who were dealing in greenbacks. Times were difficult now, but they would improve when the war was won and Jennifer had no doubt that the Confederacy would win its independence. They had whipped the Yankees to a standstill. Soon the North would become tired of it and Lincoln would be forced to end his war of aggression, she continually told herself. Until then, everyone had to make sacrifices the way Tom made the supreme sacrifice.

How many times a day did she think of Tom? He had been such a warm, loving, and passionate man. His death was a blow from which she thought she'd never recover. When she received the news that he had been killed it seemed like the end of the world. She swore to hold his memory as close as possible, but something had changed. She felt happy when General Stuart's officers came to the manor. She wanted to remove her black dress and dance. There was one officer . . . Why did she pretend not to remember Richard Jordan's name? He had such a nice smile and his blue eyes said more to her than his words. When he visited again in January they talked and he smiled and he had kissed her hand.

She wished she hadn't made the vow to stay in mourning an entire year.

"Miss Jennifer," a soft voice said.

It was the voice of Sarah, the woman who had been Jennifer's personal maid since Jennifer was old enough to have a maid. Sarah was a tall, elegant woman who moved with a natural grace. She was a "high yellow" with patrician features. She was considered more than handsome and some men had offered Jennifer vast sums for her, but Jennifer refused to sell her. Sarah was intelligent and practical, as well as completely loyal, and Jennifer relied heavily on Sarah's advice. Lately, Jennifer was wondering whether or not to give Sarah her freedom, but was terrified at the thought of Sarah leaving.

"Yes, Sarah, what is it?"

"Coppy says there's a rider coming through the grove."

Coppy was Copernicus, Sarah's thirteen-year-old son. He was a nice, happy boy who was always pleasant. Sarah never said who the father was. Jennifer thought it might be Luke since Sarah and he seemed very friendly before he ran away, but since he ran off, Sarah never mentioned him. Tom kept Coppy in the house to be with his mother, and he was turning into such an excellent house servant Tom began training him to assist Luke.

Jennifer wondered who the rider might be. She opened the desk drawer and pulled out her late husband's Le Mat revolver. The times had brought the celebrated Franks' hospitality to this.

"Let's go see who it is," she said.

Richard Jordan smiled as the young Negro boy on the porch recognized him and came down the steps to meet him.

"Good day, Captain Jordan," Coppy said. He had excellent diction. "It's good to see you again. I trust you've come to visit for a few days."

"It's nice to see you again, too, Coppy. I think two days if Mrs. Franks will let me. It's a busy war."

"Allow me to take your horse, sir."

Jordan dismounted. "Thank you."

Jordan mounted the wide wooden steps and removed his hat. He suddenly felt very nervous.

Jennifer and Sarah peeked through the curtains to see who their visitor might be. Jennifer didn't recognize him at first.

"It's that nice Captain Jordan," Sarah said nonchalantly. She had an excellent memory for names and faces and she remembered Jordan as a pleasant young man whose company Jennifer had enjoyed.

"Oh, dear!" Jennifer exclaimed. "Sarah, show him in and give him some tea or a drink or something. "I'll be down in a few minutes."

Sarah blinked. She had never seen Jennifer move so quickly, or so ungracefully. It was difficult for a lady to run up the steps holding her skirts in one hand and a large pistol in the other.

"Yes, Miss Jennifer."

Sarah arrived at the door the moment Jordan knocked. She opened the door and bowed politely.

"Captain Jordan, how nice to see you. Have you come to stay with us?"

"If Mrs. Franks is not inconvenienced, I would like to stay two days."

"Please come in, then, and I'll tell her you're here."

As soon as Jordan entered the house, an elderly black man scurried up and took his hat, coat, and saber. Sarah led him to the sitting room where she offered him a seat.

"May I get you something, captain? Tea, coffee, or something stronger?" From the tone of Sarah's voice, she obviously didn't approve of strong drink.

"I think I'd like some tea, Sarah."

She leaned over to him and said quietly. "This is Yankee coffee without a bit of chicory in it, but don't you dare let Miss Jennifer know."

Jordan smiled. "Coffee then."

Sarah disappeared and Jordan relaxed in the chair. It was going to be rough getting back in the field again after sleeping in beds and eating regular meals. It was amazing how quickly one readjusted to civilized behavior. Sarah returned quickly with the coffee and as soon as he smelled it he knew it really was "Yankee coffee."

Sarah hurried upstairs wondering what had happened to Jennifer. Sarah found her in front of the mirror trying to fix her hair. Sarah had wondered about the way Jennifer felt toward the handsome captain and now she knew. She was happy Jennifer found the man interesting. Jennifer was still young and beautiful and life, after all, was for the living.

"Sarah, what am I to do? I look awful."

"A little rouge in the right places would help," Sarah told Jennifer. "Not to mention a little jewelry, and a nice blouse that shows a little of your neck."

"Sarah," Jennifer said sounding shocked. "I'm supposed to be in mourning."

"Mourning? Most women stay in mourning for three months. You had to stay in mourning for a year. Mr. Tom's been dead nearly six months."

"I made a vow," Jennifer said.

"Vow, my foot," Sarah said. "I'll bet if Mr. Tom were here he'd tell you to put on something nice, go to a ball, and have fun. Besides, being in mourning doesn't mean you can't look nice. If you're bound and determined to wear black, why not wear a black skirt and a nice white blouse. No one can criticize that."

Sarah reached for the rouge and the powder.

"Here, put some of this on.

"Sarah, I'm not a hussy!"

"You weren't a hussy when you decided you liked Mr. Tom, either. You're just using those weapons the Lord gives every woman to help the cause."

Jennifer sat and looked at her reflection in the mirror. She drummed her fingers on the table and said, "I guess I do look a little pale. What blouse do you think I should wear?"

The maid smiled and walked to the armoire. She knew just the one.

Jordan finished his coffee and waited. It seemed a long time since Sarah had given him the coffee and gone upstairs. He began to fidget, then he got up to pace around the room. Then he began to get nervous. What if she didn't want to see him? What if she were sick? He paced the room, examining the books on the shelves, looking at the furniture, and tracing the pattern in the wallpaper.

"Captain Jordan," a soft voice behind him said. "Do forgive my manners in not receiving you right away, but there is so much to do here."

Jordan turned. Jennifer looked so lovely that he was afraid to speak at first. She was so different from when he had first seen her. There was color in her cheeks and a smile on her face. She looked radiant.

"Mrs. Franks, your company is always worth the wait. May I say that you look indeed lovely this evening." He stepped up and kissed her hand.

Jennifer felt the goose bumps go up her arm as Jordan kissed her hand. She couldn't hold back her smile. He is handsome, she thought.

"And you look most handsome in your new uniform. You must tell me of your adventures since you were here last," she said. "And what brings you here alone?"

Jordan hesitated. He blushed. She noticed the uniform. "Well, Mrs. Franks. . . "

"Wouldn't you like to sit down?"

"Yes, thank you."

He sat on the sofa and she sat across from him. Sarah brought more coffee and some cookies.

"If you don't mind, I prefer that my friends call me Jennifer," she said, trying to put him at ease.

"My friends call me, Dick, Mrs. . . . er . . . Jennifer. I think Jennifer is a very pretty name."

"Thank you, Dick. Now, you were telling me what you have done since January last."

Camp life the past three months had been boring except for one raid across Kelly's Ford in February. It was a great feat of arms. General Fitzhugh Lee crossed the Rappahannock with a hand-picked force and defeated a force of Yankees many times stronger than his own. It had been fun, but Jordan tried to tell the story from a detached viewpoint so he wouldn't seem a braggart. Jennifer looked at him as he spoke. She seems interested, he thought. It made him feel nervous. They spent the rest of that day and the following one in each other's company and Jordan felt more alive than he had in months. He had never been this conscious of the passage of time. He was painfully aware of every minute as it slipped away. Had there been a way to stop time, he would have done it. His heart sank when he realized he would have to depart the following morning. Despite the overcast sky and the chill in the air, he and Jennifer went out on the veranda.

"I wish I didn't have to go in the morning," he told her.

Jennifer didn't look directly at him. "You will be careful,won't you?"

"I'll be back." He said it seriously, without bravado.

She looked up at him then. She was terrified she'd lose someone else. He moved closer and her first thought was to move away, but she stood rooted to the spot as his arms encircled her and his lips covered hers. She felt comfortable in his arms and her arms moved up around his neck.

Jordan thrilled at the feeling of her slim waist enfolded by his arms and her body pressed against him. His reaction to her was immediate and intense. He wanted her right then, but he controlled himself and savored her nearness.

Jennifer trembled.

"You must be cold," he said.

"Yes," she said. She was still holding him tightly but her voice sounded distant. "We'd better go in."

The Road to Ely's Ford
March 4, 1863

Jordan rose early and saw Jennifer only briefly before he left. He desperately wanted to hold her again and kiss her, but there were too many servants around and he felt awkward. He barely noticed the bite of the wind as he rode toward Ely's Ford. He knew he would never love anyone the way he loved her. He was just past the deserted Wilderness Tavern when he was jolted out of his reverie. Hardly anyone traveled these roads and yet there was another rider heading his way. He nervously felt for his pistol. He breathed a sigh of relief when he saw the mounted man was wearing gray. When they drew closer, he saw the rider was a major who was spattered with mud. He looked very tired. The major reined in and waited for Jordan to ride up. The major was a man of medium height with light brown hair and a modest mustache. He had light skin and gray eyes which made him look intelligent. Jordan saluted.

"Captain Jordan, Third Virginia Cavalry, sir."

"Harvey Ferris, Eighteenth North Carolina, captain and may I say I am damned glad to make your acquaintance. I have been lost, damned near killed by some Yankee last night, and saved in a nick of time by the pickets. Could you perhaps tell me where I might find lodging, if only for a few hours?"

"There's Oakview Manor straight down this road, sir." Jordan told the major. "Mrs. Franks offers hospitality to officers of the army."

"I hope I won't be intruding. I always hate to intrude on a lady."

"It should be all right, sir."

"Thank you, captain. I won't keep you. Good luck."

"You too, sir." Jordan spurred his horse forward.

The Spy thought of killing the captain, but decided against it. This was no time to be leaving a trail of bodies. He was tired and he needed to rest, because he still had a long way to go. He spurred his horse in the direction of Oakview Manor.

Jordan rode down the hill to the bottom land near the ford. He could see the little hut that the pickets had built to keep warm. Harmon's wagon was parked near the hut. Mr. Harmon was standing by a small fire talking to Lieutenant Patterson. There were several infantrymen milling around and Jordan guessed that they were the pickets. Masters and the sutler wagon were nowhere to be seen. Jordan dismounted and Patterson walked toward him. The lieutenant saluted.

"The pickets got themselves a Yankee major a little while ago, captain," the lieutenant said.

"I know. I just met a major on the road who said the pickets saved his life."

"We shot him right in the face, cap'n," one of the pickets volunteered. "Bet his own Momma wouldn't know him now."

Jordan was suddenly curious. What poor devil was so unfortunate as to have his face blown off on a cold, dark night in the middle of nowhere? "Let's have a look at him. Where is he?"

"Behind the hut, cap'n," the picket sergeant said.

The pickets had lain the body out between the hut and the wood pile. The sergeant had placed a worn blanket over the body. Since the sergeant was wearing a new blue overcoat, Jordan assumed that he had traded with the dead man. It was a fair trade. The living were always in greater need than the dead. The sergeant pulled the blanket back. The body was wearing the uniform of a Union Army major. Jordan looked at the face. The wounds were horrible. The picket was right. The face was so badly mutilated that Jordan doubted that even the man's close friends could recognize him. The entry wound in the cheek was partially visible and Jordan bent to look at it. It had been made by a .36 caliber pistol ball at very close range. There were powder burns all over the dead man's ear.

"You say you shot this man?" Jordan asked the sergeant.

"Yes sir," the sergeant answered. "Saved the major's life."

Jordan wondered what was going on. It was obvious to anyone who cared to look at the body that Major Ferris had killed the officer himself. Why then did he claim that the pickets killed him? Was it because Ferris was so shaken that he didn't realize he had killed him? It didn't seem reasonable that a man who could put a pistol to another man's ear and pull the trigger was the kind who was easily shaken.

"Did he have anything on him? Any sort of identification?" Jordan asked the picket sergeant, referring to the dead Ellison.

We didn't take nothin' from him 'cept the coat, his blanket, and the food what was in his saddlebags," the sergeant said defensively. "I got his pocketbook here." He handed the leather wallet to Jordan. "We didn't take nothin' includin' his ring. Not that it's worth stealin'."

Jordan looked at the cheap lion's head ring on the dead man's finger. He thumbed through the wallet. There were only $20 in greenbacks and no identification. There were both Union and Confederate passes but the name lines were blank.

"Unless I miss my guess," Jordan said, "this man was a spy. Lieutenant Patterson, make sure Colonel Longfellow gets these papers."

"Yes sir," the lieutenant said, taking the wallet from Jordan.

"Sergeant, if you would please, tell me exactly what happened last night."

The sergeant told him as clearly as he could.

"You say you heard a shot before you fired?"

"Yes sir."

"Thank you, sergeant. You've been most kind."

"My pleasure, sir."

Jordan found the whole incident unsettling. Something was wrong. He was trying to sort it out when Harmon shouted.

"Here comes Masters."

Everyone looked up as the sutler's wagon rolled slowly down the steep incline toward them. The horses, the wheels, and Masters were all caked with mud. He had had a rough time of it.

"Well, I made it," he said.

"None too soon," Harmon said. "Let's hurry and get this wagon over the river."

The pickets looked curious, but made a point of minding their own business. Odd things happened at this ford from time to time and they knew enough not to ask any questions. Harmon climbed up on the freight wagon and began moving it into the ford. Patterson's men mounted their horses and trotted ahead. Jordan moved across with the cavalry and Masters followed easily in the empty sutler's wagon. The cavalry fanned out as they moved up the road. When they had gone about a mile, Harmon pulled the wagon off the road. Two of the cavalrymen opened the crates while Masters moved to the back of the sutler's wagon. The loose floorboards came up easily, revealing the storage spaces for the gold bars. The bars were transferred quickly and the floor of the sutler's wagon was nailed back in place. In the meantime, Jordan changed into a set of good quality, but well-worn civilian clothes. He was too neat to look like a sutler, but a little mud on his boots and a day or two of stubble would fix that. Jordan checked his papers. There were passes for himself and Masters and a permit allowing him to trade with the troops of the Army of the Potomac. He stepped up onto the wagon and sat beside Masters.

"Let's go," he said. When he turned to say goodbye, Harmon and Patterson were already traveling in the opposite direction.

"What do they call you?" Jordan asked Masters.

"Charley," Masters said.

"Charley? I thought your name was Tarleton."

"It is, but when I was a child, I could only say 'Tarley' which strangers thought was Charley. It stuck."

"Everyone calls me Dick," Jordan said extending his hand. "We might as well get rid of this sergeant/captain business if we're going to be business partners."

"Glad to know you, Dick," Masters said. He smiled and shook Jordan's hand.

The road was bad and they didn't get through Hartwood until noon. They saw a few Union cavalry, but they weren't stopped. By the time they reached Potomac Creek, the light was failing. They hadn't reached Accaheak Creek when the first shot rang out.

"Yankees!" Jordan said.

"I wish they were," Masters said. "They're partisans."

Another shot rang out and it hit the side of the wagon.

"Stop the wagon and you won't get hurt," a voice said.

"When I stop the wagon, get off," Masters told him. "We'll hide in the woods until we figure out what to do."

"What about the gold?" Jordan asked.

"We can't keep it if we're dead," the sergeant told him.

"But if we explain . . . " Another shot hit the wagon.

Masters brought the wagon to a stop and he and Jordan leaped into the mud on the side of the road. They hid in some underbrush. In the twilight a group of riders approached the wagon. They were armed with rifles and shotguns. Some of them were wearing pieces of uniforms, but it was obviously not a military unit.

"How many do you think there are?" Jordan asked in a hoarse whisper.

"About five or six. In this light it's hard to tell."

"It looks like they done run off," one of the riders said.

"Go after 'em, Willie," a hidden voice said. "Make sure they don't come back."

Jordan now understood why some Yankees referred to Confederate Partisans as bushwhackers. That's all this group was. The one called Willie was riding right for them. Jordan pulled his pistol out of his coat. He hoped he wouldn't have to use it.

Jordan had to make one last attempt to avoid bloodshed. "Don't shoot. We're Confederates."

Willie was obviously trying to figure out the direction of the voice as he drew nearer. Finally, he said, "You damned bluebellies expect me to believe that?" He was only a few feet away as he swung his shotgun toward the sound of Jordan's voice.

Jordan raised his pistol and fired. The bullet hit Willie in the stomach. "Oh, God," the bushwhacker cried as he tumbled off his horse.

"Willie, you all right?" a voice called.

"I'm shot, Ed. Oh, God, I'm shot." Willie's voice was pathetic.

"Al, Frank, go get Willie and kill them sutlers," Ed ordered. Two horses headed into the woods toward the sound of Willie's groaning. It was getting darker. Jordan felt the anger rise in him. This whole affair was pointless. Why couldn't these people listen to reason?

"If you can handle these two, I'm going to try to get to the wagon and see if I can find Ed," Jordan said,

Masters just nodded. His pistol was already drawn. Jordan disappeared into the dense underbrush. It was a lot lighter on the road than it was in the woods. There were two horses near the wagon held by a mounted man.

"Ain't a damn thing in here," someone said from inside the wagon. "It's empty, 'cept for some liquor."

A shot rang out.

"We'd better kill those damned sutlers and get out of here," Ed said. "Frank, burn the wagon."

"Sure thing, Ed."

Jordan moved across the road quickly. He pulled the unsuspecting rider off his horse and hit him with the heavy .44 Colt before he knew what was happening. There was another shot.

"Frank, make sure everything's all right out there." Ed was still in the wagon.

Frank walked toward the horses. He was a big man. Jordan took the fallen man's rifle and hid behind a tree. Frank walked up to the horses. Since he didn't see the man who was supposed to be holding then he called his name. "George?"

As quietly as he could, Jordan moved behind him and swung the rifle by the barrel with all his might. The stock hit Frank at the base of the skull and he collapsed in a heap at Jordan's feet. The stock of the rifle was broken. Jordan looked around just in time to see Ed emerge from the wagon.

"What the hell?" Ed said, raising his rifle.

Jordan shot him without thinking. Ed dropped his rifle and fell. Jordan didn't know whether he had hit him in the leg or in the stomach because Ed rolled over on his side and pulled his knees up, groaning, "Oh, Jesus, get me a doctor."

Masters emerged from the woods. "They're all dead in there," he said.

"Who are you people?" Ed asked. He was in great pain.

"I tried to tell you," Jordan said. "We're Confederates. I tried to tell your man Willie, but he wouldn't listen."

"He never was too bright. Oh Lord, it hurts."

"What about the others?" Masters asked.

"Back there," Jordan pointed. He walked over and kicked Ed's rifle into the brush.

Masters walked back to the horses. A moment later he was back. "One had his neck broken, the other's dead, too."

"I didn't think I hit him that hard . . ." Jordan's voice trailed off as he saw Masters' knife. Masters walked toward Ed.

Ed saw the knife, too. "Look, it was a mistake. It was dark. Oh, God, please don't," he pleaded with a pathetic sob.

"My God, Masters, that's murder!" Jordan turned his head away as Masters cut Ed's throat.

Masters wiped his knife on Ed's shirt. "We play by different rules in this game, captain. That's why I'm here. No one, and I mean no one, can be allowed to find out who we are, where we are going, or why. Now, let's get these bodies off the road and get out of here."

Jordan and Masters dragged the bodies into the woods and covered them with leaves. Then they unsaddled the horses and drove them off, hiding the saddles as well. It was after midnight when they reached Stafford Court House. Jordan was having a difficult time with the deaths of the bushwhackers. It was one thing to kill a man in battle, but when the battle was over you could conduct yourself as a human being. Even enemy wounded were treated well and captives were allowed to live. In the world of Raymond Longfellow and Tarleton Masters human beings held little importance. What were important were the secrets that had to be discovered or kept.

Jennifer Franks smiled as the newly-washed and rested Major Harvey Ferris appeared in the dining room for the evening meal.

"Mrs. Franks," he said with an elegant bow. "I am indebted to you for your superb hospitality. I confess that this morning I was at the end of my tether. You saved my life."

Jennifer smiled and nodded graciously, " My home is open to all officers of the army, major. I feel we all must do what we can to ease the burden of those fighting for our liberty."

"Mrs. Franks, if all of our ladies were as patriotic, gracious, and, if I may be so bold, as lovely as you this war would have already have been won."

Jennifer blushed slightly at the compliment. She wasn't used to men with such elegantly polished manners. It pleased her and made her feel a little self-conscious. "Please have a seat, major," she said taking her seat.

The major waited until Jennifer was seated and sat at her right.

"Where did you live before the war, major?" she asked, making conversation over the soup.

"New York, Mrs. Franks," he lied. He once had a commission in New York, and he knew the city well.

"New York? I thought you said you were from Carolina?"

"I am, Mrs. Franks," he said with his most charming smile. "I studied law at Columbia and decided to stay there and start a practice. Northerners are much more prone to litigation that we are in the South. We have much more gentlemanly ways of settling disputes."

Since serpents and Yankees occupied roughly the same position in Jennifer's eyes, she couldn't help but accept the major's statement as fact.

"Didn't you find it cold there?" she asked.

"Actually, New York can be rather charming," the Spy told her. "There was only one thing I really didn't like about it."

"And what was that?"

"The Yankees."

Jennifer laughed loudly. She thought that was very funny. Major Ferris was the first person who had made her laugh in a long time. He was so different from either of the men she'd known. Tom Franks was a happy, simple man. Richard Jordan was so serious. He was like a young boy who was trying to grow up too fast. Major Ferris was a man of the world who had traveled widely and done much. He had none of Tom's provinciality nor did he have Dick's businesslike manner. She couldn't help liking Dick, but the major was charming. Jennifer asked the next question automatically.

"Are you married, major?"

"Alas, no, Mrs. Franks."

"Not even a sweetheart?"

The Spy looked away as if the truth were too painful to tell. "There was one girl. She was from Connecticut. I confess I was strongly attracted to her and expressed my honorable intentions toward her, but when she found out that I was from North Carolina and that my family held slaves, she condemned me in no uncertain terms. I attempted to explain that our darkies were treated much better than most of the laborers in northern factories, but she continued to lash out at me. Then I tried to explain that a primitive race like the Negro benefits by his service to the white man," he said shaking his head sadly.

"What did she say to that?"

"What she said was something I never thought I would hear issuing from the mouth of a member of the fair sex. I dare not repeat it."

Jennifer flushed with anger. Yankees were always so quick to condemn the South. "Then may I say you were fortunate, sir, because it appears that the woman to whom you were attracted was no lady."

The Spy looked at her. Jennifer was angry and her eyes blazed. This woman had fire and he found that appealing.

"I know, but who can dictate affairs of the heart?" he asked with a shrug. "I was crushed and resolved to return to North Carolina. It was fortunate that I did, because the war began shortly after that."

"I apologize for bringing up such a painful subject, major," Jennifer said sincerely. She felt a little embarrassed.

"You couldn't possibly have known, Mrs. Franks," he said with a warm smile. "There's no harm done. It seems as if those days in New York were centuries ago. There is so little time for romance with this war on," he said with a sigh.

"What do you intend to do after the war, major?"

"I intend to travel, madam. I have a great desire to see all of Europe, Egypt, India, and China."

"Why those places?"

The Spy shrugged. "I suppose I have always had a fascination with the Orient. Their civilizations are so old and mysterious. I believe they have secrets that would greatly benefit us. I would like to see their ancient temples and palaces and see if that is true. I am told that there are men who can charm snakes and walk on fire. I'm not speaking of cheap carnival tricks, mind. I'm speaking of true wonders."

"That would be fascinating, traveling around the world," Jennifer said almost dreamily. She looked off into a far corner of the room. She had never been out of Virginia and when Tom was alive that had seemed enough, but she was curious about other places. She wondered what it would be like traveling to them with a man as charming as Major Harvey Ferris. It would undoubtedly be very pleasant.

The Spy looked at her as she gazed into the corner of the room. She is very beautiful, he thought. She's also very vulnerable. The Spy liked women. If it could be said he had a weakness, then that weakness was women. He enjoyed them and found their company far more fascinating than that of men. He enjoyed their favors immensely. Unfortunately, he tired of most of them rather quickly. Jennifer Franks was an agreeable surprise. She was attractive, intelligent, and beneath the polite reserve, he perceived a very passionate woman. She was very different from the women he had known. She was the kind of woman who would make an excellent lifelong companion. If she were as practical as she seemed, she would leave this place and travel with him to Europe or perhaps even the Orient. The Spy decided that when this commission was over he would return and propose. There was always the question of his commissions and his plans. He would grow old and have to give them up unless he started an agency and trained younger men—perhaps his sons. A brief smile crossed his lips. There was a possibility. The thought stayed in his mind but, there were other more immediate things to consider. He wanted her and if he analyzed the situation correctly, he wouldn't have to be too insistent.

"If I might be so bold, Mrs. Franks, may I ask your permission to walk around your home? It is, I perceive, a house built in the previous century and added to most tastefully in this one."

Jennifer looked at him without saying a word. Here was a man who was attractive, charming, and intelligent under her own roof and she was sitting there like a perfect dunce, not saying a word. "If you'd like, I can give you a tour," she said looking at his face. He was handsome and he had such lovely gray eyes.

"I don't want to put you to any trouble but I would personally find that quite delightful."

Jennifer blushed. "It's no trouble, I assure you. Come this way please."

The Spy followed Jennifer as she led him through Oakview Manor. She pointed out the original and new parts, as well as the room in which George Washington had supposedly slept. They ended the tour in the new wing, which was now unused. It was dark except for the oil lamp she carried.

"We used to have parties here before the war," Jennifer said, putting the lamp down. "But now most of the men are in the army and there isn't much dancing. Last November General Stuart and his officers were here and had a good time, but that's the only use it's had recently."

Jennifer noticed that the major had moved closer. She turned and looked at him. The lamplight reflected hypnotically in his eyes.

"I can't imagine why men don't beat a path to your door, Mrs. . . . may I call you Jennifer? You're very beautiful." His voice was a soft, husky whisper.

Jennifer watched his face as it drew closer. She wanted to say something, but his lips pressed against hers. It was a soft, gentle kiss that was, at the same time, insistent. It had been a long time since anyone had kissed her like that, if anyone *had ever* kissed her like that. This was what she wanted; what she needed. Her arms went around his neck as he pulled her to him. Her body pressed against his and she felt giddy as his lips moved from her mouth to her cheek and to her neck. When his hand moved up to caress her she suddenly felt afraid.

"Please don't," she whispered hoarsely.

The Spy relented. Ordinarily he would have pressed the matter but he decided not to. This woman was worth waiting for.

Early the following morning Jennifer told him goodbye and was overjoyed when he promised to return. After he left she tried to put her feelings into words. He had shown her more passion than she thought possible and made her think of things she had never dreamed of. China and India seem so real sitting across the table from Harvey Ferris, but in the cold light of day, Jennifer didn't know if she loved Harvey Ferris at all. If she didn't, how could she have taken such delight in his company and let him kiss her like that? What kind of woman was she? She felt she had betrayed her dead husband and Richard Jordan. How could she look at Dick Jordan's face again?

When she decided to get dressed, Sarah came in to help her. Jennifer was silent and distant, but the maid didn't ask why her mistress was so preoccupied. She knew.

"You know, Miss Jennifer," Sarah said. "We women are funny folks. Sometimes you meet a man. He may be handsome, he may be plain, he may be good, or he may be bad. Whatever he is, whatever he does, he touches something deep in your soul and for that moment there is nothing in the world but him. I feel sorry for women who never meet that man because it's wonderful, but it isn't necessarily love."

Jennifer turned, pressed her face against Sarah's shoulder, and began to cry.

CHAPTER 5

Stafford Court House Inn
March 5, 1863

JORDAN AND MASTERS slept soundly and didn't wake until nearly
8:00 A.M. They washed and went downstairs to have breakfast.
The inn was still crowded with soldiers and teamsters eating their
morning meal. Outside there was already a lot of activity. Teamsters were hitching up their teams and trying to get as far as they
could before the frozen roads were softened by an unseasonably
warm noonday sun and churned to mud by the hundreds of other
wagons on the road. Jordan couldn't tell whether this was part of a
major move or just the Army of the Potomac's daily routine. So
many civilians failed to realize that an army needed to be fed,
clothed, and munitioned even in winter quarters. Even in the
Army of Northern Virginia, where wagons and supplies were at a
premium, there was constant motion. With the Yankees and their
large armies, inexhaustible supplies, and their countless wagons it
was doubly hard to tell.

They sat down at a table and the innkeeper, a man of known
southern sympathies, placed a large plate of eggs, ham, grits, and
biscuits before each of them.

"That'll be an extra fifty cents," the proprietor said.

"Fifty cents?" Jordan asked with genuine outrage. Southern
sympathies or no, fifty cents was a lot to pay for breakfast.

"The reason it's so high," one of the teamsters told him, "is that when the Rebs come, the innkeeper here don't charge them nothin'. That way he comes out even."

The rest of the men at breakfast laughed. "If he's so secesh," another man quipped. "How come he only takes gold, silver, and greenbacks and no Reb money?"

All eyes turned toward the innkeeper, but he had ducked into the kitchen in embarrassment.

"You the fellas what have the bullet holes in your wagon?" the teamster with the sense of humor asked. He was a huge man with a large bushy beard and a red face.

"That's us," Jordan said, buttering a biscuit.

"What happened?" It was an honest question.

"We got bushwhacked last night about ten miles west of here?"

"What were you doing out there at that time of night?" the teamster asked. "It ain't healthy."

Jordan pointed a thumb at Masters. "My driver here who is supposed to know the country got us lost."

Masters, amazed at Jordan's quick improvisation, looked properly chagrined.

"Why don't you fire him, then?"

"Two reasons," Jordan said with his mouth half full. "One, he's good with a gun. Shot one of them bastards dead, which is why they stopped chasing us." He finished chewing.

"That's only one reason," the teamster said, still curious.

Jordan looked right at the teamster and said quietly, "He is also my wife's first cousin."

The room erupted into laughter.

Masters stood up, indignant. "If that don't beat all," he said tossing four bits on the table. "I save your worthless hide and all you do is complain."

"Aw sit down," the teamster said still smiling. "He was only funnin'. Are you really his wife's cousin?"

"I don't know why she married him," Masters said, still acting miffed.

"Were there really bushwhackers?" someone else asked seriously.

"Five, near as I could tell," Masters said. "I shot one, he fell off his horse, and the rest turned back."

"Damned cowards! They claim to be Reb soldiers, but they're only highwaymen if you ask me."

"Couldn't agree with you more, friend," Jordan said. It wasn't every day he could agree with a Yankee, but this was one of them.

As Jordan and Masters were finishing their breakfast a Union cavalry sergeant stepped into the inn.

"Any you boys headed north best hold off for a while. A bunch of cavalry are heading this way and they're using the whole road."

"You mean the Rebs is comin'?" one of the teamsters asked seriously.

"No," the sergeant said. "It's our cavalry."

"Didn't know we had any," the teamster quipped.

Everyone in the room laughed and the sergeant's face got red. Jordan laughed along with everyone else and for the same reason. The Union cavalry was generally laughable. The troopers couldn't ride well and Jordan remembered early in the war how some of the Confederate troopers would ride up and pull the Yankee soldiers out of their saddles and steal their overloaded horses. That was assuming the horse was worth stealing, because they didn't know how to care for their horses, either. Oh, the Yankees were brave enough, but they always fought their cavalry in dribs and drabs. You never saw a full squadron, never mind a regiment. Confederate cavalry had faced their Union opponents at odds of 3 to 1 or better and beaten them every time. J.E.B. Stuart had the best cavalry in the world and Jordan took great pride in being one of Stuart's officers. In the distance, Jordan could hear the Yankees coming. So could everyone else.

"Hey, sutler," the big teamster with the sense of humor asked. "You know the difference between teamster boots and cavalry boots?"

"No."

"The teamster boots have the horse manure on the outside."

The eating room of the inn erupted in laughter again.

"Damned cavalry again," another teamster complained. "Lately they been takin' up the whole damned road."

"This I have to see," Jordan said quietly to Masters. "Let's go hitch up the wagon, Charley," he said out loud.

The two men walked outside.

"That was very good, Dick," Masters whispered.

"Thanks. I didn't know what else to do."

The cavalry wasn't more than a half a mile away now. Jordan was grinning as he leaned against a post on the porch of the inn to watch them go by.

The first regiment moved by smartly. They were in columns of fours and their speed was a rapid walk. At the head of the column the regimental colors were flying. At the head of each company was its guidon. The horses had thick winter coats but they had been brushed and curried and their manes and tails had been trimmed. The saddles and bridles were not new. They were all well broken in, but they were in good condition. Beneath each McClellan saddle was a heavy, blue wool Yankee saddle blanket folded to add extra thickness and cushioning to the horses' backs. Beside the saddle, the horse carried a blanket roll, a feed bag, and a brush. Impedimenta such as tents and picket stakes were non-existent. The riders were also different from those Jordan was used to. They didn't have the natural grace of Stuart's men. They never would, but they were businesslike and comfortable in the saddle. Very few had the old jackets trimmed in yellow. Most of them wore the homely, but practical, four-button blue fatigue blouse worn by all Union soldiers. They had discarded the stiff black hat and wore the comfortable "bummer's" cap. Even the lowliest private had his light blue trousers tucked into good Jefferson-style boots. They were armed with pistols, sabers, and the new Spencer repeating carbine. There were two full regiments of them and there were no stragglers. They looked like two regiments that were looking for trouble and would be happy when they found it. By the time they were past, Jordan was no longer smiling.

"What's wrong?" Masters asked.

"Let's go. I'll tell you on the road."

Jordan and Masters hitched the horses to the wagon and continued their journey north.

"Did you see the cavalry that passed, Charley?"

"Of course."

"What did you see?"

"The Fourth New York and the First Rhode Island Cavalry heading south."

It was the kind of good report that a reliable scout would give. Sometimes a report like that was not enough.

"What else did you see?"

"That was it," Masters told him. "What did I miss?"

Jordan explained what he had seen. "If the rest of the Yankee cavalry is like that. It means trouble."

"You make it sound pretty grim," Masters said.

"I'm not saying we can't beat them, but it won't be a picnic."

They drove north at a moderate pace. They wanted to seem what they were—sutlers returning to get more goods to sell to the troops. They were in a hurry but they weren't going to kill their horses. Horses were expensive. On the road they passed more Northern troops. These were infantry. They, too, were well-fed and confident. Their uniforms were in good shape, their haversacks were full, and they had shoes. Most of our regiments go barefoot, Jordan thought. These weren't the same dejected Yankees that they had beaten in December at Fredericksburg.

"Fighting Joe" Hooker was reorganizing the Army of the Potomac and from what Jordan was seeing, Hooker was being damned thorough. Too damned thorough. The units were wearing the new corps badges that Hooker had devised. If he's as good at being a general as he is at being a quartermaster, it's going to be a rough summer, Jordan thought. He didn't like seeing the enemy like this. It was easy looking at him through the sights of a gun or swinging a saber. You either killed him or he killed you. This way you got to see too much.

What bothered Jordan was that his enemy no longer appeared to be flesh and blood. Flesh and blood was easy to kill, Jordan knew. He had killed a lot of them and he would probably kill a lot more. Now he was beginning to see his enemy as a machine. The machine had gotten off to a bad start, but people were beginning to adjust it and give it better fuel to burn. Now it was beginning to operate more smoothly. If the Yankees ever got an experienced engineer to run this machine, there would be hell to pay.

It was just the opposite in the South. There the machine was running smoothly, but they were running out of everything. No matter how brave and resourceful they might be, this big Yankee machine would run them over unless they stopped it. Now Jordan understood why Longfellow had stressed that 1863 was the year the Confederacy could win the war. This was the year they *had* to win the war. That was why they were going to invade the North. Pennsylvania would pay the price Virginia had paid. The Yankees would learn how it felt to have an invader on their soil and they would have to make peace. Jordan held that thought. They had to make peace. He gripped it with all his might and kept it, because he dared not consider the alternative. It was too unbearable to contemplate.

Just south of Alexandria they were stopped by Yankee soldiers. Jordan was nervous.

"Stay calm," Masters said. "This isn't for us."

"May I see your papers please?" the sergeant of the guard asked.

Jordan and Masters handed him the carefully prepared passes. He gave them a cursory check and handed them back. "Been south?" The sergeant asked.

"Sure have. We were in Stafford Court House last night," Masters told him truthfully.

"You didn't see two men on the road by any chance, did you? This is one of them." The sergeant handed Masters a handbill.

On the handbill was an unflattering likeness of Major Charles Ellison. It stated that Ellison was a spy who escaped from Forrest Hall Prison with the help of an accomplice. It offered a reward of $500 for his capture and a similar amount for his accomplice who was last seen dressed as a major of the Provost Marshal's office. No other description was available.

"Sure could use $500, but we ain't seen him," Masters said, giving Jordan the handbill.

Jordan glanced briefly at the likeness. He was about to tell the sergeant he hadn't seen the man on the handbill, but he could imagine the hairline and the bearded jaw with half the face shot away. It was the same man that he had seen dead at Ely's Ford. He was sure of it. Then he realized he had stared at it too long.

"Recognize him?" the sergeant asked suspiciously.

Jordan gave the handbill back to the sergeant and grinned. "Looked like my brother-in-law for a minute," he said. "Sure like to get $500 for him."

"Hope you catch the bastard and hang him," Masters said.

The sergeant gave them an unpleasant look and waved them through.

"Did you notice anything familiar about the man in the picture," Jordan asked Masters.

"No, why?"

"Remember the man back at the picket at Ely's ford?"

"How could he be familiar with his face shot away?" Masters asked honestly. "Besides, it doesn't hardly seem logical for a Yankee spying for us to try and kill a major in our army."

"I suppose you're right," Jordan agreed. It wasn't logical.

This was a day of disturbing thoughts, so Jordan thought of Jennifer, but it didn't help. Maybe Major Ferris was the spy. By the time they reached Alexandria they were ready for a good night's sleep.

The remainder of their trip was uneventful. Falls Church was not a big place and Wilson's Livery Stable was not hard to find. It stood on a corner not far from the main street. It consisted of a large white barn with a corral at the back. On the side of the barn, neatly painted in large red letters, was the name "Wilson's Livery." Beneath the name in smaller black letters were listed the services offered by the stable. Beneath that was another sign, also in red, that told them "Apply at Office Next Door," which had to mean the small, two-story house next to the barn. On the front door a sign said "Office. Come Right In." Jordan left Masters to watch the wagon and walked up the steps. He opened the door and stepped into what had once been a parlor. There was a railing and behind it, seated at a huge desk, was a stout man with graying sidewhiskers. He looked up through wire-rimmed spectacles.

"Yes sir. How may I help you?"

"Are you Mr. Wilson?"

"That's me."

"Do you repair wagons?"

"No, but if you need a wheel, I think I have one at the farm."

"How far is the farm?"

"Just three miles east of here. The wheels are quite reasonable."

"Can you direct me there?"

"I'll take you there myself."

Jordan just nodded. All the passwords had been spoken and things were all right. Wilson called back into the house.

"Ed, watch the office. I'm taking some customers to the farm."

"Yes, Mr. Wilson," A small clerkish man, nibbling a sandwich, emerged from the back and sat at the desk.

"Just follow me," Wilson said.

He went into the barn and climbed into a phaeton. Jordan climbed onto the wagon and Masters followed Wilson to the farm. The ride was a short one past small, picturesque farms. The scene was so peaceful that for a moment it was hard to imagine there was a war going on. Three miles from Falls Church, Wilson turned into one of the small farms with a neat white house and a barn much larger than those he had seen elsewhere. Wilson drove up to the barn and stopped. He stepped down from the phaeton, opened the doors to the barn and directed Masters to drive right in through the open doors. Masters followed Wilson's directions and pulled the sutler wagon up next to an empty hay wagon. Wilson closed the door behind them as another man lit a lamp. The other man was tall, clean-shaven, and lanky and he wore overalls. Jordan figured he was in his forties.

Wilson extended his hand as Jordan dismounted. "Welcome, Captain Jordan. I'm Samuel Wilson and this is my partner Hank Thompson. You're right on time. I see you have some bullet holes in your wagon. I trust you weren't discovered by the Yankees."

"Glad to meet you, Mr. Wilson," he said. "We weren't discovered. Unfortunately, those aren't Yankee bullet holes."

"I don't understand."

Jordan told him the story without a lot of detail. Wilson shook his head. "As if we didn't have enough problems. There are so many bandits claiming to be soldiers of the Confederacy when all they are are common criminals. It's terrible."

"You must be Sergeant Masters," Wilson said shaking Masters' hand.

"Glad to meet you," Masters replied.

"We will transfer the gold to the hay wagon immediately," Wilson said taking charge. "It has a false floor like this one. As soon as the gold is loaded we'll load the wagon with hay. After that, we'll go over to the house, have a good meal, and get you some different clothes to change your appearance. Then, the sergeant can get some rest while I take the captain to Harper's Ferry to catch the train to Baltimore."

They carefully ripped up the floor of the sutler's wagon and removed the gold. Hank threw away the old boards and replaced them with new ones. He then put dirty water on the floor to make it look as if the floor had been in the wagon for a while. In the meantime, Jordan, Masters, and Wilson carefully pried up the floor of the hay wagon and transferred the gold. Then they replaced the boards without nailing them down and loaded the wagon with bales of hay. Once they were satisfied with the result, Wilson led Jordan and Masters to the house where they ate a lunch of beef sandwiches and buttermilk.

It was easy to change Masters' appearance. Wilson dressed him in a set of workman's clothes and he became one of Wilson's teamsters. Jordan received an entirely new ensemble. He was given two handsome suits, an overcoat, and a bowler hat. Along with this new wardrobe, he was presented with a gold watch, $500 in greenbacks, a small pocket pistol, and a carpet bag with clean shirts, underwear, and shaving articles. Wilson even had visiting cards printed for Jordan. Unfortunately, when the slim cavalry captain put his new suit on, it was much too big. Wilson shook his head with a wry smile.

"I'm afraid most businessmen are not as spare as you are, captain. If Colonel Longfellow sends anymore like you up here, tell him to fatten them up first."

Jordan and Masters laughed.

"There's a seamstress in town who can take the jacket and trousers in," Wilson continued, worriedly. "I just hope she can do it on such short notice."

The seamstress altered the jackets, coat, and trousers to fit Jordan, but it took over four hours. Wilson fretted over the delay as he drove an elegantly dressed Richard Jordan to Vienna in his phaeton. Jordan wondered if this was the way Wilson always acted when things did not go exactly according to plan. By the time they reached Vienna, Wilson had calmed down. Wilson put the horses and carriage up in a livery stable, and they walked to the depot where they bought tickets to Leesburg. There, the Alexandria Railroad line ended and they would have to hire a carriage to take them to Harper's Ferry. From there they would catch the Baltimore & Ohio Railroad to Baltimore. Unlike the Southern railroads, this Northern line was not in disrepair and it ran on time. The Yankee machine was running smoothly.

Their delay forced them to stay overnight in a hotel in Leesburg where Wilson was obviously well known. It might have been a pleasant evening, except that Wilson began complaining about the delay again. Jordan wondered why the liveryman kept upsetting himself. In the morning, Wilson hired a carriage and drove Jordan to Harper's Ferry where the cavalry captain, looking very much the entrepreneur, could catch the B&O Railroad. Wilson bid Jordan goodbye.

"I'll be at Brown's Hotel in two days," Wilson said. "Good luck, Mr. Jordan."

"See you in two days, Mr. Wilson."

The ride on the B&O was one that Jordan would rather have missed. To him it was another example of the big Yankee machine. He rode the sixty-plus miles from Harper's Ferry to Baltimore in genuine comfort. The coach which he traveled in was for passengers only and it was not overcrowded. The seats were upholstered and there was a stove at one end of the coach. It was tended by the conductor, who made sure the passengers stayed warm. There was another aspect of the trip which made Jordan feel uncomfortable. As a member of Stuart's cavalry, his unit had torn up many miles of B&O track, yet the railroad seemed not to have noticed. When Southern track was torn up it took weeks and sometimes months to replace.

Jordan arrived in Baltimore at 1:00 P.M. on March 7. He took the time to buy a newspaper which he read voraciously while he ate a ham sandwich and drank a bottle of beer for lunch. He felt a little guilty about the food he had been eating recently. The ham sandwich in his hand would have served as a meal for two or more men in his company. He was beginning to put on a little weight, not that any of the well-fed Yankees around him would notice. The newspaper was interesting. The editor was demanding that the president to replace Grant and Sherman in the west. It seems that Grant was reported to have been drunk and unable to carry out his duties. Sherman, according to the article, was insane and totally irrational. What genuinely impressed Jordan were the advertisements, which offered an unbelievable array of goods and services. Spices that were unobtainable in the Confederacy were offered at reasonable prices. Salt was only 50 cents a bushel. Coffee was 20 cents a pound; in the South it was nearly impossible to get. The ad that made Jordan wince was the one that offered top horses for sale at $175 each. In the Confederacy, good horses went for $2,000.

After a short wait, Jordan boarded the train to Washington. The car was full of well-dressed men and women who went about their business as if nothing was happening in the South. The man across from Jordan was a portly man with a dark green jacket and a richly embroidered vest. Jordan read his paper trying to mind his own business, but the man seemed intent on conversation. He took a silver cigar case from his coat.

"Mind if I smoke?" he asked.

"No," Jordan said. "Go right ahead."

The man opened the cigar case and pointed it in Jordan's direction. "Cigar?" he asked.

These were expensive cigars and their rich aroma made Jordan's mouth water. He succumbed to temptation and reached for one. He drew it to his nose and sniffed.

"Cuban?" Jordan asked.

The portly man smiled. "I knew I was traveling with a man who appreciated the finer things in life."

The man cut the ends from his own with a small pen knife and handed the knife to Jordan. The cavalry captain was amazed that this little tool had gold handles inlaid with silver. It probably cost more than Jordan made in a month and that was in Yankee dollars. He cut the ends off his cigar and his well-dressed fellow passenger lit both their cigars from the same match. Jordan puffed on his cigar and rolled it in the flame to insure that it was evenly lit. Then he inhaled the fragrant smoke. It had been a long time since he had been able to enjoy a really good cigar.

"Albert Graham," the man said, extending his hand. "I'm an agent for Jennings Company in Indiana. We're contractors to the army."

Jordan took the man's hand. There was nothing flabby or weak about Graham's grip.

"Dick Jordan," Jordan told him. "I'm with Dedham & Sons. Like everyone else we're contractors to the army, too."

Graham laughed and leaned forward with a conspiratorial whisper. "This war may be bad for a lot of things, but it certainly isn't bad for business."

Jordan winked. "You can say that again."

If I had my way I'd string up every damned contractor I could find, North and South, Jordan thought to himself.

"Where are you staying in Washington, Dick?"

"The Willard."

"Good. So am I. Perhaps we can have dinner together. You are familiar with the city aren't you?"

"To tell the truth, Al, I haven't been here in years. I was working farther south when the war began, then I went west for a while. All I can remember is a dirty little place."

Graham chuckled softly. "Then you are in for a pleasant surprise, my boy. Washington isn't the sleepy little mudhole it was in '61. There's a lot going on. Be happy to show you around."

"I'd like that, Al," Jordan said. He was sincere. Being in the company of this businessman would help his cover.

The rest of the trip consisted of small talk and a nap. Jordan arrived in Washington, D.C. refreshed and curious. Graham hired a carriage and the two men set off from the railroad depot to the Willard Hotel. Graham had been correct about Washington. It was no longer the sleepy little town that Jordan had remembered visiting before the war. There were people everywhere. True, many of them were soldiers, but they only accounted for about a quarter of the people on the streets. There were hawkers, businessmen, beggars, and tradesmen. What amazed Jordan were the numbers of unescorted ladies on the street. In a Southern city, an unescorted lady would have been unthinkable, but here no one seemed to notice. Activity around the government buildings was the most hectic.

When the carriage drew up in front of the Willard, Jordan did not know what to say. He knew immediately that there was nothing like the Willard anywhere in the South—not that the South needed one. In the South business associates stayed in people's homes. Hotels, even in the large cities like Richmond or Charleston, were smaller, more sedate places than the five-story Willard with its with its rather bland exterior and sumptuous interior appointments. Jordan could not help gawking. There had been nothing like this when he had come to Washington with his father years ago.

He checked in at the desk and agreed to meet Graham in an hour for drinks and dinner. The desk clerk rang his bell and the bell boy came to carry Jordan's single bag up to the third floor where Longfellow's agent had reserved a modest room. Modest was, of course, a relative term. It was modest by the Willard's standards. The kind of place that Richard Jordan aspired to was far short of this. He unpacked his few belongings and hung up his extra suit before going down to the bar to see Graham.

Pinkerton Detective Agency
Washington, D.C.
March 7, 1863

Alan Pinkerton was not a happy man. He was furious over the escape of Major Ellison. His agency had been watching Ellison for months. He had been positive that Ellison's contact was Lydia Ratliffe. Once again the military authorities foiled his plans. When he first wanted to put Mrs. Rose Greenhow in prison for spying, they only allowed house arrest. When Pinkerton proved that she was continuously sending information to her Rebel friends, they finally agreed to put her in the Old Capitol Military Prison. There she continued to transmit information since the "gallant" officers of Washington continued to let the lady see her "friends." Some of these agents brought her information while others took it away so it could be transmitted south. Even her little daughter carried messages. Pinkerton had wanted her isolated from such contacts, but she so charmed her jailers that his recommendations fell on deaf ears. It wasn't until Mrs. Greenhow and her daughter were exiled to the South that the flow of information stopped.

It had taken Pinkerton two years to track down and stop Longfellow's buying agent in Washington itself. His success in that case was in spite of the military authorities and congress. The man knew so many congressmen that they were, to a man, willing to see the illegal traffic in arms and equipment to the enemy continue rather than admit they had been taken in by an enemy spy. The case of Lydia Ratliffe was the same. Ellison had been his only direct lead. Pinkerton's men followed Ellison for months. They were closing in when Ellison was suddenly arrested by men of the Provost Marshal's Office. The story they gave of Ellison's fiance turning him in was absurd. After they made the arrest the woman could not be found.

While Pinkerton was trying to sort out the facts, Ellison, with the help of an accomplice, escaped. This was a heavy blow to Pinkerton's case against Ratliffe. It was an uphill fight all the way because she was very popular in Washington society. However, there was still another question to be answered. Daring rescues were not Ratliffe's style. Pinkerton could only conclude that there was a new agent for the Confederacy in the capital. He had surmised that the Rebels would attempt to re-establish their front in order to buy more military supplies. Perhaps the two were interrelated. Pinkerton was interrupted by his aide who brought him an urgent report.

"Not again," Pinkerton said in disgust. "This is the third 'plot' to kill the president this week. Every time some drunk decides he wants to shoot his mouth off, the army and the police know about it. They couldn't tell a real spy if they tripped over him."

"What do you want to do?" the aide asked.

"Let the army worry about it. We have more important things to do. How many men do we have watching Ratliffe?"

"Two."

"Why only two?"

"The army requested that we help with their search for Major Ellison."

"I don't believe it," Pinkerton snorted. "Ellison is probably in Atlanta by now. Put another four *good* men on this. What I want them to look for is somebody new to the Ratliffe set. I think there's a new spy in town. If my hunch is correct, he'll need to contact Mrs. Ratliffe and then we'll get them both."

"Yes, Mr. Pinkerton." The aide left the great detective alone. Pinkerton wondered how many more spies he would have to catch before official Washington realized that every secret they gave away could be used by the enemy.

The Streets of Washington
March 8, 1863

Richard Jordan used his first and only free day in Washington
to look around. Like any military officer he wanted to learn the
lay of the land before he was required to go into action. He hired a
carriage and saw the sights. The president's mansion struck him
as terribly run down. The house occupied by Mr. Davis in Richmond, while not as large, was certainly more attractive. The
weather warmed up and in a short time the streets became seas of
mud.

Jordan went to the War Department to request information on
government contracts. He saw several officials who helpfully sent
him to other agencies. One of these was the Commissary Department, where an official gave him the exact number of rations
required by the Army of the Potomac and what Jordan's company
would have to supply on a monthly basis. The official then gave
Jordan the information he needed for submitting his bid. Jordan
picked up other useful bits of information from the medical and
personnel departments and wrote them in a small notebook.

At 1:00 P.M. he went to lunch at the Willard. There he found a
copy of *Harper's Weekly* dated February 21. The cover had a picture of Tom Thumb and his bride, Miss Lavinia Warren. It was
the first publication Jordan had seen that didn't have news of the
war as its cover story. He read about the wedding, then read
Chapter VII of "A Dark Night's Work" on page 122 and the story
"Precious" on page 126. As he paged back through the paper, one
small article on page 119 brought him back to reality. It was an
article from Newbern, North Carolina dated January 26, about
120 slaves escaping to Yankee lines because of the Emancipation
Proclamation. He wondered why people like Johnson couldn't see
what this was doing to the South.

After lunch Jordan bought a map of the city and continued his
tour of Washington. The map turned out to be nearly useless so
he paid particular attention to the layout of the streets and some
of the places he knew he would have to go, such as Brown's Hotel.
Jordan did not return to the hotel until after six in the evening. It
was already dark and he was looking forward to a drink and one

of the Willard's excellent suppers. When he asked for his key, the desk clerk smiled and handed it to him along with an envelope. Jordan thought it was a mistake, but his name was on the outside of the envelope in neat feminine script. He didn't open it immediately, but put it in his pocket and headed for the stairs.

"Dick," a familiar voice called.

Jordan turned. It was Graham and there was a woman on his arm. The woman was well dressed and very pretty. She smiled at Jordan.

"Hello, Al."

Graham stepped up, leaving the woman alone for a moment. "I was just going out, Dick. Why don't you join me. I'm sure Sally there can find a suitable friend for you."

Jordan looked at the woman. He was sure she was a prostitute, and probably a very expensive one at that. At any other time he would have happily gone with Graham, but the letter had made him nervous.

"I'm afraid I already have an engagement this evening, Al," he said with a suggestive wink.

Al grinned. "My, you do work fast. Good luck."

"It looks as though you won't need any tonight, Al."

Graham smiled and returned to Sally. Jordan went upstairs, closed the door, locked it, and opened the letter.

March 8, 1863

> Dear Richard,
>
> I was so glad to hear you were in the city. I should be very hurt if you do not visit while you are here. Perhaps you can stop by at the National Hotel and have supper with me at seven this evening.
>
> Sincerely,
>
> YOUR COUSIN LYDIA

Lydia must mean Lydia Ratliffe. Jordan looked at his watch. It was a quarter of seven already. He put the letter in his pocket and went right downstairs to hire a carriage. On the way he wondered why Lydia Ratliffe was trying to contact him so soon. Was there a problem? He arrived at the National Hotel shortly after seven. When he walked toward the entrance a colored man stopped him.

"Mr. Jordan?"

Jordan looked at him but said nothing. He tensed, ready for trouble.

"My name is Daniel. Your cousin is my employer. There has been a small change in plans. If you will follow me."

Jordan followed but put his hand on the pocket pistol just in case. Daniel led Jordan to a darker part of the street where a carriage was parked by the curb. Daniel opened the door and motioned for Jordan to step inside. He stepped up in the carriage and sat opposite an extremely attractive woman. She extended her hand.

"Good evening, Captain Jordan. I'm Lydia Ratliffe. I do apologize for this rather unorthodox introduction, but I am being followed once again. That wretched man, Pinkerton, never gives up."

Jordan took her small hand in his. He could understand why men fell under her spell. "I'm very happy to make your acquaintance, Mrs. Ratliffe."

"Please call me Lydia, captain. Now, we have much to discuss—privately. I hope you won't mind dining with me in a setting less public than the National. There is a house which I keep in Georgetown for such purposes. The Pinkertons haven't discovered it yet. I hope they don't. It would be a shame to give it up."

"Whatever you say."

"Daniel," Lydia called. "Georgetown."

The carriage started and Lydia asked him one question after another. Where was he from? Who were his parents? What unit was he in? They were all asked very politely interspersed with questions like "What are the ladies in Richmond wearing this season?" It took a while before Jordan realized she was being thorough and not just making small talk to be polite. Anyone who didn't know the answer to the questions thoroughly would have been tripped up. Jordan would not have been surprised if she had a gun in her cloak. The carriage drove behind the house and Daniel escorted them inside. It was much smaller than Jordan would have expected. It was the type of house that might be owned by a prosperous tradesman or artisan. There was a small dining room with a table that seated six and it was already set. For two.

"Please sit down, Captain Jordan," Lydia said. "Mavis will serve us our supper and we can discuss those things which need to be done."

Lydia sat at the head of the table and motioned to a seat beside her. A large colored woman served a simple supper consisting of soup, oysters, and crab cakes.

"When are you to meet Mr. Wilson?" She asked.

"He will be at Brown's Hotel tomorrow. I am supposed to tell him where the transfer is to take place and when."

"Oh, dear. That makes things a little difficult. Thanks to Mr. Pinkerton and his friends I have not been able to contact the dealer in the usual way. I am giving a party tomorrow evening. You can meet the agent for the firm there. You must contact Mr. Wilson tomorrow and tell him he will have to wait."

"Why can't you contact him?" Wilson isn't going to like another delay, Jordan thought.

"It's very simple. I am suspected by the Pinkertons of being an agent of the Confederacy. Fortunately, I have plenty of friends who look after me. As long as I don't seek out strangers, none of my associates are suspected, which is why we had to meet here. If we were to be seen together at anytime other than one of my parties you would automatically be suspected and probably arrested on principle. I have never met Mr. Wilson and don't intend to. It would be dangerous for both of us."

Jordan admired the woman. She lived her life in peril every day and seemed to take it naturally. They finished supper and the serving woman cleared the table.

"Would you like a glass of sherry, captain?"

"Yes, Mrs. Ratliffe. That would be very nice."

"You could call me Lydia," she said chiding him. "I'm not that old looking am I?"

"Why no, not at all, Mrs. . . . I mean Lydia."

She moved close to him and handed him a glass of sherry. "You don't mind if I call you Richard, do you. I think it's a very strong name."

"No, Lydia. I don't mind at all."

"Come sit beside me on the sofa and tell me about the last time you were in Richmond."

Jordan sat beside her. She was wearing a very subtle perfume and she was looking right at him. She was different from Jennifer and unlike any woman he had ever known. He tried to concentrate on his description of Richmond right after Sharpsburg. It was not at all happy considering the horrendous casualties they had suffered. He tried to make his story accurate without sounding too dismal.

"I'm sorry if I made you remember things that are unpleasant," she said softly.

Her face was closer to his and their eyes were at the same level. Jordan swallowed. If she didn't look beautiful, she looked very desirable. Maybe the word was irresistible. Jordan wondered if she wanted him to kiss her. He decided to find out. When he leaned his face toward hers she didn't retreat. Their lips met and Jordan put his arms around her waist and pulled her to him.

Jordan didn't leave the house in Georgetown until late the next morning. Daniel drove him to Brown's Hotel. Jordan knocked on Wilson's door and Wilson answered it. Masters was in the room with him.

"When do we make the transfer?" was the first thing Wilson asked.

"We can't do it for at least another day," Jordan told him and explained the reasons.

"Jordan, ever since you got here we've had nothing but delays," Wilson snapped. "I have a schedule to keep. Now I'll have to go and get another load of hay. That means keeping the gold in the wagon and I don't like it!"

The man's attitude infuriated Jordan.

"If you don't like it, then leave," Jordan told him. "I'm sick of your complaining every time something doesn't go exactly to plan. It seems you're quite a patriot when it's convenient, Mr. Wilson."

Wilson's face flushed scarlet. He opened his mouth then closed it without saying a word. The room was silent. "All right," Wilson said. "I'll get another load of hay."

"I think it might be a good idea if Masters stays here," Jordan said after thinking a moment. "We may need another person here. Besides, nobody would suspect that a high roller and a teamster would be partners."

"I agree, " Masters said, looking at Wilson.

"All right," Wilson said. "I'll be back tomorrow."

"You really know how to make friends, Dick," Masters told him as soon as Wilson left.

"All he's done is complain from the moment we arrived in Falls Church. Another fair weather patriot," Jordan grumbled. "I'm going back to the Willard. If anything happens I'll leave word at the desk for you. In the meantime, you will have a chance to taste the pleasures of this den of iniquity."

Masters smiled. "You sure do make a persuasive recruiting officer, Dick," Masters said with a grin.

"Enjoy Washington," Jordan said as he left.

Masters smiled. Jordan was an amateur, but he had possibilities. He was going to have to start watching Jordan's back. If the captain didn't know he had a backup, a tail would be less obvious to any Pinkerton who might be watching.

When Jordan returned to the Willard there was already an invitation to Lydia Ratliffe's party waiting for him. He didn't notice the large man in the tweed suit reading a newspaper across from the reception desk. The man was George Ingalls, one of Alan Pinkerton's best operatives. One of those odd coincidences that sometimes decides the fate of empires had occurred the previous evening. Ingalls had finished his supper and was just leaving the National when Daniel approached Jordan at the front door. The Pinkerton man didn't know who Jordan was, but he recognized Daniel and Daniel addressed Jordan by name. Ingalls followed Daniel and Jordan around the corner, but Jordan entered a carriage and Daniel drove it away before the detective could find a cab. Ingalls wasn't disappointed. He had a very good lead. By 10:00 the following morning, the Pinkerton Agency knew who Richard Jordan claimed to be and what room he occupied in the Willard. They searched his room so skillfully that when they left, the room appeared undisturbed. There was nothing there to indicate he was anyone but who he said he was, but he had been seen with Lydia Ratliffe's servant and that made him suspect.

Jordan returned to his room and suddenly realized that he was deliciously tired. Lydia had worn him out and Jordan laughed to himself when he wondered how Mr. Ratliffe died. If the corpse had a big grin on its face it was even money. Jordan washed up and decided to take a nap. It promised to be a long evening and he needed to rest. As he fell asleep, Jennifer's face became blurred with Lydia's. He wondered if Jennifer were as passionate as Lydia.

When Jordan awoke it was after five. He bathed, shaved, and put on his best suit. He hired a carriage and had the driver take him to the address on the invitation. The driver hardly gave a nod when he gave him the address. Lydia's parties were so famous that most of the cab drivers knew her address. Masters leaned against the side of the hotel looking as if he were waiting for someone. He watched Jordan leave and stayed to see if anyone followed him. He was relieved when no one did. There was no way he could know that the detectives assigned to follow Jordan were already in place across the street from the Ratliffe residence.

Jordan couldn't remember ever seeing such lavish entertainment. There were food and champagne in vast quantities and an orchestra playing dance music. Lydia was the belle of the ball surrounded by men in uniforms asking her to dance. Jordan watched her dance with several and her eyes made every one think that he was the one she loved. If he hadn't been in love with Jennifer he wondered if he would have fallen in love with Lydia. She was certainly alluring. After dancing with a fat colonel, Lydia walked his way.

"It's time you met some of the notables of the fair city," she said taking his arm. "It never hurts to drop a few names, dear cousin." Lydia walked up to a portly man in a general's uniform. He sported graying chin whiskers and had a receding hairline.

"General Halleck, I'd like you to meet my cousin Richard Jordan."

The pasty-faced general stuck out his hand. "Happy to make your acquaintance, sir," he said blandly.

Jordan's mouth dropped open as he shook hands with the General-in-Chief of the Union Army. "This is a rare honor, sir," Jordan finally said.

He exchanged a few pleasantries with Halleck and came to the conclusion that most did. Halleck was an ass. Nevertheless, it was a shock to stand at a party and talk idly with the commanding general of the enemy army. Lydia took Jordan by the arm and led him across the room.

"If you are going to be a contractor this is the man you should meet," she whispered.

The next Yankee general that Lydia introduced him to was no ass.

"General Meigs, I'd like you to meet my cousin, Richard Jordan. Richard, this is General Meigs, the Quartermaster General of the army."

"It is indeed an honor, sir," Jordan said. "I've heard so much about your accomplishments." Meigs was a legend in both armies. Thanks to his administration, no Yankee army ever wanted for anything including horses. Thanks to Meigs, the Union Army had no "Company Q." The Quartermaster General was an intelligent man and a good conversationalist, but no matter how much Jordan tried to steer the conversation, Meigs wanted to talk about his favorite subject.

"Mr. Jordan, are you interested in photography, by any chance?"

"No sir. Why do you ask?"

"It happens to be my hobby. A passion, really. I don't get a chance to do much of it with the war on."

"I can imagine you are very busy, general."

"I really envy this Brady fellow who travels with the army making pictures."

"I can see where you might," Jordan agreed. He didn't know what else to say.

"Ah, I see Mrs. Meigs over there. Nice meeting you, Mr. Jordan," he said bowing to Jordan and Lydia. "Nice to see you again, Mrs. Ratliffe."

"I'm impressed," Jordan told his hostess.

Lydia just smiled and guided Jordan through the throng toward a short, dark-haired man with a well groomed mustache who was surrounded by women. His body seemed out of proportion, but his clothes were so well tailored that one had to look hard to notice. His eyes were piercing and he wore a determined expression.

"Wilkes," Lydia said. "I'd like you to meet my cousin, Richard. Richard, this is Wilkes Booth."

"The famous actor?" Jordan said.

"Indeed, sir, I am flattered that you should recognize my name. Happy to make your acquaintance," John Wilkes Booth said. His voice was mellow and his gestures exaggerated, but he was an actor.

"The honor is mine, I assure you, Mr. Booth. I saw you in Richmond in *Richard III* before the war. Your performance was magnificent."

"Thank you again, Mr. Jordan. Are you in Washington for business or pleasure?"

"Business. My company is seeking a contract with the government."

"There is someone I have to see," Lydia interrupted. "I'll leave you two alone."

The gentlemen bowed as Lydia disappeared among the guests.

"You said you were from Richmond, Mr. Jordan?" Booth asked. His eyes were fixed on Jordan's face. Jordan felt a momentary surge of panic. Booth continued before Jordan replied.

"I take it, then, your sympathies lie with the South."

"I am not inimical to the South," Jordan said evasively.

"I have a plan to bring this cruel war to an end instantly," the actor said, his face aglow with anticipation. "I plan to kidnap that monster Lincoln and take him to Richmond. Then we can ransom him for the South's independence. What I need are a few reliable companions to aid me. Since you are a southerner, I thought you might like to join me in this noble cause."

My God, Jordan thought, the man's a lunatic. The last thing he needed was to become associated with a man like Booth. He was looking for a polite way to disengage himself from the conversation when Lydia came to his rescue.

"Cousin Richard would you kindly escort me upstairs, I feel a bit faint."

She looks about as faint as a cavalry horse, Jordan thought as he sympathetically took her arm. All about her looked concerned and she promised to return as soon as she had had some air. She led him up the stairs.

"Lydia, Booth is insane," he said.

"I take it he approached you about kidnaping Lincoln."

"Then you know?"

"I think half of Washington knows. It doesn't matter. He's quite harmless."

"I'm not so sure." He followed her to a room down the hall from her bedroom.

"In here," she said.

Jordan opened the door. His contact was sitting at a table, grinning. "Well I'll be damned. Hello, Dick," Albert Graham said rising from his chair. The two men shook hands.

"Hello, Al."

Lydia looked puzzled. "You two know each other?"

"We met on the train from Baltimore," Jordan explained.

"Then I'll leave you two alone," she said. "I have to get back to my guests."

"Have a seat," Graham said. "You know, I've been able to spot most of your agents a mile away. There's just something about them that smacks of spy or army. You, on the other hand are very natural. My congratulations."

"Thanks. Shall we get down to business?"

"Of course, if you have $100,000 in gold."

"We do."

"Good. Tomorrow night at eight o'clock I want you to deliver the gold to the Mahew Warehouse at the waterfront. I'll be waiting with two crates. As soon as the gold is crated I'll wire Indiana and release the shipment. Do you have the order?"

Jordan handed him the list. Graham perused it. "That's a lot of shoes," the contractor said.

"We do a lot of walking," Jordan quipped.

Graham smiled and put the list in his pocket.

"You're not one of us are you, Al?"

"You mean a Confederate, Dick?"

"Yes."

"No, not really, but I suppose you're going to ask what I'm doing selling you material with which to fight against the North, right?"

"I have to admit I am rather curious."

"Business."

"I beg your pardon, Al. You said 'business.'"

"That's right. It's business. Right now your government is paying premium prices in gold. It's only good business. It doesn't matter to me who's buying what I sell. If the country splits you people in the south will need more to conquer Mexico to make your position better. If you lose, the Union will expand and need supplies to kill Indians. So, you see, it doesn't really matter who needs my services."

"You're a remarkable person in this day and age, Al. I hope you don't get caught."

Graham smiled and lit one of his cigars. "Too smart for that."

Jordan grinned. Albert Graham was the kind of man he had been taught to despise, but somehow he couldn't help liking him. "How do you do it, Al?"

"It's very simple," Graham said. "False manifests and a few judicious bribes."

"Aren't you even afraid of being discovered?"

"Too many people with their hands in the cookie jar, Dick. It is, fortunately, a very corrupt world."

It must be, Jordan thought. He rose to leave. "I'll see you tomorrow night."

When Jordan returned to the party, Lydia was back with her guests. Jordan walked around listening to tidbits of information and hearsay. One officer in his cups bragged that the war would be over by the end of the summer. Another stated that Hooker would advance on Lee before the end of April and crush the Rebel army. Jordan walked around with a glass of champagne and listened. As the crowd began to thin, he was contemplating leaving until Lydia came up and asked him to stay. He blushed as he smiled in agreement.

When everyone was gone, they sat together and sipped some very old French brandy.

"You're very nice, Richard," Lydia said, touching his hand. "The woman who gets you is very lucky."

"You're very nice, too, Lydia. Why don't you settle down and get married again?"

Lydia laughed. "Why do men always ask that question? Maybe I will someday, but there are too many parties and too many dashing cavaliers out there. Like you," she said, kissing his cheek.

"Do you have a sweetheart, Richard?"

"No. There's one I'd like to be, but she's a widow."

"Then tell her you love her and marry her. Make each other happy."

"I can understand why so many men fall in love with you," he said. You're so honest."

Lydia laughed again. "The one thing most men don't want is honesty. I don't understand why men fall in love. There have been a lot of men who offered me everything to prove they love me. I know what everyone thinks, but most of the time I don't even encourage them and still they come to me." Lydia took a deep breath. "I don't even know why I'm telling you this."

"They say it helps to talk about things. Besides, I'm a good listener."

Lydia rested against the back of the sofa with her hand supporting her head. "You know there was one man who was so in love with me that I actually felt sorry for him. He would do anything for me. I treated him like dirt, but he always came back with more information. He was a major in the War Department."

"Was he the one who recently escaped?" Jordan asked.

"Yes."

"How did you get him out of prison?"

"I didn't," Lydia said. "One of General Beauregard's agents got him out. He came here with him and I had to hide them both."

"Who was the agent?"

"I don't know. He certainly knew his business and he was bold. I guess they made it. I wonder where Charles is now," Lydia said offhandedly. "I certainly hope the Confederate government treats him well. He is a meticulous staff officer."

Jordan's curiosity was suddenly aroused. "What was Charles' full name, Lydia?"

"Ellison," she said.

The same name on the handbill! "What did he look like, Lydia?"

"Tall, kind of good looking actually. Dark hair and beard with a little gray in it."

"Did he have a ring with a lion's head?"

"Yes, I gave it to him," she said, laughing softly. "It was a cheap ring but he thought it was beautiful because I gave it to him. That's when I felt sorry for him. How did you know? Have you seen him?"

"I don't think you have to worry about what he'll do in the Confederate Army. He's dead."

"Richard, no! How?"

"He was shot in the head at very close range with a .36 caliber pistol."

"Who did it?"

"I don't know. I assume it was his companion, but I don't know why." Jordan related the story of Ellison's death as far as he knew it.

"Oh my God!" Lydia said, sitting up. "The letter!"

"What letter?"

"Charles brought the man who rescued him here. I was terrified when they showed up. If it had been Charles alone, I would have turned him in myself, but this other man showed me a letter. It was an instruction from Stanton to an assassin to kill Robert E. Lee."

"Was the letter genuine?"

"I'd swear to it, Richard."

Jordan was silent for a moment. The conclusions he was reaching were not very comforting. "A man no one knows rescues one of your contacts in order to get access to you. No. He doesn't want access to you. He wants access to the South. He wanted a pass through the picket lines. With Ellison and the pass no one would question him."

"He panicked me," she said bitterly.

"What?"

"He panicked me into doing everything he wanted and I did it. He is the assassin and I gave him everything he needed. What a fool I was! He killed Charles, because Charles could identify him. Richard, someone has to warn General Lee!"

CHAPTER 6

Washington, D.C
March 1863

IN 1863, WASHINGTON, D.C. was a city in transition. Prior to the War Between the States, it was a sleepy southern town on the edge of malarial swamp. The town came awake only when Congress was in session and slaves were bought and sold within sight of the Capitol. It was during this time of year that the separation between the different strata of society became marked. Senators, Congressmen, and their wealthy social counterparts spent thousands of dollars on parties and entertainment, while much of the city lived in squalor. Few of its streets were paved and the Capitol and the Washington Monument were incomplete. The war changed all of old Washington. The great majority of the social scions of the city had been southern and when the southern states seceded, they left. Some remained behind because Washington was their home and others remained as spies, but the character of the city changed as new classes of people flocked to it.

The first newcomers were the volunteers who arrived to save the capital of the nation. Next came the politicians and their proteges looking for favors with the new administration. Then came contractors, engineers, swindlers, and petty criminals. Suddenly, this small town became the symbol of a young country trying desperately to survive and the nerve center of a modern nation at war.

Despite the change in influence and image, Washington still had many basic problems. There was almost no city administration in the sense that other cities of similar size had their own municipal governments. In addition to the deplorable condition of the streets, the city had problems with water and sewage that would not be solved for many years. There were twenty-five police officers and they worked only during the day. Congress in one of its moments of largess authorized the hiring of twenty-five more policemen to work at night. These were not, however, for the protection of the citizenry, but the protection of public buildings.

The sterling quality of these representatives of the metropolitan police can be amply demonstrated by one John F. Parker who was assigned to guard President Lincoln in his box at Ford's Theater on the night of April 14, 1865. After checking to see that the theater was empty, Parker decided that it was secure. When the president arrived, Parker went across the street for a drink. He was not seen until the following morning. No one on the metropolitan police seemed it odd that the man Parker was supposed to guard was assassinated and Parker continued his career in law enforcement.

Lack of law enforcement and the general run-down condition of large sections of the city made it a paradise for criminals. During the hours of darkness, it was not safe to be on the streets alone. Most citizens went armed. Pocket pistols and sword canes were the fashion with affluent gentlemen, and the derringer was considered fashionable for ladies. For those less affluent, Bowie knives, stilettos, brass knuckles, blackjacks, and even axe handles were found to be deterrents to crime. In populous, well-lighted areas of the city, crime was less of a problem than in the run-down areas where it was a way of life. In these neighborhoods, dozens of dramas were enacted every night in which men were clubbed, shot, and robbed and women were beaten and raped. In the midst of this city of contrasts were the spies. There were not only Union and Confederate spies; there were English, French, and Prussian spies, and the usual collection of double agents, opportunists, and traitors. The only agency that had any chance of sorting out this jumble was the Pinkerton Detective Agency.

As a frequent visitor to the U.S. capital, Charley Masters was quite familiar with Pinkerton and his men and he had learned to respect them. They were not brilliant, but they were businesslike and thorough and that made them very dangerous. Masters was adept at sniffing out those dangers. He was one of those wild cards that war produces. His main passion in life was books and his dream was to own his own book shop after the war.

In the fall of 1861 Captain Raymond Longfellow, passing through Richmond stopped at a book shop on Broad Street. He was immediately impressed with the clerk who waited on him. The young man had a perfect memory. Not only could he find any book in the place, but he could also tell Longfellow the books in print without consulting the publishers' lists. The captain was so impressed that he immediately hired Tarleton Masters as his civilian clerk. Longfellow soon learned that Masters was not only an excellent clerk; he was also one of his finest "scouts."

Masters would have remained a civilian except that the Confederate Congress passed the Conscription Act in April 1862. When he was due to be drafted, Masters was enlisted in the First Virginia Cavalry, with a date to show that he had been enlisted prior to April 1862. He was made a sergeant and continued to hold that rank since, seeking no reward or promotion. Masters was originally not very happy when Colonel Longfellow assigned him to watch over Jordan. He preferred to work alone. With few exceptions, the cavalry officers he had met were pompous asses.

After being with Jordan for a while, Masters had to admit that the cavalry captain was one of the exceptions. Jordan was an amateur and amateurs were usually dangerous. They became overly impressed with their roles and became conspicuous. Jordan recognized he was an amateur and was very careful. He was an excellent observer and deferred to Masters in the scout's areas of expertise. In addition to Jordan's professional attitudes, he was very likable, even if he did get irritated with fussy people like Wilson. Masters had to admit that he didn't mind trying to keep Richard Jordan alive. He was fairly certain he could keep the Yankees from killing Jordan but he wasn't sure about that pretty widow the captain was seeing.

It was nearly eight in the morning and Jordan had still not returned to the hotel. Masters stood across the street from the Willard and watched the entrance. He had changed his clothes from that of a workman to an everyday business suit. There were only four people in front of the hotel. Two were hotel employees sweeping the entrance to the Willard and a third was a colored bootblack, hoping to drum up some early morning business with new arrivals at the hotel. Masters had seen him there before. The fourth man was Pinkerton agent George Ingalls, wearing his customary tweed suit and brown hat. Leaning against the wall reading a newspaper, he didn't look as if he were a guest at the Willard and he wasn't an employee. He obviously wasn't waiting for a horse car and he didn't seem interested in hiring a carriage, so Masters decided to investigate. He walked across the street to the bootblack.

"You give good shines?" Masters asked.

"Yes, sir. Best shines in the city, only five cents."

"You make it good and I'll give you ten cents," Masters told him loud enough for the others to hear. "Gonna ask the boss for a raise today and have to look my best."

The two sweepers looked his way but Ingalls didn't even look up. The bootblack bent to his work. The rhythm of his cloth and brushes were almost musical. During the shine a carriage drove up and disgorged a cavalry captain with a very satisfied grin on his face. Masters almost smiled but he pulled his hat low over his face so that Jordan would not notice him. Jordan didn't look at anyone and strolled tiredly into the hotel. Ingalls waited a moment, tucked the paper under his arm, and went into the hotel. The bootblack was finished.

"Thank you, boy," Masters said. He gave him ten cents.

"Thank you, sir, and best of luck with your raise."

Masters nodded and went into the hotel. Jordan had just retrieved his key and was heading upstairs. Ingalls was talking to his partner, Bob Crewes, who was wearing a black suit and a flat-brimmed hat. As soon as Jordan disappeared up the stairs, Crewes followed. Ingalls took out a notebook, scribbled something in it, and tore out the page. He called one of the hotel's boys, told him something, and handed him the page from the notebook and a greenback. Masters knew he was going to have to act quickly. He strode to the stairwell and went upstairs. Crewes was standing on the opposite end of the corridor in which Jordan's room was located. He was there to prevent Jordan's escape down the back stairs. Masters thought a moment, then went up to the fourth floor. Crossing over, he descended the back steps as if he were coming from an upstairs room. Crewes gave him a suspicious look, but Masters smiled and approached him. The man tensed. Masters pulled a long cigar from his vest.

"Excuse me, sir. Would you happen to have a light?"

Crewes didn't smile but he did relax. He looked into his vest pocket. He never caught Masters' swift movement as he brought the blackjack down on his head. The detective fell to his knees and pitched forward on his face. Masters reached down and pulled him up by the armpits. The commotion aroused one of the guests in a nearby room. An older woman, her gray hair tucked into a nightcap, poked her head out of her door. Masters smiled stupidly and tipped his hat.

"Evening, ma'am," his said. His speech was slightly slurred.

"It's morning," she said. "You should be ashamed of yourself, you drunkards!" She slammed the door.

Masters dragged the unconscious detective to Jordan's room and knocked on the door.

"Who is it?"

"It's Masters. Open up and hurry."

Jordan was in his underwear when he opened the door. "What . . . " he said as Masters dropped Crewes' limp form into the room.

"Get dressed, Dick, they're coming to arrest you. Hurry."

Jordan began to dress without question as Masters rifled Crewes' pockets. "Just as I thought," he snapped. "A Pinkerton."

When Masters rolled Crewes over to check his back pockets he noticed a gash in the detective's head. Since he dragged Crewes with his head up the blood had run into the Pinkerton's collar. Masters checked to see if he had left a trail of blood in the hallway and was relieved to discover he hadn't. He was convinced that Crewes would be out cold at least long enough for them to escape.

Jordan grabbed his pocket pistol and his watch. "Let's go."

Masters opened the door and looked both ways. He motioned to Jordan and they began running toward the back stairs. He drew up short at the landing. The sound of boots on the stairs indicated they were too late. Jordan felt trapped. Masters turned down the hall and Jordan followed without question. Masters knocked on a door. The older woman who had seen him with the unconscious

Pinkerton a few minutes earlier, opened her door. Before she had a chance to speak, Masters put his hand over her mouth and pushed her inside. Jordan wasn't sure he knew what was going on but he didn't question anything. Masters pulled a knife and held it against the woman's throat.

"We are desperate men," Masters told her with a vicious snarl. "If you say nothing you'll live. If you tell them we're here, You'll be the first to die, understand?"

The woman said nothing.

"Understand?" Masters asked again.

Jordan looked at her limp form. "I think she's fainted."

"Oh, help me get her into bed."

The two men placed the unconscious woman gently into bed and pulled the covers up to her chin. There was a knock on the door.

"Mrs. Jenson," a voice outside the door called.

"The closet," Masters whispered.

Jordan opened the closet door. It was so small there was only room for one. There was the sound of a key in the lock. Masters pushed him inside and closed the door. The scout managed to roll under the bed just before the door opened. From under the bed all Masters could see were light blue trousers and black shoes. Soldiers.

"She's asleep," someone said solicitously. He was probably the hotel clerk.

"Then wake her up," a gruff voice said. Masters could see tweed trousers.

A pair of black civilian trousers with worn brown shoes moved to the bed. It was the clerk. "Mrs. Jenson." He shook the woman and it shook the bed.

Mrs. Jenson came awake with an hysterical scream. "Don't kill me! Please don't kill me!" she sobbed.

"We're here to help you, Mrs. Jenson," the clerk said. He spoke softly and held her hand.

"They were going to kill me," Mrs. Jenson was crying.

"Do you know which way they went?" Ingalls asked.

"No," she sobbed.

"We know they didn't go out the back," Ingalls said. "Continue to check upstairs," he ordered the soldiers. "I'm going to check out front."

Ingalls and the soldiers filed out of the room. Jordan and Masters could hear the troops hurrying noisily up the staircase. The clerk apologized to Mrs. Jenson and locked the door behind him when he left. Masters waited until everything was quiet before he rolled out from under the bed. Mrs. Jenson was sitting up in bed trembling. She looked at him wide-eyed.

"Thank you, Mrs. Jenson," he said politely.

The woman sighed and fainted again.

"Dick," Masters whispered.

Jordan emerged from the closet, pistol in hand. "That was close."

"We're not out of this yet," Masters told him. "We have to get out of here before they decide to come back. Follow me."

Jordan followed Masters down the back steps. There were no troops or Pinkertons there. There was an alley in the back of the hotel. It was full of garbage and trash, and from the odor it gave off, it had obviously been there a while. Jordan and Masters gagged as they looked for a way out. There were other buildings directly behind the Willard, but their downstairs doors and windows were either locked or boarded up.

Masters grimaced. "We have no other choice," Masters said in a hoarse whisper. "We'll have to take the alley to the street. Act nonchalant. Let's see if we can get into a crowd and not be noticed. If we're spotted, make for the nearest carriage."

Jordan looked at him. Maybe Masters could look nonchalant, but he was scared as hell. He would rather be shooting it out with Yankee cavalry than sneaking around the alleys of the enemy's capital city. They walked up the alley carefully, expecting Yankee soldiers to come rushing at them any minute. Masters stopped at the corner of the alley. He peered around the corner at the front of the hotel. In front of the door were several Pinkertons, including Ingalls and Crewes, who was holding a bloody towel to the back of his head. The man had the thickest skull Masters ever encountered. He had hit him hard enough to keep the average man out for hours. There was also a group of soldiers standing by a wagon at the entrance to the Willard. Masters estimated that there were at least twenty of them and an officer. Across the street a small crowd had gathered but it was too early in the day for large numbers of people to be anywhere but work.

"Let's see if we can get to that carriage," Masters whispered. He pointed to a carriage standing by the curb almost directly across the street from them. "Ready?"

Jordan refrained from saying something flippant and shook his head in agreement. Masters stepped out of the alley and walked calmly in the direction of the carriage. Jordan admired Masters' savoire-faire as he leisurely stepped into the muddy street. Jordan, not daring to look in the direction of the Pinkertons, breathed a sigh of relief. We're in the clear he thought, but then his heart began pounding as he heard someone shouting. He turned to look in the direction of the shout.

Crewes was standing in the the street. He was holding the towel against his head with his left hand and pointing at Jordan and Masters with his right. "It's them!" he yelled. "God damn it! It's them!"

"The carriage," Masters shouted.

Pandemonium erupted as the two Confederate agents broke into a run. Jordan heard shots and bullets flew over their heads. They were lucky. These were obviously new recruits and, like most inexperienced troops, they were shooting too high. Jordan and Masters reached the carriage and scurried aboard. Masters grabbed the reins and whipped the horses into a run. It didn't matter which way they were going; they just had to get away. The firing stopped and the soldiers piled into their wagon to pursue. Their officer mounted his horse and galloped after them.

"Uh oh," Jordan said. "There's a Yankee on a horse after us."

"Damn!" was all Masters said. There was no way they could outrun a single rider on horseback.

In less than a mile, the Union officer, a captain, galloped up beside them. He drew his pistol and pointed it at Masters' head. "Pull up or I'll shoot," he yelled.

Masters looked squarely into the muzzle of the Yankee captain's pistol and began to slow the horses when he was deafened by the roar of Jordan's pocket pistol. Powder burned Masters' face and acrid smoke filled his nostrils as the bullet struck the captain squarely in the chest. The impact of the bullet swept the blue-coated rider from his horse and he hit the street with a dirty brown splash into a mud puddle as his horse slowed down. Jordan looked back. The army wagon with its four horses was gaining on them because Masters had begun to rein up. He was trying to get the horses back up to speed when Jordan spotted the intersection.

"Turn here!" he shouted.

"But . . ."

"Turn!"

Masters pulled the recalcitrant horses into the side street and whipped them into a dead run. The horses took the strain and ran as foam flew from their mouths. The driver of the Yankee wagon was either inexperienced or excited. He didn't slow down and tried to take the corner at full speed. The front wheel hit a hitching rail, then the body of the wagon hit a lamp post. The wagon turned over, spilling the soldiers and driver into the muddy street. The torque of the wagon pulled the horses over and the last Jordan saw of them was the big animals on their backs squealing and kicking, trying desperately to free themselves from the harness.

"That was close," Masters said. "I owe you."

"Just evening the score, Charley." Jordan clapped him on the back. "If it hadn't been for you I'd be on my way to a Yankee prison right now."

The horses were slowing down. They were not used to pulling a carriage at full gallop and they were exhausted.

"We'd better abandon this carriage," Masters said, pulling the team up. "We can hire another one and try to get to Brown's Hotel and contact Wilson. He should be able to hide us until nightfall."

"I just hope we can still get the gold to the waterfront tonight. After that we can head south."

"I hope so, too, Dick."

The carriage ride to Brown's Hotel was uneventful. Word of the encounter in front of the Willard had not yet reached Pinkerton or the Provost Marshal's Office. Considering the stir caused by Ellison's escape, the Yankees would be trying very hard to avoid the embarrassment of having two more spies escape from their clutches in the same week. In about four hours Washington would be tightly sealed and it would be difficult to move.

Wilson was surprised to see Jordan and Masters. His face blanched as Masters explained the situation.

"This is a fine mess," Wilson snapped. "How did they know who you were?" The words were hurled at Jordan.

"I don't know," Jordan said defensively.

"Have you ever seen either of the two Pinkertons who were after you before today?" Wilson demanded.

"No!" Jordan replied. He didn't like the accusatory tone in Wilson's voice.

Wilson fumed. "That's what we get for using amateurs. You can put *your* life in danger working with him, but not mine. I'm leaving," he told Masters.

Jordan moved swiftly. He grabbed the liveryman by the collar and pinned him against the wall. "I didn't ask for this assignment, Wilson. I was told I was needed because a lot depends on the supplies that gold will buy. Neither you nor anyone else is going to foul up. If you try I'll kill you and it will give me a great deal of pleasure, because you have been nothing but a detriment since we got here." Jordan spoke between clenched teeth. "Do I make myself clear?"

Wilson, sweating profusely nodded in agreement.

"Let's calm down," Masters said evenly. He put a hand on Jordan's shoulder and the captain let Wilson go. "What's done is done. Fighting among ourselves won't change it. What we have to do is turn this to our advantage if we can, or at least minimize the damage. They probably think we will try to escape going south, so my guess is that most of the troops will be concentrated on the southern exits from the city like the aqueduct and Long Bridge. If we're careful we should be able to get the gold to the waterfront without any problem, but we've got to do it right now. If they do bother to stop us they will be less suspicious of a wagon delivering cargo to the waterfront during the day than at night."

"That's fine for us," Wilson said, gesturing at Jordan. "My pass is for two people. What about him?" Wilson had obviously decided that Jordan was the source of all their difficulties.

"I'll stay here," Jordan said angrily.

"You can't," Masters told him. "You're the only one who knows what this Graham looks like." Masters pondered the situation for a few minutes. He turned to Wilson. "Where can we get crates? It doesn't matter whether they're empty or full."

Wilson stopped to think. "I know a man who makes crates," he answered.

"Can he be trusted?"

"He's not one of us if that's what you mean," Wilson answered with a shake of his head.

Masters turned to Jordan. "Do you have any money?"

Jordan looked in his billfold. "I still have $300 in greenbacks."

"Give Mr. Wilson $100."

Jordan handed Wilson five $20 notes. They both looked at Masters with quizzical expressions. Masters was not paying attention to either of them. He went to the desk and began to write something. When he finished, he made sure the ink was dry and handed it to Wilson. It was an order to Wilson's Livery for five crates of the dimensions specified to be delivered to Mahew's Warehouse. The order was from Dedham & Sons of Baltimore. Wilson looked at it and then back at Masters. He still didn't understand.

"Get your wagon, pick up the crates, and bring them back here."

Wilson looked at the order form. "I'll be back as soon as I can," he said.

Jordan relaxed as soon as Wilson left. He suddenly felt drained. Lydia's company had been more than pleasant, but he had hardly slept. He was too tired to ask Masters why he needed the crates and he began to drift off to sleep. He smiled as he recalled the delights of the previous evening. One memory jolted him awake.

"Oh, my God," he said loudly.

Masters, who had also become drowsy, leaped out of his chair, drew his pistol, and pointed it at the door. "What's wrong?" he asked.

Jordan put his face in his hands and rubbed his eyes. "Put the gun away. I just remembered something and it startled me. It was something Lydia told me last night."

"Oh?" Masters' expression reflected a humorous, but nonetheless purient interest.

"It's nothing like that," Jordan said with a sheepish smile. "I

wish it were." He began to explain everything he knew and suspected about the corpse they had seen and what Lydia had told
him. He tried to make his explanation sound as logical as possible.
He watched Masters' face, expecting him to break out laughing at
any moment. Perhaps he was secretly wishing that the veteran
agent would laugh and explain it all away, but he didn't.

When Jordan finished his story Masters asked him, "Why didn't
you tell me this before?"

"I didn't want you to think I was crazy. Why does someone
rescue a traitor from a military prison, run the traitor all the way
through the network, and kill him when the journey's complete?
It doesn't make sense unless whoever did the killing needed the
credibility. Crossing the lines is done every day. You know that as
well as I do. If this man just crossed, his presence would be questioned every step of the way. Instead he crossed the lines with
passes signed by one of Colonel Longfellow's most trusted agents.
Now he's masquerading as a major from a North Carolina regiment and no one will question him. It's the perfect disguise."

Masters stared at Jordan. "How do you know he's disguised as a
major?"

"I saw him," Jordan said. He quickly explained the circumstances.

Masters didn't reply. Instead he sat back in his chair and began
to consider the possibilities. His experience in intelligence work
had taught him that there were usually several explanations for
any given event, but when the event was closely dissected only one
explanation was logical and therefore valid. He reviewed the possible explanations of Jordan's story.

The first possibility was what the "major" told the pickets about
a Yankee officer chasing him. It might be true. If so, why did he
tell the pickets that they had killed the Yankee officer? Masters
rejected the "major's" story for two reasons. The dead Yankee
officer was Charles Ellison. Of that there could be no doubt. Jordan, who was very familiar with gunshot wounds believed the
wound was inflicted by a .36 revolver instead of a .58 caliber
musket.

The second possibility was that the Yankees could have used
Ellison as a decoy to get into the Confederate lines. Masters rejected this also. The Union would have gotten more benefit from

questioning Ellison, and finding out who his contacts were. Then they could have convicted him and hanged him as an example to others. Killing Ellison on the doorstep of the Confederacy just to cross a ford didn't make sense. Contrary to Southern newspaper accounts, the Yankees were not cold-blooded murderers.

So, by ruling out the first two possibilities, only Jordan's account of events remained as the most logical and Masters didn't like it. He still had several questions. Was the man who murdered Ellison a hired assassin or was the letter a forgery contrived to panic Lydia Ratliffe into doing something she would not ordinarily do? Mrs. Ratliffe was an experienced agent who didn't panic easily. It seemed unlikely that anyone would go to such elaborate lengths as forging a document written by Lincoln's Secretary of War just to get across the Confederate lines. Nonetheless, Jordan's explanation of the events seemed the most logical, but Masters didn't want to accept it. Perhaps it was because he, like all Southerners, dared not contemplate what would happen to them without Robert E. Lee.

"Ferris," Jordan said out of the blue.

"What?"

"Major Harvey Ferris of the Eighteenth North Carolina," Jordan said. "That was the name he gave me."

"We have to get this information to Colonel Longfellow," Masters said with a grim determination. "This information may be more important than the gold."

There was no conversation after that. Jordan and Masters both dozed off. Jordan slept a deep, brooding sleep. When he was awakened by the sound of Wilson's key in the door, he was depressed.

"You were right," the liveryman told Masters. "The routes to the south are thick with blue bellies, but the streets in the interior of the city are only lightly patrolled. The problem is this."

Wilson handed something to Masters and gave Jordan a dirty look. Masters looked at it and passed it on to Jordan. It was a handbill offering a $500 reward for Jordan's capture. It listed him as a Baltimore businessman and a Rebel spy. There was no likeness on the handbill, but the description of Jordan and his clothing was accurate. Jordan felt a chill go through him as he read it.

"It looks like you're famous, Dick," Masters said. "Where's the wagon?" He asked Wilson.

"I moved it around back. Thought it might be safer."

"Good idea," Masters said. He began to change back into workman's clothes. "We'll go to the warehouse, deliver the gold, and then come back here. In the morning we'll check out as if everything were normal."

"What about him?" Wilson said, jabbing a thumb in Jordan's direction.

"We smuggle him out in the big crate. That's why I had you get it."

It was nearly 4:00 P.M. when the three men walked down the back steps into the alley. The alley was as filthy as the one behind the Willard.

"There's your passport to freedom, Dick," Masters said pointing to a crate slightly larger than a coffin.

Jordan looked at the crate and swallowed. He didn't like close places. "You make it sound so inviting, Charley." He said with false bravado. Jordan took a deep breath and stepped into the box. He lay in it and Masters lowered the lid. He suppressed an urge to leap out of the crate when the lid snapped shut. It's not so bad, he thought. Light filtered in between the boards and he could hear everything remarkably clearly.

The ride in the crate was rough. There was no padding in the box and one jolt sent such a searing pain through Jordan's hip that he found it difficult not to cry out. A coffin would have been more comfortable, he thought. Jordan tried to think about pleasant things to keep his mind off his predicament, but as the wagon lurched interminably through the bumpy streets, the crate became smaller and smaller. Jordan felt as if he were choking and loosened his collar. He had to fight a desperate urge to jump out of the box regardless of the consequences. He began to sweat profusely. The wagon stopped twice in traffic, but he didn't notice. Inside the crate Richard Jordan fought a battle against his own rising terror. His brain told him what he had to do. He had to be quiet until they reached the warehouse. Somewhere in his soul there was a wild beast straining at it bonds, determined to break free of its trap. Gradually the animal was gaining the upper hand.

Jordan was losing the battle when Yankee soldiers stopped the wagon outside the waterfront.

"Where are you going?" A young lieutenant arrogantly asked Wilson and Masters.

Wilson said nothing. He seemed terribly forlorn.

"We're delivering some crates to the Mahew Warehouse," Masters said. He shoved a handful of papers at the lieutenant. They contained the order for the crates, the receipt for payment and Masters' and Wilson's passes.

The lieutenant had seen so many bills of lading, passes, and receipts that he hardly knew what he was looking at. "What's in the crates?" he asked. He sounded smug to cover his indecision and confusion.

"The small one's are empty," Masters told him, spitting tobacco juice. "The big one's got Mr. Wilson's brother in it."

"Oh?" What a perfect place to hide a spy, the lieutenant thought. He began to walk to the rear of the wagon.

"He died yesterday," Wilson sobbed. "Of the cholera."

Masters was impressed with Wilson's performance. So was the lieutenant. His face blanched and he turned on his heel. He strode over to Masters. He thrust the papers into Masters' hands and wiped his own on the seat of his trousers.

"You're clear," the lieutenant said. "Move on!"

"Good day to ya, lieutenant," Masters said. He tipped his hat, spat again, and urged the horses forward.

Jordan was unaware of the entire incident. He was only aware of the animal fighting his brain. He bit into the soft flesh of his left hand between his thumb and forefinger. The pain became his only link with reality as the animal grew stronger. Only the pain kept him from leaping from the crate. Tears rolled down his cheeks. That was the way they found him when they finally pulled the lid off the crate.

"What the hell . . . " Wilson said.

Masters grabbed Jordan by the lapels and pulled him to a sitting position. "Dick, it's us. You're out. You're all right."

Jordan stared at him uncomprehendingly, then he looked around and burst out crying in relief. Wilson looked at him with contempt.

"What's the matter with him?" Wilson asked.

"He obviously has a mortal dread of being closed in," Masters replied. "I've read about it before. This trip must have been sheer horror for him. It's a wonder he didn't just jump out of the box. Look at this," He said lifting Jordan's left hand.

Wilson looked wide-eyed at the swollen hand turning blue around the teeth marks. "What did that?"

"He did. He bit his hand to control the terror. He probably would have bitten it off to keep from betraying us."

"My God," was all Wilson could say. His expression softened and he leaned down to help Jordan out of the crate. It took a long time for Jordan to stop crying and calm down.

"That was a hell of thing you did, Dick," Masters said softly.

Jordan looked up at him. His eyes were red, but there was a steel hardness to them. "I'm not going back in there," he told them. "I'll die first."

Masters knew he meant it.

"How the hell are we going to get him out of here now?" Wilson asked.

"Maybe I can get a ride on Graham's boat to Baltimore," Jordan said wiping the sweat from his face. "Then I can catch the train to Harper's Ferry."

"It's a thought," Wilson agreed.

They pulled the wagon into the warehouse and waited. Jordan hated the wait. He was tired and he wanted to sleep, but he was afraid if he went to sleep the animal would seek him out and he would dream of the terror he had faced in the crate. It was the kind that most men can't imagine and although he had controlled it, he was now afraid of being afraid and showing it. Masters came over and sat beside him.

"Medicine," Masters said, handing Jordan a silver flask.

"Where did you get this?"

"I carry it for snake bite."

"Thanks," Jordan said. He took two healthy swigs and coughed as the liquid burned from his throat to his stomach. He was expecting bourbon but this stuff burned like fire. "Jesus, what is this?"

"Cognac. Smooth isn't it?"

Jordan shook his head. "No," he coughed.

"Look, Dick," Masters said sympathetically. "I know what you're going through."

"Do you?" Jordan was very defensive. He had shown weakness in front of his companions and he was embarrassed.

"Yes I do, only with me it was snakes. How's your hand?"

Jordan lifted it. It was badly swollen. "Hurts like hell."

"I'll bet. You saved our lives back there. Even Wilson realizes it."

"I did no such thing."

"Dick, there's a lot written about courage and most of it's pure trash. It doesn't take all that much courage to face another man in battle with a sword or a gun. Most of us really don't have a choice. You either face the danger with dignity or you run away. If you do that you live in disgrace for the rest of your life, cut off from those you love, wishing you were dead. I don't think anyone considers that living."

"What are you driving at?"

"There's something other than battle we have to face and that's ourselves. Inside each one of us is a demon and that demon is there to eat your soul and destroy your very being. Most men never learn that theirs exist, but some of us do. Few of those that do can defend themselves and the demon winds up destroying them, piece by piece. Some drink themselves to death trying to escape. You faced your demon today and he didn't break you. Don't let him make you think he did." Masters put his hand on his friend's shoulder.

"Thanks, Charley," Jordan said letting out a sigh. "What happened to you?"

"I was thirteen. I ran across a nest of king snakes. There must have been half a dozen and they were crawling all over themselves trying to get way. I froze and filled my pants. I was that terrified. My father thought it was ridiculous because the snakes weren't poisonous. He beat me in front of my mother, my brothers, and my sisters for being a 'sissy.' It still hurts."

Jordan nodded. He didn't understand it all, but he felt better and slept. He didn't dream.

Albert Graham was about as quiet as the average steam engine. The three Confederate agents could hear him long before he came close to the wagon, tripping over boxes and cursing. In addition, Jordan could smell Graham's expensive cigar. After a few moments, Wilson lit an oil lamp and Graham sighed in relief. Jordan wondered how Graham survived in this arena of clandestine sales.

"Good evening," Graham said. Jordan had to smile. Graham was in evening clothes. He looked at Jordan and moved closer. "Are you all right, Dick? You look like hell."

Jordan grinned. "I'm all right, Al. I'd like you to meet my partners."

Jordan made quick introductions and they began removing the false floor of the wagon. It took them less than an hour to transfer the gold to two crates Graham had in the warehouse. Once the crates were packed and nailed shut, they hoisted them onto the wagon and followed Graham to a paddlewheeled steam yacht moored to one of the piers. With the help of the crew and a small hoist, they lowered the cargo into the hold.

"It's a pleasure doing business with you gentlemen," Graham said without a trace of sarcasm. "Rest assured that the shoes and other supplies will be at Vicksburg by the first week in May. If there's nothing else, I'll bid you all a fond adieu."

"Al, I need a favor," Jordan said.

"Anything that's within my power," Graham said. His arms were spread wide in a gesture of generosity.

"Take me to Baltimore with you."

Graham, who had not yet seen the handbills began to laugh. "So you're the ones who caused the ruckus at the Willard, this morning. You woke Sally and me out of a sound sleep. The Pinkertons are sure mad at you. Sure, come along. Do your friends want to come along, too?"

"No, the authorities don't have their names and they have passes."

"Okay, let's get going."

Jordan said goodbye to Masters and Wilson. "See you in Harper's Ferry day after tomorrow, Mr. Wilson."

Wilson nodded in agreement and they shook hands. "Good luck, captain," he said sincerely.

Albert Graham's yacht was nothing less than a floating palace. It was well stocked with food, wine, and cigars. Jordan would have been surprised if Al didn't have at least one beautiful woman on board. He had two. Graham graciously offered the company of one to Jordan but he declined. Jordan took advantage of other aspects of Graham's hospitality, however. He washed himself and his underwear, then he brushed off his other clothing. He cleaned and reloaded his pocket pistol, ate a light supper, and went to bed.

Before Jordan left the yacht in Baltimore, Graham offered him a job with his company.

"That's very generous, Al, but you know I have to get back."

"Look me up after the war then," Graham said. "I could use someone like you. Here," he said handing Jordan a box of Cuban cigars. "A little present."

Jordan smiled. "Thanks, Al. I'll be sure to look you up after the war."

Jordan hired a carriage to the railroad station in Baltimore. He bought a ticket for the first train to Harper's Ferry but discovered that the train didn't go directly there. He had to change trains at the relay point just south of Baltimore. To make matters worse he had to wait. He spent his time buying newspapers and a new bag to replace the one he had left at the Willard. He then purchased some new underclothing and shaving gear. He wanted to travel with some luggage. Jordan boarded the train with a feeling of relief. It would be restful to get back to the simple business of waging war. He would never look askance at reports again, he thought. Well, maybe that was going too far.

George Ingalls was one of Alan Pinkerton's most experienced operatives. He operated by hunches and one of his hunches told him that not all of the spies from the Willard Hotel were going to escape south. He reasoned that they would go to Baltimore, which was a hotbed of secession and leave Baltimore by boat. Operating on this premise, he took a train to the relay point and positioned himself at the rear of the platform. There, in his tweed suit he would be inconspicuous and he could observe everyone on the platform. Whenever a train stopped on its way to Baltimore, he boarded it and walked through the cars looking for someone suspicious. He was waiting on the platform for the northbound train when the southbound train arrived. He wasn't that interested in it, but he was a detective and he watched the passengers leaving the train as a matter of course. His jaw dropped when he saw Richard Jordan get off the southbound train. It didn't matter to Ingalls that his logic had been faulty. His hunch had been correct.

Ingalls decided against trying to apprehend Jordan on the platform. There were too many people on the platform who might get in the way and make it easy for Jordan to escape. An enclosed speeding train was a better place. Even if the suspect tried to escape by leaping from the train, he would probably break an ankle in the attempt. Ingalls watched Jordan the entire time he was on the platform. He also looked around for any sign of Jordan's accomplices. There didn't appear to be any.

An hour after Jordan stepped onto the platform, the train to Harpers Ferry arrived and he boarded it. He took a seat by a window on the side opposite the platform and didn't see the man in the tweed suit board the train at the last minute. Ingalls waited until the train was up to speed to make his move. He pulled his pocket pistol and concealed it in his newspaper. Jordan was sitting a third of the way up in the second car from the end. There weren't many people going to Harpers Ferry and the seat next to Jordan was empty. Ingalls walked up the aisle and sat next to Jordan. Before the cavalry officer could turn to see who had sat next to him, he felt a gun in his ribs. His blood ran cold as he turned to face Ingalls. How had the man found him?

"Good morning, Mr. Jordan, if that's your name."

"It is. Good morning, Mr. . . . ."

"Ingalls," the Pinkerton detective said, supplying his name.

Jordan turned to look at him. "Mr. Ingalls."

"Mr. Jordan, my orders are to capture you alive if I can, but if I can't it would please me to blow a very large hole in you for all the discomfort you and your henchman have caused my partner and me." Ingalls voice was very matter-of-fact and Jordan had no doubt that he would kill him, given the slightest provocation. "Now, in order to remove you from the temptation to escape, we are going to move to the area between the cars. There I will shackle you to the railing and have a clear shot at you should the need arise. I don't like shooting innocent bystanders."

"What do you want me to do?"

"I am going to get up and step back. You will get up and head for the back of the car. If you make the slightest false move I will kill you."

"I understand." Jordan watched as Ingalls backed out of the seat. Then he followed. He walked slowly up the aisle to the door. Jordan felt off balance. He had never been captured before. It was almost like being in the crate. He had to think. The best time to try something was at the door. No. Ingalls would expect that. Wait until you're through the door, he thought.

Jordan opened the door and actually held it open for the Pinkerton man. Ingalls stepped out onto the platform with him and reached for the manacles on his belt. He moved the gun slightly and Jordan kicked him in the shin as hard as he could. No matter how big a man is, his shins are sensitive. Ingalls bent over in pain and Jordan hit him as hard as he could. The detective dropped his gun, but he didn't go down. Jordan was amazed. The man was hard. Ingalls was also amazed. He had thought that Jordan was just another soft businessman, and the force of the blows from the tough cavalry officer surprised him. Ingalls fell back against the railing, using the fraction of a second to clear his head. Jordan didn't come after him to finish the job so the detective lunged forward again. He was a very muscular man and when he hit Jordan he nearly knocked the wind from him. Jordan fell back, unable to keep his balance. Ingalls landed on top of him and hit him with a short jab to the head. The side of Jordan's head went numb and he realized he had to do something quickly. He managed to reach his pocket pistol. It was a tough shot because he couldn't see and he would have to shoot toward himself and up. He pulled the trigger. The heavy slug hit Ingalls in the buttock and it flung him forward. The detective hit his head on the rail and slumped off Jordan. Groggily, Jordan got to his feet and grabbed the dazed Ingalls by his shoulders. He raised the detective to his knees and bashed Ingalls' head against the railing until the detective was limp. Then Jordan lifted him to his feet and pushed him over the railing. He watched as Ingalls hit the ground and bounced. Jordan leaned against the rail and took deep breaths of the cold air and dusted himself off. Everything hurt. The conductor came out to get his ticket.

"Sir, are you all right. You look awfully pale. Are you motion sick?"
"I think so."
"Where's the other gentleman who was out here?" The conductor asked.

"There was no other gentleman out here," Jordan told him. "But. . . "

"Believe me. There was no other gentleman out here."

Jordan went back in the car and returned to his seat. He hoped the rest of his journey would be less eventful. He needed to get back to the peace and quiet of fighting the war.

CHAPTER 7

Headquarters, Chief of Scouts
Army of Northern Virginia
March 16, 1863

WHEN RICHARD JORDAN put his uniform back on, the sensation was so splendid that he felt like dancing a jig. Once again he was a member of a recognizable, organized army and that was the way he preferred it. He was happy even though his first task upon his return was to submit a report of his activities in Washington. There was another reason he was happy. In the time that he was gone, the weather had begun to change. There was less of a nip in the air and buds had begun to form on some of the trees. Spring was in the air and Jordan smiled. Perhaps he would be able to see Jennifer before he returned to the Third Virginia Cavalry.

There was another, less attractive, aspect of spring. Soon there would be grass for the horses to eat and that would put meat on their bones. Once that occurred, the troopers would be able to properly exercise their mounts and the cavalry would be ready for another campaigning season. The skirmishing and raiding would begin. In a few weeks there would be more fighting and, perhaps, the major battle that would end the war. Nevertheless, it made him feel comfortable. This was a way of war he understood. The danger of open battle was preferable to moving in the shadows with Colonel Longfellow's minions. It wasn't that he thought they were dishonorable. It was just the opposite. He admired Longfellow and especially Charley Masters, but he never again wanted to be one of those shadow people who operated behind enemy lines, exploiting the unwary and dealing with those to whom personal and national honor were nothing. Jordan, anxious to get back to the Third Virginia Cavalry, submitted his report, thinking that would be the end of it. It wasn't. Colonel Longfellow asked him to wait. He wanted to read the captain's report personally, then review it with Jordan face-to-face.

Longfellow chewed on his cigar and read Jordan's report for the second time. It gave an excellent account of what had transpired since Jordan and Masters headed north in the sutler's wagon. Most military men would have been delighted with the results. The two scouts had traveled to the enemy's capital, purchased the supplies for the upcoming offensive in the north, and outwitted Pinkerton and the Provost Marshal of Washington. Then they had returned with the sutler's wagon full of badly needed medicine. Any conventional commander would have congratulated his men and rewarded them, but Colonel Longfellow was not a commander of conventional forces. To a person whose subordinates operated behind enemy lines, results were measured in a number of ways. One very important measurement of results was how unobtrusively the mission was handled. Jordan had performed like the proverbial bull in the china shop. Heroic escapes make great storytelling, but they indicate sloppy intelligence work and, in the long run, do more harm than good. One of the strengths of the Confederate spy network was that most officials in Washington were either blissfully ignorant of its existence or were embarrassed by it. The public escapes of Ellison and Jordan in the space of a week were bound to make even the most blase official aware that there was something going on. Worse, it could force those embarrassed officials to take some action. The only bright spot that Longfellow could see was that Wilson's network had been left intact. He was no longer sure about Lydia Ratliffe's.

There was something else that bothered Longfellow and that was the Ellison business. If Longfellow disliked notoriety, he disliked unsolved mysteries even more. Jordan had come to the conclusion that Ellison's murder had something to do with a plot to assassinate General Lee. If Jordan had been the only one to come to that conclusion, then Longfellow could have dismissed the report as the untrained notions of an amateur. Unfortunately, the source was Lydia Ratliffe, one of the colonel's most trusted agents. She kept her fingers on the pulse of official Washington and provided consistently reliable information. To make matters worse, Charley Masters, an experienced agent whose judgment Longfellow trusted implicitly, had come to the same conclusions as Jordan. The conclusions, if one chose to accept them, were, to put it mildly, alarming. An enemy agent, whose ostensible mission was to murder Robert E. Lee, had freed Ellison from prison and used the major to penetrate Lydia's network. When he was safely through the lines, he callously murdered Ellison and then went on his way. Ten days had elapsed, but no attempt was made on Lee's life. If—and it seemed to be a big "if"—Lydia's network had been penetrated, why hadn't the authorities arrested her and shut down her operation? Longfellow was baffled. But as the days passed and no assassination attempt occurred, he became less concerned with the "Ellison business."

There was another problem that weighed heavily on Longfellow's mind. While it was not directly related to Jordan's trip to Washington, or the Ellison business, it was always in the background and indirectly influenced every operation he undertook. No matter how well he did in providing information about the enemy, there was still a group who considered Longfellow's work dishonorable and distasteful. Stuart had named Longfellow "Chief of Scouts" to avoid the stigma that "spy" held to most people, but it hadn't helped. There was a growing number of officers who wanted Longfellow's operation shut down. Some of these were motivated by their sense of honor; some were jealous. In January their complaints reached the Senate in Richmond. It had not taken much effort for Longfellow to prove that he was a scout and not a spy, but Congress was not content to stop there. Its meddling continued and the strain of running a comprehensive intelligence operation and fending off Congressional investigators was beginning to take its toll.

Longfellow decided to interview Masters and Jordan personally. By taking the role of devil's advocate, perhaps he could discover something face-to-face that he couldn't discern from their reports. Longfellow decided to interview Masters first because he was a known quantity. Masters strolled casually into Longfellow's office. He was unmilitary in his posture and he did not salute. Longfellow was not upset. He employed agents who did well in the field. Saluting wasn't part of their responsibilities.

"Have a seat, Charley," he told Masters.

Masters sat in the chair next to the desk and stretched his legs to their full length. "Is this about the trip to Washington?"

"Yes."

"You have my report. What else do you need?"

"Sometimes reports can be misleading even though the party writing them tried his best to write them clearly. Sometimes it's because the writer is so familiar with the events that he assumes that others are too."

"This is about the Ellison murder, isn't it?" Masters said, bringing the conversation right to the point.

Longfellow smiled. There was no use beating around the bush with Masters. "Yes."

Masters grinned. "I thought so. What's the matter?"

"Nothing, really. I'd just like to clear up some things in my own mind."

"Like what?"

"First I need to ask you some questions, Charley," Longfellow explained. "I realize that you're a step ahead of most men and that usually includes me, but I need to ask these questions in a specific order and I need a truthful answer to each one."

Masters shot him a quizzical look. "Have I ever lied to you, colonel?"

"No. Maybe 'truthful' was a bad choice of words. Give me your honest opinion, how's that?"

"Fine."

"Keeping in mind that Jordan is an amateur, I want you to give me your impression of him."

Masters pursed his lips, and considered his words carefully.

"With all due respect, colonel, you know the old saw about the cavalry officer who was so dumb that even the other cavalry officers noticed. In my experience most are lucky enough to remember which side of the horse to mount on. Well, Dick's the exception. He's intelligent, observant, decisive, and courageous."

"That's a pretty broad endorsement," Longfellow said. "It sounds like you're impressed with him."

"I am."

"Let's talk about his qualities. You said he was observant. How was he observant?"

Masters cited Jordan's analysis of Ellison's wound and the observations he made about the Yankee cavalry at Stafford Court House.

"I would expect that," The colonel said a little testily. "That's his area of expertise. He didn't seem to notice the Pinkertons even though they seemed to know who he was. How do you explain that?"

"I can't. I don't know how they recognized him unless they happened to see him with Lydia Ratliffe by accident. I really don't know."

"If he had been more observant he wouldn't have had to kill a Pinkerton detective on the Baltimore and Ohio Railroad either." It was obvious that the colonel was not pleased with Richard Jordan.

"Do you want me to sit here and defend him?"

"You like him, don't you, Charley?"

"Yes, I do."

"Is it because he saved your life?"

"That's part of it. The rest is because he's a decent man and you don't meet too many of those in this business. He also tried very hard to do the right thing."

"Like what?"

Masters related the story of the crate and Jordan's improvisation in the inn at Stafford Court House.

"Then you think he's credible?"

"Very."

"Then why doesn't his theory about this Ellison business hold water?"

"What do you mean it doesn't hold water?"

"If you assume that every one of these speculations . . . "

"Just a minute, colonel," Masters interrupted. "I would hardly call them speculations. You've always said that good intelligence work depends on gathering facts."

Longfellow held up his hand. "Bear with me Charley. If you assume that Jordan's 'theories' are correct, then the assassin, if that's what he was, crossed the river into our lines on the fourth of March, right?"

"Yes, of course."

"Today is the 16th. It's been twelve days and no one has so much as cocked a pistol in General Lee's presence, much less tried and kill him. How do you explain that?" Longfellow smiled. His logic seemed flawless.

"It's simple. This assassin is determined to kill the general and get away," Masters said.

Longfellow's expression changed from smug satisfaction to uncertainty. "What are you saying?"

"It's just that General Lee is a very approachable man. The lowliest private in the army can walk up to him and ask for a plug of tobacco. Even enemy prisoners have been known to walk right up to him and ask for redress for some grievance. You and I have both seen it."

"So?"

"So what would happen to the man who tried to kill him?"

"He'd be torn from limb to limb, of course," Longfellow said.

"That's just my point. Let us, for a moment, 'speculate'." Masters paused as he emphasized the word but Longfellow didn't react to it. Masters continued. "Let us speculate that the assassin is not a crazed fanatic determined to kill General Lee, even if it costs him his own life. Let us suppose that he is a professional killer, who has been offered a substantial sum to do the job. A man of that sort doesn't kill from a sense of patriotism. He does it so he can survive and enjoy his reward. My guess is that this assassin knows as well as we do if he tries to kill General Lee now, he will die even if he succeeds in the attempt. He's probably somewhere in the army right now becoming a familiar face in the command. He will stay there and wait until Lee is in a dangerous situation. Then, when he murders the general, it will seem as if the general were struck down by an enemy bullet. In the tragedy and confusion, the assassin will disappear and return to the north to enjoy his blood money."

Longfellow looked at Masters for a moment and let the impact of what he had just said sink in. "I'm glad you're on our side, Charley," he said. "I want you to do something for me."

"Yes sir."

"I'm going to call Captain Jordan in here. I'll leave the side door open. I want you to sit on the other side and listen to the interview."

Masters looked a little pained as if he were being required to betray a friend.

"I know what it sounds like, Charley, but I have to be sure about this. You and Jordan are telling me that the Yankees have sent an assassin to kill our finest general. If I'm going to report this to anyone I have to be absolutely certain. May I remind you that we are not exactly looked upon with fondness by some officers of this army? And there are many who would love to see me—us—humbled, and our operation curtailed. We can't afford to have that happen."

"I understand, sir," Masters said.

"Good. Go get Jordan and sit behind the door."

Masters rose and left the room. A few minutes later Jordan walked in the door and reported to the colonel.

"Captain Jordan reporting as ordered, sir." He said giving a proper military salute.

Longfellow returned his salute, and motioned to the chair that Masters just vacated. "Have a seat, Dick," he said gesturing to the chair Masters had just vacated. "Cigar?"

"No thank you, sir."

The colonel didn't speak immediately. He rose and stuck the end of a fresh cigar in the chimney of the oil lamp. He drew on it, rolling the cigar until the end glowed evenly. He then puffed two clouds of fragrant white smoke before sitting down again.

"This is going to be a mighty rough war if I ever run out of these," he said trying to put Jordan at ease. "I'll bet you're anxious to get back to your unit, eh, Dick."

"Yes sir, I am."

"Well, I'll try not to delay you any further, but I do want to talk with you personally about your report. What you've written is that we have a very dangerous situation. I wanted to interview you personally because I am concerned and, to be frank, I'm not sure what my next move should be."

"I understand, sir."

"Now that you've had a couple of days of rest, do you still believe that this Major Ferris has crossed our lines to kill General Lee?"

"Yes, sir, I do."

"I realize that for you it must be redundant, but I'd like to hear your conclusions from you personally. Please believe me. It will help."

Jordan repeated his report verbally. He tried to present his case as logically as possible and he was relieved to see that Longfellow's interest in what he had to say didn't flag. When the colonel mentioned the fact that no attempt had been made on Lee's life, Jordan used the same explanation as Masters, but the colonel was still skeptical.

"Sir, may I say something?"

"Go ahead. That's what this interview is for."

"I can understand your skepticism. Were I in your place, I probably wouldn't believe me either. Therefore, I would check out my story with hard evidence."

"How do you propose I do that?"

"First, check to see if there's a Major Harvey Ferris in the 18th North Carolina or anywhere else in the army. A major should be easy to find since there aren't many in a regiment. Next, have someone exhume Ellison's body to see if the wounds were made by a pistol ball or a .58 caliber rifle ball. Those are two facts you can establish objectively."

Longfellow drew on his cigar and looked at the cavalry captain. Jordan was right. He couldn't afford to overlook the hard evidence, even if it made things look bad. Longfellow put his cigar in the ashtray and looked at Jordan. He tried to make his voice as pleasant as possible. "I'd like to thank you for everything you've done for us, Dick," he said extending his hand. I intend to write a letter to General Stuart telling him how valuable your help has been. I would just like your word that you that you'll keep everything that's happened strictly confidential."

"Of course, sir. You have my word."

"Good. I knew I could rely on you. There is one favor I'd like to ask. I have some dispatches for General Stuart. Would you mind taking them to him?"

"I'd be happy to."

The General is at Culpeper attending a court martial. You can go to Orange Court House then put your horse on the train. That will save you both a trip. Once you deliver them you can return to your regiment."

Jordan rose to shake the colonel's hand. "Thank you, sir. The Third Virginia will seem mighty restful after this."

"Best of luck to you, Dick."

"You, too, sir." Jordan saluted and left.

Masters waited a decent interval before coming through the door. "Well?" The sergeant asked.

"I think I'll do exactly as he suggested," Longfellow said. "We should be able to put this thing behind us once and for all."

"I hope you're right, colonel," Masters said. "Now, if you don't mind I'll say my good-byes."

"Certainly."

Masters walked up the path to headquarters. Jordan was signing the receipt for the dispatches. He smiled when he saw Masters.

"I've come to see you off, Dick."

"That's nice of you, Charley. I just had a talk with your boss."

"So I gathered."

"I don't think he believes me," Jordan said.

Masters shrugged. "He's a hard man to read sometimes, Dick. There are a lot of people who don't understand what he's trying to do. He has to be very careful with what he says. People only remember when we're wrong, not when we're right."

"I think he's doing his best to bury this," Jordan said with a tinge of bitterness. "But it's no longer my problem." He put his hand on Masters' shoulder. "Anytime you're around the Third, stop in. I mean it."

"I will, Dick. I'll let you know how this whole thing comes out."

"I'd appreciate that. Next time you're in Washington say hello to Mrs. Ratliffe for me."

Masters' face broke into a grin. "I surely would like to have that opportunity. Take care of yourself."

"You, too, Charley."

The two men shook hands and Jordan mounted his horse. He waved as he steered the animal in the direction of Orange Court

House. If he were lucky he would be there by evening. Then he could get back to being a soldier. He couldn't help wondering where Major Harvey Ferris was; who he was and what he was doing in the Army of Northern Virginia. He had stopped at Oakview Manor. Perhaps Jennifer could add something to the solution of the mystery. Perhaps he had said something that might give himself away. Jordan was tempted to go to Oakview, but the strap of the courier case reminded him that he was back in the army and he decided not to. Perhaps he should have mentioned that he had seen Ferris and that he had given Ferris directions to Oakview Manor, but he didn't want to involve Jennifer. Was it because he didn't want Jennifer to know he had been a spy?

The ride to Orange Court House was pleasant. Jordan admired the country with its thick forests and rolling hills. He was alone with his own thoughts on a tree-lined country road. It seemed as if he had not been alone to think things out for at least a century. The last time he had been able to let his thoughts drift he was alone in his tent. That was when Bobby had brought him the package from home and the letter from Dana. He decided to read his brother's letter again as soon as he had a chance. There were still the pickles unless Bobby had stolen them.

Life had been much simpler before he made the trip to Washington. Now there was an assassin loose somewhere in the Confederate camp. At a moment known only to the assassin himself, he was going to strike down the great hope of the South, Robert E. Lee. Jordan felt the anger rise in him. Why couldn't Longfellow see? The evidence was there! The Yankee Major Ellison had been murdered. The reason he was murdered was that he could identify the assassin. It was that simple. The evidence was there. All Longfellow had to do is open his eyes to see it. Masters believes me, Jordan thought. Why can't I make Longfellow understand? The thought of Ellison's murderer running around freely depressed Jordan. He found it difficult to think of anything else. The man was there and he was going to kill Lee. Jordan had never been as sure of anything in his life. There had to be a way of finding the assassin and stopping him.

The depot at Orange Court House was busy, but there were few civilian passengers going north. Culpeper had already changed hands numerous times during the war and only those with ultimate faith in the Confederacy or those who didn't care remained. There were plenty of soldiers going to Culpeper. Some were returning from furlough and some were returning to their units after being sick or wounded. There were very few new recruits. A year ago, the rail depots thronged with new recruits. Jordan got his ticket from the ticket agent and then went down the platform to the express agent who took his horse for transport to Culpeper. Realizing that he had well over an hour to wait, Jordan looked around the depot for a newspaper, but there were none. In Baltimore and Washington the newsboys were shoving the papers in his face. In the South paper was getting scarce. He didn't feel like sitting down so he walked out on the platform.

"Dick. Dick Jordan," someone called his name in a mellow Alabama accent.

When Jordan turned in the direction of the voice his face erupted in a broad smile. Walking toward him was Major John Pelham, the tall, blond chief of Stuart's horse artillery. Pelham had been nicknamed "the Gallant" and no one begrudged him the epithet. He took artillery pieces where most men wouldn't or couldn't take a mule. Thanks to Pelham, the Confederate Cavalry was never without artillery support. Pelham was also modest to a fault, and everyone who knew him liked him. Even General J.E.B. Stuart treated him more like a younger brother than a subordinate. Despite his military accomplishments, Pelham was more widely known for another talent. He was the best-known flirt in the Army of Northern Virginia.

"John Pelham," Jordan said shaking the major's hand. "What are you doing here?"

"I've been visiting friends."

"Lady friends no doubt," Jordan said.

Pelham blushed slightly. "General Stuart's cousin, Miss Nannie Price," he said. "Now tell me what brings you here? I thought you were with your regiment. Did you manage to get a furlough?"

"Nothing quite as much fun. I was temporarily assigned to Colonel Longfellow's organization."

"Longfellow the spy?" Pelham asked.

"The same."

"What did he want with you?"

"I have been doing some scouting for him for the last two

weeks," Jordan explained evasively. "I'm returning to the Third. What's been happening while I was gone, John?"

Before Pelham could answer, the whistle of the approaching train blew. The artillery major looked at his watch. "Not bad. Only ten minutes late."

The train was typical of those that traversed the South. It had two passenger coaches, two boxcars loaded with ammunition, and a flatcar with four guns under canvas. Behind the flatcar was a dilapidated caboose. Jordan and Pelham climbed aboard the passenger coach. They took a seat next to one of the intact windows and Jordan watched as the coach filled with troops. He had to admit one thing; the troops returning from home and hospital looked a lot better than the troops he had left in his company. At home they had been fed. Jordan admired them for returning to such appalling conditions. The coach itself was shabby. The glass in the broken windows had not been replaced. The windows had been boarded up. The upholstery on the seats was torn and in some cases had been removed entirely, leaving plain wooden seats. There was neither water nor heat in the car. The whistle blew and the train lurched forward. As the train left the station, the car swayed. The springs were bad and the roadbed was uneven. To Richard Jordan, it was a far cry from the luxurious railroads of the North. No one else seemed to notice. Pelham was looking absentmindedly out the window.

"How did you manage to get to Orange Court House for a visit, John?" Jordan asked. He was anxious to continue their small talk. "I thought General Lee discouraged officers from leaving the army for visits?"

It was Pelham's turn to grin. "I have been inspecting batteries along my journey, so I've really been on official business. There's no prohibition against being a guest in a private home."

Jordan smiled and laughed softly. "That's one I'll have to remember."

"Unfortunately, General Stuart has asked that I return. I received word that he was in Culpeper at a court martial so I am going there to join him, instead of returning to headquarters," Pelham continued.

"Who's in Culpeper, John?"

"You seem to be reading minds today, Dick. What makes you think I'm going to see anyone in Culpeper?"

"Because Culpeper is a place that's been devastated by the war and has less charm than Fredericksburg these days. If I were to go out of my way to Culpeper, it certainly wouldn't be to see General Stuart."

Pelham looked at him with a sheepish smile. "All right. I'm bursting to tell someone, but if you breathe a word of this before it's finished . . . "

Jordan held up his right hand. "You have my word."

"If I can avoid General Stuart for a few hours, I am going to Judge Shackleford's to ask him for the hand of his daughter in marriage."

"Oh, dear," Jordan said with all the solemnity he could muster.

"What's the matter, Dick?"

"You obviously haven't considered the effect of your decision on our country then, have you?"

"What do you mean, Dick?" Pelham was puzzled and very concerned.

"If you marry, then every single woman between here and Texas will go into mourning," Jordan explained, just barely maintaining a straight face.

Pelham stared at Jordan for a moment and blinked. Then he blushed and began to laugh. "You had me half believing you, Dick," he said clapping him on the shoulder.

Jordan burst into laughter with him. "In all seriousness, John, best of luck."

"Dick, you're worse than General Stuart. He teases everyone. Did you hear what he did to 'Old Jack' last Christmas?"

"No."

"Jackson has his headquarters in the plantation office of the Corbin place. It's separate from the house and the whole place is decorated with pictures of race horses and fighting cocks. When General Stuart saw this he began teasing Jackson about his taste in decor and told Jackson that he was glad the newspapers didn't know how a hero of the South lived. By the time he was through 'Old Jack' was tongue-tied and blushing."

"No."

"Yes."

Jordan laughed again. The image of the forbidding, eccentric "Stonewall Jackson" standing tongue-tied and blushing was too hilarious for words. Pelham joined him in the laugh.

"He's really not a bad person, Dick," Pelham explained. "You know he actually likes to drink whiskey?"

"I never would have guessed it."

"It's true," Pelham insisted. "To tell the truth I'm as nervous as a wet hen about seeing Judge Shackleford. I hope this business of my supposed flirting won't hurt my chances. I really don't mean anything by it. It's just that when a lady looks at me I like to look back." The artilleryman took a deep breath. "It's one thing to flirt, but with the woman that's close to your heart you get so nervous you can't talk. Dick, I think I'd rather charge into a brigade of stirred-up Yankees than do this."

"Why is it we're more scared of romancing our own ladies than we are of fighting the enemy, John?" Jordan asked the question absentmindedly while he gazed out of one of the few remaining glass windows in the car. He was thinking of Jennifer. Perhaps he should propose the next time they met.

"Sounds like you have someone in mind yourself, Dick. Anyone I know?"

"You do. It's Jennifer Franks."

"Tom Franks' widow?"

"The same."

"She's a fine woman, Dick. Have you asked her?"

"No. I don't know I really should. I've only seen her three times. The first time was when she let General Stuart have his party at Oakview Manor."

Pelham didn't reply and Jordan didn't continue. For a while neither man said anything. Jordan felt awkward and didn't want to break the silence. Pelham was staring out the window at the gray countryside.

"Do you think the weather will clear soon? It's almost impossible to move a battery over roads like this," Pelham said. He sounded far away.

"Or wagons, either," Jordan added. "The forage hasn't been getting through. We should be getting grass soon."

"I hope so. I'm tired of sitting around waiting for the mud to dry. We can only defeat the Yankees during campaigning season. I think we will finally whip them this year, Dick." Pelham was smiling. "I hear they're totally demoralized and most of their two-year volunteers are going home. If we could go north and beat them on their own soil, they would have to give us our independence."

You haven't seen them the way I have, Jordan thought. "Are you looking to break the hearts of the ladies in the North, too, John?" Jordan said trying to change the subject.

"Northern women, bah," was Pelham's reply. "The trouble with the Yankees is their women. They're dowdy and they have no fire. I'll take a Southern girl any day."

"I agree with you on that point," Jordan said with a sigh.

The rest of the trip passed in small talk. Pelham was reading *The History of the War in the Peninsula and Southern France,* Napier's famous account of Wellington's war against the French in Spain. Pelham thought that the defensive lines of the Army of Northern Virginia compared favorably to the defensive lines of Wellington at Torres Vedras. Jordan agreed with him even though he had no idea what or where Torres Vedras was.

The train arrived in Culpeper late. As Pelham looked out on the platform he recognized someone.

"Uh, oh," he said.

"What's the matter, John?" Jordan asked.

"It's Stuart. If he sees me, I'll never get over to the Judge's house."

Jordan thought for a moment. "Why don't you get off the train on the side opposite the platform. I can distract the general by giving him the dispatches I'm carrying."

"I'll be forever in your debt, Dick."

Pelham got up to go to the rear of the coach. "Too late," he said with a groan.

Jordan looked up. The dashing J.E.B. Stuart himself was walking down the aisle.

"John Pelham, what a pleasant surprise," Stuart said. "I assumed you would be on your way to headquarters. All the better. We're going to have a little sport tomorrow. Our scouts tell us that the Yankees are trying to cross the river at Kelly's Ford. General

Fitzhugh Lee assures me that the ford is well protected, but should they manage to get across we'll give them a hearty welcome. Would you like to go along?"

Jordan thought Pelham would be disappointed, but he seemed to brighten. "I'd love to, general."

"Good," Stuart said. "And who is this?" he asked, looking at Jordan. "I feel I should know you."

"Captain Jordan, 'C' Company, Third Virginia Cavalry, sir," Jordan said, identifying himself.

Stuart's smile broadened. "Oh, yes. You've just returned from service with Colonel Longfellow in more northerly latitudes. You'll have to tell me everything. Sometimes I think Longfellow even keeps secrets from me."

Everyone chuckled. Some secret, Jordan thought. They began to file out of the car.

"General," Jordan said. "I have some dispatches from Colonel Longfellow for you."

"Dispatches and reports. I dare say if we spent as much time fighting the enemy as we do making reports we would have whipped them in '61. Very well, have Major Price sign for them, then you can join us for supper."

"I have my horse on the train, sir. I'll be returning to my regiment tonight."

"My boy," Stuart told him. "The Third Virginia can do without you for one more evening."

"Yes sir." Jordan went to get his horse.

As soon as his horse was stabled, Jordan joined the officers of Stuart's entourage at the house of an elderly woman. With Stuart were his servant Jim and Bob Sweeny with his banjo. They had a light supper and retired to the parlor where they clustered around the piano and sang songs. Jordan only knew the words to "Bonnie Blue Flag" and "Lorena", but Stuart knew all the words to all the songs. It constantly amazed Jordan that Stuart, the world's finest cavalry commander, had a beautiful voice. It was a pleasure listening to him.

The gathering broke up early and they went to bed. The cavalry captain and the artillery major shared a room.

"Do you think there'll be some action tomorrow, Dick?" Pelham asked.

"Probably not, John. If Fitzhugh Lee says the ford is secure, it's secure."

"I would like to get into a cavalry charge," Pelham said. "I've never done that before, but I'd like to."

"What about Judge Shackleford?"

"That can wait. I'm sure Miss Shackleford would want me to do my duty before calling on her and her family."

"I suppose you're right," Jordan said. He was looking forward to the morning. By tomorrow afternoon he would be back with the Third Virginia and he could forget about everything except fighting Yankees. He fell into a relaxed sleep.

They were awakened by an orderly at 5:00 A.M.

"The Yankees are at Kelly's Ford," he shouted. "Wake up."

Jordan and Pelham tumbled out of bed and dressed quickly.

"I hope they have a horse for me," Pelham said. He was worried. "I don't want to miss a fight."

"I'm sure the general has one for you," Jordan said to reassure him. "He needs one himself."

Pelham was the first out the door. Jordan followed him downstairs. The officers had assembled in the kitchen. They were drinking chicory coffee and eating coarse bread for breakfast. Jordan only had a sip of the coffee. Without a word they began filing out of the house.

"God bless you boys," the woman told them.

They made their way to the barn where a number of horses were standing. Among them was Jordan's. Pelham's eyes seemed to light up as he mounted the large black mare that Stuart had procured for him. A Stuart's signal they mounted and headed east into the brightening sky. The morning was bitterly cold.

Kelly's Ford, Virginia
March 17, 1863

As Stuart and his party rode to meet General Fitzhugh Lee, nephew of the Commanding General of the Army of Northern Virginia, the Yankees were making their presence felt at the little ford that provided a way across the Rappahanock River. The attack was a reprisal for the raid that Fitzhugh Lee had led across the ford on the 24th of February. Lee had led a force of 400 picked troopers and horses in the raid. He routed the Union

Cavalry at Hartwood and drove them for several miles, killing many in the process. Orders to counter-attack Lee were not obeyed and Lee was able to get his small force away without significant loss, even though his men and horses were very tired. It was the same old story and the Confederates were jubilant.

General Joseph Hooker was not the kind of man to take that sort of thing lying down. He ordered General Averell to launch an attack and destroy Lee's force. When he learned that Lee's force was at Culpeper, Averell planned to do just that, but Lee was ready for him. The wily Confederate cavalry commander was not about to be surprised himself. He had his troops fell trees in the ford and then posted sixty sharpshooters to cover the ford.

What Lee had not counted on was the Yankee desire for revenge and the resources they could throw into the enterprise. At 1:00 A.M. he was notified that there was activity across the river. At 5:00 A.M. he learned that Union forces had attacked the ford with more than 2,000 troopers. Lee alerted his brigade which consisted of the First, Second, Third, Fourth, and Fifth Virginia Cavalry and Breathed's Battery. Unfortunately, he could only mount 800 of his entire brigade due to the condition of the horses. He expected the Yankees to move southwest to Orange Court House. That would have given him time to react. Instead they were heading west toward Culpeper.

It was noon by the time Stuart and Lee and all their men arrived near the ford. By this time the Yankees had swept Lee's sharpshooters aside and cut up the trees blocking the ford. When Lee's brigade came up they found the Yankee force already deployed a half mile from the ford. Jordan didn't wait to hear what the generals were saying. He galloped off to join his regiment. Pelham had already gone to see what he could do to help Breathed's Battery. Jordan was too late to join his company so he fell in at the rear of the regiment with Major McClellan, the adjutant, and drew his saber.

"Looks like you got back just in time, Dick," the major said. "The Yankees have taken up position at Brook's Farm about a half a mile from here."

McClellan pointed in the direction of Brook's Farm and Jordan could see that some of the Yankee cavalry had dismounted and taken up a position behind a stone wall. Their left was anchored in some woods and their right was anchored near the Wheatly Ice House. A staff officer came galloping up to Colonel Owen. Orders were shouted and Bobby Maysfield's company dismounted. They began to move forward as skirmishers. Jordan watched as the skirmishers moved confidently forward. Suddenly the stone wall erupted in smoke. The Yankees with their breech loading carbines began pouring a hail of fire into the hapless dismounted Confederates some of whom began to drop. The Confederates, armed with muzzle loaders, couldn't match the firepower of the Yankee repeaters and began to fall back. Jordan was concerned about Bobby, but he didn't have time to dwell on it.

The order was given to the mounted troops to advance in column of fours. Jordan hated being in the rear of the regiment, but he had no choice. Just as the regiment began moving forward, Pelham came galloping forward. He waved at Jordan and moved toward the front of the column. The bugle sounded the shrill call for a charge and the regiment rapidly picked up speed. They were charging straight for the stone fence lined with Yankees. Jordan couldn't see if there was a gate in the fence or not. Troopers began to fall out of their saddles as the Yankees increased their rate of fire.

The regiment swerved to the left still looking for an opening. The Confederate cavalrymen drew their pistols and traded shots with the Union soldiers behind the wall. The Yankee artillery began to fire. The regiment had found a gate and began pouring through. Pelham stood in his stirrups at the gate and shouted encouragement as the troops galloped past him. Overhead shells burst in the air. Jordan saw Pelham's horse shy and raise up. The young artilleryman tumbled from the saddle and his horse bolted. Jordan reined up without thinking.

Pelham was lying on his back, smiling. His face was covered with soot from the blast. At first Jordan thought he was dead, but Pelham groaned. Jordan couldn't see where the artilleryman was wounded so he tried to lift him up. Pelham's body was totally limp. Jordan heard the sound of the fighting change and he peered over the wall. The Yankees were preparing to counter-charge. A chill ran up his spine. He looked at the Yankee line. It was straight and disciplined. As if they were a single man they drew their sabers. Although he couldn't see their regimental standard Jordan knew this had to be one of the regiments he had seen at Stafford Court House. If he didn't hurry, he and Pelham would be taken prisoner. He tried desperately to get Pelham on his horse, but he couldn't manage it. Just then Major McClellan rode up.

"What's wrong, Dick?"

"It's Major Pelham, sir," Jordan shouted over the din. "He's wounded."

"Good God!"

McClellan dismounted and helped Jordan get Pelham over the bow of the saddle. Jordan mounted and he spurred his horse to the rear. Only then did he notice the wound in the back of Pelham's head. Half a mile south of Newby Shop, Jordan handed Pelham over to other officers and hurried back to his regiment.

Things were getting much hotter. The Yankee cavalry had moved forward almost a mile. The Third Virginia formed and charged again. This was definitely not the Yankee cavalry of old. His own regiment took on the First Rhode Island which was commanded by a dapper little colonel. Jordan's blood was up. He raised his saber and followed his regiment into the melee, angry that he wasn't in the front.

The two units met with a crash. Blue uniforms were everywhere. The sunlight was reflected in the flash of sabers and the air was thick with pistol smoke. Jordan hit one Yankee in the shoulder and the man went down. He ducked as he sensed rather than saw the blow coming from behind. A unknown friend shot the enemy soldier behind him. Then Jordan crossed swords with a Union officer. The man knew how to wield a saber and the two of them dueled for a long time. Jordan cut him at least once and the Yankee cut a deep slice in Jordan's new uniform, but the Third Virginia was being pushed back and the officer he was dueling with was lost in the melee and the dust.

Blue uniforms lapped around him and Jordan knew if he didn't act quickly, he would be surrounded. The captain drew his pistol and looked for a way out. A Yankee lunged for him just as Jordan fired his big .44 caliber revolver. The man's face disappeared and he fell out of the saddle. Jordan pointed his pistol at another Yankee just as the other man raised his pistol and fired. Jordan felt the tug of the bullet as it passed through his sleeve. It was enough to deflect his aim and he missed his target. He saw light and spurred his horse forward, firing twice more before he was clear. He cantered after the regiment as it fell back.

The Third Virginia rallied behind some trenches filled with Confederate infantry and backed up with a battery of artillery. They waited for the Yankees to charge again and press its advantage, but the blue coats hesitated and began to fall back. Soon it was evident that they were withdrawing their artillery. Jordan waited for the order to pursue, but it never came. The Northern troops were allowed to get across the ford unmolested. Jordan felt cheated. They should have pursued. He couldn't know that it was only Averell's caution that had saved Fitzhugh Lee's brigade. The unthinkable had occurred. Yankee cavalry had come looking for trouble, acquitted itself well, and had withdrawn in good order, but the result did not satisfy Hooker. Averell was relieved.

A few days later, Jordan learned the unvarnished truth of what had happened at Kelly's Ford. Only three of Jordan's men had been wounded in the action, but 130 other Confederates had been killed or wounded. The Yankees hadn't suffered near that many casualties. Pelham died of his wound and Stuart wept openly, saying the artilleryman was irreplaceable. Pelham wasn't the only irreplaceable casualty. Jordan was heartsick when he learned that Bobby Maysfield had been killed on the skirmish line that morning.

This was the first time that an intimate friend of Jordan's had been killed in battle and the war was suddenly different and more frustrating. If they had only had enough supplies to keep their horses healthy this would not have happened. They would have been able to put more troopers into the battle and destroy the entire Yankee force. It made Jordan wish he had set fire to Washington while he was there. He took the responsibility of shipping Bobby's body home at his own expense and prepared to write a letter to Mrs. Maysfield. What would he say to her? What would he say to his own mother? Bobby was like another son to her.

When Fitzhugh Lee issued an order congratulating the brigade on its victory at Kelly's Ford, Jordan could hardly believe it. He wondered if the army hierarchy had all gone mad. Longfellow refused to believe the facts behind the Ellison murder and Lee had announced a victory for an action which every trooper knew was a close call.

**The Treasury Department
Washington, D.C.
March 18, 1863**

Salmon P. Chase looked at the ledger and got up from his desk. He walked across the thick carpet to the window and looked out at the snow flurries. It would soon be a full-fledged storm. He had never done a dishonest thing in his life and the thought that he was about to do something that some might consider so, weighed heavily on his conscience. Nevertheless, it had to be done if the Spy were to be paid.

There was also a certain irony in the act. Pinkerton agents had seized over $250,000 in Confederate gold when they caught the Rebel purchasing agent who had been operating in the capital. No one quite knew what to do with it. It didn't fit into any account listed, so the clerk who received it put it in a separate account. The ledger for that account was on Chase's desk. All he had to do was change one digit and the $100,000 required to pay the Spy was his.

In the last bit of good daylight, Chase sat down and took a large magnifying glass from the top of his desk. He held it in his left hand while he picked up a swab moistened with a bleaching solution. Carefully he rubbed it over the "2" in the ledger and it gradually disappeared. He let the paper dry. Half an hour later he inked in a "1" that looked very similar to the original clerk's "1". When the ink was dry the secretary closed the ledger.

The Confederates were paying to kill their own general and they would never know it.

**Colonel Longfellow's Headquarters
March 20, 1863**

Colonel Longfellow stood on the porch of his headquarters and gazed out at the landscape disapprovingly. The entire vista was one endless blanket of white. It had snowed the last two days depositing nearly 10 inches on the ground. All military and civilian traffic had ceased and it would take days before it returned to normal. Regardless, he couldn't wait. He had to have answers and he had to have them quickly. He already had one answer and it wasn't the one he wanted. When Masters had inquired about Ellison's body he spoke with the mortician who had prepared the body for burial. The man had found a .36 caliber pistol ball in Ellison's skull.

Longfellow went back to his desk and penned a dispatch. Most of his colleagues and probably all of the citizens of the Confederacy would have been shocked and outraged if they saw the addressee. It was Major General Henry Halleck, General in Chief, United States Army. Communication between the two sides was not routine but it did happen. Even General Lee had recourse to it occasionally but this was unofficial and if word leaked, Longfellow could be summarily dismissed—or worse. Longfellow knew Halleck before the war. To say that he disliked Halleck was putting it mildly. Halleck was pasty-faced and irritating. However, Halleck had a great intellect, hence his nickname "Old Brains" and he would answer a question honestly. Longfellow decided it was worth the gamble.

March 20, 1863

Dear General Halleck:

During routine military matters evidence has come to our attention of a plot to murder one or more high ranking officers in our army. Since I am convinced that a man of your honor would have no truck with a scheme so utterly opposed to the civilized rules of warfare, I am requesting that you inform me of any evidence you may have of such a dastardly plot should one exist.

Your obedient servant,
RAYMOND LONGFELLOW
Colonel, C.S.A.

Longfellow sealed the letter with wax and tapped it on the desk. He hesitated for a moment.

"Get me Lieutenant Patterson," he called.

Half an hour later the lieutenant was on his way to a designated meeting place where he would hand the dispatch to a Yankee officer whose position in the Union Army was similar to his own. In less than 48 hours the dispatch would be on Halleck's desk.

CHAPTER 8

Colonel Longfellow's Headquarters
March 25, 1863

MASTERS WAVED AS Jordan reined up in front of Colonel Long-fellow's headquarters. The captain tied his horse to the hitching post and stood on the porch while Masters ambled over. The two men shook hands.

"How's it feel to be back in the army, Dick?" Masters asked.

"Very comforting compared to traveling with you, Charley."

"It doesn't look it," Masters said, pointing to the sewn-up slashes in Jordan's uniform. "You need to stop using those Yankee tailors."

"Well, at least he was wearing a different uniform and I knew he was trying to kill me. That's very different from the people you associate with. How are things with you?"

"The same. Actually, it's been kind of dull since you left. The colonel has been most gratified."

Jordan laughed. "I can believe that. Have you any idea why he sent for me?"

"He didn't even tell me you were coming, Dick. I'll bet it's about the Ellison business, but I wouldn't get my hopes up if I were you."

"Let's see what he wants, then."

Jordan and Masters walked into the main room of the head-quarters. Jordan walked through the turmoil and then stopped

for a moment. When he had left the headquarters ten days before, all the maps had been of Virginia. Most of the maps on the
table now were of Maryland and Pennsylvania. Longfellow's door
was open and the colonel waved Jordan in.

"Sit down, Dick," he said pleasantly. He closed the door behind
the captain and offered him a cigar.

Jordan accepted the cigar and lit it with a match from a box on
the colonel's desk.

"I have some good news, Dick. It seems that your assassin was
just a ploy to frighten Lydia Ratliffe," Longfellow said. He sounded very sure of himself.

Jordan stopped in mid-puff and looked at him.

"I have proof," Longfellow said reassuringly. "But I have to
have your promise that once you've seen this you'll forget it and
not discuss this matter again.

"Of course, sir."

Longfellow handed Jordan the dispatch.

> HEADQUARTERS, WAR DEPARTMENT
> March 23, 1863
>
> Dear Colonel Longfellow:
>
> Reference your letter on the 20th instant. I have this day
> discussed the matter with the Secretary and he confirms that
> at no time has there ever been any plan to carry out any form
> of warfare other than that ascribed to by civilized nations.
>
> Your Humble Servant,
> HENRY W. HALLECK
> General in Chief
> U.S.A.

Jordan's jaw dropped and his cigar fell to the floor. He had seen
too many captured dispatches and knew too much about Longfellow to doubt that the dispatch was genuine. He didn't even ask
how Longfellow happened to be able to correspond with the head
of the Yankee army.

"In addition to this," Longfellow continued, "there is not now,
nor has there ever been a Major Harvey Ferris in the 18th North
Carolina or any other unit in the Army of Northern Virginia.

"In fairness, I have to admit you were correct in the manner of

Major Ellison's wounds. He was indeed killed with a .36 caliber pistol, but that seems to be the only part of your theory that was correct. I appreciate your concern and your services, but I think we can put this whole business safely behind us."

Jordan sat there staring at the colonel. Longfellow couldn't possibly believe what he was saying. He was ignoring the entire reasoning behind the murder of Ellison.

"As far as the murder of Ellison," Longfellow continued. "We can only assume that his death was the result of some personal matter. Perhaps it was an affair concerning Mrs. Ratliffe. We shall probably never know. I am now convinced that there is no plot to assassinate General Lee, and, I imagine so are you."

Jordan mumbled a "Yes sir," and rose to leave. Longfellow opened the door for him and wished him good luck. Once he was gone, Longfellow opened the top of the stove and dropped the dispatch from Halleck inside. He felt genuinely relieved. Now he could concentrate on the invasion of Pennsylvania.

Jordan walked out on the porch in a daze. Masters watched him for a moment then walked up. "Let me guess. There is no plot to assassinate General Lee."

Jordan grinned crookedly. "That's what he says and he's got a lot of evidence to prove it."

"But you still believe the plot exists, don't you, Dick?"

"Yes, Charley, I do." Jordan let out a huge sigh. "In fact, I'm more convinced than ever that a plot does exist. I just don't know what I can do about it."

"Let's walk," Masters said.

They headed away from the house and the barn toward a nearby grove. The ground was partially covered with melting snow and their boots squished as they walked.

"What did he tell you?" Masters asked.

Jordan told him briefly what had happened, but left out the note from Halleck. Masters looked out toward the snow-covered fields and was silent for a moment. Then he continued.

"He's been awfully concerned with this Pennsylvania offensive, Dick," he said. "I'm sure if it weren't for that he'd give it more attention. He's been under a lot of strain lately."

Jordan tried to understand what Masters was feeling. The sergeant obviously admired Longfellow and he was having a difficult time coping with the fact that the colonel may have made a grievous error. Jordan put his hand on Masters' shoulder.

"One man can't do everything, Charley, and he can't be right all the time. He's only human."

"I know, but why can't he see this?" Masters asked. He was almost pleading for an answer. "I know you're right, Dick. The more I think about it, the more I know it. The man we're dealing with is a snake. He's laying out there hibernating, waiting for spring to strike at his prey. When he does strike it will come at the worst possible time."

"Then how do we find him and how do we stop him?" The question was serious.

"Just the two of us?" Masters asked.

"Who else? To whom can we turn? The only man who can help us is convinced there's no danger. What else can we do?"

"I really don't know. But how do we find a man we don't know, then recognize him and expose him for what he is? If Major Ferris is a disguise you may not even know him the next time you see him."

"True. It's all true, but we have to try, Charley. Even if it's just the two of us. We have to keep our eyes and ears open. That's all I think we can do right now. You're a lot more experienced in this sort of thing than I am. What do you think we should do?"

"I don't know, Dick. I'm as stymied as you are. If I think of anything, I'll let you know, all right?"

"Sure." Jordan was feeling deflated and there was nothing either of them could do about it.

Jordan and Masters walked back to the house and Jordan mounted his horse.

"Good luck, Dick, and stay away from those Yankee tailors," Masters said, managing a grin.

"I'll try," the captain said.

Just Charley and I against this assassin, Jordan thought. It didn't seem like very good odds. None of us knows the other, but I saw him once. Jordan tried hard to remember the details of Ferris' face. He could recall every detail of Jennifer's face and hands and the clean scent of her skin that morning, but the major's face was just a blur.

Second Corps
Army of Northern Virginia
March 27, 1863

The soldiers looked up as they heard the sound of hoofbeats in the camp. The gray day was dying and the sound was unusual. They were not the hurried hoofbeats of a dispatch rider's horse. Neither were they the sound of a team pulling a wagon. To those familiar with animals, and there were more than a few among the North Carolina troops of A.P. Hill's Light Division, they were the hoofbeats of a mule.

Soldiers poked their heads out of tents and huts to see what the mule carried. A captured Yankee mule might mean extra rations. The North Carolina men were disappointed in the mule and its rider. The animal was one of those universally known as a Missouri Mule, but it no longer exhibited any of those characteristics that made the breed famous. Instead of possessing a shiny black coat with a powerful body, this one was swayback and its coat was gray with age. The rider was no prize either. He wore an old top hat and had a blanket thrown around his shoulders to ward off the rain and the cold. The reins he clutched were made of rope and there were pathetically few belongings strapped to the cheap, worn saddle.

"He damn sure ain't a peddler," said an infantry corporal. His voice had the pleasant twang of eastern Carolina.

"I'll bet he's another preacher," a sergeant said taking a chew of tobacco.

Most of his comrades nodded sagely. The man did look like one of the hundreds of itinerant preachers who visited the army. In October of 1862 a large revival movement had sprung up and it was sweeping through the Confederate forces. Since few regiments had chaplains assigned, itinerant and volunteer clergy were welcome. They assisted by preaching and baptizing those who wished to draw closer to Christ. It was sometimes questionable how much good it did. Officers still reported that their camps were rife with card playing, gambling, drinking, and other diversions known to soldiers since biblical times. Nevertheless, devout commanders such as Robert E. Lee and Thomas J. "Stonewall" Jackson encouraged the revival to continue.

The mule rider stopped by a group of soldiers and tipped the worn beaver hat. "Good evening, gentlemen," he said. His voice was soft and raspy. "Could you please tell me where I might find the Reverend Lacy's dwellings?"

The soldiers looked at him, mildly bemused. "Over yonder is headquarters," one of them answered. He pointed to a house with light showing in the windows. "They can tell you where he is."

"I am obliged to you," the man said returning his hat to his head. "God bless you." He put his heels in the mule's flanks and it plodded forward.

"Preacher," the sergeant said, spitting into the fire.

The Reverend Dr. Beverly Tucker Lacy was the most unusual man in either of the armies facing each other across the Rappahannock. He alone was responsible for the revival sweeping the Confederate army. Since there was no official chaplain of the army, Lacy's good friend and parishioner, General Stonewall Jackson, had made him unofficial chaplain-in-chief of the Second Corps. In addition to weekly services and sermons, Lacy was responsible for coordinating efforts among the various denominations and faiths, insuring that regiments that did not have chaplains were visited by clergy whenever possible.

Lacy was well thought of throughout the army. He was an ardent secessionist and a raconteur. These attributes combined to make his sermons anything but dull. After one of Lacy's sermons the audience usually broke up into groups which held long, and sometimes heated discussions about the sermon. This was especially true among Jackson's officers, many of whom looked upon a Lacy sermon as the high point of the week. Lacy and Jackson shared morning devotions daily in Lacy's tent.

On that Friday evening of March 27, Lacy was very tired. Coordinating a revival as large as the one now taking place was a strenuous chore. It was one he performed gladly, but found the resistance of some of the generals very frustrating. General A. P. Hill was one of those he would have liked to have on his side. It wasn't that the Light Division commander prevented his men from taking part in the revival, it was just that he refused to take any of it seriously. Perhaps Hill's attitude was due to the harsh feelings between him and Jackson. On occasion Jackson could be most unforgiving, yet he was a great man and a great general. He was the sword of the Confederacy and a good Christian. Lacy put down his pen and rubbed his eyes. He decided he must get to bed early this evening. Saturday was a busy day and he had to get ready for his sermon on Sunday.

"Reverend," his aide said entering the tent. "There's someone here to see you."

"Who is it?"

"He says his name is Jeremiah Bailey, and he has letters of introduction from Dr. Israel Wilkinson of Chattanooga. He's a little on the shabby side," the aide emphasized.

Lacy smiled. Dr. Wilkinson was an old colleague and dear friend. They had spent many pleasant evenings debating scripture. Lacy had not heard from Wilkinson in months. Anyone recommended by Dr. Wilkinson would be more than welcome.

"Show him in," Lacy said eagerly.

"But . . . " the aide said.

"Show him in," Lacy repeated.

Lacy's jaw dropped slightly when his aide led the man into the tent. The visitor was hardly the type of man Lacy would expect to be bearing letters of introduction from Israel Wilkinson. But these were unusual times and, Lacy reminded himself, one must always maintain a Christian and not a worldly view of others.

"Reverend Lacy?" the man asked, removing his hat. He looked briefly at Lacy and then shyly toward the floor. "I am Jeremiah Bailey. These letters will explain my presence here." He handed Lacy two sealed envelopes.

"Please sit down," Lacy said gesturing toward a folding chair near his table.

As the man sat down Lacy took a few seconds to look at him. He was one of those young men who look very old. He wore a worn, but clean dark brown frock coat over a patched, checked shirt. His trousers were Yankee light blue, a fashion adopted by many on both sides. His shoes were black and well-worn. His watch fob was a shoe lace. His face was intriguing. He was clean shaven and there were signs of premature aging in his pale and wan face. It looked as if the man were a heavy drinker and there were bags under his eyes. Despite that, Bailey had an expression of utmost sincerity and perhaps piety. He sat with his hands folded, gazing curiously around the tent. When he saw Lacy looking at him, he smiled nervously. He looked tired and hungry.

"Please get Mr. Bailey a cup of coffee," Lacy told his aide.

Both the aide and Bailey looked surprised.

Lacy looked at the envelopes and recognized the handwriting immediately. He opened the first and read it.

> Chattanooga
> March 19th 1863
>
> My Dear Tucker,
>
> My humblest apologies for not writing. As you are well aware, these are not the best of times. The bearer of this letter carries a personal one for you so I shan't dwell on those things here.
>
> This letter of introduction is for Mr. Jeremiah Edward Bailey who was born in Paw Paw, Virginia, but until recently served in the Army of the Tennessee, where he was mustered out after suffering a wound in the right lung. His story is quite remarkable and I would prefer he tell it to you personally. He is proof that the Lord still walks among us. He would like to go home, but of course he cannot since it is occupied by the enemy. Since he can neither serve as a soldier nor go home he has asked to be of use in the army of his home state. He has been of great use to us here and we wanted him to stay, but a man does wish to be among his kin. Speak with him and find useful work for him. He will be an inspiration to those around him.
>
> > Your devoted friend in Christ,
> > I. WILKINSON, REV.

Lacy put the letter down and looked at Bailey. "The Reverend Wilkinson speaks very highly of you, Mr. Bailey, but he doesn't say why. He wants you to tell me your story."

Bailey shifted uncomfortably in the chair and looked back at Lacy. "The reverend is a wonderful man. He was most kind in writing the letters and I would appreciate any useful work you have for me to do." The aide brought the coffee and Bailey thanked them both for the kindness. He cradled the cup of chicory coffee as if it were the most priceless of gifts and continued. "I am not an educated man or a man of means. I am, in fact a sinner, reverend. In my youth I killed a man in an argument over a woman of easy virtue and ran away to Tennessee. I was—am—a drunkard. I was drunk when I volunteered for the 12th Tennessee. I don't suppose I was a very good soldier, but I wasn't a coward. Last December I was shot in the lung at the Battle of Murfreesboro. The doctor told me I was going to die. They told me I was unconscious for days and they expected me to go any minute, but during the time I was unconscious God spoke to me."

Lacy was deeply impressed by the man's sincerity. "What did He say, Mr. Bailey?"

"It wasn't like He said anything. There was this bright light inside my soul and while it was there I felt . . . I guess uplifted is the word but that don't come close. He made me realize that I was a sinner, but the most uplifting part was that I knew I could redeem myself. Never was I threatened with eternal damnation or punishment. Before I had been so empty, but when His spirit entered me I felt whole and I knew that to be empty again would be worse than damnation."

Lacy didn't say a word. There could be no doubt that Jeremiah Bailey was telling the truth. There was an aura about the man that you could almost touch. Despite his other misfortunes, Lacy envied Bailey's encounter with The Redeemer.

"How may I assist you, Mr. Bailey?"

"It is I who want to assist you, reverend. Reverend Wilkinson was kind enough to find me place in a hospital as an orderly. I had no training in that direction, but I seem to have an aptitude for it and the work gives me great comfort."

"I'll talk to Dr. McGuire in the morning. Until then I assume you are tired from your journey. I will find a place for you and something to eat. Do you have a horse?"

"I have a mule, sir."

"Then we will find a place for your mule also." Lacy called his orderly.

"Yes sir?"

"Find Mr. Bailey a place to stay and bring him here tomorrow morning."

"Yes, sir. Follow me, Mr. Bailey."

Doctor Hunter McGuire was to medicine in the Second Corps what the Reverend Lacy was to religion. General Jackson may have been eccentric but his staff were not. They were honest competent men who thought very highly of their chief. The doctor did not question Bailey about his religion or his motives when Bailey was brought to him in the morning. The army always needed medical orderlies and he was happy to get one.

"I'm recommending you to the army hospital south of Fredericksburg, Mr. Bailey."

"Thank you, doctor," Bailey said graciously.

"Don't thank me until you've seen it," McGuire said. "It's a vile place and if I had my way, I'd burn it down and shoot the staff. Unfortunately, the hospital is not within my area of authority."

"The Lord will find a way, doctor. I suspect that is why he led me here."

"Good luck, then, Mr. Bailey."

Bailey mounted his mule and rode to the hospital. He quickly discovered that Dr. McGuire was not exaggerating. The hospital was a converted barn and it stank. It reeked not only from leftover manure, but also from rotten bandages, festering wounds, and human excrement. In addition, there was only one small stove to heat the large mass of the barn. Bailey walked into the place and down the rows of pallets. Three of the patients had been dead for at least two days and had not been moved. The patients who were alive were filthy and vermin-ridden. He found one surly orderly sitting by the stove trying to keep warm. There was no doctor to be seen.

"Who is in charge here?" he asked the orderly.

"Doctor Lingle," was the man's reply.

"Where is he?"

"Verdiersville, I guess."

"What is he doing in Verdiersville?"

"He knows a woman there."

"That makes you the one in charge, doesn't it?"

"Of this mess?" the orderly said. "Not on your life."

"Then that puts me in charge."

"Yeah I guess it does."

"Then pick up that ax."

"What for?"

"You're going to chop some wood."

"Why? I already have enough."

"Your patients don't."

The orderly looked at him for a moment. He looked as if he were about to say something, but he picked up the ax and went out to chop wood. Bailey turned to the patients. They were staring at him.

"Which of you can walk?" he asked.

"If we could walk, do you think we'd stay here?" asked one man dressed in rags.

"No, I don't suppose you would, but this place is a mess and the Lord helps those that help themselves," Bailey told them.

"You a preacher?" one of the men asked.

"No sir. I'm just another child of God, like all of you. Now, I need anyone who can walk and carry."

"Hell, I guess I can," one man wrapped in a filthy blanket said.

"Me, too," others said.

"Let's find some buckets. We need water to clean this place up."

Some of the soldiers started to move. Bailey moved through the mass of prostrate men. Several of them were obviously dying and there was nothing he could do for them. Many were so weak that they were laying in their own excrement. He had to have clean straw and blankets as well as food and medicine, but that would come later. Now he had to save as many men as he possibly could by making them care enough to save themselves.

"Help me please," cried a pathetic voice.

"What's your name, son?"

"Gilbert, Horace Gilbert. I haven't had any water. Please may I have some water?"

Bailey pulled back the man's blanket. He had a bad stomach wound and would probably die very soon. "I can't give you water, son. Just a minute." Bailey wet a cloth and put it to the man's lips. He sucked it greedily.

"Can you write a letter for me, mister?"

"Certainly, let me get a pencil and paper." Bailey returned with a pencil and paper and wrote the letter that Gilbert dictated. It was a simple goodbye to his mother in Alabama. Gilbert was dead before nightfall.

The rest of the day was no different. Counting the three who were already dead, they carried out ten before the next morning. With the help of four men who could walk and others who could crawl, Bailey had some of the floors cleaned. At four in the morning he fell asleep by the stove, totally exhausted. The rations arrived at 6:00 A.M. The meal consisted of nothing more than watery gruel and some bitter chicory coffee that was hardly worth drinking. Bailey continued to clean.

At 8:00 A.M. he left without a word. Everyone assumed he had just become discouraged and quit. Six hours later he returned with a wagon full of clean hay and pine needles. He made each man in turn empty his mattress, wash it, and dry it by the stove. Then, he had them wash the rags they called clothes and their bodies. It was a long process because all of the clothing and blankets had to be dried by the stove. He needed more stoves. He left again one morning and returned with enough pieces to patch together three stoves. They weren't pretty but they worked.

It was then that Bailey could begin paying attention to the wounded. He began by bathing those who couldn't move. The sores on their bodies were large and festered, but Bailey persisted. Patients who could walk or crawl helped him. From his meager belongings, he produced some cheap pens and paper as well as some ink. These he gave freely to those who needed them. On the first of April, less than a week from the time he arrived, he held a service. All of his patients took part. From that time on, Bailey was affectionately known by the patients as "The Reverend." He still had not seen Dr. Lingle.

The only doctor to visit the hospital was the tireless Dr. McGuire who was curious to see how Bailey was doing. He was amazed at the results Bailey had achieved.

"This place has improved immensely, Mr. Bailey. I take it Dr. Lingle is pleased with your efforts."

"I wouldn't know, doctor," Bailey said shyly.

"What do you mean you don't know?"

"Well . . . " Bailey hesitated.

"What he means," the orderly interrupted, "is that we ain't seen the doctor since before the reverend come here. He done this all hisself."

McGuire looked around at the group of patients who had gathered in curiosity.

"That's right, doctor," another volunteered. "He got us stoves and fresh straw."

"Bailey done it all."

McGuire fumed. "This may not be my area of responsibility, but I'm going to see this condition corrected. I promise you that! I commend you for your efforts, Mr. Bailey."

"I cannot take credit, doctor. It is the Lord's work. God bless you."

A short time later, Dr. Lingle was arrested at his mistress' house and charged with dereliction of duty. Dr. Amos Warren, a pleasant and enthusiastic man with experience in running a large hospital, was appointed as head of the Fredericksburg Army Hospital. He was conscientious and thorough and reported that dozens, if not scores of men would have died had it not been for the efforts of Mr. Bailey. He requested that Mr. Bailey remain as his chief orderly. Stories of Bailey's works spread from the hospital to the camp. He rapidly became a legend in the Army of Northern Virginia. One afternoon, he was summoned to Headquarters of the 2nd Corps. The Reverend Lacy was one of the persons waiting in the room. Bailey removed his hat and looked at Lacy.

"I was summoned here from the hospital, reverend," Bailey, said sounding somewhat fearful. "I trust that I haven't done anything to upset anyone."

Lacy laughed warmly. "No, my dear sir. Believe me you have upset no one. There is someone here who has wanted meet you, that is all."

Lacy turned to a man in a gray uniform with lots of gold braid. He had kindly eyes and a full beard. "General Jackson, this is the man I told you of. Mr. Bailey, I'd like you to meet General Jackson."

The general stepped forward and extended his hand.

"*The* General Jackson? *Stonewall* Jackson?" Bailey's voice was incredulous. Tears began to roll down his cheeks as he shook hands with the great general. His voice was choked with emotion. "Oh, this is an honor, sir. A great honor."

"The honor is all mine, Mr. Bailey. The reverend here told me of your transformation and the fine work you have done at the hospital."

"It is not my work, general; it is the work of God. I am but an insignificant agent of His will."

The general smiled warmly. "If it will not take you away from your important work, Mr. Bailey, the Reverend Lacy and I would be honored if you would take morning devotions with us and then we could, perhaps, discuss some of your experiences with us."

"The honor would be all mine, general, I assure you."

"Fine, then shall we say Sunday next?"

"Yes sir. And thank you." Bailey wiped the tears from his eyes, bowed slightly, and backed out of the room.

"I see what you mean, reverend," Jackson told Lacy after Bailey had gone. "He is truly a remarkable man. He is uneducated, yet he is obviously in a state of Grace. He is an example that many of our soldiers should be exposed to. The Lord does indeed work in mysterious ways."

"Amen, general, amen."

Headquarters
Third Virginia Cavalry
March 31, 1863

March 31 was a bad day for Richard Jordan. It had nothing to do with the war or with the Yankees. It was the end of the month and, because of his assignment with Colonel Longfellow, he was behind in his reports. On top of that it was payday. Normally, Lieutenant Hall would have taken care of that chore, but he had been seriously wounded at Kelly's Ford, leaving Jordan to handle all of the company administration himself. The reports were especially difficult because they had to contain the results of the action at the ford. "C" Company had gotten off lightly. Besides Lieutenant Hall, the only other serious casualty had been Private Wilkins who had died of his wounds. Jordan had just completed writing a letter to the man's family. The entire regiment had suffered a loss of fifty-one horses and that hurt. Fortunately, the men of "C" Company were more adept at picking up battlefield strays than others, so "C" had come out of the action only a few horses short. Among the other prizes they captured were some of the new Spencer carbines. They were wonderful weapons but there was not enough ammunition available to make them worth carrying. Jordan was nearly finished with the report on the condition of his horses when Simpkins interrupted.

"Begging the captain's pardon, Sir, but the regimental commander requests his presence immediately," the orderly said, saluting smartly.

Jordan returned the salute and stared out the open flap of the tent. What does the colonel want me for? Was there something he had done wrong or overlooked? Captains were seldom called before august persons like regimental commanders for a polite cup of tea. He had already told the adjutant that his reports would be late so that couldn't be it. He quickly tried to remember what he might or might not have done as he buckled his belt and put on his saber. Jordan thrust his hat on his head and walked smartly across the muddy field to the headquarters tent. Major McClellan, the adjutant, looked up from his paperwork as Jordan entered the tent. His expression was grim. When Jordan looked around at the other officers and the clerks, they refused to meet his gaze. Jordan swallowed hard.

"Captain Jordan to see Colonel Owen," he told the major.

McClellan nodded toward the flap that separated the colonel's portion of the tent from the adjutant's. Jordan screwed up his courage.

"What's happening, sir?" he asked McClellan.

The major shook his head. "I'm afraid the colonel will have to explain this one, captain."

Captain? Major McClellan always called him "Dick."

The major pushed the tent flap back. "Captain Jordan, sir."

Jordan stepped before the colonel's desk and reported. The colonel looked positively hostile.

"I'm glad to see you are at least prompt, captain," Colonel Owen said.

Captain again. This time it sounded almost nasty. The colonel picked up a sheaf of papers on his desk. All Jordan could see from his vantage point were that they looked very official.

"Captain Jordan," the colonel said solemnly. "I feel it is only fair that we review the facts of this case before we begin the proceedings."

Facts? Proceedings? Wasn't he allowed counsel? Maybe I should ask for counsel, Jordan thought. He decided to wait until the charges were read.

"On March 1, 1863, Captain Jordan was attached to Headquarters, Cavalry Division, Army of Northern Virginia, for special duty . . . " The colonel droned on, listing everything Jordan had done from the time he left until Kelly's Ford. Jordan tried to understand what negative connotations there were to the list of events. It must be more serious than he thought.

" . . . In addition to these accomplishments, Captain Jordan acted with great heroism in the recovery of a wounded comrade under fire.

"I hereby authorize the promotion of said Captain Jordan to the brevet rank of major.

"Signed James A. Seddon, Secretary of War and Robert E. Lee, General Commanding."

Jordan was standing rigidly. He was so prepared for the question "Guilty or Not Guilty?" that it took a moment for what the colonel had said to sink in. When he saw the colonel chuckling and the major laughing his cheeks began to burn. As soon as the colonel began to pump his hand in congratulations, Jordan began laughing, too. They had had a good joke at his expense and they carried it off perfectly. It had been worth it.

"Congratulations, Dick," the colonel said, getting serious for a moment. "But, unfortunately you won't be staying with us."

"What do you mean, sir?"

"You are now a major and we have no opening for a major in the regiment. Second Corps needs an assistant adjutant in the Light Division and you have been tentatively selected for that position. It's a grand chance for you to move up. The Light Division has a great reputation."

"I really don't want to leave the Third, sir." Jordan was slightly dismayed.

"I'm gratified to hear that, Dick, but this is the army. Powell Hill is a good man and his star is rising. You'll have a great future with him, I'm sure."

For a moment Jordan was tempted to decline the promotion in order to stay in the regiment, but he had been in the army long enough to want to advance and this was his chance.

"Thank you for your confidence, sir. If you will allow me, I have some Cuban cigars in my tent."

"Cuban?" The colonel looked at Major McClellan.

"I don't think we ought to ask where he got them, sir," the major said.

"I think you're right. Cuban, eh? By all means."

When Jordan returned the officers relieved him of most of Albert Graham's good cigars and they produced a jug that Jordan knew would be drunk at his expense. War or no war, there were certain military customs that could not be overlooked and one of those was that the promoted officer always buys the whiskey and the cigars.

Jordan found it difficult to say goodbye. He even found it difficult to bid Simpkins farewell. He signed the company over to a lieutenant from "A" Company and went to headquarters to pick up his orders. He grinned when he saw the date. He was not due to report until the second of April. That gave him a day en route and Oakview Manor was on the way. He saddled one horse and packed his few possessions on the spare. He was on his way before the afternoon began to fade.

Jennifer decided to write Jordan a letter. It had been a few weeks since he had visited her and she wanted to see him again. She wanted the letter to be a carefully worded invitation for him to visit her again. She didn't want to seem too anxious to see him yet she wanted him to know that he was welcome. She had started the letter twice, pondered what she had written, and decided to start over. She carefully tore off the imperfectly written parts and saved the good paper. It was too expensive and too scarce to waste. She was thinking of the way she would word the next version when Sarah entered the room.

"I don't think you're going to need that letter, Miss Jennifer," Sarah said.

"Why?"

"Because Captain Jordan is riding this way right now."

"What? Are you sure?" Jennifer got up, went to the window, and peered out. He was so close that there could be no doubt. "Sarah, would you see to it that the captain is entertained?" Jennifer disappeared into her bedroom.

"Yes ma'am," Sarah said.

Jordan dismounted and gave Coppy his horse. He ascended the wide steps to the house with mixed feelings of excitement and apprehension. What if she didn't want to see him? The rush of panic passed quickly, and before he could knock on the door, Sarah opened it.

"Good evening, Captain Jordan," she said bowing graciously. "Welcome to Oakview Manor. Have you come to call on Miss Jennifer?"

Jordan smiled at the pre-war formality. "Yes, Sarah, I have. Is Mrs. Franks at home?"

"Please come in. I'll tell her you're here."

Jordan entered and the same man came to take his coat, hat, and saber.

"If you wouldn't mind waiting in the parlor, captain, I'll bring you some more of that wicked Yankee coffee."

"I'd love some, Sarah. Thank you."

Sarah disappeared in the direction of the kitchen. Jordan, expecting a long wait for Jennifer, went to the bookcase to see if he could find something to read. Sarah returned with the coffee and he perused a book on agronomy. He wondered if he could ever be a gentleman farmer like Tom Franks. He was leafing through the book when he felt Jennifer's presence in the room. He looked up and there she was, floating in the room, a beautiful apparition. Suddenly he realized it was really her. He jumped to his feet blushing.

"I . . ."

She stood there in a brown merino skirt and a white linen blouse open at the neck. Around her shoulders was a crimson silk shawl.

"It's nice to see you again, Dick," she said, extending both her hands to him.

He took her hands in his and kissed them. He stood for a moment looking at her smiling face. "You look beautiful," he whispered. Her face, the feel of her hands, and the scent of her perfume were almost more than he could bear. He drew her to him and pressed his lips to hers. Then he dropped her hands and encircled her waist with his arms. Any fears he may have had melted when her arms went around her neck.

"I was writing you a letter," she said softly. She leaned her head against his shoulder.

"What did it say?"

"I wanted to see you again."

"I always answer the letters of the woman I love, promptly and in person," he said with a chuckle.

"Do you mean that?"

"What?"

"That you love me."

"With all my heart."

"I love you, too, Dick."

He kissed her again and the war, the spies, and the assassin were forgotten.

"How long can you stay, Dick?"

"Just for tonight. I'm on my way to my new assignment."

"What new assignment?"

"It slipped my mind," he said, blushingly. "I've been breveted a major. I've been assigned as an assistant adjutant to the Light Division."

"A major? That's wonderful!" Jennifer stepped back, looked at him with a scowl, and shook her head.

"What's wrong?" he asked.

"You're out of uniform, major," she said with mock severity.

"What?" He looked at his boots and coat.

She put her finger on his collar. "I'm an army widow, remember? Three bars doth not a major make."

Jordan blushed. He had completely forgotten. He couldn't report to his new assignment with the wrong rank on his collar, but where was he going to get a pair of gold stars to show his proper rank?

"Give me your tunic," she said.

"What?"

"Give me your tunic."

"But . . . "

Jennifer reached over and began undoing the gilt buttons on his gray coat.

"The servants," Jordan said, blushing.

"If it bothers you that much, I'll stop," she said.

"Sarah," she called.

"Yes ma'am," Sarah said, appearing from nowhere.

"Would you get old Mr. Franks' smoking jacket? It should fit Cap . . . Major Jordan. I think it's in the trunk with his clothes."

"Major?" Sarah asked with obvious pleasure. "Congratulations, sir."

"Thank you, Sarah," Jordan replied, bowing graciously.

Sarah disappeared and returned with a burgundy silk smoking jacket. "This belonged to my late father-in-law," Jennifer explained. "It will be a little large on you because he was portly. Tom's clothes wouldn't fit you. You're too large in the shoulders. Now, the tunic please."

Jordan removed the tunic, handed it to Jennifer, and put on the smoking jacket. It was large in the middle but it fit.

"Have a seat. Sarah and I will return in a minute."

Jordan returned to his book on agronomy. He was amazed that there were so many different kinds of dirt. He didn't know how long she was gone, but when she returned, his tunic had the gold star of a major on each side of his collar.

"Try this on," she said. "I took the stars off one of Tom's old uniforms."

Jordan put the tunic back on and went in front of a mirror. Was that really him wearing major's stars?

"Now take it off again. I'll have one of the women clean it and press it. Besides, I like you in the smoking jacket."

Jordan grinned and removed the tunic. He put on the smoking jacket as Jennifer gave the tunic to Sarah. "Have Jewel patch up these cuts, clean it, and press it."

"Yes, ma'am."

When they were alone, Jennifer looked at him with a concerned expression. "Those are saber cuts, aren't they?"

"Yes," he said.

She trembled slightly and he pulled her close again. She slid into his embrace, putting her arms around his waist. She said nothing. Jordan thought she was thinking about Tom Franks, but she was thinking about him. Was it wrong to care so much so fast?

"Would you like supper, Dick?"

"That would be nice," he said, not really willing to let her leave his arms.

"I'll be back in a minute," she said slipping away.

Supper was simple fare compared to the lavish meals served at Oakview Manor prior to the war. It was simply boiled chicken with cornbread and yams. Jordan didn't care. He was so happy he really didn't care what he was eating. He would have been content to just look at Jennifer. They spoke of pleasant things before the war and the plans they had for after the war. Jordan was screwing up his courage to ask her to marry him when he was reminded of a very ugly part of the present—Major Harvey Ferris.

"Jennifer, when I left last time, I met someone headed this way. He was a major named Harvey Ferris. Did he stop here by any chance?"

Jennifer froze. Her cheeks flushed as she remembered the shameless way Harvey Ferris kissed her. A hundred questions raced through her mind. Did Dick know about Ferris and her? How could he? Should I lie to keep him?

Jordan looked at Jennifer. She seemed so far away.

"Jennifer?" Jordan asked.

"Yes?" She returned to the present. "I'm sorry. I was far away. What did you say?"

"Did a Major Ferris stop here after I left?"

I can't lie, she thought. If he knows we might as well end whatever we have right now. "Yes, he did."

"I don't know how to tell you this," he said.

Jennifer stiffened in panic.

"I—that is we—think he's a spy."

Jennifer looked at him. He was concerned about Ferris as a spy, not her paramour. Relief flooded her. "A spy?" She began to cry.

"I'm sorry, Jennifer," Jordan said, rising and moving to her side. He put his arm around her. " I didn't mean to frighten you."

Jennifer buried her face in his arm. "It's all right," she said. "Believe me it's all right." One day, she vowed, she would tell him, but not now.

Jennifer stopped crying and wiped her eyes. "A spy?"

"Yes," he said. "Can you tell me anything about him, that might help us catch him?"

"Not really," she said. "He was really quite ordinary." Jennifer wondered if she sounded convincing. "He was of medium height, brown hair, and gray eyes."

"Gray eyes?"

"Yes," she said, remembering Ferris' almost hypnotic gaze. "It seemed like he could look right into your soul."

"Hmm." Jordan pondered the information. "Gray eyes. That's something anyway."

"What has he done, Dick?"

"Nothing that we know of so far," he said. "We're trying to find him before he does, but he seems to have vanished into thin air. Did he say where he was going?"

"To Culpeper to deliver dispatches to General Fitzhugh Lee, I think," Jennifer said. That checked with what Ferris told the pickets.

"Do you remember anything else he may have said?"

Jennifer told Jordan what she knew about Ferris, but there weren't any hard facts. Ferris probably lied to her the way he lied to him and the pickets. Jordan tried to imagine what else someone like Ferris would be doing behind Confederate lines, but the only thing a cold-blooded killer could be doing was planning a murder. Since that was the case, why was Ferris waiting so long and where was he hiding? Could he really wait that long? Where could he hide almost indefinitely? Eventually someone was bound to notice that he wasn't who he said he was or that he really didn't belong. Socially, an army is a very small place. Everyone went through a rite of passage and there were hundreds of personal relationships. Any new person would be asked what regiment he came from and there was invariably someone who asked if the newcomer knew so-and-so from his old regiment. That kind of society made it nearly impossible for a stranger to walk in and establish himself. You had to belong. You couldn't just pretend. How Ferris could disappear within the army was a puzzle Jordan still had to solve.

Jennifer watched him without saying a word. This was a side of Jordan she had never seen before. He was so engrossed in the problem of Ferris he hardly realized she was there. On the one hand she was impressed that he was obviously a much deeper and more thoughtful person than he seemed outwardly. On the other hand, she didn't like being ignored for a spy who had done nothing and who could not be found.

"Would you like a brandy, Dick?"

At first he didn't respond so she repeated the question.

"Oh, sorry. I guess I just have a lot on my mind. Yes, I'll have a brandy."

Jennifer rang a small bell and a servant appeared. "Bring two brandies please, Caesar."

"Yes, ma'am," he said. In a moment he was back with two snifters.

Jordan was delighted with the amber liquid. It was so much smoother than the cognac Masters had given him. "This is wonderful, Jennifer."

"Tom had it imported from France before the war."

She was talking about Tom Franks as if he were just an old friend and it made Jordan feel self-conscious. But he said nothing. It was best having Tom Franks out in the open than in the shadows.

"I'd like to go for a walk," he said.

"It's a bit too cold to go outside tonight," she said. "But I could show you the rest of the house. You've never seen all of Oakview Manor, have you?"

"No I haven't."

"There's even a room that George Washington slept in."

"Really?"

"So they say."

"I'd love to see it."

Jennifer showed him through the the house. When they came to the room she had let General Stuart use the previous November, he stopped.

"What's the matter?" she asked.

"Nothing's the matter. The first time I saw you was in this room. You were wearing a black dress and you looked so sad."

"I must have looked a fright."

"No, you looked beautiful and I thought how terrible for someone who was so beautiful to be so sad."

Jennifer laughed softly. "Did you really think I was beautiful?"

"No, I think you are beautiful," he said pulling her close to him.

Jennifer didn't resist as he kissed her. She molded her body against his and slid her arms around his neck. For Jordan she was the ultimate woman. She was there clinging to him, his arms encircling her slim waist. He wanted her and the wanting became almost more than he could bear. He kissed her neck and his fingers touched the long, silken softness of her hair. He inhaled the sweet, clean scent of her skin. The temptation was almost too much to bear. Jennifer took his hand and kissed it.

"I love you, Jennifer." He was surprised at the sound of his own voice.

"I love you, Dick," she said holding his hand against her cheek.

"Will you marry me?"

"You don't have to . . ."

"I know I don't have to. I want to. Will you?"

"Give me a little time, please."

"You know I will."

Jennifer showed him the rest of the house and he kissed her goodnight. She seemed a little distant and he wondered if he had acted like a boor. He went to his room and got ready for bed. I'll have to apologize in the morning, he thought. How could I have been such a cad? But she had been so tempting. He climbed beneath the covers and fell asleep wondering how he could make amends before he lost the woman he loved.

At breakfast Jennifer seemed distant and he was at a loss for words, especially with the servants around. Suddenly they were alone and he was terrified. It took all his willpower to say her name.

"Jennifer . . ."

She looked at him and he couldn't tear his eyes away from hers. "Yes?"

"About last night . . ."

A hint of a smile passed her lips and she blushed.

"If you still want to, Dick, the answer is yes."

CHAPTER 9

Old Orange Turnpike
April 2, 1863

RICHARD JORDAN RODE away from Oakview Manor aware that his life had changed radically and it bothered him. Life, before he had gone to Washington, had been simple. He was a cavalry officer and his duty was to fight the enemy. The war still had a veneer of adventure and the enemy were those men in blue who would quit after you shot enough of them. That the Confederacy would win the war was an article of faith. How could it be otherwise? They were in the right and their soldiers were braver and smarter. The only complication in his personal life was the fact that his brother was in the Union Navy and that would be resolved as soon as the South achieved its independence. Women were worshipful creatures who provided a delightful diversion when one was away from the field of battle. Everything fit, and if some aspects of his life were not pleasant they were at least easy to comprehend.

All of that comfort had been swept away. Fate turned a page in the book of life and Jordan found himself staring at reality. The war was a contest of national survival and Jordan knew that the North was better equipped for the struggle. Instead of a clear, open contest between armies, the conflict permeated every strata of society, destroying families and corrupting individuals. Regardless of the outcome, his world would never be the same. His father and brother hated each other and there would be no more Bobby Maysfield to steal pickles. Jordan was now aware of a plot that had the potential to cripple his country with a single blow and he was powerless to do anything about it. Then there was Jennifer. Jordan had never been in love like this before. "Love" had just been the name of a game that was fun to play. He chuckled at other men who were crushed when their sweethearts found other men more attractive. Now he understood how they felt, because life without Jennifer would be hollow and empty. He found it almost impossible to pull himself from Jennifer's arms when he had to say goodbye.

It was only when he was well away from Oakview Manor that he began to think about his new assignment. He had been ordered to report to Army Headquarters instead of directly to Hill's Division. That way they could have a look at him before they sent him to his actual assignment. If they felt he didn't belong, they could always assign him elsewhere. Jordan wondered about the rift between Stonewall Jackson and A.P. Hill. The bad feeling between the two men was common knowledge in the army. It was even rumored that only the intervention of Lee prevented a duel. The army was a place in which gossip ran rampant, but it was a matter of public record that Hill had been placed under arrest by Jackson and the arrest had to be suspended before Hill could march to Maryland and save the army at the Battle of Sharpsburg.

Hill wasn't the only one whom Jackson had arrested. There was also Garnett. It wasn't a pleasant situation by any means and Jordan didn't want to get caught up in it. He was a soldier and he was determined to do his duty. He wondered how men could let themselves be consumed by private matters and self-delusion when the South was in danger. He also wondered if Jackson and Hill had the same capacity for self-delusion as Longfellow.

Jordan arrived at Army Headquarters early in the afternoon. He was ahead of schedule, despite the fact that he had stolen a day, and that made him feel a little smug. Army Headquarters was as unassuming a place as a major military headquarters could be. It was just a collection of tents in the midst of some trees. The only thing that betrayed its importance was the frenetic activity common to any headquarters. Personnel of all ranks carried papers in the open or in cases from one tent to another and dispatch riders dropped off or picked up messages. There was a telegraph office in one tent, and in another, a group of generals huddled over a map. Jordan found the adjutant's tent and went in.

A staff captain much older than he looked up and smiled as he walked in. "Yes, sir, what can I do for you," he said.

The "sir" and the obvious deference in the captain's voice caught Jordan a little off guard until he remembered that he was now a major and captains were subordinates.

"My orders instruct me to report here," Jordan said, handing the captain his orders.

The captain looked at the orders and pursed his lips. "If it's all right with you, sir, I'll take you to see Colonel Taylor right away."

"That will be fine, captain."

The captain rose and told a sergeant at another desk where he was going. "You probably won't get to see General Lee, sir," the captain said. "He has a very bad cold. Colonel Taylor will probably be the one to confirm your assignment."

Jordan followed the captain across to another tent and the captain pulled the flap back so that Jordan could enter first. Rank does have its privileges, Jordan thought. Colonel Taylor was a slim man with dark hair and beard. He had a serious, but pleasant expression.

"Welcome to headquarters, Major Jordan," he said. "I'm Charles Taylor."

"Thank you, sir. Dick Jordan. Nice to meet you. I'm happy to be here." It was a lie, but a diplomatic one.

"Unfortunately, you won't be having an interview with the general right away. He has a slight cold and the doctors have prescribed warmth and bed rest, so he's been staying at the Corbin house. He does like to meet as many officers as he can, so you'll have a chance to meet him as soon as he's on his feet. If I know the general that won't take too long. In the meantime, I'll have someone take you over to General Jackson's headquarters and from there you'll get your assignment."

"Thank you, sir."

The captain who had escorted him to Colonel Taylor's tent took him to the plantation office of the Corbin house where Jackson had his headquarters. The captain introduced him to Major Pendleton, Jackson's adjutant.

"Sandy Pendleton," the adjutant said introducing himself.

"Dick Jordan."

"Glad to have you with us, Dick. You're early. We were told you wouldn't be here for a day or two."

"I could have used the leave," Jordan told him.

"We don't talk about leave for officers around here," Pendleton said with a grin. "Neither General Lee nor General Jackson have left the army since the war began and they frown on officers taking furlough. I realize that it's different in the cavalry when you have to find your own remounts, but the generals are very dedicated to the cause."

"I understand."

"Well, why don't we take you over to see the general right away. He's looking forward to meeting you."

"General Jackson?"

"Of course. Don't pay any attention to his reputation. He's a firm leader, but he is also a pleasant man when you get to know him. This way."

Jordan followed Pendleton to a smaller house on the grounds, knocked on the door, and walked in. Apprehensively, Jordan followed the adjutant through the door. Jackson was sitting at a table writing. On the table next to a stack of papers was a half-chewed lemon. The decor was just as Pelham had described. There were pictures of race horses and fighting cocks all around the room.

"General, this is Major Jordan," Pendleton said. "He's the new assistant adjutant assigned to General Hill's headquarters."

Jackson smiled briefly and rose to shake Jordan's hand. "Happy to meet you, major." The general had a firm grip.

"The honor is all mine, sir, I assure you."

"Don't take worldly reputations too seriously, Major Jordan. The work already accomplished could not have been done without the direct intercession of the Lord. It his to Him that we must give thanks and to Him whom we must pray for the victory which will give us independence. That is why I encourage all my officers to conform with the strictures of their religions and be faithful in the observance of their daily devotions. It is only through prayer that we will find salvation and victory. Some of our senior officers don't seem to understand this, but I pray for them also."

Jordan wondered if the last comment were a reference to A.P. Hill.

"The one thing that I demand in this corps," Jackson continued, "is immediate and strict obedience to orders. When an order is given, it has already been considered and need be considered no further. Some of our officers don't understand that either. You, as an assistant adjutant, must understand that."

"Yes sir," Jordan replied. Jackson was looking him right in the eyes.

"I trust we will see you at devotions on Sunday, Major Jordan. Good day."

Jordan saluted and left feeling very uncomfortable. Jackson's references to Hill were obvious. If Jordan had any doubts about the rift between the two generals, they were gone. Pendleton appeared not to notice. As they stepped out on the porch, a figure in a battered top hat and a frock coat came toward them. Jordan was surprised to find such a shabby man at headquarters. The man removed his hat and bowed stiffly.

"Good day, gentlemen," he said in a soft, raspy voice.

"Good evening, Mr. Bailey," Pendleton replied, as the man went into the general's office.

"Who is that?" Jordan asked.

"That is Mr. Jeremiah Bailey. The troops call him 'The Reverend.'"

"Is he a preacher?"

"No, not exactly, but the soldiers look upon him with awe and affection. They feel he brings them good luck." Pendleton explained briefly how Bailey had come to the army and what he had done. "It's too bad we don't have more like him," the adjutant concluded.

Jordan looked at the door through which Bailey had passed. "I have to agree with you. Apparently, the general does, too."

"Oh, yes. The general, Reverend Lacy, and Mr. Bailey often observe their daily devotions together.

"Now, I suppose, you're anxious to get to your new home," Pendleton said with a smile.

"Yes, I am."

"The Light Division occupies a place called Camp Gregg. It's about ten miles east of here, near the river. You can't miss it."

"Thanks, Sandy. I suspect we'll be seeing a lot of each other."

"It's report writing season," Pendleton remarked with a pleasant laugh. "I suspect we will. General Jackson and General Hill have at least one thing in common. They both hate to write reports." This was the first time Pendleton alluded to the friction between Jackson and Hill. Jordan pretended not to notice.

"That's one thing we all agree on. I hate reports, too."

"Unfortunately, as adjutants, that's our business," Pendleton said with a smile and a shrug.

The light was beginning to fade as Jordan found Hill's headquarters. He found Colonel Palmer, Hill's chief of staff, and the colonel took him directly to the general. The famous commander of the Light Brigade was sitting at a table smoking a pipe with two other men. At first he didn't realize who Hill was. The general was wearing a calico shirt and talking with his companions as if they were three friends having a friendly discussion at one of their homes or a local tavern. Before Jordan could salute and report to Hill, Palmer introduced him to the general. Hill smiled, rose, and offered his hand.

"Welcome to the Light Division, Major Jordan. We're glad to have you with us. Let me introduce you to generals Dorsey Pender and Henry Heth."

The two generals rose. Heth was a man of medium height with a bushy mustache. He was the commander of a brigade of Virginians. Pender was tall and had olive skin and a pointed beard. He was the commander of the North Carolina Brigade. Both men were already famous.

"I'm honored, gentlemen," Jordan told them.

Hill offered Jordan a seat and the new major sat down. Hill asked him some general questions. Jordan couldn't help liking Hill. He was polite and charming and seemed very congenial.

"Have you visited General Jackson, yet?" Hill asked.

"Yes sir."

"Was he on his knees or standing up?" Jordan was a little nonplussed and the other two generals made no effort to hide their mirth. "No matter, I suppose he asked you to join him Sunday."

"Yes, sir, he did."

"Well, you can go if you feel obliged to," Hill said. "A man's religion is his own business. From now on you can tell General

Jackson that you have work here. Now that we have that over with, where are you from, Major Jordan?"

"Richmond, sir."

Hill looked at him strangely, then he asked, "Are you Jordan the draper?"

"It's my father, sir."

"I thought you looked awfully young for that. Your father is quite a gentleman, major. Mrs. Hill must have spent four hours in his shop picking and fussing. I swear I was ready to throw her out myself, but your father never once got rattled or impatient." Hill turned to the other two generals. "I have honestly never seen the like. Mr. Jordan was absolutely charming and Mrs. Hill came away delighted and we had a most pleasant afternoon. You must thank him for me, major."

"My father will be glad to hear that, sir."

"He is in good health, I presume?"

"Yes, sir. Unfortunately, he's had to move the majority of his business to Wilmington now that the Yankees have Norfolk."

Hill shook his head understandingly. Then he reached out his hand. The interview was obviously over. "Welcome, again, to the Light Division, Major Jordan. Colonel Palmer will show you to your quarters and show you your duties."

"Thank you, sir. Gentlemen," he said bowing to Heth and Pender. They nodded and Jordan left.

Colonel Palmer took him to a small hut where he met his roommate, Major Lindsay Walker, Hill's chief of artillery. He was a large man who wore his hair long. A flowing mustache and imperial beard seemed to accentuate the man's friendliness and humor. As a whole, Jordan liked artillerymen. They had pleasant dispositions and they were always ready to have a party. The trouble was when two of them got together they began speaking a strange language about charges, fuses, weight of metal, and other subjects foreign to any but themselves. The hut that Jordan was to share with Major Walker was just that. There was space for two cots, a stove, and a table which Walker, as chief of artillery, needed full time. Two cracker boxes served as chairs.

"It's not much," Walker admitted, "but, it's warm and it's dry."

"These days those two factors override everything," Jordan said with a grin.

"Where were you before you came here?" Walker asked. It was a typical army question.

Jordan briefly explained his background in the cavalry and his promotion.

"Congratulations, then. I'm sure you'll like it here. Hill is a fine general and a good man. This is the best division in the army and we're not the only ones saying it."

"It's certainly going to be different being in the infantry."

"You can say that again," Walker said with a warm laugh. "I've been here two years and I'm still not used to it."

Jordan's first duty was to compile the dispatches and records of the Battle of Second Manasass into an after-action report for army records. He was given a copy of the report of the Battle of Cedar Mountain as an example he could go by. Hill's notes for the outline of the report made Jordan very uncomfortable. With great glee the division commander described the flight of the famous "Stonewall Brigade" from the field as his division moved up to save the day. Jordan knew that it was meant as a barb for Jackson. This kind of bitter wrangling was unhealthy for the army and the Confederacy, but Jordan was only a staff officer and as the new man in the headquarters, there was little he could do about it.

On Sunday, April 5, Jordan rode to Jackson's headquarters and went to the service held by the Reverend Lacy. It was held in a tent near the headquarters and the seats were crude benches and cracker boxes. The tent was packed with officers. Jackson, his staff, and the odd Mr. Bailey were in the front. They all knelt in prayer, then Reverend Lacy rose to give his sermon. It was powerful and interesting and Jordan had to admit that he enjoyed it. When it was over, the assembly filed out of the tent and broke into small groups which began discussing the sermon. Jordan watched Jackson, Lacy, and Bailey walk toward Jackson's quarters. It seemed a curious trio. Here was a great general with his friend, a famous clergyman, and a stooped man who seemed old before his time. There was something about Bailey . . .

"Dick Jordan," someone called.

Jordan turned. It was Sandy Pendleton.

"Hi, Sandy. Nice to see you again."

"How did you like the sermon?"

"Reverend Lacy certainly makes you think, doesn't he?"

Pendleton laughed. "He certainly does. We spend most Sundays discussing his sermons. Sometimes the arguments get very heated. Why don't you join us?"

"I'd like to, but I have to get back. I have a lot of work to do. I really don't fit in just yet, and I'm trying to learn."

"I know how that goes. When you get settled please come. We'll be glad to have you."

"Thank you, Sandy."

Jordan looked in the direction of Jackson and his two companions. They had already disappeared into the house. Jordan wondered about Bailey. Perhaps it was just that these strange times and they made for strange bedfellows. He mounted his horse and returned to Camp Gregg.

Jordan could hardly call his work interesting, but he was kept busy. He was in great demand when it came to horses and mules, since he was more familiar with their maladies and idiosyncrasies than others in the staff. A few days later, Major Edward B. Hill, the general's brother, took him on a tour of the other headquarters in the army so Jordan would know where he would have to go, and whom he would have to see when he had to deliver dispatches or transmit orders. The entire trip, Jordan knew would take two days. They rode upriver to Jackson's camp and then south past the hospital. It certainly looked like an efficiently run place. Bailey, wearing a white smock over his clothes, was outside chopping wood.

"You should have seen this place before that crazy old man got here," Major Hill said. "It wasn't fit to be a kennel."

"Bailey did all this?" Jordan asked.

"He certainly did. The men think the world of him. He doesn't ask for anything except to be useful. He sleeps on a little cot in a corner and eats once a day. He's really amazing."

"Does anyone know why he does it?" Jordan asked. Even though he had heard the story from Sandy Pendleton he was interested in hearing it again.

Bailey finished cutting the wood and laid down his ax. He picked up an armload of wood and walked past the two mounted officers toward the hospital.

"Good day, gentlemen," Bailey said, recognizing Major Hill. "May I help you?"

"I'm just giving Major Jordan a tour of the area, Mr. Bailey," Hill said. "He's our new assistant adjutant."

Bailey smiled at Jordan. He had the expression of a man who was at peace with himself. "God bless you, major," he said. "We must all do God's work in our own way. If I may be of any assistance, please do not hesitate to call on me."

"Thank you, Mr. Bailey. I will."

Bailey bowed deferentially and carried his wood into the hospital. Jordan watched him for a moment. "Where to next?" he asked.

"We're supposed to go to your old stomping grounds in Culpeper."

"Mind if we swing by Oakview Manor?"

"Not at all. Any special reason?"

"One very special reason."

Hill smiled and they started their long ride. They were only a few miles from the hospital when Jordan began thinking about Bailey. There was something he couldn't put his finger on. Perhaps it was because Bailey looked familiar. Jordan froze and his horse stopped. The implications of what he was thinking flowed rapidly to a frighteningly logical conclusion. That was it. Bailey *did* look familiar. Jordan tried to imagine him with a reddish mustache. He recalled Bailey's face as he looked at him. Bailey had gray eyes. Bailey was Major Harvey Ferris!

"Oh no!"

Major Hill had not seen Jordan stop. He had ridden on a few yards ahead when he heard Jordan's voice. He turned and looked at Jordan, then rode back. Jordan was only vaguely aware of Hill's return. He was positive that Bailey was Ferris and if that were so then he was dangerously close to Lee's headquarters.

"Jordan?" Hill asked. "Are you all right?"

"What?" Jordan asked as he became aware of Hill next to him.

"Are you all right? You're pale. You look as if you've seen a ghost."

"It's nothing; really nothing," Jordan told him evasively. "A touch of fever probably." There was no way he could let Hill know what he was thinking. I have to see Charley, Jordan thought. I have to see him right away.

Hill looked at him in genuine concern. "Maybe you should see a doctor when you return."

"Yes, I will. Thank you. We'd better get going."

Fredericksburg Military Hospital
April 10, 1863

Jeremiah Bailey sat at the bedside of one of the patients in the hospital. His name was Virgil Sands and he was so young that it wouldn't have been inaccurate to describe him as a boy. Like so many, he was a recent amputee and he had a bad fever. If it broke during the night he had a good chance of living. If it didn't, he would be dead in less than twenty-four hours. Bailey wiped his head with a clean, damp cloth.

"Reverend?"

"Yes son?"

"Would you write a letter for me?"

"Certainly. I'll get a pen and paper." Bailey rose, walked to a table a few yards away, and picked up a lap desk. He returned to the patient's bedside.

"Now what would you like to say?" Bailey asked soothingly.

"I want this to go my Momma and Daddy," the boy said, turning his face away from Bailey. "This may be the last time you hear from me. . . ."

Bailey dipped the pen in the inkwell and began writing. This boy was going to die. Like so many others he had a premonition of his own death and he wanted to say goodbye before he lapsed into delirium. Bailey had seen it too many times before. It could almost be predicted. His hand wrote the dying boy's words, but his mind dwelt on more important matters.

The major had not given any outward sign that he had recognized Bailey, but Bailey was certain that he had. He sensed it as surely as he sensed the coming of the rain. They had met on the road south of Ely's Ford the morning he killed Ellison. Most men would not even have noticed the similarity between Jeremiah Bailey and Harvey Ferris, but Jordan had. That meant that Jordan was far more observant than most men and far more dangerous to his plans. It also meant an unseen development, but it was something that could be dealt with. The campaigning season was rapidly approaching and it would soon be time to act. He would have to kill Jordan to insure a clear approach to his target, but killing Major Jordan would require only a minor change in the plan. Bailey finished the letter.

"Thank you, Mr. Bailey," the boy said. "God bless you."

"Get some rest, son," he told the boy. "Sleep will help you get well."

They both knew it was a lie.

Jordan and Hill arrived at Oakview Manor in time for lunch. Jennifer was very reserved with Hill present, but with her eyes she made Jordan forget Bailey, Hill, and the war. Jennifer sent Hill on a tour of the house with Sarah so she and Jordan could be alone.

"I've missed you so much since you left, even if it's only been a few days," she told him as he held her.

"As soon as I get settled we can be married. I haven't even had time to write to my father and mother yet. Perhaps I can get to Richmond on furlough to buy a ring."

Jennifer smiled. "How is your new assignment, dear?"

"Too many reports," he said with a grin. "But it is fun having captains calling me 'sir'. I have actually met Stonewall Jackson."

"Really? Is he as strange as some of the officers say he is?"

"No, he's quite an ordinary person, even though he does have some strange habits. I wish he got along with General Hill a little better, but I suppose its hard to have so many brilliant and proud men in one place without a little friction. That's what makes General Lee so amazing."

"Couldn't you invite me to camp for a Sunday. I understand quite a few officers have their ladies visit."

"Of course," Jordan said. Then the idea hit him. Jennifer could identify Ferris. Dare he ask her or should he just have her take a look at Bailey? Then he wondered if he would be putting her in danger by doing so. He decided to let her visit him and let things happen as they would.

They exchanged kisses and held one another until Sarah returned with Major Hill.

The two officers left to continue on their way. Before they had gone much further, it became evident that Jordan knew the area much better than Hill, so Hill let him lead the way. It was no accident that they found themselves at the Johnson farm at sundown.

"Well, Captain Jordan, isn't it?" Johnson said.

"I'm flattered you remember me, sir."

"Never forget a face," Johnson told him.

Probably from identifying runaway slaves, Jordan thought. "There has been one change however, Mr. Johnson," he said.

"What's that?"

"I've been breveted major, sir."

Johnson looked at Jordan's collar and beamed. "So you have," he said pumping Jordan's hand. "Congratulations, my boy," he said with genuine good will.

"May I introduce Major Hill, Mr. Johnson."

Hill bowed graciously. "Honored, sir."

"You look very familiar, major," Johnson said. "But I can't place you."

"Perhaps you're thinking of my brother Powell, sir."

"Ambrose Powell Hill is your brother?"

"Yes sir."

"This is an honor. Please, you must have supper with us."

The two officers accepted the invitation. They dined with the Johnson's and some of the officers from Longfellow's headquarters. One of them was Patterson who was now a captain. He recognized Jordan and they shook hands.

"Is Charley Masters around?" Jordan asked.

"He should be at headquarters," Patterson said. "If you're looking for the colonel, I'm afraid he's been called to Richmond."

"I was looking forward to seeing him, too," Jordan lied. He was relieved that Longfellow was nowhere near the place.

As soon as it was polite to do so, Jordan excused himself from the supper table and made his way over to the headquarters building. As usual, the place was in chaos. He almost walked by the lieutenant leaning over a map.

"Charley?"

Masters looked up and smiled. "Dick, what are you doing here?" he said. Then he added, "Maybe I'd better not ask."

"Am I seeing things?" Jordan asked.

"What? Is something wrong?" Masters looked at his boots.

"You've been promoted."

"Oh, that. I was breveted, same as you."

"That's great."

Masters shrugged. The promotion honestly meant little to him.

"Can we talk somewhere private?"

"What's this about?" Masters was concerned.

"Private," Jordan insisted.

"The colonel's office. He's not here." Masters led the way to Longfellow's office and closed the door. Before he could say another word, Jordan told him.

"I found Ferris," he said excitedly.

It took Masters a second before he realized whom Jordan meant. "Where?"

"He isn't using the name Ferris any longer, Charley."

"What name is he using?"

"Jeremiah Bailey," Jordan said confidently.

Masters looked at him, stunned. "Bailey? Dick, are you crazy? That man is a legend in the Army of Northern Virginia. Even President Davis wants to give him an award, but he's too humble to accept anything."

"It's because he's Ferris. He doesn't want any notoriety."

"Dick, I don't know what it is about you. You definitely have a nose for this business, but this time I think you're reaching too far."

"Let me acquaint you with a few facts, then. As a good friend of mine once remarked, this assassin, or whatever you want to call him is probably making himself comfortable, waiting for the right opportunity to make his move. In order to be 'comfortable' he would have to be accepted in the army yet also be able to move around. An officer would be accepted, but his flexibility would be severely limited by his prescribed duties. This man is not only accepted, he has an incredible amount of flexibility. He prays with Jackson and Lacy, yet he is accountable to no one. I don't know for certain, but he probably has a pass that allows him to go anywhere, whenever he pleases. There you have it. If I were in Ferris' business, I'd probably do the same thing."

"It's too perfect," Masters said, trying to find a hole in Jordan's conclusions. "I can't believe Bailey would be the kind of man that would do that sort of thing. He tends the sick and wounded, writes their letters, and prays with them. It's damned hard to swallow, even for me."

"That's just the point," Jordan said, emphasizing his opinion with the point of his finger. "Charley, everyone thinks of him the same way. The kindly old so-and-so is a little strange, but he's a wonderful person. Just think for a moment; what do we know about him?"

Masters thought for a moment then looked at Jordan with a new understanding. "We don't know anything about him. He appeared from nowhere. Like a ghost."

"Chameleon, you mean. We know a lot about this man. Maybe we don't know his name but we know a lot. We know he masqueraded as a Yankee officer to get Ellison out of prison. That had to take some kind of planning, not to mention audacity. Also, you need papers to get someone out of prison. Where did he get them? Next he convinced Lydia Ratliffe, an experienced agent that he was one of Beauregard's agents and then panicked her into giving him a pass to cross our lines. When he does cross, he murders Ellison in cold blood and makes it look as if the pickets killed him. If we hadn't come along, no one would have known. Then, he mysteriously disappears and this eccentric, saintly man appears and offers his services—with a letter of introduction that I'll bet is forged."

"You know what your problem is, Dick."

"What, Charley?"

"You're too damned persuasive for your own good. What do you need?"

"I need someone who can find out about Jeremiah Bailey. Is he actually from Paw Paw? Did he serve in the Army of the Tennessee? Was he wounded in the lungs? There are a thousand questions, but those will do for a start."

"I'll see what I can do. Colonel Longfellow is consumed with this Pennsylvania business. I may even be able to get a trip to the Army of the Tennessee. Who knows?"

"Just be careful, Charley. The Yankees hold most of the state."

"Don't worry," Masters quipped, grinning broadly. "There won't be any cavalry captains around to get me into any adventures."

"Thank God for that."

Headquarters, Second Corps
Army of Northern Virginia
April 4, 1863

The Spy watched as they carried the body of Virgil Sands out of the hospital on a stretcher. The tears that flowed down Bailey's cheeks were genuine. The actor who taught him how to use makeup had also taught him other tricks of the profession. While he stood, head bowed, his mind was occupied with the problem Richard Jordan had created. Anderson had planned everything carefully and could not allow a few coincidences to stop him from fulfilling his greatest commission.

Jordan had been heading toward Ely's Ford when they met. That meant he was going north. One could deduce, then, that he was at least a scout if not a spy for Colonel Longfellow. From that, one would have to assume that Jordan saw Ellison's body and knew that Ellison was not killed by the pickets. The Spy then decided to carry his suppositions to their worst case scenario. He would have to assume that Jordan went to Washington and, since he was one of Longfellow's men, he would have seen Mrs. Ratliffe who would have related the story of Ellison to him. Jordan would then have a fairly complete picture of the Spy's activities.

In addition, Jordan had seen his face. It had been made up, to be sure, but Jordan had seen him. Why then didn't there seem to be a more active effort to ferret him out? This question also had to be answered by speculation. One could only assume that Jordan had presented his findings to his superiors who didn't believe him. One could always count on military officials to do precisely the wrong thing when an action required imagination and intellect. Therefore, the Spy thought, Jordan is working alone, or perhaps with no more than two additional companions. Bailey will have to be very careful, the Spy thought. *Very* careful. He will have to watch and observe.

Bailey followed Sands' body to the grave, read the burial service, and said the appropriate words about nobility and sacrifice. The men were comforted. The Spy was not.

Jeremiah Bailey was a brilliant masterpiece of the Spy's inventive mind. The Spy knew from past experience that he could never masquerade as an army officer for very long. Army officers belonged to specific regiments and had specific duties. For good or ill they were extremely well known by hundreds, and, in the case of higher ranking officers, thousands of people so there was more than an odd chance that someone an officer knew would enter the picture sooner or later.

These facts made it impossible for the Spy to masquerade as an officer. That left a limited number of occupations open to Anderson as he took the train to Kentucky. The reasons for Anderson's destination were as well thought out as the rest of his plan. Everyone would be leery of someone coming from the north, no matter how impeccable his credentials might be. Therefore, he would have to be seen entering Virginia from the south. The Spy ruled out North Carolina. It was not in the war zone and was not in turmoil. Since there was not a large number of strangers passing through, residents had time to question any stranger who entered their community. Anderson, no doubt, could have passed for anyone he wanted but decided not to take the chance and chose Kentucky.

Anderson saw three distinct possibilities. He could fit himself out as a sutler, but these were becoming rare in the South due to the lack of goods for sale. He could get a job as a correspondent for a small newspaper and use those credentials to get into Jackson's camp. This was also a lesser choice because reporters were not uniformly well liked. The third choice appeared to offer the best possibilities and that was posing as preacher or other purveyor of religion. Anderson noticed that these men usually passed in and out of army camps with little notice. The Spy had always been interested in religion. Personally, he found religion boring, but a thorough knowledge of the subject allowed him to take advantage of the delusions of the religious and the self-righteous.

Posing as a writer of religious tracts, he visited a large army camp and watched as thousands of soldiers gathered to hear ministers preach for a revival. It was during this prayer meeting that the Spy saw the real Jeremiah Bailey.

Bailey was a young man grown old before his time. He helped with the services and tended the sick and wounded. His eyes shone with the light of the newly-saved. Anderson, the writer of religious tracts, began asking about Bailey. Everyone with whom he spoke had a very high opinion of the man. He was a reformed drunk who had seen the light and was now doing the work of the Lord. The Spy found this intriguing, so he arranged to meet Bailey personally. There was nothing pretentious about the man. Bailey was semi-educated and a bit on the seedy side. He was an unusually humble man whose sole pleasure in life was an occasional drink of whiskey prescribed by the army doctors for his cough, which was the result of being shot through the lung at the Battle of Stone's River. The interview took place on a couple of ammunition crates. The Spy procured a bottle of potent whiskey and requested to meet Bailey. He was sitting on one of the crates when Bailey walked up. The man had the expression of one at peace with himself. Anderson was not surprised. He had seen it before in the eyes of the devout.

"You, Mr. Anderson?" Bailey asked.

"Yes," the Spy said, rising. "You must be Mr. Bailey."

"I am."

The Spy rose and the two men shook hands. Then the Spy motioned for him to sit down. Bailey glanced enviously at the bottle at Anderson's feet.

"I realize that you are a busy man, Mr. Bailey, so I won't beat around the bush. I am a writer of religious tracts currently engaged by the Franklin Steam Printing House in Atlanta. My purpose in visiting the camp is to find inspiring examples of faith among our soldiers. Thus far I have not been pleased with what I have seen. The lurid stories of gambling, drinking, and other vices which a gentleman need not acknowledge are, alas, true. When I came here I was, to say the least, pleasantly surprised to find that many of our gallant soldiers had pledged themselves anew to God, helping display the righteousness of our cause. I realize that you are now invalided, but the stories others have told me of your salvation would be of interest to our readers."

"Do you think so?" Bailey asked innocently.

"Is it not written that there will be more joy in heaven over one sinner who repents than over ninety-nine persons who need no repentence?" Anderson asked. "It would be an inspiration to everyone, I assure you."

"If you think it will help . . ."

"Do not be anxious how you are to speak or what you are about to say," the Spy said. "For it is not you who speak but the spirit of thy Father speaking through thee."

"Amen," Bailey said.

The Spy reached for the bottle of whiskey. "Do you indulge, Mr. Bailey? I am told that spirits ward off the less salubrious vapors of camp life."

"I take if for my wound," Bailey said flatly.

"Ah, yes." Anderson pulled the cork from the bottle with his teeth and filled two tin cups with the amber liquid. Bailey drained his with several large gulps and Anderson generously refilled it. Anderson produced a notebook and a pencil from his coat pocket. "Now, Mr. Bailey, if can tell me your story in your own words."

"Ain't much to tell, really. I was raised in Paw Paw, Virginia. It's a small town on the C&O Canal. Big tunnel there. I wasn't much good, if the truth be told. Oh, I worked hard when I was sober, but that 'tweren't often. Mostly farmin'. One day my friend Jack and me, we had us a little money and we bought us a jug an' went up to this place across the river 'bout half way to Cumberland. They had women there. I took a fancy to this one an' Jack, he took a fancy to the same one. We started on the jug and before I know'd it she was takin' Jack upstairs. I got mad an' pulled her away. Then Jack got mad and we commenced to fightin'. The woman was screamin' for somebody to come break us up, but nobody came. I was real mad and picked up the leg of a chair we'd smashed and hit Jack real hard. Sounded kind of like when you hit a man with the butt of your rifle. I know'd I'd killed him and the woman started screamin' I'd killed him. I took fright and run off. I just started wanderin' and finally I got here."

"Did anyone help you along the way?"

"Oh, yes, sir. They was kindly Christian folk. I guess the Lord was trying to show me the way even then. I suppose that's why I never stole nothin' from them.

"When I got here the war was just startin' and I was hungry and cold so I figured I'd join up. At least it was a place to sleep and something to eat, although we didn't always have somethin' to eat. I stayed in the army 'til I was shot at Stone's River. It was terrible painful and them doctors told me I was goin' to die. Afterward they said I was out of my head, and they was ready to carry me off, but I wasn't out of my head. The Lord spoke to me."

"What did He say, Mr. Bailey?"

"He told me I was a sinner and showed me how bad I'd been."

"How did he do that?"

"He showed me my soul. It was ugly and twisted and I was ashamed of myself. I wanted to die and told the Lord to take me, but he said he couldn't. He said I had to repent my sinnin' ways, else I was goin' to hell. He showed me that, too. I asked him what he wanted me to do. He told me that I had to be humble and do good works, and when I was ready He'd call me home and that I wasn't to be scared. When I got better, the doctors told me it was a miracle. I told them that I spoke with the Lord and they looked at me funny, but I was alive and they couldn't deny that. Even the skeptics what don't believe in God have to see His miracles. That's the way the Lord works."

"That's truly amazing, Mr. Bailey. It will be an uplifting experience for my readers to learn your story. What are your plans now?"

"I want to go home, or as near home as I can. I have a letter of introduction from Reverend Wilkinson to Reverend Lacy who is with the Army of Northern Virginia. I'm going there to do whatever good work I can."

"That's very admirable, Mr. Bailey. Does anyone know you there?"

"I think not. Most of my people are in Morgan County and they are all Yankees, God forgive them."

The opportunity was too good to be true, the Spy thought. "When are you leaving, Mr. Bailey?"

"Next day or two, why?"

"It just so happens that I am also on my way to Virginia. Perhaps we can ride together." Anderson uncorked the bottle and poured a generous amount into Bailey's cup.

"Would be nice havin' someone to talk to," Bailey said.

"It's agreed, then. Shall we leave tomorrow morning?"

Bailey nodded.

They left on a cold, clear day after Bailey said his morning prayers. Anderson knelt beside him and listened carefully to the man's devotions. They made excellent time because it was cold and the roads were hard. Anderson watched Bailey carefully until he was convinced that the man was, indeed, genuine. The Spy kept an adequate supply of whiskey and shared it generously with Bailey. Just after they crossed the Virginia border, they spent the night in an abandoned cabin. Anderson made sure that Bailey had plenty to drink and when the man fell asleep, Anderson strangled him and stripped the body. Bailey's wound had caused two scars. There was one in the front where the bullet entered and one in the back where it exited. Another detail.

Anderson buried the body in the morning and made certain there was no trace of the grave. He applied enough makeup so that people would think him a drunkard. There was one thing he had to change. On Bailey's discharge, it said that he had brown eyes. Anderson forged the discharge to read "gray." He took his horse and Bailey's mule and headed for his commission. There were additional details, to be sure, but he would take care of them as the need arose.

Headquarters, Light Division
April 17, 1863

Jordan stared out the door of his little hut. It had been raining since Wednesday, the 15th and didn't look as if it were going to stop anytime soon. It was one of those cold, driving rains that makes a soldier feel as if he's been cold and wet his entire life. The headquarters complex was a quagmire and, for once, Jordan was glad of it. The weather meant that neither army could move and it gave him time to gather the evidence to ferret Bailey or Ferris out and foil his plot to kill General Lee. At first he didn't recognize the bedraggled civilian who splashed his horse through the mud of Camp Gregg and stopped at his door.

"Good morning, Dick," Masters said with sarcastic cheer.

"Charley, my God, you look a fright. Come in and get dry."

"Thanks, I've been riding day and night for a week. I'm done in. I've just come back from Tennessee. The whole place is crawling with Yankees. That's why I'm wearing civilian clothes."

Jordan called for the orderly to take care of Masters' horse and made way for his friend to stand by the stove. He produced a flask of whiskey and handed it to Masters who gratefully took a drink.

He stripped off his coat and hung it by the stove and removed his wet boots. Jordan gave him a blanket to wrap his feet in. Masters' eyes were red-rimmed and bloodshot. Jordan waited until he was comfortable.

"You were right, Dick," he said sullenly.

Jordan was silent. He looked at Masters then looked out at the rain.

"He is a chameleon, I'll give him that. His story checked out all the way. Even the Reverend Wilkinson letter was real. You lost your bet. I'll drink the whiskey as payment."

"The letter was real?"

"Sure was."

"Then how . . ."

"The eyes."

"Eyes?"

"Our Bailey has gray eyes. I checked the discharge records. The real Bailey had brown eyes."

"Had?"

"No proof, just speculating. Our friend Ferris or Bailey doesn't leave any witnesses. I'm just using Ellison as an example. Anyway, our Bailey is very close to the real article. He acts talks and preaches the same way. Only the eyes are different."

"Damn!" Jordan swore.

"What's the matter? I thought this was the evidence you wanted."

"It's convincing enough for me, but what about anyone else? Nobody is going to take our word on the basis of discharge papers. There are always errors on those things. I'll bet Bailey's copy says gray eyes. It'll take more than that to convince someone like Longfellow that a difference in eyes is significant. He didn't want to believe that Ellison had been killed by a pistol, and once he found out the facts he ignored them."

Jordan heard a soft clink. He turned. Masters had fallen asleep on Jordan's bed and dropped the empty flask. Jordan picked up Masters' feet and put them on the bed so he would be more comfortable. Then he covered him with another blanket. He didn't know what he would do without Charley Masters. Throughout the entire episode Charley was the only one who believed him. Now, Masters had confirmed that he was not crazy and that was quite a feat. They were faced with exposing a ruthless killer who would happily murder both of them in order to be able to kill his next victim. Jordan needed Masters' help but he wondered if he had the right to ask his friend to risk his life in such bizarre circumstances. I need time, Jordan thought. It has to keep raining, if only for another day or two.

CHAPTER 10

Guiney's Station, Virginia
April 20, 1863

IT HAD BEEN raining without letup for the past six days and this third Monday in April made it seven. Despite the rain, a crowd waited patiently on the platform at Guiney's Station and Richard Jordan was among them. The throng was there to greet passengers arriving on the train. From the notables on the platform one might think that the passengers were dignitaries from Richmond, but they weren't. Everyone was waiting for a woman and a five-month-old child. They were the wife and daughter of General Thomas Jonathan Jackson. "Old Jack" stood anxiously on the platform, awaiting their arrival. It had been months since he last saw his wife and he had never seen his daughter, Julia. Jackson had switched his headquarters from the plantation office at the Corbin place to the Yerby house where there was enough room for him to maintain his headquarters and house his family. Jackson refused to take a leave during hostilities, so he had his wife join him whenever it was possible. It was obvious from the way he fidgeted that he was anxious to see them.

Among the well-wishers on the platform were Dr. McGuire, Reverend Lacy, Sandy Pendleton, and Jeremiah Bailey, alias Major Harvey Ferris. As usual, Bailey stood in the background. "Humble" Mr. Bailey was in a position to observe everything, Jordan noted. Jordan watched Bailey from one end of the platform and Masters watched him from the other, but both pretended not to pay any attention to him.

The whistle blew and Jackson and his entourage turned in the direction of the sound. Bailey had his eyes peeled on Jackson. It was something Jordan had noticed recently. When no one seemed to be looking, Bailey was intently watching Jackson. Why? Why wasn't he observing General Lee, his target, Jordan asked himself. Could it be that Lee was not the target, after all? Bailey was spending more time at Jackson's headquarters than he was at Lee's. Usually, Bailey would take his daily devotions with Jackson. What could be a better cover? It made good sense not to spend too much time around Lee if Lee were the target. Otherwise the Spy might give himself away. These new suppositions bothered Jordan. Had he discovered a new aspect to the plot or was he complicating the issue needlessly? There was nothing substantial upon which to base a decision and his instincts were unclear.

The train pulled into the station and Jackson climbed into the coach impatiently. When he emerged, there was a pretty young woman, a baby, and a colored maid. The crowd clapped and cheered as Jackson proudly held his new baby up for them to see. Jackson led them to a carriage and they left for their quarters. Gradually the crowd dispersed. Bailey was one of the first to leave. Jordan waited until he was sure Bailey had gone and walked to the other end of the nearly empty platform. Masters was waiting for him beneath an eave out of the rain.

"He certainly looks harmless enough, doesn't he?" Masters said.

"I guess he does," Jordan agreed, shivering in the cold.

"What's wrong?" Masters asked. He knew when his friend was mulling over a problem.

"I don't know. There's a piece of this puzzle eluding me and I can't seem to find it."

"Do you mind if we look for it where it's dry?" Masters asked with a chuckle.

"Sure," Jordan said with a forced smile. "I guess I get carried away."

"There are some other people in this army who should get carried away like you do, Dick."

The two men walked over to their horses and mounted them. They rode them at a slow pace down the muddy road back to

Camp Gregg. Neither of them noticed the shadowy figure in the livery stable they passed. The man stood back away from the door and held his hand over his mule's muzzle, watching them intently. Bailey had assumed that the young man at the opposite end of the platform was Jordan's companion: this confirmed it. He waited until they faded into the rainy afternoon before he mounted his mule and rode for the hospital.

The Spy was pleased by this turn of events. He had never had a commission in which an adversary knew what he was going to do. It lent an air of interest to the mission that the Spy found exciting. It was now one against two. This was far from boring and made the entire mission worthwhile. He would now have to find out who Jordan's companion was. Whoever the young man was, he seemed to share Jordan's interest in Bailey, and for that he would also have to die. The time and place of his death, like Jordan's, had to remain open, but at the earliest opportunity he would kill both of them. It was only a minor change in the plan. He had already decided upon one change. He would stop at Oakview Manor and take Jennifer Franks with him. He had thought about her a great deal lately and decided he wanted her permanently. After their evening together, he was sure she would go with him. How could she do otherwise?

When Masters and Jordan arrived back at camp, the orderly took their horses and the two men went to Jordan's hut.

"We still have to get some sort of evidence that can convince the authorities Bailey is a spy or an assassin," Jordan said.

"What about his wound?" Masters asked. "How can you fake being shot in the lungs? He would have to have scars where they sewed him up, wouldn't he?"

"Yes, he would."

"Then let's just get him to take his shirt off. That should settle it right there," Masters said.

It sounded so simple that Jordan found the idea tempting. But, on second thought he decided that taking direct action would not be a good idea. They had to remain discreet.

"Is there anyone we can get to do it for us, Charley?"

"Why don't we just go do it ourselves?" Masters asked impatiently.

Jordan shook his head. "Bailey isn't a stupid man, and I'm sure he knows we're on to him, but I don't want to tip our hand any more than we have to."

Masters thought a moment. "If we could get the Provost Marshal to believe that there was a deserter who fit his description, we might get them to act. We'll just have to be there when he takes his shirt off."

"Can you do it?"

"I think so. There's someone at Longfellow's headquarters who's a close friend of an officer in the Provost Marshal's office. He owes me a favor so maybe we can work something out. I'll leave for headquarters right now and get things rolling. I have to make an appearance anyway. Otherwise they'll think I'm absent without leave."

Jordan smiled with satisfaction. "I knew I could count on you, Charley."

"It isn't done yet, Dick," Masters told him, warily.

"I have confidence in you, Charley."

"I'll let you know if it can be done as soon as I can, Dick. Take care of yourself."

"You, too, Charley." Jordan watched Masters go down the muddy walk to his horse and felt elated. They were close. Soon they would be able to expose Bailey for the murderer he was.

Charley Masters didn't waste any time. On Tuesday, April 22, a lieutenant from the Provost Marshal's Office, accompanied by a detail of five armed guards, arrived at the hospital. The lieutenant had a handbill for a deserter with a description that closely matched Bailey's. The description listed no significant scars. Masters followed at a discreet distance as the lieutenant arrived at the hospital. When the officer from the Provost Marshal's office presented his credentials to Doctor Warren, the chief of the hospital exploded.

"Just who the hell do you think you are, lieutenant? Mr. Bailey is a medically discharged veteran who has been working voluntarily in this hospital for over a month. How dare you come in here and accuse him of being a deserter? He was shot in the lungs and he's still serving his country. How can you even think of charging him with desertion?"

"Doctor, all I have to go on is this report," the lieutenant said calmly. "The man described on this handbill has never been shot."

He gave the handbill to Warren. "Either I can take him with me to the stockade at headquarters, or you can let me see the man's scars. If he has, in fact, been wounded he is not the man I'm looking for and I'll be on my way."

"It's degrading. Simply degrading," Warren fumed.

They were still arguing when Bailey, who had heard them discussing him, walked up.

"What seems to be the problem, doctor? I heard my name mentioned."

"This officer seems to think you're a deserter, Mr. Bailey," the doctor snapped.

"I've been accused of many things in my time," he said with a modest smile. "But this is a first. Is there anything I can do?"

"The doctor says you were shot in the lung," the lieutenant told him. "The man I'm looking for has no such scars. Show me yours and I'll be satisfied you're not he."

"That sounds reasonable," Bailey said in his raspy voice.

"I think you should protest such treatment, Mr. Bailey," the doctor insisted. "It's degrading."

"Now, doctor," Bailey said soothingly. "I appreciate your concern for me and I am indeed thankful for it. But, the lieutenant here is only trying to do his duty."

Masters watched the proceedings carefully. Bailey was certainly a cool one. He didn't act like a cornered man. Masters' hand dropped to his pistol. Any moment he expected Bailey to bolt for the door. Masters held his breath as Bailey began to unbutton his flannel shirt. What the hell is he trying to do, Masters asked himself. Bailey removed the garment, tossed it over a chair, and began to unbutton his undershirt. Masters nervously licked his lips. His heart was pounding. When Bailey removed his undershirt, the livid red scar below his right nipple was clearly visible. Even from a distance away, Masters could see the stitch marks. This wasn't happening. It was impossible. The odds of two men having the same scars were incalculable.

"This is where it went in," Bailey said. He turned around. "And this is where it came out."

"Can you see them clearly?" the doctor demanded, angrily. "Or do you want a full medical explanation? I can assure you that these are the scars of a man who was shot. Are you satisfied?"

"Yes sir," the lieutenant replied. "This is what I came for. My apologies, Mr. Bailey."

"No offense taken, lieutenant. You were only doing your duty. God bless you."

The lieutenant left as Bailey began to put his undershirt back on. He looked directly at Masters and smiled. The expression on his face was one of derisive contempt. He's mocking me, Masters thought. The bastard is mocking me. How on earth did he do it? Before he lost his temper, Masters strode out of the hospital.

The Spy watched Masters leave. He had every reason to gloat at this small triumph. His planning and attention to detail had, as usual, paid off handsomely. Now his enemies would have to reconsider their position. The scars were indeed real and they were recent. After killing Bailey, the Spy found a doctor who specialized in providing medical exemption certificates for those wishing to avoid the draft. For an additional fee, the doctor was prepared to provide a scar to go with the certificate. The doctor made two small, superficial incisions and then sewed them up. It had been a painful process, because the Spy did not trust the doctor and would not allow him to use chloroform. As soon as the operation was finished, the Spy paid the doctor for his work and a little more to ensure that he kept his mouth shut. The Spy then continued his journey to the Army of Northern Virginia. Men who left their fate to chance were fools. Jordan and his friend had tried to trap him. Now, it was time for the Spy to set a trap of his own.

"How did he do it?" Masters asked, still in disbelief.

"You actually saw the scars, Charley?"

"I saw them and they were real. Then he grinned at me, the bastard. He was laughing at me. I couldn't believe it." Masters was angry.

"He's more clever than either of us could imagine, Charley. I've heard of doctors giving men scars so they wouldn't be conscripted. That's probably what he had done. God, that man is clever."

"What are we going to do now, Dick?"

Jordan shrugged. "I don't know." He sounded embarrassed. "I guess we'll just have to keep an eye on him and jump him when he tries to make his move. It isn't going to be easy, but I see no other choice. Unless he makes a mistake, we'll have to catch him red-handed."

"I don't think he makes too many mistakes, Dick." The bitterness in Masters' voice was evident.

"Let's not make him a god, Charley. He's only human. He's bound to make a mistake somewhere along the way. Just don't let him get to you. We don't need to make any mistakes, either."

"I just don't like being mocked like that," Masters said.

"Calm down," Jordan said, putting a hand on his friend's shoulder. "We'll get him before he has a chance to kill anyone. I promise."

"I hope you're right, Dick." Masters wasn't convinced.

The Yerby House
April 23, 1863

Masters watched as the Reverend Lacy, General and Mrs. Jackson with little Julia, the general's staff, and a host of well-wishers filed into the Yerby house for Julia's baptism. One of the well-wishers was Mr. Jeremiah Bailey.

Masters was not an invited guest so he remained outside to watch for Bailey. Jordan was the field officer of the day and could not be there. He had advised Masters to stay away because he was certain that Bailey was not ready to kill Lee. Jordan tried to convince Masters not to make himself conspicuous, but Masters wouldn't listen. He was still smarting over Bailey's mocking smile and he was determined to catch the assassin. He remained hidden in a grove outside the Yerby house and watched carefully.

Only a short time after he entered, Bailey emerged from the house. He looked around carefully and then mounted a horse instead of his mule and rode south. Masters mounted his horse and followed him down a series of muddy wooded country lanes. Masters had tracked men before and he was careful not to be seen. Several miles south of the Yerby house, Bailey turned off the road onto what could only be called a cowpath. The trees and underbrush were so thick that Masters lost sight of Bailey. He dismounted and followed Bailey's trail on foot.

The ground was soft and it was easy to do see where the assassin's horse had gone, but Masters had to hurry. The sky was overcast and it was late in the afternoon, so there was very little daylight left. Masters was not foolish enough to try and track Bailey in the dark. He thought he might have to return the following day when he saw the house or, rather, what was left of it. The structure had burned and the roof had collapsed, leaving only one wall standing. The hoof prints led past the house, but Masters' instinct told him that the house and Bailey were somehow connected. It was probably the place that he hid his Confederate uniform and other passes that he might need. It was also a good place for a trap.

Masters tied his horse to a tree and carefully skirted the house from the tree line. There was little chance of anyone hiding in the house itself. It was nothing but charred timber, but there was an open cellar door. Masters was excited, but he carefully weighed the possibilities. His instincts told him that this place was being used by Bailey. If so, then he could go in alone or wait and bring Jordan back the following day. He decided to go in alone. If he went for help, then Bailey would have time to move whatever was in the cellar.

Masters drew his pistol and walked toward the open cellar door in a crouch. When he reached the door, he stood outside for a moment and looked around. Then he picked up a piece of charred wood, tensed, and tossed it inside. It hit the dirt floor with a thud. There was a scurrying sound and Masters raised his pistol. He let out a sigh of relief as a squirrel fled the cellar. Masters descended the steps slowly. Fortunately, they were stone and didn't creak. Inside, the cellar was pitch black. There was an oil lantern hanging by the door. Masters picked it up and sniffed it. It had been used recently. There was oil in it, so Masters carefully took a match from his vest and, standing back from the door, lit the lantern. Holding the light high above his head with his left hand and holding his pistol with his right, he stepped into the cellar.

The lamp illuminated stone walls and a dirt floor. The cellar was about half the size of the house. There was a stairway leading up to the house, but it was blocked by rubble. Masters walked around the heavy gray stone walls which made up the foundation of the house. He held the lantern high, making sure that there were no doors or additional rooms where someone could hide. He even looked up and checked the ceiling. Only the beams covered by a floor were above his head. When he was convinced that the door he used was the only entrance to the cellar, he began to search the cellar itself. The cellar contained a cot with blankets, a stove which looked recently used, and an open trunk. There were also some shelves on the wall which contained preserves and vegetables in jars. They looked edible and Masters deduced that the fire that had consumed the house occurred relatively recently. Ordinarily, one would be able to tell by the smell of the burnt timbers, but the rain washed away any chance of that.

Masters turned his attention to the open trunk. During his initial search he had glanced inside. It posed no threat so he continued to explore the rest of the cellar. Satisfied now that he was the only occupant of the cellar he was drawn to it. He hung the lantern on a hook in the beam above the trunk placed there just for that purpose. Masters took one more look around and holstered his pistol. He knelt by the trunk and smiled. Inside was a Confederate major's uniform, a suit of civilian clothes, a wallet, and a small leather case. Masters picked up the wallet first. It contained over three thousand dollars in Yankee greenbacks. It was enough to buy the bookstore of his dreams. The leather case was the most amazing piece of evidence. It contained passes from both the Army of Northern Virginia and the Army of the Potomac. They were issued in several names and they were genuine. The last item he looked at took his breath away. It was a letter of instruction from U.S. Secretary of War Edwin Stanton to an unnamed party to kill Robert E. Lee prior to the Union advance on April 5.

The Spy watched Masters from his hiding place behind the shelves and held the .44 caliber Colt at the ready. He had learned his lesson after shooting Ellison and opted for the heavier caliber. The Spy smiled. Masters had swallowed the bait. The old couple who occupied the house before the Spy murdered them were members of the Underground Railway and had hidden escaped slaves in this very cubby hole. A small, nearly invisible hole allowed anyone hiding there to observe most of the cellar without moving. The Spy had ingratiated himself to the couple and they told him of their loyalty to the Union. Anderson had, of course, confessed his own loyalty to the "Grand Old Flag" and they boasted of the slaves they had hidden. The Spy smiled in approval when they showed him their "hidey hole." He killed them both that night, and after arranging the cellar to suit his needs, he burned the house down the following morning. The bad weather made the fire less conspicuous and the smoke was hidden in the drizzle. This was where he had "found" the stoves he took to the hospital.

The Spy's horse was stabled in a small shed hidden in the woods. He dismounted and headed quickly for the cellar while the horse plodded to its familiar stall. Anderson expected Masters to follow the horse, but the Confederate lieutenant headed directly for the house. The Spy had barely enough time to close the opening of the "hidey hole." Anderson waited until Masters was absorbed in the trunk and pushed the door to the hidden chamber open. He took three quiet steps and stood far enough behind Masters to prevent the young Confederate from leaping at him.

"Don't move," the Spy said quietly.

Masters froze, wondering where the assassin had come from.

"Raise your hands and turn around but don't stand up," the Spy said calmly. "If you understand, nod your head."

Masters nodded. He had to follow directions until he could see where the assassin was. It would be his only chance. He did as he was told. When he turned on his haunches he recognized Bailey. The man was too far away to try to knock him off balance. Perhaps he could distract him enough to find an opening or a chance to jump for cover.

"Who are you?" Masters asked.

The Spy smiled. "Lieutenant Masters, isn't it?"

"That's right," Masters said, glancing around for something to help himself with.

"Lieutenant Masters, one thing I never do is explain."

It is doubtful whether Tarleton Masters was aware of anything else. The Spy's bullet caught him squarely in the forehead. His kepi went flying and he sprawled back on the cellar floor. The Spy walked over to ensure that Masters was dead, then went quickly to the door of the cellar and listened. He couldn't hear anyone riding away. He was positive Masters had been alone when he followed him, but he had to make sure. He left the cellar and skirted the wood line. There he found Masters' horse. The Spy returned to the cellar, dragged Masters' body by his feet to the trees, and hid it under some leaves because he didn't have time to bury it. When he returned to the cellar, he retrieved the cap. There was blood on it and that would serve the purpose. Next he retrieved the letter from the trunk. This should do the trick for Major Jordan, he thought.

Jordan returned from his work late that evening. The Light Division was getting ready to go to war. Supplies were still short, but the regiments were beginning to drill and men who had been absent without leave were beginning to return to their units. As a result there were a rash of court-martials. The army went through a charade about taking away a man's pay when the money was worthless and confining him to camp when there was no place to go. The court-martials were done more for the benefit of the men who stayed than anything else. Their commanders, for the most part, were glad not to have the absent men to feed in the winter and they were happy to have them back for the campaign season. The Confederacy could not afford to squander its manpower. There were, of course, cases in which deserters were shot, but these men usually had committed some serious crime in addition to deserting.

All this activity kept the headquarters very busy and drew Jordan further away from where he could observe Bailey. He relied on Masters to keep him informed and was concerned when Masters didn't come to see him. Jordan thought about looking for him, but he was tired and hungry. He decided to get something to eat, but he needed to think. He stretched out on his cot and closed his eyes for a moment. When Jordan awoke it was early Friday morning. It was nowhere near reveille, but he was refreshed after the first long sleep he'd had in days. Walker was not in the hut. He was probably off on another inspection. Jordan sat up and rubbed his eyes. It was dark and still raining, but he had to relieve himself and wash up. He put on his coat and walked down the duckboards to the latrine.

Bailey carefully opened the door to Jordan's hut. He was prepared to strangle the major in his sleep if given the chance, but Jordan wasn't there. He was tempted to wait for the major and surprise him when he returned, but when he heard the officer of the guard talking to a sentry, he decided to adhere to his original plan. Jordan's quarters were too public. He placed the items on the cracker box near Jordan's bed and slipped away.

When Jordan returned he lit a candle and saw Masters' kepi and a piece of paper on the box. As soon as he saw them a chill ran up his spine. When he picked up the cap, Masters' blood came off on his hand and Jordan knew that his friend was dead.

"Oh, damn!" Jordan said, fighting back the tears. "Why Charley?"

He picked up the paper, hoping against hope that it might be a ransom note; that Masters was injured and not dead, but Bailey didn't need hostages. It was the letter of instruction from Stanton to the assassin to kill Lee. A vicious anger welled up in him and Jordan grabbed his pistol. He was going to ride to the hospital and kill Bailey right then. He was actually checking the charges in the big revolver when he stopped himself. He took a deep breath and sat on his bunk. His hands were still shaking with rage but he put the pistol down. No, that's what he wants me to do, Jordan thought. That why he did this. He wants me to be angry enough to go after him, but I won't do it. That was the way he killed Charley, but I'm not going to let him kill me. I'm going to kill him, but not in rage. He's had all the advantages until now, but he's made his first big mistake.

Jordan dressed and asked the orderly who put the items in his tent on the off chance that the man might have seen something. He hadn't. Bailey was too smart for that. Then Jordan asked the orderly to saddle his horse while he grabbed a mouthful of corn-bread and some chicory coffee for breakfast. A few minutes later he was on his way to Colonel Longfellow's headquarters.

The colonel was at his desk which was covered with papers. He looked as if he had been up all night. The look he gave Jordan was not one of welcome. Jordan didn't salute and the colonel didn't seem to care.

"What do you want?" Longfellow asked.

"Charley's dead," Jordan told him.

"How?" The colonel's expression of fatigue changed to one of genuine sorrow.

"Bailey, Ferris or whatever his name is killed him." He put the kepi on the colonel's desk. Longfellow picked it up and looked at it.

"Did you see it?" Longfellow asked.

"No," Jordan said flatly.

"How did you get this?" Longfellow's tone was accusatory.

"It was in my tent this morning. This was with it," Jordan said, handing the Stanton letter to Longfellow. "That's the letter that Mrs. Ratliffe saw, colonel. I'm convinced of it."

The colonel read through the letter and looked at him with contempt. "So, the great Major Jordan who is such an expert on intelligence matters that he turned the entire city of Washington upside down is convinced this is the letter Mrs. Ratliffe saw." Longfellow's tone was snide and mocking. "This is what I think of you and this letter." Longfellow tore the letter in two.

Jordan's pent-up anger and frustration boiled to the surface. "That's evidence!" he shouted. He reached for the letter but he couldn't get it away from Longfellow.

"Evidence, my foot!" Longfellow shouted. "Now, I'll tell you for the last time. This is an intelligence headquarters. We don't deal in fairy tales. I'm heartily sick of your supposed assassination plot. There never was and there is not now any evidence to indicate a plot to assassinate any of our generals."

"Are you going to ignore Masters' murder the way you ignored Ellison's?" Jordan snapped.

"Ellison's death is of no concern to me," Longfellow said regaining his composure. "As for Masters', if I can connect you with it in any way, I'll see that you are court-martialed and hanged for it. Is that clear?" Longfellow's red-rimmed eyes stared at him in unmitigated hatred.

"Go ahead, draw up the papers," Jordan retorted. "All we need is Lydia Ratliffe here to testify. Then the court-martial can see how you've ignored everything to do with this case and got one of your best men killed!"

"Get out!" Longfellow was no longer calm. He screamed hysterically. "Captain Patterson!"

Captain Patterson came rushing into the room.

"Get him out of here!" Longfellow was in an uncontrollable rage.

"I think you'd better go, sir," the captain said softly.

Jordan backed out the door. Longfellow looked as if he were about to have apoplexy. "I think you're right."

"I'm sorry, sir," Patterson said as he escorted Jordan to the porch.

"How long has he been like this?" Jordan asked.

"I don't know," the captain said with a shrug. "He works night and day. General Stuart tried to get him to take a short furlough, but he refused. The colonel said there would be plenty of time after we won the war this summer. "Do you think we will, Major Jordan?" His question was almost a plea.

Jordan who was trying hard to calm himself down hadn't heard the question. "What?"

"Win the war?"

"With the likes of him we'll be lucky if we don't lose it," Jordan said bitterly. He mounted his horse and rode back to Camp Gregg. Could he stop the assassin alone?

On Saturday, the rain stopped and the sun came out. The day was bright and clear and warm and everyone held his breath. Each man knew that the beginning of the campaigning season was only days, perhaps hours away. As if to reinforce that fact, a Yankee observation balloon rose high above the trees and swayed gently in the sky. Anxious messages were telegraphed to Longstreet to return from Suffolk. Lee needed his veteran divisions immediately. Couriers came and went and the regiments of the Light Division made ready to march. Then, nothing happened. The ground was still too wet. It needed to dry a little more. It dried in the sunshine of Saturday, and Sunday dawned warm and clear.

Jordan attended a tent service given by the Reverend Lacy. Lee and Jackson both attended. Jackson naturally brought his wife and the baby. They sat on the plain wooden benches and listened to the service, then Reverend Lacy rose and gave his sermon. The scripture he had chosen was the parable of The Rich Man and Lazarus. The two generals were deeply moved by the sermon and wept openly as they thought of family and home. Jordan only caught bits and pieces of it. He was too busy watching Bailey and Bailey was watching Jackson. Jackson and Lee sat side by side and it would have been quite natural for Bailey's attention to switch from one general to another, but the assassin looked only at Jackson. Why? The answer was more disturbing than the question. Jordan left the service before Bailey could see him. He didn't want to give himself away. He needed to discuss his dilemma with someone, only the someone he needed to discuss it with was dead.

Jordan couldn't shake the feeling that he had been deceived. In fact, he was convinced of it. Think, he told himself. Think! He had to take each conclusion in a logical sequence, regardless of where it led.

Lee is the commander of the Army of Northern Virginia. Except for Sharpsburg, he has won every battle he fought against the North. If he isn't the target then who is?

The answer was plainly Jackson. But why? Lee was the guiding hand of the army. Why indeed. When he began to look at the logic of his own supposition, every piece fell right into place.

Jackson is the most victorious general in either army. He moves his troops so fast that they are called "foot cavalry" by both sides. Europeans refer to him as the "new Napoleon." If Lee were killed who would replace him? There are only three generals senior enough. Joseph Johnston has not fully recovered from his wounds so he wouldn't be able to take command. Longstreet is the next choice but he has not done well enough in independent command. Jordan thought of the mess that Longstreet had gotten into in Suffolk County thrashing around in the swamp and fighting the Yankees over that worthless Fort Huger. I can't imagine Jackson getting involved in a mess like that, Jordan thought. So, Jackson would be the only one who could replace Lee.

The next step in the logical process was more disturbing. Jackson was always the one who made Lee's tactical and strategic vision a reality. Who could replace Jackson if he were badly wounded or killed? Jordan knew of no one. No general in the Confederacy had his sense of space and timing or his spirit. If Jackson were to be killed there would be no one who could turn Lee's concepts to reality. Jackson was Bailey's target; Jordan was sure of that. The only problem now was how to stop him.

Camp Gregg, Virginia
April 29, 1863

On Monday and Tuesday, there were reports of the movement of large numbers of Union troops moving behind the Yankee lines. On the morning of Wednesday, April 29, 1863, the Army of Northern Virginia woke to the sound of gunfire. General Stoneman, commander of the Yankee cavalry, opened the campaigning season by forcing his way across the Rappahannock. He had been attempting to get across the river since the fourteenth, but he had been frustrated by the weather. Now he was across the river and driving south. Large numbers of Federal troops were at Banks' Ford west of Fredericksburg. There could be no doubt now. The Union Army, over 100,000 strong, was on the move. Unlike its previous campaigns, it was not heading for Richmond. It's target was the most valuable prize in the Confederacy, the Army of Northern Virginia. If any doubted the seriousness of the situation, he must surely have been convinced when the Reverend Lacy escorted Mrs. Jackson, little Julia, and their colored maid to the depot at Guiney's Station so they could catch the earliest train south.

In the afternoon, three Yankee corps crossed the Rappahannock at Kelly's Ford. Meade's Fifth Corps, which some said were the toughest troops in the Yankee Army, crossed at Ely's Ford. The Confederate left flank had been turned and the Yankee corps were converging on the road junction which was named for the small farm of Chancellorsville. This position offered a number of roads that led to the rear of Lee's army. More Union troops had crossed the river at Fredericksburg. Lee, with 61,000 men, a force roughly half that of Hooker's, viewed the situation with concern. However, he refused to panic and declined to be drawn into a general engagement. The division commanded by Dick Anderson was ordered to occupy the high ground east of Chancellorsville.

On the evening of April 29, Jackson ordered his corps to the trenches near Hamilton's Crossing, while he performed a reconnaissance of the area with his chief engineer. The Light Division began the twenty-five mile march as it began to drizzle. On the last day of April, the troops huddled in the same wet position they occupied during the Battle of Fredericksburg. It was there that General Gregg was killed holding off the men of Meade's Corps. It had been an anxious day for the Light Division and they had no desire to repeat it. Jordan was kept busy carrying orders and dispatches, but Bailey was never far from his mind. How was he to prevent the assassin from carrying out his work without any idea of his whereabouts?

The doctors and the orderlies at the hospital began preparing their instruments for the avalanche of casualties that was bound to occur when the two armies met in battle. They were surprised to see Bailey saddling his mule.

"Where are you going, Mr. Bailey?" Dr. Warren asked.

"I am going to the battle where I can do the most good."

"But you can do the most good here, sir," the doctor insisted.

"I have spoken to the Lord and he has instructed me to go with the men in danger and offer them His comfort in this holy struggle."

The doctor shook his head. He was very fond of Bailey but he had no hold over him. Bailey didn't even draw a salary. "Be careful," he said.

"Fear God, dread nought, doctor," Bailey said, placing his hand on the doctor's shoulder. "I will return unless He wills otherwise."

Bailey rode his mule to the ruined farmhouse. If the Yankees advanced, the house would be in the middle of the coming battle and that might be awkward. It was one of those things that could not be controlled. Bailey let the mule have its head. The animal knew the way even in the dark. The Spy now had to make a decision, and it was not an easy one. Should he enter the battle area as Bailey, the trusted civilian, or as Ferris, the major from the 18th North Carolina. Bailey would certainly not be questioned but he might be considered in the way. Ferris, on the other hand, would be another person in a gray uniform, noticed but ignored.

Anderson tied his mule up at the cellar door and lit the lantern. He changed into the Confederate major's uniform and lifted a bundle of cloth from the bottom of the trunk. He carefully unwrapped it. Inside the bundle was a seven-shot Spencer repeating carbine. He wiped the excess grease from the weapon and worked the action. Next, he loaded the carbine with a tube of cartridges. He took several other tubes from the trunk and went to get his horse. When he was convinced that everything was in order, he ate some hardtack and laid down to rest for an hour while he reviewed what he planned to do.

On the morning of May 1, there was a skirmish between Dick Anderson's Division and the Yankees of Meade's Fifth Corps. The

Union commanders were itching for a fight and they were bringing one on. Suddenly, they received an order to disengage and withdraw from the strategic road junction which they occupied. Prior to the battle, Hooker had bragged that God had better have mercy on Lee, because Joseph Hooker would not. Now the boastful Yankee general had lost his nerve.

The Union corps commanders were amazed at the the order to withdraw. They protested, and for a moment it looked as if Hooker's subordinates might deliberately ignore their commander's orders. It might have been better for the Union cause if they had, but these men were disciplined soldiers. They obeyed the hated directive and the Yankee soldiers began to withdraw at 11:00 A.M. This gave Lee the chance he was looking for.

Stonewall Jackson, A.P. Hill, and their staffs were shown to a hill by an officer from one of the regiments in the area. The view from the hill took Jordan's breath away. He could see the Union lines clearly. The Yankees were digging in with the Rappahannock River at their backs. It would have been bad enough if the river ran parallel to their line, but it didn't. It was in the shape of a "V" with the open end toward the Confederate lines. Their right flank hung in the open. It didn't take a military genius to discern the solution to the problem. All one had to do was strike them on their right, funnel them into the "V", and crush them against the river. It would be a slaughter.

This was the battle the Confederacy had been hoping for. One big question was, could they do it with only 61,000 men to cover the entire battlefield? If so, which troops would make the attack? Another question concerned the roads: were they capable of supporting such an advance? The entire area was covered with thick undergrowth and was nicknamed "The Wilderness." This was where the genius counted. As the first of May drew to a close, Lee and Jackson sat on Yankee cracker boxes and sipped coffee. They were joined by Major Hotchkiss, Jackson's map maker. Jackson had sent him out to scout the route hours before. Hotchkiss unfolded the map and traced Jackson's proposed maneuver.

"And what do you propose to make this movement with?" Lee asked.

"With my whole corps," was Jackson's calm reply.

Jackson's corps was almost 28,000 strong. That meant nearly

half of Lee's force would strike the enemy on his exposed flank. Lee would be left with only two divisions—roughly 14,000 men— to cover his front against 50,000 Yankees. The remainder would have to cover the Union feint at Fredericksburg. It was a gamble, but Lee decided it was worth the risk. Jackson's troops would begin marching at 4:00 A.M. the following morning.

Light Division Headquarters
Hamilton Crossing
May 2, 1863

Stonewall Jackson made his plan and issued the order of march for his corps. D.H. Hill's Division under the command of General Rhodes would go first; Trimble's Division under the command of General Colston would march second; and the Light Division would bring up the rear. All units must be ready to march at 4:00 A.M. Jordan got very little sleep that night.

The Light Division, like the other divisions, was a smaller version of the corps. There were plans to be made, marching orders to be issued, and dispatches to be delivered. From A.P. Hill down to the junior captain on the staff there was work to be done. Hill was now wearing his battered slouch hat and his battle jacket which had no rank. He didn't need any. Everyone knew exactly who he was. The order of march for the Light Division was Pender's Brigade, Heth's Brigade, Lane's, McGowan's, Thomas', and Archer's. Only the soldiers got any sleep and there was little of that. Every man in the army knew that a great and, no doubt, decisive battle was not far off. The veterans wrote last minute letters home, checked their equipment, and grabbed what little sleep they could. The new recruits fidgeted and worried.

At 4:00 A.M. the Light Division stood ready to march and waited. D.H. Hill's division began it's march at 4:30, but Jackson's Corps was marching along a single route and it took time for all the units to get on the road. Jordan stood at headquarters and waited with the rest. He was impatient to strike at the Yankees but he also wondered where Bailey was. Jordan was worried and was tempted to go and look for the assassin, but he knew he couldn't. He was needed at his post. Perhaps this was the battle that would win the war.

The Light Division began to move at 7:30. The day was warm

and with first light came a ground fog that hid Jackson's great turning movement from the Yankee balloon. Soon the weather cleared and the sun shone down from a cloudless sky. There were no enemy observation balloons to be seen. The roads were dry enough to support artillery and wagons, but damp enough to keep down the dust. Conditions were perfect. It was a long march, but the soldiers hurried. Like their corps commander, the great Stonewall Jackson, they knew that time was of the essence.

To the layman, a march looks very simple. All one has to do is walk from one place to another in a given time. For an individual it is, indeed, a simple act but for tens of thousands, it is as complex an undertaking as battle itself. Each brigade must know its proper place within the division and each regiment must know its proper place within the brigade. Unit integrity must be maintained so that each regiment is ready to be deployed in battle without interfering with the regiments to its right and left. Rest periods must be coordinated so that units do not become intermingled. Communication has to be maintained with all parts of the column, so dispatch riders and staff officers from the regiments, brigades, divisions, and the corps are constantly in motion. They move up and down the column, keeping it in order, reporting changes, and rounding up stragglers who couldn't—or wouldn't—keep up the pace.

The Spy, dressed as Major Harvey Ferris, understood the mechanics of the march, and he hovered on the edge of it, riding up and down the columns of marching men, carrying a small dispatch case. He looked like all the other staff officers and no one questioned his presence. He easily learned what the objective of Jackson's Corps was and had to admit it was a bold plan which strongly suggested genius. Should it succeed, it would no doubt become a classic for future generations of military men to study. Success, of course, depended on the commander, and if the Spy had his way, the commander would be dead before dawn. Salmon P. Chase was right. Kill Jackson and you kill the South's ability to wage war. As the afternoon wore on, the Spy drew closer to the head of the column. There he saw Jackson impatiently urging his men forward.

There was only one uncomfortable moment during the march. In the afternoon, Yankee troops attacked the 23rd Georgia at

Catherine's Furnace, thinking they were retreating. Thomas and Archer deployed their brigades, beat off the half-hearted attack, and double-timed to catch up with the rest of the Light Division. At approximately 4:00 P.M. only two-thirds of Jackson's force were at the point of departure for the attack. Except for Heth's, all of the Light Division's brigades were still on the road. Jackson realized it would be dark soon and he was determined not to let this opportunity slip away. To the units already in position, he gave the order to deploy. He would begin his attack with the forces at hand and let Hill come forward when he could. In the thickets, deployment was agonizingly slow. Jackson rode forward and made a final reconnaissance. He could see the Yankee soldiers in their camp with their arms stacked, waiting to cook their evening meal. Jackson returned and with a smile of grim satisfaction and gave the order to advance.

The Yankees were taken completely by surprise. The first indication they had that something was amiss was a stampede of wildlife rushing from the woods. The second indication was the long gray battle line screaming the terrifying "Rebel Yell." The first onslaught was devastating. The troops of the Union XIth Corps panicked. No organized resistance was offered as thousands of blue-clad troops bolted to the rear seeking safety. In less than an hour an entire Union division ceased to exist.

It is an axiom that no military plan survives the first contact with the enemy. In some ways, the success of the plan was its undoing. Units became inextricably intermixed and the advance slowed. The only unit left intact was the Light Division, minus Heth's Brigade. Hill was without orders, but he could sense victory and was eager for battle. Impatient as usual, he called Jordan to his side.

"Major Jordan!"

"Yes sir!"

"Find General Jackson and ask for directions for our advance."

"Yes, sir." Jordan saluted and galloped toward the advancing divisions of the corps.

The Army of Northern Virginia was on the verge of a great victory, perhaps the greatest of the war. Jordan rode forward. All around him was wreckage—Yankee wreckage. Prisoners plodded to the rear by the hundreds. Fires, started by exploding shells, were burning throughout the forest, consuming everything in their path including helpless wounded men who couldn't move out of their way. The forest was alive with shouts, gunfire, and terrifying screams. The smell of gunpowder mixed with the smell of burning timber and sometimes burning flesh. It was a nightmare, and even though the moon rose in a clear sky, it was impossible for Jordan to tell where he was. That's when he saw him.

Jordan was not the only one having a difficult time in the chaos of the Battle of Chancellorsville. The Spy was finding it hard to locate his target. He had never had to track a man in the middle of a battle, but he remained calm. He found a quick solution.

"Dispatches for General Jackson," he would call whenever he came upon a unit. They invariably waved him forward. He felt he was getting close. Then he heard someone call his name.

"Ferris!"

The Spy didn't hesitate. He drew his carbine and swung in the saddle. Jordan had already drawn his pistol, but he had misjudged the distance in the dark. He fired and the bullet flew over the Spy's head. The Spy fired and his bullet gouged the bark in the tree next to Jordan's head. Instinctively, he pulled back behind the tree and fired again.

"Give up, Ferris," he called. "We know who you are."

The Spy's answer was another bullet which slammed into a branch above Jordan's head, showering his hat with bark. Jordan fired again and moved his horse around to see if he could get behind the man he knew as Ferris, but, by the time he reached the spot where Ferris had been, the Spy had disappeared in the darkness. Jordan spurred his horse forward. He found the Hazel Grove Road and followed it toward the sound of the firing. The night was growing cold, but he couldn't stop to put on his overcoat. He found Jackson at the intersection of the Hazel Grove and Plank roads. He was ordering General Lane forward. As soon as he rode up Jackson recognized him.

"Major Jordan, where is General Hill?" Jackson demanded. Before Jordan could answer, Jackson said, "Ah, there he is."

The restless Hill was riding toward them. The commander of the Light Division could not even wait for his own staff officer to report to him. Jordan wondered if Hill were angry with him for getting lost, but Hill didn't seem to notice him. The division com-

mander and Jackson seemed to have no differences. Both were
were excited with the prospects of the battle.

"Press them," Jackson told his subordinate anxiously. "Cut them
off from the United States Ford. Press them."

"My staff doesn't know the ground, general," Hill replied.

Jackson told Captain Boswell, his engineer, to go with Hill's staff
and show them the way. Hill and Jackson rode forward together,
following a scout who was a native of the area. Jordan, with no
specific instruction, followed behind them. After a short ride Hill
left Jackson. Jordan knew he shouldn't leave Jackson.

"Should I stay with General Jackson and report any changes,
sir?" Jordan asked Hill.

"Good idea, Major Jordan. Rejoin us as soon as we cross the
Plank Road."

"Yes sir." Jordan saluted and rode after Jackson.

Jackson had already moved ahead of his own troops to a piece
of high ground where he could hear the Union troops digging in.
Jordan was unable to see Jackson, but in the corner of his eye he
saw something glint in the moonlight. A chill went up Jordan's
spine. He knew exactly what it was. Nearly invisible in the trees
was a mounted man with a drawn carbine. Jordan drew his pistol
and urged his horse toward Ferris. Just then a group of riders
came toward him. It was Jackson and his staff. Their route would
bring them between Jordan and the assassin. Jordan holstered his
pistol and spurred his horse toward the general. When he drew
even with Jackson, he grabbed the bridle of Jackson's horse.

"General," Jordan shouted. "Don't expose yourself! You are in
danger!"

Jackson pulled his horse away from Jordan. "There is no danger, sir. The enemy is routed. Tell General Hill to press on!"

Jordan wanted to tell the general that the danger was not from
the enemy, but he didn't have a chance.

The Spy watched as Jordan cantered up to Jackson. He was
blocking the line of fire. For a moment the loudest sound was the
call of the whipoorwills. It was louder than the sound of the dying
battle and the shouting of the officers. The Spy took a rest against
a tree. When Jackson pulled clear and started for the lines, Anderson fired. Jackson, hit, swayed in his saddle. Suddenly, the nervous Confederate troops to their front began firing at Jackson's

group. One man fell from his saddle. Anderson, unable to see Jackson, worked the lever and fired at Jordan. The bullet struck him square in the shoulder and the force of the impact threw Jordan from his horse. He hit the ground hard and lay there, stunned.

"Cease firing!" someone shouted. It sounded like Hill. "You're firing at your own men!"

"It's a lie!" the Spy shouted. "Pour it on 'em boys!"

There was another volley and Jackson staggered again. Another of his staff fell. The Spy was about to take another shot when Jackson's horse plunged into the brush. The general hit his head on a branch and pulled his horse into the open. Then he leaned over in the saddle. One of his staff caught him and led him behind a tree.

"Damn!" the Spy swore. He could see nothing of his prey. He knew he had hit Jackson, but was he dead?

Jordan lay on his back. He was only semi-conscious and he felt dizzy and sick to his stomach. Was Jackson all right? Jordan tried to sit up, but his left shoulder erupted in pain. He reached over to the spot that ached and felt the blood. He decided to roll over on his stomach and get up on his hands and knees. He rolled over on his right side, fighting the nausea. Then he managed to get to his knees. He crawled over to a tree and sat up against it. He could see a group gathered around someone lying on the ground. Hill was cradling the man's head in his hands while someone else held a flask to the man's lips. The man on the ground was Jackson.

"Oh my God," Jordan moaned.

Someone heard Jordan's moan and went over to him. Jordan didn't recognize him, but his benefactor seemed to know him. "We'll have an ambulance here any moment, Major Jordan," the man said. He pressed a canteen to Jordan's lips.

"Thanks," Jordan said. Jordan could hear the sounds of guns being unlimbered. The sounds were muffled as if they came from another room. Suddenly, the Union artillery opened with a hail of canister which cut down trees, shredded brush, and made sparks fly on the rocky ground. Jordan lost consciousness.

The Spy was caught unaware by the Yankee artillery. Even though he was not in the direct line of fire, a blast of canister hit his horse. The wounded beast threw him and then fell dead. The Spy lay

stunned for a moment then kept still while the hail of iron continued to fly over his head. There was still work to be done. He
couldn't leave until Jackson was dead, and for personal satisfaction
he wanted to make sure that Jordan was also dead. While the
greatest general in the Confederate Army was being dragged to an
ambulance under fire, the Spy began removing the uniform of
Harvey Ferris. Once again, he had to become Jeremiah Bailey. A
new legend was about to be born in the Army of Northern Virginia.
Several men would later testify that "the Reverend" Bailey had
saved them from the flames in the thickets of Chancellorsville.

CHAPTER 11

Army of Northern Virginia
Second Corps Field Hospital
May 6, 1863

FROM SATURDAY, MAY 2, 1863 to the following Wednesday, the Army of Northern Virginia attacked a foe nearly twice its strength and sent it reeling back across the Rappahannock River licking its wounds. It was one of the most incredible victories in military history. The South was jubilant, but many held their breath because the architect of that victory lay seriously wounded in a bedroom of the plantation office of the Chandler Farm near Guiney's Station.

On the night of May 2, the wounded Jackson was carried to an ambulance and taken from the scene of his wounding to the Second Corps Field Hospital. There, Dr. McGuire leaned over Jackson and told him they would have to examine him.

"We might find the bones so badly broken that our only choice will be amputation," McGuire told him truthfully.

"Do what you think best," the general said impatiently.

Jackson was given chloroform and went to sleep with the word "Blessing" on his lips.

McGuire and the other physicians began their examination of Jackson shortly after 2:00 A.M. on the morning of May 3. A smoothbore musket ball was found in the general's right hand. Some of the North Carolina regiments still had smoothbore muskets. McGuire held the ball in his palm and looked at the other doctors.

"Our troops," he said.

It was an honest mistake. The only person who could refute McGuire's conclusion was laying a few yards away from where the examination was taking place, but he was unconscious. Despite the bullet, the right hand was not badly injured and could be saved. The left arm was a different story. The conical Spencer bullet had done its work well and had badly shattered the bones. The doctors had no choice. Dr. McGuire and two other doctors performed the amputation quickly and efficiently. Jackson lay mercifully asleep while McGuire cut away the damaged tissue and sawed through the bone. Another doctor tied the arteries while a third monitored the general's heart with a stethoscope. Half an hour later Jackson was awake and able to take some coffee. At half past three he was able to take a message from Sandy Pendleton. A.P. Hill had also been wounded. Jackson was lucid but weak. He was told that Stuart had assumed command of his corps.

"Tell General Stuart to do what he thinks best," Jackson told the adjutant.

Shortly after Pendleton left, Jackson fell into a deep sleep. He awoke, took breakfast, and told everyone he was going to get well. Then he sent his aide and brother-in-law, Joe Morrison, to Richmond to bring back his wife. Jackson received a note from Lee lamenting that it would have been best for the South if Lee had been wounded instead of Jackson. He also congratulated Jackson on his victory.

"General Lee is very kind, but he should give the praise to God," Jackson said.

The battle was still in doubt on Monday, May 4, so Lee ordered Jackson moved to a safer place. Just after daylight on Tuesday, he was placed in an ambulance for the day-long ride to the Chandler Plantation. The trip was not unpleasant. Engineers preceded the wagon, filling in potholes and pulling up roots. The walking wounded cheered as he went by and the people offered pails of milk and other delicacies. Some knelt beside the road and prayed for Jackson's swift recovery. Inside the ambulance, Jackson analyzed Hooker's plan and told Dr. McGuire where the Union commander had gone wrong.

When Jackson arrived at the Chandler plantation, McGuire decided to put him in a bedroom in the office. There were sick soldiers in the house and the doctor didn't want to risk infection.

The bullet that struck Richard Jordan had passed through the fleshy part of the major's shoulder without hitting bone, so that he was in no danger of losing the arm. Unfortunately, he contracted a bad fever and the doctors feared for his life. Jordan passed in and out of delirium for four days. On the afternoon of May 6 he opened his eyes and attempted to sit up. The pain in his shoulder numbed his body. He groaned loudly.

"Don't exert yourself, Dick," a soft voice told him. "You need rest."

Jordan focused his eyes. "Jennifer?"

"Yes. Are you awake?"

"If you're actually here and I'm not dreaming, I'm awake." He was suddenly aware of his surroundings. There were men groaning all around him and the stench was bad. It was the field hospital. "You shouldn't be here," he told her. "This is no place for a lady." She didn't answer and he saw there were tears in her eyes. "You're crying."

"It's because you're going to be all right. You've had a bad fever. The doctors were worried, but it broke last night."

"My arm?" he asked warily.

"The doctor told me the bullet didn't hit bone and the wound is clean. If you rest, it will be all right." She spoke gently and soothingly and wiped his head with a cool, damp cloth.

"What day is today?" he asked, suddenly.

"It's Wednesday, the sixth. Why?"

"Jackson?"

"He was shot by his own men and his arm had to be amputated, but he appears to be out of danger."

"Still in danger," he said. It was difficult to talk. His mouth was dry. "Water."

Jennifer raised his head and put a glass to his lips. He took three large gulps of the cool liquid.

"Jackson is still in danger," he said more clearly.

"Why?"

"He wasn't shot by his own men. Not at first, anyway. He was shot by Ferris or Bailey or whatever his name is. I think he shot me, too."

"Dick, Dr. McGuire found a Southern bullet in his hand. He's positive that General Jackson was shot by his own men."

"There may have been a Southern bullet in his hand, but the one that took his arm came from an assassin's carbine. I saw it. I have to warn him."

He tried to sit up again, but Jennifer gently pushed him back down. "You can't. You've had a very bad time. You've had a fever for three days. You must rest. The doctor says that you lost a lot of blood and you must have lots of rest. Please, Dick. If you won't rest for your sake do it for mine. There's nothing you can do. The doctor says you won't be fit for duty for at least three months. I'm arranging to take you to Oakview to recuperate. I just hope your parents won't mind."

She smiled so tenderly and sweetly at him that Jordan couldn't help but return the smile. She looked beautiful, but something still had to be done to warn Jackson. He grabbed her wrist but he had no strength.

"You must warn them, please!" The effort of talking was exhausting him.

"All right," she agreed.

"Promise?"

"I promise."

Jordan was drained. He lay back on his pillow and closed his eyes. Sleep came immediately.

The Chandler House
Guiney's Station, Virginia
May 7, 1863

"The general is sleeping comfortably," Dr. McGuire said. "He really should not be disturbed. The other doctors and I feel that he's now out of danger and that with a proper period of recuperation he may once again command the soldiers of our nation. Unfortunately, I must advise against anyone except family and close friends paying him a visit at this time, Mr. Bailey, though I am sure he will be gratified to hear of your good wishes."

"Thank you, doctor," Bailey said. Tears were forming in his

eyes. "We are all praying for him. God bless you for what you've done."

"You, too, Mr. Bailey. Your services have not gone unnoticed."

"I am only doing that which the Lord commands me to do, doctor. Good day."

"Good day to you, Mr. Bailey."

The doctor watched Bailey walk away. He liked Bailey and knew the general did, too, but he was concerned about Jackson. The general had pneumonia in his right lung. With plenty of rest he would get over it, but McGuire couldn't afford to take any chances.

The Spy, hat in hand, bowed graciously and left the Chandler house. He mounted his mule and rode away without looking back. Things were not as well as Dr. McGuire made them seem. The doctor himself looked totally exhausted. That meant he was by Jackson's side day and night. Nevertheless, the news that the general had a good chance to recover was not what the Spy wanted to hear. He couldn't leave until Jackson was dead. There had to be a way to get in and finish the job. He first thought of entering the house at night to smother Jackson with a pillow, but that was a bad idea on two counts. The first was that smothering someone took time. The second was that Jackson was constantly attended by someone, and even a weakened person could create a ruckus when frightened. What the Spy needed was a method that was quick and silent.

The mule plodded back to the hospital while Anderson pondered another unsolved problem. During his sojourn around the battlefield and the hospitals he tried to locate Major Richard Jordan. He had been told that Jordan was wounded and underwent treatment at the Second Corps Field Hospital. By the time Anderson arrived at the hospital Jordan had been moved. No one knew exactly where. As long as the meddling major stayed out of the way, Anderson was satisfied, although he preferred Jordan dead.

Despite the fact that Sarah and Coppy had lain a thick mattress in the back of the wagon and covered him with blankets, Jordan's journey to Oakview Manor was very painful. Jordan would wake for short periods and then drift off to sleep again. He desperately wanted to tell someone at headquarters about the danger to Jackson, but he couldn't. He was away from his place of duty—weak and utterly helpless, and he hated it. Jennifer rode in the back of the wagon with him, holding his hand and making sure he had water.

"Did you tell anyone about Bailey, Jennifer?"

"I tried to visit General Heth who has taken General Hill's place, but he couldn't see me. I then tried to see General Stuart and General Lee, but they were all too busy with the battle."

"There has to be something we can do," he said. His voice was tinged with despair.

"There are some things we have to trust to God, Dick." She didn't know what else to say. Right now all that really mattered was making sure Dick Jordan got well.

Fredericksburg Army Hospital
May 8, 1863

Bailey sat on his cot by the stove, wracking his brain for a way around his dilemma. Many solutions presented themselves, but each time he thought of one, its logical conclusion was a dead end. He considered every option, from burning the Chandler house down to waiting until the general was moved elsewhere. Every course of action he could think of was either too risky, too messy, or too uncertain.

He was becoming increasingly frustrated when he looked up and watched one of the orderlies remove a bottle from the medicine chest. The orderly carried the bottle to a bedridden patient and sat beside the bed. He uncorked the bottle and poured some of the medicine into a spoon. The orderly gently lifted the man's head and put the spoon to his lips. The patient made a face, then asked for a drink of water. Something in a dark corner of Anderson's brain whispered "poison." The Spy had never used poison. "Accidents" and "suicides" were more his style. The inept police departments which investigated his commissions easily recognized accidents and suicides and accepted them. Poison was a dimension he hadn't considered until now. There was one way to learn.

"Excuse me, Dr. Warren," Bailey said, entering the doctor's office. "I hope I'm not disturbing you."

The doctor, sitting at his desk, put his pen down and smiled.

"Of course not, Mr. Bailey. Have a seat," he said, indicating a chair.

Bailey sat down.

"What can I do for you?" the doctor asked pleasantly.

"Well, we have a lot more wounded than we've ever had and some of them ask for medicine. I am totally ignorant of that subject and am afraid of dispensing the wrong thing. With all of the other orderlies so busy, I thought I might offer some assistance if I could."

"You're right to be concerned, Mr. Bailey. Some medicines can be very dangerous if given in the wrong doses or with the wrong things."

"I don't understand. Aren't all medicines supposed to be good for you?" Bailey asked innocently.

"Yes, they are," the doctor explained carefully. "But sometimes when you mix two medicines together they make a different substance which is harmful."

Bailey gave him a puzzled look.

"I'll give you an example," the doctor explained helpfully. "Take laudanum and alcohol. Laudanum is used for relieving pain and alcohol is used as a mild stimulant. Both are used in medicine, but if you mix them together and give them at the same time, then it causes a shock to the heart. If the patient were in a weakened condition, it would probably kill him."

"Oh, my Lord!" Bailey said, looking shocked. "I shall certainly not dispense any medicine then."

"It's not that bad," the doctor reassured him. "I will put you with a formally trained orderly and you can learn from him."

Bailey smiled gratefully. "That's very kind of you, Dr. Warren. You've been a great help to me."

"Always happy to be of assistance, Mr. Bailey."

The Spy went back to his duties and thought very carefully about the information the doctor had given him. Laudanum and alcohol were just what he needed, but how would he get Jackson to take it? When the orderly gave the patient a spoonful of medicine it tasted bad. It would be difficult to get Jackson to take something that tasted bad. How could he make whatever he gave Jackson taste good? He had not even finished the question when he knew the solution. Jackson's favorite drink was whiskey, lemon, and powdered white sugar. All the Spy would have to do was add laudanum. It shouldn't be any problem to get a half-conscious man to drink something he already liked.

Whiskey was abundant in the army and laudanum was available in the hospital, but the lemon and the sugar were difficult to find. The Spy used all his persuasiveness as Bailey and not a little gold to encourage those who had the items he needed to part with them. He already knew the routine at the Chandler house office because he had been observing it since McGuire moved Jackson there. There were no guards in or outside the office itself. Mrs. Jackson went to bed in the main house before eleven. Dr. McGuire and the general's servant, Jim, stayed with him. The doctor usually dozed on the sofa across the room from the general's bed. At approximately 11:30, Jim went to relieve himself. This took from ten to fifteen minutes. This nightly routine at the Chandler house never varied by more than a few minutes. The reports of Jackson's improving health made it necessary to act quickly, so the Spy decided it had to be done that very night. He mixed the laudanum, sugar, and lemon in the whiskey bottle and recorked it. In addition to the bottle and a glass, the Spy carried a pistol and a blackjack just in case.

The Spy rode his mule to the Chandler house and dismounted a hundred yards from the office in a grove. He tied the mule to a low branch and walked carefully up the road. The sky was overcast and it was very dark. The Spy stood in the shadows across from the office and waited patiently. Jim left the small frame building at 11:40 and headed for the privy. The Spy hurried across the yard to the office. He quietly opened the door and closed it behind him. Nothing could be heard except the sound of heavy breathing coming from the room on the far right. The Spy stepped carefully to the open door of Jackson's room and smiled.

The general was resting peacefully and the exhausted doctor was sound asleep on the couch. Anderson uncorked the bottle and poured some of the liquid into the glass. He stepped to the bed, gently lifted Jackson's head, and put the glass to the general's lips. Jackson came partially awake and took several swallows. Dr. McGuire stirred but continued to sleep. The Spy laid Jackson's head down carefully and recorked the bottle. Slipping the glass back in his pocket he left the room. He heard Jim's footsteps and hid in the empty office. He fingered the blackjack while Jim returned to the general's bedroom. Then, as silently as he entered, the Spy slipped out the door.

The Chandler House
Guiney's Station, Virginia
May 10, 1863

At 3:15 in the afternoon of May 10 1863, the Confederate States of America suffered their gravest military disaster. General Thomas Jonathan "Stonewall" Jackson, the "Southern Napoleon," died after uttering the words "Let us cross over the river and rest under the shade of the trees." The greatest tactical genius in the history of America and perhaps the world was dead. The South wept. Jefferson Davis, in a telegram to Lee, wrote, "A great national calamity has befallen us." General Robert E. Lee did not exaggerate when he wrote that he had lost his right arm. He would never find another. In the midst of the tragedy, few, if any, noticed Mr. Jeremiah Bailey pack his meager belongings on his mule and ride away.

The Spy rode to the cellar that had been his base of operations for so many weeks. Exhausted, he lay down on the cot, barely noticing the trace of stench that drifted into the cellar from Masters' unburied body decaying in the warm spring air. The Spy smiled as he thought of Jennifer Franks and fell asleep. He awoke late the following morning feeling totally refreshed. He dressed in civilian clothes and selected papers that identified him as a neutral English journalist. His other possessions included a small single-shot pocket pistol and the appropriate passes.

He strode over to the shed where he kept his horse, walked the animal back to the cellar, and saddled it. The Spy left the mule saddled and let it go, knowing it would plod back to the hospital and lend additional mystery to the disappearance of Jeremiah Bailey. He made one last check, then took the rest of the oil and spread it liberally around the cellar. Anderson walked up the stone steps for the last time and made a small torch with a stick and a few rags. He soaked the rags in oil, lit the torch, and tossed it down the steps. He mounted the horse quickly and spurred it forward. The fire built rapidly and exploded with a "whoof" as the flames consumed the evidence of his occupancy. A satisfied smile spread across his face. His work was finished. Now it was time to turn to personal matters.

The Spy arrived at Oakview Manor a little past three in the afternoon. Coppy didn't recognize him.

"I'd like to see Mrs. Franks if I may," he said, tying his horse to the hitching post.

"Whom shall I say is calling?" Coppy asked.

"My name is Anderson. I'm an English journalist," the Spy said with an upper class English accent. "Mrs. Franks and I have met before and she offered her hospitality if I were ever in the area."

Jordan's room was in the front of the house overlooking the veranda. The window was open so that he could enjoy the warm May air. He was half asleep when he heard the voice. At first he thought he was dreaming, but then he pinched himself. The voice wasn't raspy, and it had an accent, but he recognized the essence of it. It was Bailey! What was he doing here?

Jordan rolled over on his good arm and pushed himself to a sitting position. The effort made his wounded shoulder throb. When he swung his legs over the side of the bed, he felt dizzy. He hadn't tried to stand on his own since he had been wounded. He grasped the bed post and, with his good arm, pulled himself to a standing position. He locked his knees and closed his eyes to fight off the nausea that the dizziness had brought on. He found that as long as he held on to something he could stand. Moving was another matter. He took one tentative step and then another. First he leaned on a small table, then he leaned against the wall. He tried to look out the window but he could see nothing. Just this small effort exhausted him and he sat in a chair to rest. As soon as he felt better, he made his way sluggishly to the armoire where he found his pistol. There were still three charges in it and the caps were in place. It would have to do. It felt awfully heavy as he made his way to the door, leaning against the wall for support. He would worry about the stairs when he came to them.

Sarah met Anderson at the door and the old black man took his hat. Sarah led him to the parlor and went to get her mistress who was in the office.

"I don't remember any English journalist, Sarah," she said.

"Well, he's sitting downstairs."

"Perhaps there's been a mistake," Jennifer said. "I'd better go see."

The Spy smiled and stood as Jennifer entered the room. She is, indeed, beautiful, he thought.

"It's a pleasure to see you again, Jennifer," he said.

Jennifer was offended by this stranger's use of her Christian name. "Sir, I don't believe we've been properly introduced."

The Spy smiled. "If we had only met socially, I couldn't blame you for not recognizing me, but after what we shared I feel a little slighted."

His voice had a strange warmth and Jennifer suddenly realized who the man was. She flushed as she felt herself drawn to him again. "You. I—I thought you were in the army," she stammered.

"I've come for you, Jennifer," he said softly.

"What?"

"I've come to take you with me. I have enough money for us to go anywhere in the world." He took her hand and drew her to him.

Jennifer remembered the evening he had spent with her at Oakview Manor. Warmth rushed to her cheeks and she wanted to close her eyes and melt in his arms, but Dick Jordan meant more to her than mere passion and she resented the way this man manipulated her feelings. As Anderson's face neared hers, Jennifer put her hands against his chest and pushed away from him.

"No," she said. "You killed General Jackson! I'm not going anywhere with Yankee vermin like you!" she hissed.

"That's not what you said last time I was here," he said, grabbing her wrist. "You're a remarkable woman, Jennifer, and you're going with me even if I have to throw you over my shoulder and carry you."

Jordan stood in the doorway, amazed at what he was hearing. "Jennifer, is this true?"

The Spy was still holding Jennifer's wrist as both he and Jennifer stopped in amazement and stared at Jordan. Jennifer's cheeks flushed red. Was there any way she could convince Jordan she didn't care for this man now? She took a deep breath.

"He tried to take advantage of me when he was here. I wanted to tell you when you got better." Tears were forming in her eyes.

Jordan did not have to be convinced. He knew she was telling the truth.

"Take your hands off her, Ferris or whatever your name is."

"Well, well, Major Jordan," the Spy said nonchalantly. "I've been looking for you."

"I bet you have," Jordan said. He leaned heavily against the door frame to conserve his dwindling strength.

"My compliments on your survivability, major."

"No thanks to you."

"You have no idea how I regret not having finished the job. You have been nothing but a thorn in my side during this commission, and now I find you interfering in my personal life."

The Spy moved quickly. In a single motion he pulled Jennifer in front of him and drew his pocket pistol.

"Dick," Jennifer gasped.

The Spy pointed his gun at Jennifer's head. "Throw away your pistol and she won't get hurt."

"Is this your way of showing me you love me?" Jennifer asked defiantly.

"You can't love if you don't survive, Jennifer," Anderson told her. "If you give me a chance I'll give you far more than this wreck of a man can." The Spy raised his pistol.

Jennifer felt his hold on her relax as he pointed his weapon at Jordan. "I doubt that," she said, pushing his arm with all her might. The Spy's arm went wide and the pocket pistol went off. The bullet buried itself in the ceiling. He recovered quickly and shoved Jennifer into Jordan as hard as he could. The pain of Jennifer slamming into his injured shoulder made Jordan gasp. Jennifer sprawled face down on the floor and Jordan went to his knees. The world began to turn purple and close in on him. He could see only a shape in the rapidly closing circle of his vision. He raised his gun, pointed it at the blurred figure in the circle, and pulled the trigger. The .44 caliber Colt bucked in his hand as the room exploded. The shape was thrown against the wall. Jordan cocked the pistol and fired again, but he was already passing out.

"Dick," the voice came from far away. "Are you all right? Please say something." She was wiping his face with a damp cloth.

"Jennifer?" Her face slowly came into focus. His shoulder throbbed. "Are you all right?"

"Yes. Are you?" There were tears in her eyes.

He wanted to say something to make her stop crying. "I'm fine." For the moment there was only the two of them. Then he remembered. "Ferris?"

"You killed him," she said, gesturing with her head. "He's lying in the corner. . . Oh, no!"

"What?" Jordan raised himself to a sitting position. The corner was empty save for a pool of blood on the floor. From it a trail of blood led down the hall to the front door.

"How could he?" she whispered in panic.

Jordan grabbed his pistol. "Help me up."

Jennifer helped him to his feet and they followed the trail of red to the front door and down the steps. Lying beside his horse grasping the reins was the Spy.

"He looks so small," Jennifer said.

Jordan nodded in agreement. Who would believe that the small man lying before them had mortally wounded a nation?

About the Author

Author Benjamin King is a former military historian for the Casemate Museum at Fort Monroe, Virginia. He served with distinction in Vietnam as a member of the 101st Airborne Division, winning the Bronze Star at the Battle of Hamburger Hill.

A graduate of the University of Connecticut, he lives in Newport News, Virginia and is a designer for the U.S. Army Transportation School.

A Bullet for Stonewall is his third book.

About the Author